INVISIBLE DEAD

INVI
SIBE
D

LE
DEAD

SAM WIEBE

 RANDOM HOUSE CANADA

PUBLISHED BY RANDOM HOUSE CANADA

Copyright © 2016 Sam Wiebe

www.penguinrandomhouse.ca

Random House Canada and colophon are registered trademarks.

LIBRARY AND ARCHIVES CANADA CATALOGUING IN PUBLICATION

Wiebe, Sam, author
     Invisible dead / Sam Wiebe.

Issued in print and electronic formats.

ISBN 978-0-345-81627-6
eBook ISBN 978-0-345-81628-3
     I. Title.

PS8645.I3236I58 2016   C813'.6   C2015-908560-8

Book design by CS Richardson

Cover image: © Nagib El Desouky / Arcangel Images

Printed and bound in the United States of America

10 9 8 7 6 5 4 3 2 1

Penguin
Random House
RANDOM HOUSE CANADA

悄悄是別離的笙簫

Silence is my farewell music

XU ZHIMO, "Saying Goodbye to Cambridge Again"

VANCOUVER

I don't know why this city sees fit to kill its women.
Answers won't be forthcoming.

PART ONE

OMEGAS

ED LEARY NICHULLS was serving eight counts of second-degree murder up in Kent. "Scrapyard Ed" lured runaways and prostitutes out to his family salvage lot, killed them, eventually, and eventually disposed of the bodies. He didn't avoid the authorities for long, once they'd started looking. But that had taken years.

I generally don't like serial killers, don't find them interesting, though I could name a couple exceptions. Nichulls wouldn't be one. But a client had received a tip-off that Nichulls knew something about her daughter's disappearance, so I made the drive to Agassiz to see if it was true.

The Kent Institution is two hours east of Vancouver, past sprawling townships that seem intent on chewing through their farmland, regurgitating strip malls and noose-shaped cul-de-sacs of tract housing. Kent is federal and maximum-security, a large brown bunker flanked by caged-in exercise yards. Next door is the medium-security Mountain lockup. Corrections is the town's chief industry.

A tall guard with a scar on her cheek walked me through the checkpoints, down the long hallway, concrete walls painted white and green. A conference room had been arranged. Inside was another guard, stone-faced, and a thin man in an expensive pinstripe that hadn't been taken in. His two-button vest flopped about his midsection. He rose to shake my hand.

"Tim Kwan. Nice to meet you, Mr. Wakeland. I'm his counsel. For today, anyway." We shook and Kwan sat back down, smoothing out trousers that hadn't been pressed. "He gets a lot of requests for his time."

"I won't take up much of it," I said.

We waited while the guards fetched Nichulls. Kwan sketched runic-looking figures in the margins of his Day-Timer. I studied the two photos that I'd brought with me. The first was of a young blonde seated in front of an antique bookcase, her posture square and erect, one elbow propped on a desk next to a globe. It was a yearbook photo—I could see ripples in the backdrop on which the bookcase was printed, the shadow of the next kid in line falling across the globe.

The other photo showed a much older woman, leaning into a graffitied brick wall. Not older—aged. Rough, defiant, sexual. Eyes heavy-lidded and suspicious. Black hair, black eyeliner, overdrawn crimson mouth. A sneer levied at the camera lens.

That these were the same woman was just one of the contradictions of Chelsea Loam. Her adopted mother had provided ample details about the adolescent who'd been brought into the Kirby family. None of it explained why she'd left home. Or who she'd been before she arrived.

The door opened and Kwan tensed, snapped shut his notebook. Nichulls appeared between two guards. They sat him down and uncuffed him. Then they hovered behind his chair, each taking a shoulder, an angel and devil in matching uniforms, attending on some poor sinner.

"Howdy," Nichulls said to me.

I wanted to find something in Nichulls's appearance that would justify revulsion. True, if he'd set his heart on a modelling career, he'd never suffer scheduling conflicts. But homely as he was, whatever sickness resided in him didn't reside in his face. His thinning white-blond hair and orange beard, colourless eyes and overbite, made him look at worst like a disreputable uncle. Like someone at home at flea markets or the track. Jail hadn't faded his deeply tanned forearms, which suggested a liver or endocrine problem. Tattooed on his right arm was a blue crucifix.

Kwan leaned forward and introduced himself, informing Nichulls that Kwan worked for his usual lawyers. Nichulls smiled and watched amused as Kwan studied his hands, the floor, the textured cover of his notebook. Nichulls briefly looked over at me to see how funny I found the lawyer's agitation. I stared back at him, waiting.

They conferred for a moment, discussing minor points of treatment and privilege. Minor for those on the outside, at least. Nichulls's grievances had chiefly to do with meal selection.

"Three hots and a cot," Nichulls said. "What I'm owed. Least get me some choice, y'know?"

"I'll petition the warden," Kwan said.

Nichulls's eyes focused on me and he nodded and smiled. "Might as well get down to it," he said. "Down to the nitty gritty titty. What'd you want to ask me?"

I held up the photos. He reached for them, pulled them toward him. I let go.

"First," Kwan said, "let me reiterate that nothing you say to my client or he to you can in any way be interpreted as an admission of wrongdoing. If, however, said information proves valuable in locating someone, whether living or deceased, we would expect that information to be made available to various parole boards, committees and appellate courts, preferably in the form of written affidavits or spoken testimonials from yourself or your office, to be used on my client's behalf at his discretion. We're clear?"

"Clear," I said.

"Clear," Nichulls echoed, grinning. "Clear as mud. Who's this cutie?"

I told him her name. Nichulls examined the second photo. He had no problem marking the blonde student and the grey-complexioned runaway as one and the same. I didn't read recognition in his face. Only a casual lust.

"Looks young," he said, tapping the corner of the yearbook photo.

"She was twenty-four when she disappeared. That was eleven years ago."

"This girl a whore," he said, a funny inflection on the last syllable.

"Are you asking or telling me?"

"Asking. If I ask you, I'm asking. She a whore?"

"She trafficked," I said. "You're familiar with the strolls. Have you ever seen her before?"

"Don't think so," Nichulls said. "No."

"Then we're done here."

I rose and put out my hand for the photos. He kept them at arm's reach from me, the way a bully might. The guards inched closer. Tim Kwan pushed his chair back slightly.

"Now hold on a minute, hold on here." Nichulls gestured for me to sit. "I said I didn't think so. Think's not the same as certain. Gimme a minute. Eyes aren't so good anymore."

He squinted and stared at the photo of the young girl in her chiffon dress, posed in front of the cheap backdrop, arm near the prop globe. Him holding the picture felt obscene. I sat and waited. I don't wait well.

"And?" I asked.

"Hold your horses." He tapped his temple. "Gears don't turn as fast as some people's. 'Specially not after what I been through."

"Either you know her or you don't."

"And I said I'm thinking. Takes as long as it takes. Where is it I know you from?"

"I'm a private investigator," I said. "One or two cases have made the papers."

"Don't read 'em."

"I was a cop before. Briefly. That must be where."

"Nah." He squinted at me, then nodded to himself. "The Astoria. You and that old man."

I nodded, no use hiding it. Kwan looked at me, curious.

"I used to box in the basement of the Astoria hotel," I told the lawyer. "Sometimes after training my father would take me upstairs for a drink." I pointed to Nichulls. "We'd see him in the bar, time to time."

A grin of absent-minded nostalgia played out on Nichulls's face. He was a celebrity and loved being one. Back then, though, he'd been one more drunk, twisting quarters into the guts of a candy dispenser, grinning at my father the cop and my sweaty sixteen-year-old self. The grin took in the square-shouldered man sitting with the exhausted boy in the hotel bar and assumed the worst. The grin said: you are my tormentors and you are no better than me. The grin aimed beyond us, at the world, and still gracing the contours of his face now.

"Those were the times," Nichulls said. "Not like now. You still fight?"

"No."

"Why's that? Not good enough?"

"Partly," I said. "Once my father died I had no use for it."

"Sorry to hear that, him dying."

"I appreciate your sympathy. Could we get back to Chelsea Loam?"

"Never left her," Nichulls said. "Kind of body'd she have? Tall, thin, fat, what?"

"Slight."

"She dress like a whore? Real obvious-like, bright red lips?"

"I didn't drive out here to give you beat-off details."

His brow crinkled. "No call for salty language. Remember it's you asking me for help."

"You're right."

"Catch more flies with honey—your dad never tell you that?"

"If you ever saw her, or did something with her, tell me. Please. If not, tell me that." The *please* was hard to get out.

Nichulls held up a pair of stubby fingers. "Hold on two secs. You're working for who, 'zactly?"

"Her mother," I said. "Foster mother. She'd like to see her daughter buried, if there's anything to bury. And if not, then at least know what happened to her."

Nichulls nodded. He'd put the photos down on the cheap wood coffee table. Tim Kwan spun them toward himself and stared, as if he hadn't looked at them before. I wondered what kind of lawyer he was.

"The mother put up any kind of reward?" Nichulls asked.

"No."

"But she's paying you something, right?"

"Yes."

"What?"

"Something."

"Was just curious," he said, hands flying up to underscore the harmlessness of his query. "Your girl takes a nice photo. Can I keep these?"

"No."

"Guess I'll have to get Timmy Boy to bring me some." He wet his bottom lip. "Dangerous world out there. You hoping your girl turns up, nice and safe and sound?"

For the second time I stood up. "I didn't think you knew anything. Or would say if you did."

Nichulls didn't rise to the bait. "You afraid?" His tone was scornful, mock curious. "Think I'm bad, there's people out there put me to shame. Believe you me."

"What people?" I said.

"Real bad people."

"Do you know what happened to her?"

Nichulls leaned forward and cleared his sinuses. One of the guards touched his shoulders and Nichulls slouched back.

"Leaving now," I said to the guards.

Kwan passed me the photos. From the look on his face, he seemed genuinely saddened that nothing had come from the meeting. That raised him in my estimation, though I didn't share the feeling. It had gone the way I knew it would.

The killer had the last word.

"I'll be here if you need me," Nichulls said.

2

IT WAS MUGGY and overcast as I drove back to the city. Even with the windows down and the odd spatter of rain dancing on my forearm, I was sweating. July in the Lower Mainland: the sun transient, the rain lukewarm and viscous.

I drove straight downtown, touched my pass to the sensor on the parkade gate, slid the Cadillac into its spot. Then I rode the elevator up to the office.

It had been a strange transition from self-employment to being one half of a partnership. Wakeland & Chen Private Investigations had a plush office suite in the Royal Bank building, on the stretch of Hastings where addicts and panhandlers are politely discouraged. We had several corporate clients and a full-time office staff, even if that staff was Jeff Chen's second cousin Shuzhen. Gone was my cubbyhole of an office, with its cobbled-together furnishings, and the staircase that smelled perpetually of piss, no matter how often I bleached it. Partnering with Jeff Chen had turned my career around.

At the same time, I didn't like dealing with white-collar types, other than to hand in my work and cash their cheques. I don't golf, I don't schmooze, and when I drink it's usually alone with my stereo. A smarter person would keep quiet and start saving for a Porsche. I was beginning to feel unsuited for about eighty percent of my profession.

Jeff was tolerant. He'd spent a decade navigating the corporate security world. He'd worked for Aries, a company so shady they could only call staff meetings during an eclipse, run by a crook who thought scruples were for the weak. Jeff knew I was eccentric, but also that I would deliver. A successful missing persons case netted the kind of publicity you couldn't purchase.

So we struck a compromise: I was free to work the cases I wanted, provided I donned a suit and glad-handed every once in a while.

I dropped the mileage log on Shuzhen's desk, then headed to my office to scoop the mail off my table. The only thing that had accompanied me on the trip to the profitable end of Hastings was that oak dining table, chipped and scarred and pocked with cigarette burns. Someone had once broken into my old office and set it on fire. That tank of a table had withstood the blaze, and I'd had it refinished. It still served as my desk, incongruent as it was with the tasteful, flimsy office decor around it now. Furniture that can survive arson has untapped potential.

My office door was unlocked. Standing inside with her back to the door was Marie, Jeff's fiancée. She was a good person. I reminded myself of that as she turned and shot me a look that seemed to ask what business I had being here.

"When will you let me pick out a real desk for you?"

A witty rejoinder would only lead to squabbling. I shrugged. "I'm comfortable with it. What are you up to?"

"Seeing if you billed Gail Kirby."

"Heading over there now."

"Because it's been a month already, and when I phoned she said she'd just received the invoice."

"Heading over there now."

"And I didn't know if you'd been late handing it in, or if it was disorganization on her part."

"I'll give her the invoice today," I said. "And I'll tell her, cancer or no, she doesn't pay within forty days I break her knees."

"You do that," Marie said. "Try to remember this is a business, not a charity. People who won't do business aren't worth doing business with."

"You learn that at the School for Culinary Arts?"

My stupid mouth. Marie frosted over instantly.

"I'm twelve credits from my MBA," she said. "And yes, before that I explored other career options. How well did you do in college, Dave, you want to talk academic achievement? What did you accomplish?"

"I drank a lot in libraries."

I put the file on the desk. Marie looked at the photo of teen-aged Chelsea Loam. Her face softened. "I thought this girl was a prostitute," she said.

"That's an old photo. Other than the street shot, the only others are from arrest reports. I don't like using mugshots—gives the impression she's a criminal, sends the wrong message." I tapped the yearbook photo. "So does this one, but having people think she's a doe-eyed innocent is better than seeing her as a harlot who got what was coming to her."

"People think that?"

"People think a lot of shit," I said.

Jeff came down the hall, spied us and turned in. He kissed his fiancée and took his sweet time coming back down to earth.

"You went and saw that asshole today," Jeff said. "Anything useful?"

"It was a long shot. She worked in the same area where Nichulls took his victims, but so did a lot of people."

"So it's not Nichulls," Jeff said. "What next?"

"Next is telling Gail Kirby it wasn't him." I looked at Marie. "And giving her the invoice."

"And then back in the rotation?"

"More than likely," I said. "She had the one anonymous tip about her daughter. Now that that's a bust, there's not much left to the case."

"Good," Jeff said. "Not good, but—you know what I mean. The VP of Solis Developments asked about you personally."

"Goody."

"They're thinking of ditching their in-house security, taking up with us. Their boss, Utrillo, is on the fence. But the sales VP Tommy Ross is a fan of yours. Wants you to bodyguard him on his trip to Winnipeg."

"Pass."

"No passes allowed."

"I hate Winnipeg."

"Have you ever been?"

"It seems the kind of place I wouldn't like."

Jeff shook his head. "I do a lot of things I don't like. For you this is mostly a vacation. Free plane, free hotel. While you're out there you can see the world's biggest Coke can."

"No," I said.

"They're a big account, which makes them more important than a small account." He held in his arms a thick file in a faux-leather accordion folder with a gold foil decal in the shape of a sun. He spoke to me in the voice you'd use for a small child or a large dog, pointing between the file in his arms and the open folder with the two photographs. "Big account. Little account. Little. Big. See how that works? If the big account is happy, you can afford to work on the little account. If not, then we'll all need squeegees and cardboard signs."

I said I'd think on it.

"And please get rid of the table. I will pay to replace it. Get a whole office suite."

"There are some nice rosewood desks at the India Imports on Broadway," Marie said. "You can use my discount."

I waxed noncommittal and took the big brass elevator eight floors down to street level. Half the battles I fought, I fought only to fight them. Why not ditch the table? It was just something familiar.

On Hastings I unlocked my Cadillac and drove west down Seymour, working out what I'd tell Gail Kirby. I wondered what she'd expected from Nichulls. What she expected from me.

I looked at the file on the passenger seat, a corner of the black-and-white photo reaching out past the beige cardboard to graze the beaten leather. A few strands of black hair, the edge of a jawline.

Chelsea Loam.

I doubted very much we were done with each other.

3

MRS. GAIL KIRBY once told me, "When I was calling Missing Persons every day to ask what they were doing to find Chelsea, they used to say, 'She's just a whore, it's not like she's anyone important.' The first reporter I went to told me if Chelsea was the daughter of some grey-haired lady from Kerrisdale, everyone would put a lot more effort into finding her. Well, now I *am* a grey-haired lady from Kerrisdale, and before I finish I'm going to know what the fuck happened to my daughter."

She'd come to me reluctantly, a month ago, prompted by her other daughter, Caitlin. "She thinks I'm not strong enough to face this monster," Gail Kirby had said. "Caitlin should know what I faced in my time. But I see her point."

Caitlin had thought the whole effort a waste. After my first meeting with her mother, she'd told me, "There's simply no way Chelsea could be alive and not call us. Not with the amount of money my mother shelled out to her, unconditionally. No way she'd go all this time without coming back for more of that. Plus Gail loved her. Chelsea's dead, she's dead, and let that be the end of it."

"But why hire me?" I'd asked.

"Because," Caitlin had said. "Gail shouldn't have to deal with people like that. Her life's been arduous enough as it is. If this 'clue' is as bogus as it appears, she shouldn't be tormented by Ed Leary Nichulls."

The clue referred to a letter the Kirbys had received through the doggie door of their palatial house in Shaughnessy Heights. No stamp, nothing written on the construction-paper envelope. The envelope itself unfolded into a note written in blue magic marker. All caps. ASK SCRAPYARD ED ABOUT YOUR DAUGHTER.

False leads weren't uncommon. The Ghoshes, other clients of mine, had received notes claiming if Mrs. Ghosh stood by her bedroom window naked, rubbing herself for three nights in a row, her daughter would be brought back. Jeff and I found the writers, a couple of high schoolers whose parents took a boys-will-be-boys attitude to the incident.

I parked my Cadillac in Gail Kirby's driveway and headed to the door through a trellised archway. The clematis that weaved through it had bloomed ivory-coloured flowers, but patches of the front garden remained dead heaps of brown and grey, last year's untended bark mulch. Gardening was Mrs. Kirby's very favourite hobby and she hadn't been attending to it.

I let myself in. I found Gail and Caitlin in the solarium, playing cribbage and drinking Pimm's. Gail smiled as I approached.

I gave her the news. It didn't seem to dampen her spirits. Caitlin involved herself in her cellphone.

"It was worth a try," Gail said. "Sit down for a minute."

I sat in a white wicker chair and flicked a spider off the armrest. Watering cans and gardening supplies littered the tiled floor of the solarium. Bags of calcite and fertilizer, stacks of red clay pots, floral-patterned gardening gloves and a trowel and shears tucked into an overturned straw hat. All of it filmed with dust. One of the pots had been repurposed to accept cigarette butts. It lay next to Gail Kirby's chair, beside her oxygen tank.

"Gail has something she wants to ask you," Caitlin said. She didn't look up. Her tone made it clear that she'd lost an argument on the same subject before I'd arrived.

Gail lit a cigarette and looked at her daughter with a mixture of sadness and pride. Only a parent could pull off such a look. She said to me, "What would you do, David, if you were working this case full-time? Where would you start?"

"With the police," I said. "They have resources a private firm can't compete with. I'd work up as much info on your daughter as I could from friends and family. At the same time I'd start with her disappearance and work backward. Find out who she worked with, lived with, who she went to for help. A lead might emerge. But I'd start with the police."

"The police don't care," Caitlin said.

"Lot of cases they're effective, whether they care or not."

"I care," Gail said. "I have the money. Would you put up a reward if you were me?"

"No, but I'd pay for information. Let people know a solid lead is worth money, but keep the scammers and lunatics away."

"I want Chelsea found," Gail Kirby said. "I'm prepared to pay."

"Money pissed away," Caitlin muttered.

"There will be plenty left for you when I'm gone," Gail said.

"That's unfair." Caitlin pushed away from the table and made a show of tossing her cards in. "Know what? I refuse to deal with this any longer. I have a life of my own."

As she stormed out, Gail said to me, "She may have a point."

"There's no guarantee," I admitted. "And it's not cheap."

"I don't care about the money. Do you know how it came about, this fortune?" She took a whiff of oxygen and set the mask back on the table's edge. "Lew—my husband—died in an industrial accident on an oil rig in Fort St. John. The settlement was generous. Caitlin had finished school and Chelsea had left us. I put all of it into real estate. This was before the housing boom. Now I'm worth skillions."

She crushed out her cigarette on the glass table and consigned it to the pot with the others. "And now I have cancer," she said. "Stage three. It's not going to get better. I want my daughter found, David. Chelsea only lived with us for five years, but she's as much my daughter as Caitlin is. It kills me not to know. And since I have this money, I'm going to use it."

"It's been eleven years," I began.

"I know she's probably dead. I have no illusions. I just need to know."

Gail took an envelope from the pocket of her button-up

sweater. She meant to sail it across the table to me, but her strength failed and it glanced off the pitcher in the middle of the table. I reached over. Inside was a cheque for two hundred thousand dollars.

"Your time and expenses," she said. "You find her or what happened to her."

"I can't take that much from you," I said.

"Sure you can."

I pushed the invoice toward her. "Pay this and I'll draw up a contract."

"And you'll find her?"

"I'll do my level best."

"Do everything," she said.

Caitlin was waiting in the driveway. I'd boxed in her Beemer, but she lingered by the side panel of my Cadillac like she wanted some words. I'd had enough of words for the day, but it wasn't my choice.

She eyed the Cadillac, a decade-old XLR in dire need of a wash, like it was the model of conspicuous consumption. "You probably have a fleet of these made off of swindling old ladies like my mother."

"Let me ask you a question," I said, opening the door and resting an elbow on the roof. "What do you think it's worth, finding your sister?"

"She wasn't my sister," Caitlin said.

"But what price would you allow your mother to put on that?"

She shook her head. "It was my idea to hire you. Otherwise Gail would've had to follow up on this mess herself. She didn't think you were necessary. Now," she said, "she thinks you're worth two hundred thousand dollars."

"You didn't answer my question."

"It doesn't matter because you're not going to find her because she's not around because she's dead. Something happened to Chelsea."

She paused and turned to examine an unkempt rose bush in the front yard. Wilted yellow petals, tendrils of thorns snaking out across the path. I waited her out.

"Chelsea messed up everything," she said. "Everything she touched. Even my mother knows it deep down. Hiring you is only out of guilt for Gail finally being happy—which she won't be for much longer if the doctors are right."

"How long does she have?"

"She doesn't tell me those kinds of things," Caitlin said. "She doesn't want me to worry. That's a laugh, isn't it?"

"I'm sorry," I said.

"It's simply how it is," Caitlin said. "What it means to you is if you're going to swindle her, you'd best do it in the next few months."

Rather than return to the office, I drove to St. Augustine's, had a pint of Black Plague Stout, and began piecing together what I knew of Chelsea Loam's life.

Lewis and Gail Kirby had adopted her just before her thirteenth birthday, taking her out of a group home. There wasn't much on her before that. Single mother, unknown father. Ethnicity predominantly white and aboriginal, possibly Métis. Chelsea was well-behaved at the home. Her self-portrait, age seven, showed the black-and-white outline of a girl, faceless but wearing a long dress, in the midst of a Crayola field of daffodils, tulips and sunflowers. MY NAME IS CHELSEA. MY SECOND NAME IS ANNE. MY FAVOURITE FRIEND IS PAULINE. MY FAVOURITE SONG IS CALLED HOLIDAY BY MADONNA. MY FAVOURITE BOOK IS MY SIDE OF THE MOUNTAIN BY I DON'T KNOW THE AUTHOR. I wondered cynically if the adoption centres encouraged children to cutesy up their drawings in order to attract a family, like a matron instructing a stable of debutantes how best to land a beau.

Chelsea had done well with the Kirbys. Appropriately trepidatious during eighth grade, being locked in classrooms and gymnasiums with so many unfamiliar strands of DNA. Grade nine saw her settle into a group of friends, play in concert band, land on the honour roll. More of the same in ten and eleven, a widening of her social circle to include boys. She'd joined jazz choir and sung a solo in "Get Your Kicks on Route 66."

In grade eleven there was trouble—relatively speaking. She'd pulled a C in geography, a C- in pre-calc. Incompletes for PE and Career and Personal Planning. Gail suspected drinking. Lew suspected drugs.

Lew's accident and death and the resulting confusion made it hard to account for where Chelsea was at, physically and spiritually. As Gail had told me, one day she just wasn't there.

What followed were late-night phone calls every few months. Chelsea needed money for a procedure—"Don't make me say it," she pleaded with Gail. She'd been arrested and needed money to retain competent legal counsel, "not these legal aid shitheads." She'd tested positive for hepatitis and could use a few bucks for her prescription. She was getting clean. She was trying to get clean. She was thinking about trying to get clean, really trying this time.

And Gail always paid her. Both wept at every transaction.

Then the calls stopped coming and Gail reported her missing. That was eleven years ago. Chelsea would be thirty-five now. Six years older than me. And yet looking down at her photo I saw a girl half my age.

I had no real perspective on Chelsea Loam. If I delved into her childhood I might find skeletons—abuse, violence—but then I might not. There's no formula for why people stray from the righteous path.

It was going to be a messy case, I could sense that much. I A-B'd the two photos I had, the smiling blonde in her yearbook dress, the defiant professional with eyes of wet flint. Separate existences. Separate friends.

It was so damn easy to lose the way.

4

THE WAITER BROUGHT our sushi in elegant wooden ships.

"So . . ."

"Dave."

"Dave, right. What do you do for a living, Dave?"

"Private investigator."

"Really? That's neat."

"I like it. What about you?"

"You know what I do. I work with Marie in the shop."

"Right. How's that?"

"Well, it's not my dream job, but it could be worse. The cus-tomers, though. Sometimes they're totally unreasonable. People expect so fucking much, they're so entitled. Drives me—huh."

"What?"

"Huh, nothing. Sending Abby a note about tomorrow."

"Ah . . ."

"Abdul. He works in the office with Marie and I. Nice guy but a little scatter-brained."

"Sure."

"I'm just gonna type this and go pee. Order me another Asahi when she comes back, 'kay?"

She walked off, nearly bumping into the table next to us. I wondered if she texted on the toilet.

It was quarter past nine. Ryan Martz would be off work by now, tossing them back at the Cambridge. I wondered if it would be bad manners to walk out without saying anything, without leaving payment or a note. Probably.

I walked down Thurlow and made a right on Pender. The office buildings were mirrors reflecting fire as the sun bobbed at the horizon, causing a surprisingly cloudless sky to light up teal in that final hour before dark. The I-Don't-Give-a-Shit hour.

Located on the ground floor of a hostel, the Cambridge was a hamster den for slumming college kids and backpackers. Every surface in the place had a tacky coating of spilt beer and ketchup. Why would a cop drink there, away from his own kind? Maybe that was the explanation. I'd gone through training with Martz. I knew his parents had been hippies, the overly permissive and disorganized kind, and his entire square-john, shaved-head, Metallica-driven existence was an edifice raised in defiance to them. Maybe by downing Winchesters in a beer parlour populated by sociology majors with dreadlocks and smug utopians in trilbies and kerchiefs, Martz had found a way to commune with his anger. Drinking, after all, is one of the best forms of perseveration.

I slid onto the picnic bench across from him. Waited for him to notice me. Martz didn't react, other than to hold up his pint to the barkeep as a signal to bring a fresh glass.

"Wakeland," he said. He was half gone already. "What're you doing here?"

"Just here for the music," I said. "My day's not complete without a few hours of white guy reggae."

"I bet," Martz said. "I bet you come here all the time." He launched into a laughing fit, rapping on the table with a bandaged hand.

"What's so damn funny?"

"Picturing you dressed up like the Terminator, black jacket and shades. 'Rasta la vista.' Get it?" And he collapsed back into laughter.

"That's good, Ryan. For you it's brilliant."

"So you came to see me."

"No shit."

"About?"

"A woman, a young lady who disappeared eleven years ago."

"Chelsea Loam," Martz said. "I heard about your visit to Nichulls."

I had some beer. It tasted like rust and water and beer. The Cambridge was filling up. The barkeep was coordinating with the doorman over cheap wireless headsets to keep the standing crowd from blocking the entrance.

"The mother asked me to look into a tip she got."

"Chelsea Loam was an orphan."

"Foster mother. So I did, I looked into it."

"We had that same tip," Martz said. "Someone saw Chelsea Loam out with Nichulls. Turned out to be garbage. Or maybe not. But who can prove it?" He shrugged helplessly. "Hookers."

"It's not her fault if someone did something to her."

"What do you know?" Martz said. "You don't fucking know. She could've gone skiing down the wrong hill. Happens."

"Now you're reaching, Ryan, and it's sad."

"This one I dealt with today," he said. "I spent all day up in her shitty fucking roach-infested room. Other day she and her roommate had a fight. The officer who caught the code three tells me they were trying to kill each other. Roommate walks out, and when she doesn't come back the next day, the other one calls Missing Persons, all boo hoo hoo. And I get to take her statement. Rat shit everywhere, Burger King wrappers. And while I'm doing that she walks through the door, the missing roommate, and the two of them go at it again. And I get stabbed in the hand with a fucking pen trying to separate them. They can both get themselves killed, far's I'm concerned."

"Good thing they're not who I'm looking for," I said diplomatically.

"Don't pretend you don't know what I mean. Any one of them would take your fucking eyeteeth out for a paper's worth of skag. Animals, Wakeland."

"Keep your voice down."

"I got roaches, silverfish crawling on my uniform. And these two don't give a shit if they fucking kill each other. But I've got to. And these sheltered cunts—" here he craned his neck in the direction of the college students sharing the bench with us, the gesture not lost on them "—they act like, oh, the cops don't care, they use stormtrooper tactics, why don't they just ask these nice, innocent addicts not to rob and steal and suck prick for fucking dope. And I cut myself again going through that bitch's medicine cabinet. And who were we talking about? Chelsea Loam. I read that file. She's just the same."

"Focus on her. Tell me what you know."

He smiled. "Why don't I just give you her file?"

"I'd like that."

"I know you would. But it'd be wrong."

"Only legally."

"Which means I'm not doing it," Martz said. "I bent the law enough for you already. Or have you forgotten that Salt mess? That whole—what's the word for a bunch of fucked-up shit?"

"Fiasco? Debacle?"

"That whole debacle cost me my promotion. Most likely I'm CFL now. Constable for Life. Lucky fucking me."

"My father never moved past constable."

"And he was a great cop," Martz said, pointing unsteadily. "Because he knew the difference between—know what? I'm sick of arguing with you. Sick of the whole schmozz. What do you want to know?"

"Any leads, for starters?"

"If there were, don't you think we'd've followed up on them?"

"Missing Persons is a small unit," I said. "Can't do everything."

"Damn straight. Tell that to—tell that to everybody."

"Do you have her DNA on file?"

"DNA, fingerprints. Dental records."

"LKA?"

"One of the flophouses downtown. The Baltic, maybe."

"Who'd she run with?"

"Who'd she run with," Martz repeated, almost mystified at

the question. "Who the fuck do you think? Junkies, pimps—"

"She had a pimp?" Chelsea hadn't struck me as the pimp type.

"I'm just saying, when we looked into her, that's the calibre of people she hung with."

"Soiled doves and men of low character."

"In so many words, Wakeland."

"How hard did you look?"

He glared at me. The vein that ran up his temple over his shaved head pulsed. "Fucking hard," he said. "You think we wouldn't look for her hard?"

"I don't know, I'm not a cop—"

"Fucking A you're not."

"—anymore," I finished. "And it doesn't matter, you know I have to go back through everything. I need to know everything about her. Everyone she met in detention or in rehab, every roommate, every friend."

"Every prick she ever sucked."

"That's right," I said. "Every goddamn one of them, that's what it takes."

"Is prurient a word? You're prurient, Dave."

"I'll also need to find her parents. Her birth parents."

"All that to find her probably lying dead in a ditch somewheres."

"You're not going to talk me out of it."

"No," Martz said. "I know that won't happen. I don't even think it's all that stupid. I—listen. You know how these—women—get reported missing?"

"Loved ones."

He shook his head. "Most of the time it's care workers, calling 'cause they haven't picked up their welfare cheques. Or the health clinic 'cause they didn't refill their scrips. That's the quality of person you're dealing with, Dave. They're hanging on as it is. You really think you're gonna find someone like that? You think you're helping anyone by poking around in all that piss and come?"

Outside on the patio, a jittery panhandler moved around the tables. The sun had disappeared. The foot traffic toward Gastown and the waterfront was heavy.

"Do you really want an answer to that?" I said.

"No," Martz said. "I want to go home and have a shower and clean all this skin off."

"Clean what off?"

"All this shit—roach shit, rat shit, human shit—fucking petrified diarrhea nobody bothered to clean up."

"You said skin."

Puzzled, Martz stared into the glasses and pitcher, a forest of distorted reflections of himself.

"I don't understand the significance," he said.

5

NO ONE HUSTLED LIKE JEFFERSON CHEN. At eight the next morning we were in the lobby of a financial building on West Georgia. Jeff was pacing, going over his pitch. He was wearing a bespoke suit he'd brought back from Savile Row, grey pinstripe with wide lapels, white silk shirt, no tie. He looked a bit like a villain from a Ringo Lam film. I was wearing the same black suit–black tie combination I'd worn yesterday, and looked like an arena security guard right after the Big Game.

Dunham Insurance wanted to outsource their claims investigations. They were "exploring all their options." Jeff wanted the job, wanted it badly. It would mean hiring another full-time investigator. Maybe an office manager. Jeff was determined to grow the business up and out, to not only get it off the ground, to not only see it soar, but to construct an entire floating city of commerce.

We waited in the lobby. I listened to him run through his sales pitch again and again. I was there as a mascot, an old hockey player trotted out to press the flesh at the grand reopening of a supermarket.

The elevator doors opened and a man and woman, both in blue suits, came out and shook our hands and herded us into the elevator and up to the eleventh floor and through glass doors into a conference room where another two suits smiled and made small talk about the Canucks and told us we could start whenever we were ready.

Jeff wasted no time.

"Wakeland & Chen and Dunham Insurance are a perfect match because both companies are dedicated to excellence. Not good or good enough but excellent service is what we provide, and it's what we provide consistently. Not only that, but we're more cost effective than our competitors. Our typical invoice is sixty-five percent of what Aries, our leading competitor, charges. We are mobile and flexible, our technology is *beyond* state of the art—Dave, pass them each a complimentary pen camera—and every member of our hard-working staff is hand-chosen and personally trained by David Wakeland, who you may have seen on the CBC in conjunction with one or two high-profile cases."

On the elevator ride down, Jeff shook his fist in triumph. "Fucking yeah. Nailed 'em, Dave."

"It was the pen cam. Everyone loves the pen cam."

"You did good, too. Didn't say anything to embarrass us. I'm glad at least one of them watches local television."

"I'm going to need more time on the Kirby case," I said. "At least another few weeks."

"You're remembering to send out the invoices, right?"

"Of course."

"And you'll be around for the hiring interviews?"

"If I can."

"You have to. I promised them back there."

"You also promised that we're cheaper than Aries."

"We are, given how you're under-billing the Widow Kirby."

The elevator dinged. We pushed our way into the lobby through a throng of young professionals. They packed themselves into the car as if there'd never be another.

We walked down toward the waterfront, Jeff mindful of the bloated gulls sailing low overhead. I'd always felt about five blocks out of place in the financial district. Whoever had called Vancouver a city of glass hadn't been talking about my city.

But as we passed yet another mirrored window, I caught our reflection. We looked at home.

"I appreciate the effort you put into running the business," I said.

"I know you've got your own way of doing things, and that's cool."

"Are we lying to each other?"

"No," said Jeff. "We're on our way up, we're making moves, and we're doing things our own way. What could be better than that?"

I didn't answer. We crossed Burrard at Pender, passing a homeless man with a violin, a ghetto blaster and a somnolent dog.

"You know I've got your back," Jeff continued. "But you know I can only have your back if we have steady work like Dunham and Solis rolling in. For you, that means sometimes you have to put on a suit and smile and pretend to be human."

"I can do that," I said.

"Good. Where you going next with the Kirby case?"

That I didn't know. Martz had told me what I'd expected to hear—that as far as the police were concerned, Chelsea Loam had disappeared for no reason, and with no possible leads. Neither could I get a sense of who she was from her foster family. Gail Kirby and her daughter had been bludgeoned by Chelsea's swift slide into addiction. To Gail, who had adopted the head-in-the-sand approach, she was a troubled innocent, struggling to find herself. And to Caitlin, who'd seen the effect Chelsea's struggle had had on her mother, Chelsea was a lost cause. It would be facile to say that the truth probably lay between the two. Maybe the better answer was that they were both right.

I had a cigarette before following Jeff up to our office. His cousin Shuzhen was up there already, sorting through the previous night's emails while the coffee brewed. She was in her second year of pre-law at UBC, temping during the summer. She hadn't yet taken off her coat, a white beltless Burberry that clung to her plaid skirt.

"Chinese donut?" she asked.

I set the kettle down on its base and flicked it on. She handed me a pastry. With the donut wedged into my mouth I ripped open a yellow teabag, set it down in the tiny clay pot.

"How come you don't drink coffee?" Shuzhen asked. "You look like you should drink coffee. Black coffee. In a big red 7-Eleven mug. Every day, same teabag, same pot."

I had to put the donut down on the corner of the saucer to answer her. "I'll tell you why," I said. "Coffee shrinks your testicles to the size of raisins."

"Seriously? That's not true."

"A doctor told me for your balls to maintain optimum fluff and buoyancy, the body needs a daily pot of Earl Grey."

"You're full of it, Dave."

"Yes I am." I poured out the water, watched the string on the bag pull taut. "I don't know why I like anything. Good citizen of the Commonwealth, I guess."

"You know it's the Chinese that invented tea," Shuzhen said.

"Now *that* I don't believe. Next thing you'll be trying to tell me they invented gunpowder and the printing press."

I set the tea service on my office table and dumped out Chelsea Loam's meagre file next to it. Two photos. A few documents. My handwritten notes on my meeting with Nichulls. I needed an entry point into her life, somewhere to begin piecing her last weeks together.

What I needed was a guide. Someone who knew the stroll and the secret places where people congregated. I'd worked there, but the knowledge I had as an ex-cop wouldn't help. I needed access to the world kept hidden from cops.

Chelsea had lived ten minutes on foot from where I sat now, drinking my Twinings. It was five minutes from where my old office had been. It was another world.

I took off my tie, still knotted, and looped it over the back corner of my chair. I changed into a hoodie and jeans and beaten-up Red Wings, took my lockbox out of the bottom drawer of the file folder, and stuffed my pockets with fifty-odd dollars in change. I ran off copies of Chelsea's Missing flyer, making sure to circle my cell number on each of them.

Jeff and Shuzhen were huddled in conversation as I headed to the elevator.

"Balls feel nice and fluffy now?" Shuzhen called to me. I didn't need to turn around to know the look Jeff was giving her.

I started at the Baltic, hoping the manager had miraculously preserved a box of Chelsea's possessions. But she shook her head when I showed her the poster, had actually started shaking it even before her eyes locked on Chelsea's face. I asked if Chelsea had been a resident and she looked and said no one of that name had stayed here, but the guest logs didn't go back that far.

I left a poster with her and asked her to display it. She said she was only the day manager and would have to square that with her boss.

I tried the nearby hotels and SROs in case Martz had his details wrong. I met with similar non-answers. It had been eleven years. For the vulnerable underside of the city, eleven lifetimes.

Outside the needle exchange I watched a woman sitting on an overturned bucket as she held her lighter to a square of tin-foil, inhaling the fumes through a Slurpee straw. She had on a purple pro wrestling sweatshirt, yellow lettering, THE CHAMP IS HERE. I waited until she'd finished before approaching.

"Morning," I said.

"So?"

I passed her a flyer and a business card. I went through my spiel. She considered both pictures.

"I used to see her," she said. "Way back. Her name was Charity."

"Her street name, you mean."

"Whatever. I heard she got clean."

"Who'd you hear that from?"

"Fuck I remember a thing like that for?"

"She's missing," I said.

"I realize that from the big word over her picture says 'missing.'"

"Anyway," I said, "can you tell me anything about Charity? Who she hung around with? What she was like?"

"I didn't really know her that well," the woman said. "We had the same social worker is how I know her name. She was young. Real pretty, too."

"What's your case worker's name?"

"It's Beverly now but it used to be Vivian. And Shirley before that, but it was Viv who was me and Charity's case worker."

"Vivian have a last name?"

"Yeah and you should look it up. And ask her about Charity 'cause she'd know."

"I will."

"I only saw her here an' there. Didn't know her well."

"Appreciate the help," I said. "Can I ask your name?"

"You can but I'm not giving it to you, Mister Policeman. Mister Pleece-man. Mister Puh-leeze-man."

I gave her ten dollars in bills and ten in change and told her to call the number on my card if she needed anything.

"I need new blood," she said. "A new head of hair. New veins. New lungs."

"Least your mind works," I said.

"That was true," she said, "would I be sitting here?"

6

VIVIAN FEATHER HAD RETIRED from social work a few years after Chelsea Loam's disappearance. She now ran an artist's colony on Quadra Island. The miracle of the internet robbed me of an excuse to take a trip up there, but I got through on Skype soon after looking her up.

"Broke my heart," Feather said. "Chelsea wasn't all that different from me at her age. Fierce young aboriginal woman, beautiful, everything going for her after a rough patch or two. And then . . ." Her voice trailed off.

Vivian Feather was a heavyset woman with long straight silver hair. She wasn't looking quite into the lens of the webcam, but downward as if peering over imaginary glasses. She looked younger than her seventy years, but old enough that talking to her reminded me to visit my mother.

"You must have known her pretty well," I said, leaning forward in my office chair. "Who else did she confide in?"

"I don't know if she had that many people to talk to."

"Did she have a man in her life? Was she heterosexual, homosexual?"

"That's all very private," Feather said. "What she told me in confidence I don't mean to break."

"Of course not, and I wouldn't want you to. But without making you uncomfortable, Mrs. Feather, could you tell me what you can?"

"I'll say this," she said. "The man who dropped her off and picked her up from my office was always very rude. I assume that was her boyfriend."

"What was his—"

"Even if I remembered, I wouldn't feel comfortable saying."

"Okay," I said. "I heard a rumour she got clean."

"From who'd you hear that?"

"Lady on a bucket. She said you'd know."

"When Chelsea stopped coming," Vivian Feather said, "she'd been talking about rehab for ages and ages. Never made a serious attempt that I saw, but that's no judgment on her. I haven't walked in her shoes. I know she was under pressure."

"One day she just wasn't there," I prompted.

"That's right. I told her several times I would gladly come to her, meet her where she wanted to. But she liked my office. I always had Tootsie Rolls, fruit leather. Back when I could metabolize that stuff."

"You remember when she stopped coming to see you?"

"October sixth was the last appointment she kept. I remember the date. I couldn't stand that nobody'd bothered looking for her."

"Did you go to the police with that info?" I asked.

"I don't recognize the police," Vivian Feather said.

"Meaning?"

"I mean I don't recognize their authority. They're the paramilitary wing of an occupying force on unceded land belonging to the Coast Salish peoples."

"So who'd you tell?"

"Anyone who'd listen," she said. "God, mostly. I still pray for Chelsea every night."

"Was she religious, Chelsea?"

"It wasn't my business," Feather said. "Religion is complicated. More so for us—it's political, it's something that was taken from us. White man's god, the Christian god, and Chíchelh Siyám—it's hard enough to get your head around one of them, let alone both."

"Is there anything else you can tell me about Chelsea?" I asked.

"It was a while ago."

"Do you think the man that dropped her off was her boyfriend or her pimp?"

"Honestly, I'd rather—"

"What was his name? I think you can tell me that without compromising."

"I'd rather not."

"I'd rather not have to ask," I said. "But finding her is the task in front of me. I understand your reluctance. I'm asking for your faith."

"You don't strike me as religious," Feather said.

I scratched my ear. "My parents were cultists. What I do believe, you have an obligation to the living that supersedes any promises you make to the dead. Chelsea's mother is very sick. She'd like to know what happened to her daughter before she passes on. So please tell me the boyfriend's name."

Vivian Feather sighed big time.

"She never used his proper name," she said. "That was a thing with her. She preferred to be called Charity. As if Charity and Chelsea were different people."

"What'd she call her boyfriend?"

"Kamikaze."

At two I walked down Water Street to a restaurant called Peckinpah. I threw down two shots of Bulleit bourbon, a brisket sandwich with slaw and cornbread. Then I walked to the parking lot next to Waterfront Station and stared out across the bay toward North Van.

If I was to conduct my own guided tour of the city, I'd start here. Looking out through the fence and over the rail yard, past the docks with their orange loading cranes, past the Seabus route and the cruise ship moored by the convention centre, past the sulphur barge, to the roll of cityscape slowly unfurling up the North Shore mountains. That tableau tells you everything. It tells you that beneath the trappings of civilization and the damage done by industry lies something in hibernation. Something that will shrug us off, all of us, as easily as a sunbathing father will destroy the sandcastle his children build over him while he sleeps.

On the days when you can't quite believe how cruel and insensible the human experiment is, that passed for a comforting thought.

I took my time getting back to the office, walking off the calories and the bourbon haze. When I got back I noticed a car illegally parked out front. A silver Mercedes, cream-coloured leather upholstery, a crack in the front fender repaired with electrician's tape. I'd seen the same car outside Kent.

Tim Kwan was sitting in the waiting area, eyeing Shuzhen over a week-old B-section of the *National Post*.

"We should talk," he said.

I directed him into my office. Jeff followed us in. We all took seats.

"Coffee?" I asked.

"I'll tell you what I'd really like," Tim Kwan said, "is a drink, a *drink* drink, if you have one."

"We don't keep any alcohol in the office," Jeff said.

I opened the filing cabinet. At the back was a bottle of Botanist gin and a mickey of Crown Royal. I poured a slug of rye into a paper cup, topped it up with water from the dispenser in the hall, and set it down in front of Kwan. I was saving the Botanist for something special.

"You're not joining me?" he asked.

"Had one earlier," I said.

Jeff hadn't stopped glaring at me since I'd produced the bottle.

"With lunch," I clarified.

"Anything else I don't know about? Heroin, maybe? A grenade launcher?"

"Nope." Turning back to Kwan I said, "Are you here on behalf of your client?"

"I'm here on behalf of yours," Kwan said.

"Care to explain that?"

Kwan sipped his drink. He didn't down it like someone who needed it, who was accustomed to a midday sloshing. More like someone who was embarking on a dangerous course of action, and had heard enough about liquid courage to want some for himself.

"I've been a lawyer for fifteen years," Kwan said. "I hate my own kind. They all went to the same Richie Rich schools, yacht clubs. Oh, they're happy to have me on board to fill their diversity mandate, but as far as making partner and getting a place in the country club, I'm still not their kind of people. I wouldn't go the same career path again, I truly wouldn't. I don't think there's anything worse than being a lawyer."

"Lawyer-turned-poet," I offered.

"None of them care about right and wrong," he said. "About morality and ethics. And least of all justice."

"This isn't news."

"The partners would fire me if they knew I was here, no doubt. But I have to tell you—and it can't get back to me—I saw your missing girl."

"Chelsea Loam?"

Kwan nodded.

"Alive? When?"

Kwan said, "Our firm has another client who's been fighting a prohibited weapons charge. We had it thrown out of court. Wasn't hard—the Mounties really wanted this guy, they rushed things and botched procedure. They disclosed surveillance photos of our client in his clubhouse during one of his parties. They would have been taken around the time your girl went missing. I was going through those photos, on account of a civil suit the client is launching against an associate-turned-informant. I think she's in one of the photos."

"Are you sure?"

"I think so, yes."

"Can I see the photo?"

"You can come with me and I can show it to you. I can't give you a copy and I can't verify any of this legally or I'd lose more than my job. You can't tell anyone this came from me. Fair?"

It wasn't, but that didn't matter. "Fair," I said.

"If you're ready we can go. I'll drive us to my office and bring the photo out to you. You can take a look at it, verify, but then that's it."

"You're being a bit sly with regards to this other client," I said. "I assume we're talking about someone in organized crime?"

"It's Terry Rhodes," Kwan said.

I sighed and rubbed my forehead. "Nothing can ever be fucking simple."

"You understand why the precautions," Kwan said. "Why the—why the drink. If this gets back to my boss, I'm fired. If it gets back to Terry Rhodes, I'm fucked."

"The last thing we need is the Exiles involved," Jeff said to me.

"Agreed. But all the same I've got to see that photo."

"I guess you do," Jeff said. "Just talk to me before you do whatever else you're thinking of."

7

KWAN'S MERCEDES WAS IN NEED OF NEW SHOCKS. As we stop-started through the midday traffic, Kwan talked about everything but the law or Rhodes or Chelsea Loam. The firm's offices were on Melville Street. It would have been quicker to walk.

"Your partner gets it," Kwan said. "On the one hand you've got the white establishment, on the other, your own kind. And neither can understand why you don't swear allegiance to them exclusive."

"Jeff's his own man," I said.

"No one's his own man. Second you're born, you're an owned commodity."

"I disagree," I said.

"You're young."

Kwan left the sedan double-parked and dashed inside. I sat in the artificially cool climate and thought about how to proceed. If it was Chelsea—big if, but it made a sick type of sense when I thought about it—I'd have to talk to Terry Rhodes.

Rhodes was an east coast biker who'd survived the Montreal motorcycle gang wars. He'd come west, decided he liked it and stayed. He had homes in Campbell River, Surrey and Abbotsford, but business often brought him to the city. He ran a security company, of all things. Corporate swine paid extra to have their galas and soirees protected by a bona fide full-patch member of the Exiles.

Nothing conceals a great crime like a smaller, flashier crime. Beneath the hard-living exterior of every biker lies a calculating business mind. They import black tar heroin and cocaine via the docks, farm the high-risk grunt work out to ethnic gangs or associated bike clubs. They run sprawling, massive dope farms up north, some buried deep in the earth, and swap it with the Americans for guns. The public sees rowdies and easy riders and doesn't give a shit. The city has been don't-give-a-shit territory for forty years. By the time people wised up, most of the old-time bikers had bought into straight businesses and gone semi-legit. Not only strip clubs and online poker sites, either, but clothing boutiques, music stores, car dealerships.

Terry Rhodes was past fifty, had money enough to buy an island, if he'd been that kind of asshole, and could have retired comfortably. But the grin he wore when his picture landed in the paper betrayed something more irrational than greed. The purpose of money wasn't to have enough. It was to take it from the other guy. The money only existed to pay off those institutions that needed paying off so he could continue doing things his way.

And what was his way? There were rumours. Rhodes still personally dished out punishment, still went on hits, still did the bidding of those wealthier and more influential than he was. A "Terry Rhodes" was a type of disfiguring torture or punishment involving the right eye and several teeth. All of it hearsay—or mythology.

Kwan came out of the office. He approached the car and made a window-rolling motion. He was sweating.

I pressed the roll-down switch, but without the ignition key the powered windows were just windows. Kwan looked both ways, tentatively, then held up his phone and pressed the screen against the glass.

In pixilated form, the photo showed a crowded bar scene. A corner of a stage was visible, part of a drum kit and the keyboardist's arm and shoulder. In the centre two figures moving through the crowd, a man and woman both in leather. Kwan turned the phone long enough to zoom in on the faces. They were holding hands, the man leading her—or pulling her, it was hard to tell—away from the stage. The man had the hatchet face, long hair and beard of Terry Rhodes. The woman was definitely Chelsea Loam. Cheekbones jutting out of sunken features, hair cut short and returned to its natural black, casual smear of lipstick and kohl-rimmed eyes. She looked haggard, partially digested by her lifestyle. But it was her.

I stared until Kwan took the phone away and went back inside the office. I climbed out and stood near the car.

Nothing can ever be fucking simple.

After ten minutes Kwan emerged with a cigarette in his mouth. He made an elaborate deal out of patting his pockets before asking me for a light.

"Left my Zippo upstairs. Do you mind lending me yours?"

So we had a smoke and played out Kwan's cover story, two strangers enjoying a late afternoon nicotine fix. I thanked him.

"I hope she turns up all right," he said.

"You know the exact date the photo was taken?"

"October twelfth. Big party at the old Law Courts Pub in Port Coquitlam."

"You know the place?"

"Knew of it," Kwan said. "Exiles hangout by reputation. Long gone now."

Kwan tossed down his cigarette and ground it into Melville Street with the point of his loafer. The cigarette had barely been touched. I wondered if Kwan actually smoked or if it was another precaution. I wondered why I found his precautions so amusing.

"Remember you can't say it came from me. And if you talk to him you can't say you saw a photograph. Do you need a ride back?"

"Quicker if I walk," I said.

"You'd think I never learned ethics," Kwan said. "I just broke every rule in the book."

"Rules and books don't draw breath."

"The truth is, I used to have to go to places like the Law Courts all the time. Ms. McKechney used to send me on errands. Rhodes and his hangarounds would make me wait, call me names like gook, commie. More often than not I wouldn't get paid for it. Well, fuck them. Fuck. Them. I hope you find that dead girl under their floorboards and they go away forever."

"And your firm would represent them, naturally."

Kwan smiled. "Kind of a win-win, isn't it?"

Shuzhen left first, saying her goodbyes and slinging her white trenchcoat over her shoulder. Jeff came into my office and treated me to the spectacle of watching him change ties.

"Taking Marie to Bard on the Beach tonight," he said.

"What's on?"

"*Macbeth* and some comedy. We're seeing the comedy."

"Enjoy that."

He shot his cuffs. "It'll be all right. They serve wine." He looked at the paper cup half full of whiskey, still sitting on the corner of the table. "Yeah, drinking is a lot of fun. Under the right circumstances."

"That's about as subtle, Jeff, as if you'd tattooed it on your foot and kicked me in the face. I'm not an alcoholic."

"No, I know that. Alcoholics are happier."

"Lot on my mind," I said, trying to end the discussion.

"You'd do better, Dave, to leave your work at work. Get some sort of personal life, then when you come back in the morning, you come back refreshed."

"Compartmentalize," I said.

"Exactly. It's better for your health and better for your work. Forgot to ask how your date with Marie's friend, what's her name, went."

"Brianna. She has a really neat phone. Lots of neat programs on it."

"They call those 'apps.' Five years older and I'm telling you." He checked his reflection in the window. "You work too damn much, Dave. Not too hard, just too much. And when an Asian tells you that, it's time to listen. Go fucking watch the sunset or something. Go to the beach. Get laid."

"Enjoy your Shakespeare."

After he left I phoned the Cambie Street police station and asked for the Missing Persons desk.

Ryan Martz's gruff voice answered, "Yup?"

"This is Dave Wakeland. Do you have any record of Chelsea Loam associating with bikers?"

"Wakeland. This is a line for police business, not private eye wankery."

"Chelsea Loam and Terry Rhodes?"

"Christ almighty."

"A pimp named Kamikaze?"

"If I hang up you'll just phone back, won't you?"

"I've got a couple leads. I'm following up on them."

"Fine." Martz sighed into the phone. "Bikers and hookers are sometimes found in each other's company. Match made in scrote heaven there. What else you got, Rockford?"

"Kamikaze?"

"Right. Pimps and dumb-ass names go together like fucked-out hookers and biker scum. Hope you got paid in advance, Wakeland. That all you called for?"

"Actually, I wanted to see if you felt like coming with me to talk to some of Rhodes's crew."

Martz laughed to himself. "Scrapyard Ed Nichulls and now Terry Rhodes. You could write a book, Dave. Fucking Audubon. *Migratory Shitbirds of British Columbia.*"

"I'll be at the Northwestern Inn in Burnaby and then back in town for La Grange."

"Tell you what. Do the titty bar first and I'll come for that part."

"All right. I'll meet you over there."

"Don't worry, I'll find you. I'll just ask for the only guy in the bar with an erection from staring at the bouncer."

"Gay jokes now?"

Martz's sharp laughter over the phone.

"Lighten the fuck up, Dave. Tell you what, I'll ask this chick I know in Sex Crimes does she know a Kamikaze. I'll even buy the first round. Domestic only. How's that?"

"Goddamn miraculous," I said.

8

GIRLS. HOT WET LIVE DIRTY DESIRABLE GIRLS. Big tits
and shaved pussies. Raunchy, naughty, crazy, explicit, wild,
party-loving hot bitches. All of them yours. Turned on by you.
Created, in fact, for your pleasure.

Ignore the scars from the tit jobs and C-sections. Ignore the
accents, South America and Eastern Europe, hinting at a life
that makes one of constant leering and menace seem liberating
by comparison.

La Grange was doing brisk business for a Thursday night.
A bachelor party held court at the front near the stage. The
betrothed sat goggle-eyed, the best man hyping the action.
The others took turns flipping the girls tens and twenties.
And the fiancée, keeping pace with the boys, as if to prove she
could be fun, too.

I didn't see Terry Rhodes, but then I didn't expect to find
him. I was looking for cronies. On this night, though, there
were no leather vests in the place. Maybe in a back room, but
not out on the floor.

The girls took a short break and the bachelor party moved
into the VIP lounge. The best man and fiancée were debating
whether or not to buy the lucky stiff a private dance.

"I mean, it's totally fine with me. I mean that."

"Because we don't have to. It's not that big a deal."

"Oh, I know that. We'll be right in the next room."

"Oh, totally. But again, it's up to you."

"He doesn't need my permission. I'm not that kind of girl-friend, oops, I mean wife."

"Let's see what he wants to do. Jerry? You up for a little—"

I had a Bulleit and soda and moved through the bar. Some of the girls were gorgeous, the sweat and vulgarity and their imperfections making them somehow more than the plastic image they projected.

I sat and watched a brunette who left her heels on during her act. She moved gracelessly on the heels, unused to them. She was shorter than the others, lithe and undernourished. Small-breasted, high-hipped, not a stripper's body. But there she was.

Martz was late. No surprise. I bought a beer and watched the bachelor party trickle out, some sort of discord among them. The brunette was swapped out for a blonde Vietnamese girl with D-cup breasts. Hers was more of a balancing act than a dance.

On the next changeover I saw the brunette stroll casually out of the washroom. There was something familiar about her. She saw me. I pointed to my nostrils. She wiped a dribble of coke-snot off her upper lip.

"That could've been embarrassing," she said. "Thanks for the catch. Maybe the next time your fly's open I'll be around to repay the favour."

"What high school did you go to?"

She said, "I'm not really allowed to socialize with the customers. But thanks, babe."

And up on stage she went in a rhinestone bra and panties, disrobing to the throb of Nine Inch Nails. The Vietnamese girl wobbled as she knelt near someone's face, accepted his dollars out of his hand with her mouth.

I felt a hard thwack on the back of my neck.

Martz stood behind me, holding two beers with his other hand. All his most genuine smiles seemed lupine at heart.

"This is my kind of investigation," he said. "Who we interrogating first?"

"I'm thinking it was a mistake coming here."

"It's early yet. These places don't even get going before ten."

We took a table and watched the dances. After a while the brunette came back out. She dipped and swayed. Smiled at me. For a moment I didn't do anything. At a nearby table three East Asians were whooping and clamouring, wads of dollars already out. She smiled and pursed her lips in a mocking pout, then moved away to shake for the other table.

"Fuck's the matter with you?" Martz said. "Give her some money. Or did you run out? There's an ATM at the back."

"We're here for work."

"Fucking tits, dude. She should be shaking that shit for us."

I walked over to the bartender. He looked at me the way a bartender in a strip club looks at a patron who's been drinking for the past two hours. This'll be fun.

"Do you know Ken Everett?"

"Sure," he said.

"He ever come in here?"

"I don't tell people 'bout other people's comings and goings."

"I used to spar with him."

"Hey, whatever, man."

I pointed at the stage, which now featured two redheads in Catholic schoolgirl outfits, the MC hyping them. "Give it up for Vancouver's own weird and wild sisters, make some noise for . . . the Bobbsey Twins!"

"The girl who was just up there," I said to the barkeep. "The brunette. What's her name?"

"That's Shay," he said. "She's not a regular. She's only filling in this week 'cause Keisha caught a stomach flu." He took a bucket of limes out of the mini-fridge and dumped the old bucket's contents on top.

I put two twenties on the bar. "What's her real name?"

"Save your money for the girls." He turned back to his citrus work.

Martz had returned from the ATM with a stack of twenties. He'd lured over one of the Bobbsey Twins and was making her snatch the bills from his hand by clasping her thighs together. It was difficult labour and had the success rate of a coin-operated crane game.

Outside I had a cigarette and thought about what to do. It was still early enough I could make it out to Burnaby. I'd had more to drink than I'd planned. And anyway the plan itself was nothing special. I wanted to find Ken Everett or one of Terry Rhodes's other stooges, ask him to ask Rhodes. I didn't want to butt heads with a motorcycle gang, demanding answers and making accusations. I wanted to make it a request, go through the proper channels to get an audience. There's a corporate hierarchy to most gangs. Like companies. Or police departments.

It had started raining, big hot drops of oily water.

I finished the smoke and turned and saw the brunette tucked under the awning, her own cigarette giving off the smell of burnt vanilla. She wore an old-school Hudson's Bay flannel coat and she'd changed into rubber gumboots.

"Want one?" she said, offering me the pack. I took one and accepted her match. I noticed her nails, cracked and spottily covered with glitter polish. "I normally get menthols but I thought I'd try these for a change."

"You're a good dancer," I said lamely.

"I try."

"I don't normally come to these places."

"Why not? It's fun."

"Yeah. I don't know."

She finished her smoke but made no move to go. She said, "If you're here to bust Amory, he sold it all and got out of the growing business like three weeks ago."

"I'm not a cop. Who's Amory?"

"Never mind," she said, throwing up her hands. "I'm so sorry. You're just regular citizens who look nothing like cops even though your buddy's packing his pistol and you haven't spent a dime, you cheap fuck."

"I'm not a cop," I said.

"Whatever."

"He is." I pointed at the club, indicating Martz. "I'm a private investigator. Are cops notoriously cheap?"

"In my experience they tip for shit and want all sorts of freebies. There's one cop comes in here, makes every new girl suck his dick on the house."

"Jesus."

"Yeah." A hint of a smile came to her face. "I told him I had hep C and an open sore in my mouth. That wilted his rod like old celery."

We shared a laugh. "Smart thinking," I said.

"Nah, it was the truth. I remember getting vaccinated back in grade school, but I guess it didn't take."

"That's where I know you from," I said. "You went to Emily Carr. We went to the same elementary school."

"Oh my God." She pressed her face to her hands. "I am so embarrassed right now." Laughing as she said it. "I haven't thought about that place in years."

"Remember the big red fire truck they used to have instead of a jungle gym? You know they tried to take that away? Guess too many kids got hurt."

"I remember you pushing me off that—David Wakeland."

"I did?" That broke my reverie. I searched for the memory, the name. "Sharlene?"

"Remember, I was teasing you for not having a mommy or daddy and you shoved me clean off the hood. I hit the wheel well. There was blood everywhere."

"Sorry," I said. "It's not a habit. I mean I haven't hit anyone since then. Women."

"I probably deserved it," she said. "Anyway, private investigator, huh. You're all Sam Spade and shit now. What are you doing here?"

I told her.

"Terry Rhodes doesn't come in all that much. Ken and the others, usually once or twice a week. You might try their club in Burnaby."

"Going there next."

She nodded. It was a warm night but she was swaying on her feet, keeping her coat tight around her.

"There like a big reward for information?" she asked.

"No," I said. "But if you hear anything, I'll pay."

"How much?"

"I don't know."

"A thousand?"

"That's a bit steep," I said. "If you find out where she is, or what happened to her, and it's verifiable, I might go three hundred."

"Wouldn't that be doing your job for you?"

I wanted to talk more. There was more to say. But a limo pulled up, a stretch Hummer, and spewed its contents onto the pavement in front of the club. Three suits, all in various stages of shit-facery, tossed back the dregs of their beer cans and dropped them in the gutter. One of them groped for the door handle. He noticed us and walked up to the mouth of the alley.

"Shay, how's the action tonight, babe? Action hot?"

"Totally super fucking hot," she said.

"Right on." He went back to his friends and they passed inside.

"They were here last night," she said.

"Good tippers?"

"At the beginning, sure."

As the door wheezed shut on its pneumatic hinges we heard Rob Zombie's "Living Dead Girl" start up.

"I'm back on in two numbers," she said. "Nice catching up."

"Maybe we'll see each other again."

"Come by anytime."

"Right." I gave her my card. "And if you happen to hear anything."

"I will, David Wakeland."

"David. Or Dave."

"Dave."

She banged on the side door. One of the red-headed Bobbsey Twins opened it, glowering at me as Shay passed under her arm. Sharlene Nelson who'd moved to Aldergrove in fifth grade, who'd once brought a cassette tape of the *Commitments* soundtrack for show and tell and had tortured us all with a rendition of "Mustang Sally" in fake Irish brogue.

I texted Martz: YOU GOING TO DEGRADE WOMEN ALL NIGHT OR ARE YOU COMING TO THE INN?

Then without waiting for his reply, I drove out to Burnaby.

9

IT WAS A FIGHT NIGHT, and the Northwestern Inn's parking lot was packed for the pay-per-view. I circled, looking for a space, making sure first that the bikes were there. A row of them, Softails and Ultraglides, along the side of the building diagonally. This was the Burnaby chapter's favourite dive. I slotted the Cadillac in beside the dumpster and walked inside.

A roar from the patrons greeted me. On the flat screens around the establishment I saw a fighter ground his mohawked opponent, mount him and pummel the challenger's face until the ref called the fight. A drunken clamour filled the place, cheers and I-told-you-sos.

I looked for Ken Everett in the roped-off section on the mezzanine. He was standing on the fringe of a party of bikers. Narrow-shouldered and slightly gangly, dressed in denim and leather to match the others. I wanted to talk to him alone. That wasn't likely to happen.

I walked up to the bartender, a gin mill veteran in a sweat-stained tank top. "See that man with the shaved head?" I pointed at Everett.

"Couple with shaved heads."

"But the one standing up. He's an old friend. What's he drinking?"

"They're all drinking the same. Black Tooth Grins, doubles."

I slid her the same two twenties I'd tried to give the other bartender. "I want to play a joke on him," I said.

"Son, those aren't joke playing type people."

"He'll understand. On the next round I want you to substitute his drink. One shot of the cheapest Scotch you have, one of the cheapest tequila. One part lemon vodka and one part dark rum. Top it up with Orange Crush."

"Nobody serves Orange Crush anymore."

"Root beer, then, or diet cola. And a squirt of peppermint schnapps. When he asks, direct him to where I'm sitting."

The bartender sighed and took the money. I had a seat. Eventually the next round went over. On the TV was a light-heavyweight bout that no one seemed to care about. It went to the third round before a Superman punch brought down the younger-looking fighter. It caught the crowd off-guard and the eruption was a slow build that culminated with the instant replay.

Everett stepped over the velour rope and dropped down onto the main level. He was carrying his drink and the front of his shirt was stained with liquid. I watched the dumb show play out.

The bartender stretched out her hand in my direction. Everett looked my way, walked over curious and angry. I grinned at him and he noticed who I was and grinned back.

"Dave Wakeland."

"The Thundering Left Hand of Ken Everett."

"And what's left of the rest of him." He sat down, extending out his right knee. "That was a fight," he said. "You gave me hell."

"If we'd been eighteen they would've let us go eight."

"And you'd've won."

I shook my head. "I didn't need it the way you did."

"You catch that fight a few minutes ago? Now there's a guy needs it."

"He's pretty sound."

"Sound. He's a fucking beast. Like Castillo. Remember Castillo? Wiped the floor with the both of us. Didn't set the world on fire when he went pro, but going up against him, and him a year younger than us, and fighting that good? Fuck." He pawed at the shirt stain with a napkin. "Why is it, Dave, you only think about the times you lost?"

"'Cause you don't learn anything from victory," I said.

"Maybe. Terry's bodyguard's ex-MMA. I appreciate it—how can you not appreciate a ground and pound like that last fight?—but I don't feel the love for it. Boxing was—you had a good day in the ring, in the gym, everything felt right."

"Maybe they feel that way about mixed martial arts," I offered.

"But I don't. All these years, you know, I think I was happiest working the speed bag in the Astoria. Your old man buying us beer afterwards."

"He passed a couple years ago," I said. "Drunk driver."

"Right. I remember hearing something about that. Meant to call." A nostalgic smile crossed his face. "Your dad—step-dad, whatever—toughest man I ever met, not counting Terry's bodyguard."

"He liked you. Always said you had a great left."

"I did," Everett said. "It's just the rest of me." He shook his head vigorously, warding off regret. "So. What'd you come here for?"

"I'm a private investigator. I'm looking for a woman named Chelsea Loam. She went missing eleven years ago. Her mother wants me to find out what happened to her."

"And what happened to her?"

"Someone dropped the mother an anonymous tip saying she was seen with Ed Leary Nichulls."

Everett grimaced. "That fucking guy. Never understood what the older guys saw in him."

"Turned out to be a bum steer," I said. "But I have to look into every tip."

"Right." He shifted slightly back from the table.

"I got another tip, also anonymous, that says she was at a party with Terry Rhodes before she vanished. That makes Rhodes one of the last people to see her."

Everett's reaction was slow but intense. His posture shifted another inch, and suddenly we were acquaintances, not old friends. Unthinking, he took a sip from the concoction in his hand, tasted it and scowled.

"Yeah. Can't help you there," he said.

"I need to talk to him, Ken. Ten minutes. Off the record. He chooses the time and place."

"Goes without saying."

"I'll ask him myself if I have to."

"You don't want to do that." Everett looked over at the VIP lounge, then back at me, a pained expression on his face. "How soon's this got to be?"

"Soon."

He sighed. "All I can do is ask."

"All I'd want you to do."

"It'd be a favour to me, him talking to you."

"And I'd owe you one for doing it."

He nodded. "I'm seeing him tomorrow. I'll ask, 'less he's in one of his moods."

"Appreciate it, Ken."

"Yeah. Maybe someday we'll get in the ring again."

"Maybe."

I bought him a real drink and together we watched the post-fight analysis. I thought of the time he'd broken my jaw. It was the first real injury either of us had caught. The look on Ken's face, surprise and shock, like he'd been the one hurt. He'd apologized all the way to Emergency.

"My kid wants to get into this," Everett said, pointing to the female fighters touching gloves for the main event. "She's twelve. The one I had with Joanna. Ever meet Joanna? Doesn't matter. My kid loves the fights."

He ran a hand over his scalp. When he swallowed the faded ink from his neck tattoo bobbed amidst the stubble. I realized he was holding back tears.

"That kid," he said. "Wants to be just like me. Do what I do. I don't know where the fuck I went wrong with her."

TEA AND WARM BREAD at CRAB Park before dawn. A cigarette in the light rain as I walked up Alexander Street toward the office. Even these didn't break the funk I'd worked myself into.

Shuzhen was out for the morning. Jeff leaned on the radiator by the outer office window, looking smug as only the well-sexed can.

"Managed to stay awake through the play," he said. "Had some nice Pinot Noir, and I got a blowjob on the drive home. Now that's the life, huh Dave?"

I lifted the pot off the percolator and poured myself a paper cup full of Jeff's decaf. "You don't drink coffee," he said. "Something up?"

I took out my phone and showed him the last text I'd received.

It said MY HOME 3 TODAY DONT SHOW LATE.

"You know the number?"

"I know who it's from," I said.

"Terry Rhodes?" Jeff poured a coffee for himself, added a shake of Coffee-mate and two generic sweeteners. "You said you'd talk to me before moving ahead on this."

"Well, I didn't. And don't pretend you expected me to."

"So how are you going to handle it?"

As if I hadn't been thinking about that all night. The text had come in at four, the noise jolting me awake. I hadn't gone back to sleep but had paced my cramped first-floor apartment until dawn.

I'd thought I'd have time to prepare. I'd thought I'd have some measure of control. I saw now how stupid those thoughts had been. Proof positive I'd exceeded my depth.

I answered Jeff's question by saying, "I'm going to ask him questions."

"But what's your tone going to be?" He topped up my coffee cup unbidden.

"My tone."

"Your general attitude," Jeff said. "Are you gonna go in demanding answers, all pissed off, or be professional?"

"Play it by ear," I said.

"With Terry Rhodes you're gonna play it by ear?"

"When your enemy attacks as a mountain, you attack as the sea," I said.

"Don't quote martial arts manuals to me, gwai lo. Take me through how you think the interview will play out."

Marie and I knew about the manuscript in Jeff's bottom drawer. For the past two years he'd been trying to author a textbook on interrogation strategy. Alternatively titling it *Advanced Techniques for the Contemporary Interviewer* and *How to Get People to Tell You What They Don't Want To*, Jeff had been trying to codify what he knew into a ten- or twelve-step system. Every so often he fixated on using me as a guinea pig.

Step Two was, "Prior to the interview, play out all possible outcomes so as to prepare yourself for every eventuality." It was classic Jeff Chen—smart, well thought out and deeply flawed.

"I'll play Rhodes, you play yourself," Jeff said.

"Fine."

"What y'all wanna know 'bout—why are you laughing?"

"Nothing. You're a master of dialect, Jeff."

"Fine. What do you want to know about?"

"I'm looking into the disappearance of a young woman."

"Don't know her."

"She went by Charity."

"Right. Don't know anything about her."

"There's a reward."

"Really?"

"Yeah. If you tell me what I want to know, my partner Jeff Chen will give you a pot of the world's most wretched coffee, plus any sexual favour you can name with a straight face."

Jeff sighed. "Fine," he said, walking a half-circle around me. "I'll be you, you be Rhodes. I need information."

"What's that got to do with me?"

"I have it on good authority that a young girl was in your company on the evening of October twelfth, year two thou—"

"I'd never say I have something on good authority."

"Shut up and say you don't know."

"All right. I don't know anything about that."

"Are you quite sure?"

"I am."

"All right, then."

I blinked, waited for Jeff to add something. He didn't.

"That's it?" I said. "What fucking good does that do me?"

"I'm showing you how to ask your questions, do it respect-fully, and not invite any reprisals."

"Christ's sake. The whole point, Jeff, is to get the information from Rhodes. To find out where the woman ended up."

"And what I'm teaching you, Dave, is how to come up with an exit strategy for when you don't get that info. 'Cause it doesn't benefit Rhodes to talk, and he's not so stupid that you'll be able to trick him. More than likely he's only meeting with you to see how much you know."

"You think I don't know that?" I said. "What do you think I've been turning over in my head the last five hours?"

"Maybe you shouldn't go, then."

"Can't do that."

"I'll go with you."

"'Preciate the thought."

"Dave—"

I reached for the box of Twinings. "I'm going to wash out the taste of this swill," I said. "Then at three o'clock I'm going to show up at Rhodes's house and ask him if he knows what happened to Chelsea Loam. Alone and unarmed, which is what he expects. That's the job. Given the inherent risk in what we do, I'll be as safe as I can."

"There are other people at risk too," Jeff said.

With my window open and my chair propped slanted against the wall, I waited out the clock. Martz's acquaintance from Sex Crimes, Constable Jane Henriquez, called to say she'd never heard of a pimp named Kamikaze, and the name didn't hit when she ran it through CPIC. I thanked her. Decent of Martz to follow through with that, I thought, considering the state I'd left him in the night before.

I drank my tea, tried to concentrate on work. From outside I heard the wheeze of a train whistle above the Doppler tremors of passing cars. I looked outside, saw below me a dump truck amidst the stalled moving traffic, its exhaust pipe belching foulness into the atmosphere.

Somewhere above or below ground was a woman who'd vanished when she was twenty-four and would be thirty-five this year. The world hadn't paused. Hadn't even noticed. With all the global positioning satellites and surveillance cameras that now blanketed the city in a unified field of transmissions, we were no safer—maybe much less so. Our technology makes us blind to the fact that we're humans, with an inborn need to wreck and transcend any system we come up with. Cameras can't stop us from disappearing—they're one more thing to hurl angrily into the approaching void.

I was waiting out the time, updating my correspondence on the Ghosh case, making sure that when I spoke to Mr. Ghosh next month I could assure him that nothing had developed. The emails I wrote on his behalf all began with "I know it's only been a month since our last correspondence" and ended with "and of course if you hear of anything please don't hesitate to contact me." Hundreds of agencies and associations received those emails on behalf of Jasmine Ghosh, who'd be well into her teens now. If she were alive. I wondered how many of those agencies consigned my monthly correspondence to their trash bins.

It was some kind of world.

Sharlene Nelson entered my office without a heads-up from the intercom. On that system of outdated technology and faulty cabling we'd been sold a bill of goods by a friend of Jeff's who had quite literally flown by night. By the time Shuzhen said, "Someone to see you," Shay was sitting in my guest chair, running a hand over the scarred hide of the table.

"Fancy furniture," Shay said. "I like the rest of the office."

"It's uncomfortably nice," I said.

"Why do you say that?"

"Because I'm uncomfortable in it and it's nice."

"I like it. The elevator has brass panelling. All the doors are oak. Nothing looks like that now. There's even a post office drop in the lobby."

"It's not bad," I admitted. "Beats my last office."

"You should see some of the places I've worked."

I refilled the teapot and brought the service back to my desk. She accepted a cup, stirred in skim milk and three dollops of honey. Stirred it and stirred it.

"Is there something I can help you with?" I asked.

"I need money. I want to make a change. I was kind of thinking maybe I could help you."

"Did you find out something about Chelsea Loam?"

"No, but I could," she said. "I know that area and I know those people. And no offence, but you still look kind of like a cop, so a lot of people probably won't talk with you but might talk to me."

"It's a fair point," I said. People speak to cops out of fear and a primal need to please authority. An ex-cop doesn't inspire those same feelings. There were worlds open to Shay that weren't open to David Andrew Wakeland.

Shay said, "Okay good, I'll need a thousand dollars and I'll need a little bit of it up front."

"I told you," I said. "A thousand—"

"You're not going to poor-mouth, are you, Mr. Brass Elevator?"

I caught myself and smiled. "No, ma'am."

"Good. Like I told you I need money to make a change. A thousand bucks isn't even life-changing money. It's foot-in-the-door money. So?"

"Are you going to spend this on drugs?"

"You're spending it on finding that missing girl you said you want to find so much."

We eyed each other over the table. I had the better view.

"Ask me," she said.

"Ask you?"

"What you want to ask. Am I a hustler? Do I do drugs? Why yes, David, I do drugs. Yes, for a while I did sell my body to the night. And I'm going to take your money now and buy drugs. And I'm going to do those drugs with other people who do drugs and ask them questions and find out what you need to know. And once it's over you'll pay me and I'll clean up and go back to school, because I'm twenty-nine and I can't do this forever. But I can do it short-term and help you. If you can get over your delicate bourgeois sensibilities."

"How much are you asking for?"

"Three hundred."

"And then seven when you tell me what happened to Chelsea Loam."

"No," Shay said. "Then a thousand. The three hundred is expenses. That's what private eyes always charge in movies, it's always fifty dollars a day plus expenses, hundred seventy five plus expenses. That three hundred is my 'plus expenses.'"

"How about one hundred?" I said.

"How 'bout you go fuck a jug?"

I held up my tea, saluted her and took a sip.

"See," I said, "it's not my bourgeois sensibility, it's my bourgeois pocketbook. I give you three hundred dollars, no collateral, no receipt, I've been hustled. I take that back. I've hustled myself."

"I'm not full of shit. You've known me since grade school."

"How about this," I countered. "Sort of a trial run. I'll give you two hundred and you bring me back something useful. Something I didn't know."

"Like?"

"For starters, I need a line on a pimp named Kamikaze. I need Chelsea's last known address. I'd like to see her personal effects. Info on her birth parents. Pictures of her from around the time she went missing. Names of people who knew her. Anything like that. Concrete tangible information, not the runaround. Then I'll give you your 'plus expenses,' and if it turns out right, the thousand."

"And what if I find her?"

"Then I'll give you the thousand and kick Jeff out, and I'll go to work for you."

She grinned and stuck out her hand. "If you ever get sick of private eyeing, you could probably last on the street. I know a lot of girls that don't have your business sense."

I cut her a cheque for two hundred dollars, made it out to cash, and wrote out a receipt for Gail Kirby. "I'll put 'Misc. Expenses,'" I said. "'Drugs for hustler' might offend her bourgeois sensibilities."

"It's one of those words," Shay said. "Bourgeois. If you say it to someone under forty who has more money than you do, you can pretty much shame them into doing anything you want."

I passed her the cheque. She inspected the numbers.

"Usually I only take cash," she said. "But since there's a Royal Bank in the building, any problems I'll just say the guy on the eighth floor used a bad cheque to pay me for letting him lick my butt."

I walked her to the elevator. As we waited she said, "Are you having regrets?"

"Maybe a little buyer's remorse," I said.

"Don't," she said. "It'll pay off."

"Hope so."

Shay opened her purse and rummaged for cigarettes. I heard the sound of pills rattling in their plastic vials. She caught my look.

"It creeps up on you. I used to feel so fucking good, Dave. I'd wake up at noon with nothing to do till night. And there'd be dope around, and I'd be like, this'll pass the time and let me chill." She caught sight of herself in the brass. "That probably sounds really stupid."

"Not at all," I said. "Sort of. I mean, I used to feel juiced working patrol in District Two, and then come home to this quiet house with my girlfriend asleep, and want to go back out."

"Why'd you quit?"

"I was sort of asked to resign. Long story."

"Some other time, then."

"Some other time."

The elevator was waiting. Getting on, she said, "I'm not trying to put one over on you, Dave."

"My experience, people who say they're not trying to put one over on you are usually trying to put at least one over on you."

"Maybe, but I'm not. I'm going to find that lead and we're going to find that girl and then I'm going to dry out and get my nursing certificate."

"Hope it works out," I said.

What I didn't say: My experience, people who say they're not trying to put one over on you, who aren't in fact trying to put one over on you, are quite often putting one over on themselves.

The door closed. I went back to my office. Finished my emails. By then it was half past two, and time to meet Terry Rhodes.

11

MEET HIM WHERE? was a question I didn't think I'd need to ask. As I rolled out of the underground lot in my Cadillac, I thought I knew. Rhodes had a home on the Island in Campbell River. He had access to the clubhouses and hangouts of the Vancouver, Surrey and Coquitlam chapters. It wasn't like an Exile in good standing didn't have places to stay.

But Rhodes had a piece of property at Adanac and Skeena, over the city limits into Burnaby. A quiet residential neighbourhood. On paper the place was owned by a company out of Montreal, leased to Rhodes for a nominal fee. He didn't conduct business there, and not so much as a noise complaint had been connected to the address. I learned this from a call to an ex-colleague named Laal who'd been assigned to the Outlaw Motorcycle Task Force.

So I drove toward Burnaby. But when I turned off Hastings onto Skeena a text came in from the same number. It gave an address in North Surrey plus the nonsensical phrase KEY IN PANDA.

As I crossed the Alex Fraser Bridge, I started thinking about Shay. I didn't care much about the two hundred dollars. The transaction made me anxious because I didn't like Shay putting herself at risk for me.

Even more, I didn't like the idea there were places she could go that I couldn't. As a cop I'd always prided myself on being

INVISIBLE DEAD • 61

of the street. The call-outs other cops hated—2 a.m., shitbox
flat, yet another junkie domestic, insolent roaches that don't
even scurry—I'd done them happily and earned my scars.
Yet now that world was closed off. I could occupy the same
space, the same geography, without sharing that world anymore. And maybe I never had. It was like immigrating to a
country and decades later finding out all the time you'd spent,
all the taxes, had granted you no citizenship, no status. Other
people, all other people, were more and more incomprehensible.
And I wondered whether I wasn't approaching the time to quit.

Of course this was just a feeling, fleeting and mutable. But as
I drove to meet Rhodes I found the idea of doing something else
more appealing.

The house Rhodes had brought me to was a three-storey
McMansion in a quiet cul-de-sac, light blue with white trim.
The roof had been capped with some sort of polymer and looked
artificial, like a gingerbread house. A big empty driveway fed
into a two-car garage.

I parked at the end of the cul-de-sac and approached the
front steps. Baskets and chimes hung above the railing. Beside
me, a kidney-shaped flower bed was cut into the pavement.
Among the lettuce and roses sat two garden ornaments, a
pewter Buddha and a plastic panda. The panda was balanced
atop a slug trap. I lifted it up and found a key driven into a rip
on its flank.

Inside, the lights weren't on, and nothing happened when
I turned the dimmer switch. The hallway extended in front of
me in darkness. In the living room to my right, none of the TV
components were lit up, nothing blinking or telling the time.

I pocketed the key and walked down the hall toward the
kitchen. I called out hello and my name.

The kitchen was empty. There was no table in the dining
room. Just one black chair and sitting in it, a man.

Behind him, the blinds on the sliding door leading outside
were twisted so that irregular slashes of light fell across him.
He was sitting in shadow. A big man, wearing cargo pants and

an orange wife-beater that clutched the contours of his torso.
He had a fighter's physique. He was barefoot.

"He said three."

"I know," I said. "I didn't get the address till ten to."

"Late."

"The last half hour you've been sitting here waiting in the
dark?"

"It's not dark," he said.

His voice was calm, his body almost motionless. I couldn't
see any tattoos. His hair was cut short, in a flat-topped style
that looked like an exaggeration of Eisenhower-era respectabil-
ity. An expensive-looking watch hung off one wrist, and two
of the fingers on his left hand were taped. He was maybe forty.

"Is Terry Rhodes coming?" I asked.

"Why would he come here?"

"We're supposed to meet. I'm supposed to ask him some
questions."

"That won't happen."

"Then I'll be going."

"Don't be stupid," he said.

We waited. I waited for him to speak. He seemed to be waiting for me to see if I'd disobey. After a solid eighty seconds
I started for the hall.

"I told you, don't."

I stopped. I said, "You don't scare me."

"How would you know?"

"I've known a lot of yous," I said.

He took a deep breath and nodded very slightly, as if I'd
made an interesting point. I noticed he didn't blink all that
often. Someone in a neighbouring yard was cutting grass with
a gas-powered mower. Outside it would be loud.

"I think we need agreement on things," the man said.

He stood up and came at me, swift. I didn't mean to back
up but I did. He stopped arm's distance from me. He was well-
tanned and his skin had almost a jaundiced tinge to it.

"Do you think I'm for real?" he asked.

"Yes."

"Do you think I could hurt you if that's what I wanted to?"

"Probably."

"Yes, right?"

"Yes."

"You're a private detective?"

"Yes I am."

"Would you want to know what I am?"

"What."

"What I do?"

"You can tell me if you want."

"I take things."

"Kind of things?"

"Things you'd rather keep."

I said, "Is this where I say, is that a threat? And you say, no it's a promise? And I say, oh yeah? And you say, oh yeah?"

I'd slipped my weight to my back foot. The man stood straight and still. The look on his face looked strangely like concern. I was starting to wonder if his thoughts and expressions matched up at all.

"Mr. Terry Rhodes doesn't know any girl that you're looking for," he said. "Stop looking for her. Stop right now when you leave this house. Will you stop?"

"I'm kind of getting the sense he does know," I said.

"I need you to answer me yes or no. Will you?"

"I can't," I said.

"Can't stop or can't answer yes or no?"

"How 'bout I say yes and go ahead anyway?"

"I need you to say yes and mean yes."

"Yeah. Can't do that."

"Go over to the kitchen."

I waited for him to swing at me. The punch didn't come. Instead a kick swept out and clipped the side of my knee, too fast to deflect. I was off balance, rocked by the pain. I swung anyway. He batted my fist away, seized my shoulder and propelled me backward into the kitchen, back until my spine hit the countertop.

"Stick your hand in the drain," he said.

I didn't. His grip on my shoulder tightened. I tried to shrug him off but his forearm came up into my throat and he bent me back over the sink so the back of my head pressed against the drape over the window and shook it down.

"Stick your hand into the sink."

I did.

"Fingers into the drain. All the way. Until your hand's stuck."

I complied.

There was a switch over the drain. He flipped it. Nothing happened. He flipped it back down.

"Stay there," he said. "Don't move and don't take your hand out."

He turned and left the kitchen. I heard his feet on the stairs. I tugged my hand. I could have probably pulled it out but I didn't. I wondered why I didn't.

Time passed and then the lights went on. I heard thumps on the steps and he came back. Now I spun my wrist to try and free my hand.

"The fuse box," he said. "That's where I was."

I was sweating. Suddenly my hand was free.

"Put it back in there," he said. "All the way. That's it."

He walked up close and reached over for the switch. He kept his face close to mine. He had brown eyes like anyone else's.

"I'm supposed to hear you say you won't pursue this," he said.

"I won't."

"Won't what?"

"Chelsea Loam. I won't look for her anymore."

His hand reached for the switch and I flinched. My other hand groped at the countertop blindly but there was nothing.

The man flipped the switch. The garbage disposal roared to life. My hand—

Nothing.

The man dropped a small gear and some rusted screws into the other basin and turned off the disposal.

"That's your warning," he said. "Put the key back where you found it."

He walked out of the room. I unstuck my hand. I took some breaths. Then I left, placing the key back as I went.

Fear is the least-understood phenomenon. A study of fear would be interesting to read, if you were the kind of person who read studies. What makes it so unappetizing is the nagging sensation that it is the proper state of things. That anyone without fear in their hearts has simply been enveloped in a comforting fantasy.

I drove to the office, going slow and making a nuisance of myself to the rush hour commuters humping over the Alex Fraser. I tried to think of the last time I'd been bullied so successfully. It felt as if someone had erased part of me, as if I'd really lost my hand.

Ken Everett must have known what I was walking into. Rhodes might have forced him to set it up. Or kept him in the dark, it was hard to say. Much as I wanted to confine and segregate my fear, there was no sense to be made, no way to process it.

Outside the office on the eighth floor I heard the strains of an argument through the door. I unlocked it and went inside, went to my office and locked myself in. I sat down and opened the filing cabinet and took a pull off the Botanist. I listened to Jeff and Marie bicker in his office, their voices as clear as if the doors had been open.

"—why you have to be so damn morose—"

"Me morose? Let me know the proper reaction for you saying you'd leave me."

"It was a joke, Jeff. It was—"

"Wasn't a joke. I heard—"

"You always—"

"I heard the tone and you were not—"

"Well it's not like it's gonna happen—"

"Not the point—"

"He's a movie star for crying out—"

"Not the point, Marie."

"Well what is. The point. Jeff."

"We've been talking marriage."

"Yes?"

"Which is a pretty big commitment for me."

"Oh, and it isn't for me?"

"And I'd like to not waste all this time—"

"Who said—"

"—only to find out you'd rather be with somebody else."

"Jeff, it's a thing people say—"

"Those are called words."

"—a funny way to say someone's cute."

"Funny to who?"

"I'm not allowed to say I find other men attractive?"

"Not the same—"

"It's *exactly* the same—"

"Oh, it is, of course, I'm just stupid."

"Brianna asked was I happy with you, if everything was going all right—"

"You said I'd do till you left me."

"I said you'd do till Tom Hardy asked me to run away with him. Don't you see?"

"I guess I really don't."

And so on and so on and so forth. I drank gin and listened to them squawk, and I dreamt of ways to hurt someone whose name I didn't even know.

12

I DID NOTHING THAT WEEKEND. Laundry, swept the patio, reaffixed a towel rack that had ripped through the drywall. I ordered in sushi and drank tea and worked my way into the back recesses of my liquor cabinet.

And on Monday I still hadn't reached a decision. I drove to the Kirby house to let them make that choice for me, to tell me how much I should value my neck.

Gail Kirby was out. A mother-daughter team of Vietnamese maids were working through the house. I asked them when Mrs. Kirby would be back.

"Don't know," the mother said apologetically. "I'll get her daughter, please you wait."

So I waited in the living room and moved a couch so the younger cleaner could vacuum behind it. She wore earbud headphones that snaked down into the pocket of her uniform. She didn't make eye contact, but nodded her thanks as I slid the couch back.

Eventually Caitlin came down the stairs. She wore a sleeve-less button-up shirt and capri pants, and carried a wine glass with two half-melted ice cubes tumbling around inside it. I followed her into the kitchen.

"I'm having sangria," she said.

"No thanks."

She poured herself one, catching a couple of fresh cubes as they tumbled from the ice machine built into the fridge.

She leaned against the large island in the centre of the room, tasting her drink with no apparent enjoyment. I stopped in the entryway, still on the hall carpet rather than the blue mosaic tile of the kitchen.

"I'll simply say this," Caitlin said. "We both know what my mother has allotted for this silly errand. If you're here for more money I can tell you I have conditional power of attorney, and it's my preference to wait and consult with Gail before I authorize any further expenditure."

"Is she all right?"

"She's having a round of aggressive radiation therapy, if you must know."

"Sorry to hear that. The cleaners said she was out."

"Oh, yes." Caitlin waved her hand in dismissal in the direction of the cleaners. "They don't speak much in the way of English. It seemed easier to tell them Mrs. Kirby was out than to explain a medical procedure."

"The daughter is pre-med at UBC," I said.

"How on earth do you know that?"

"Because I'm a really, really good detective."

If her nose had crinkled any more it would have been cellophane.

"She has a UBC lanyard around her neck," I added by way of explanation. "Medical textbooks on the back seat of their station wagon. Her name's Deanna Tranh, if you want to talk to her sometime."

"I'll do that," Caitlin said. She ran her tongue over the edge of her bottom lip. "So is this about money?"

"It's about seeing if I should continue."

I told her only that I'd linked Chelsea back to a well-connected biker who was reluctant to talk.

"It's more than enough for me," Caitlin said. "However, I can tell you that my mother would only redouble her efforts. But then she's always been very single-purposed."

"Listen to you," I said. "You're a couple years older than me and you sound like Jane Eyre."

"Books and film raised me. My parents certainly weren't around."

"You wouldn't spend a dime looking for Chelsea, it was your decision, would you?"

She bit her lip and looked for one moment as if she would have liked to throw something at me. Then she smiled. The kind of smile that has no smile in it.

"You must think I'm some haughty stuck-up lesbian," she said.

"I hadn't given much thought to your sexual preference."

"Come upstairs," she ordered.

I followed her up, temporarily disrupting Deanna and her mother's efforts to steam-clean the stairs.

Upstairs we passed through Gail Kirby's bedroom, tidy and antiseptic, a medical bed with fold-down rails occupying the centre. A plastic gripping rail reached floor to ceiling. Through the next door we entered a sort of office and craft room, with a computer desk and photo printer, a table covered with patterns, various half-finished sewing projects, and on the floor, three dusty boxes and two green garbage bags.

The flaps of one box had been separated. Nestled within were ribbons and trophies, a childhood's worth of art projects, now just so much construction paper, stale macaroni and glitter.

"Were these Chelsea's?" I asked. But the era was wrong. The trophies were gaudy and plastic, too ornate for the early eighties when Chelsea came of age. This was late-nineties childhood ephemera.

"These," Caitlin said, "were Kevin's."

I pulled out a framed portrait of a boy around seven, with dark hair and olive-coloured skin. He wore a Winnie-the-Pooh sweater. His mouth was open as if caught in a moment of wild ecstatic joy, as if some force had touched him in the pure pleasure centre of his brain.

"He was Chelsea's?" I asked. There wasn't a great likeness between Chelsea and Kevin. Maybe about the eyes, which both seemed brighter than their dark colour would allow.

"She gave birth to him," Caitlin said.

"Where is he?"

"With Father, in Mount Pleasant Cemetery."

"I'm sorry," I said.

"He was born with a heroin addiction, as well as develop-mental issues," Caitlin said. "No one thought he'd survive. Chelsea's careful parenting ensured that Kevin was diabetic by the time he was walking. She wanted to get rid of him, put him up for adoption. My mom said she'd take him. Which meant that I would take him."

"Did Chelsea see him often?" I asked. But Caitlin wasn't listening.

"I had no choice in the matter. I was only a child myself. I never wanted to be a mother, least of all a mother to someone who needed so much more than I could give. The doctor swore that with his accumulation of ailments, it was only a matter of making Kevin's time comfortable. But he lived into his teens. He passed a year ago."

"Did Chelsea spend time with Kevin? Get to know him?"

"She'd phone. Sometimes I'd let her talk to him. Other times I'd hang up on her."

"Who was the father?"

"If Chelsea didn't know, how would I?"

"How did she feel about that?"

"Honestly, Mr. Wakeland, I don't care in the slightest. Sometimes she was remorseful and ashamed, other times she was only acting penitent. After the fifth time she vowed on Kevin's soul to clean up and take responsibility, I told her I didn't want her to see him."

"And your mother knew about that?"

"Yes, though she was busy tending to her holdings. It's only since her retirement and diagnosis that Gail has become con-cerned with doing the decent thing, and not just what seems decent in the eyes of her neighbours."

"Parenting is difficult," I said.

"I'm thirty-nine now, probably past the opportunity to have kids of my own. My biological clock and all of that. Only now am

I realizing what I don't have. I wasted the better part of my life caring for my sister's child, so that cunt—you see, Mr. Wakeland, I do know how to speak your language—could waste her life getting high and break my mother's heart. Please go."

She was staring out the window, over the neighbouring roofs and through the netting of power lines. Maybe toward the Coast Mountains, looming blue against a blue sky. I thought there might be tears but she was clear-eyed, standing there among the keepsakes of a life she no longer cared for, looking out at something else.

"Do you think she's special?" Jeff asked.

We were sitting on a bench in Coal Harbour, a few blocks from Denman where Jeff's condo was. I'd suggested we take the morning off and walk the Seawall. That eight-kilometre circuit finished, I'd collapsed on the nearest bench and lit a cigarette.

I'd been hoping to sound him out on the Loam case, hoping he'd either say something that made sense, or something that pissed me off enough to do the opposite. Instead I'd been treated to a two-hour soliloquy on the premarital relationships of Jefferson Chen.

The heat was pleasant. It was a good day away from the office.

"Do I think who's special?" I said.

"Marie. Who else were we talking about?"

"I wasn't really listening," I said.

He shook his head. Everyone who passed us was beautiful—trim fit spandex blondes, sculpted shirtless men in drawstring shorts, dark-skinned women, lithe under their summer dresses.

I took a long drag off my cigarette. "Why do you smoke in this day and age?" Jeff said.

"Makes me look cool," I said.

"Right, sweatpants and a Screaming Trees T-shirt and a cigarette, that's the cover of *Esquire* right there."

We sat. "I don't know what you should do," I said at length.

"Yeah, we'll figure things out. How's your love life?"

"No movement on that front," I said. "Remember that Audrey Hepburn calendar I had hanging in my old office?"

"Yeah, we ditched it. Why?"

"It was a gift from my last office assistant. Sometimes when I was in the office for days on end I'd masturbate to that calendar."

"Don't tell me that," Jeff said.

"It's not the point of the story. Just a salacious detail."

"Well, I don't need those details."

"My point," I said, "I used to imagine having a relationship with someone like that. She always seemed so happy, so alive."

"Vivacious."

"Good word, yeah, exactly. And I used to wonder how long it would take, her being in a relationship with me, to suck every ounce of enjoyment out of her. Leave her a bitter old husk, wandering around a mall somewhere."

Jeff nodded very seriously. Three women eating gelato walked past the bench. A ways along the path, a cyclist in a lemon bodysuit wove his bike through the foot traffic. A heron exploded out of the water, coursing through the air toward Stanley Park.

"Hanson Brothers are playing the Rickshaw tonight," Jeff said. "Any interest in coming with?"

"With you and Marie? You probably need some alone-together time." Jeff took his punk rock seriously, dancing with abandon. I'd spend three hours stranded, holding his jacket and beer.

He didn't argue the point. I tossed away my cigarette.

"I don't know how to proceed," I said. "My instinct, someone tells me to do something, is to do the opposite, just to fuck them up. But you can't fight bikers. Their money, their connections. And if Chelsea Loam is dead, and it was Rhodes that's responsible, how in hell does it benefit anyone knowing that, if there's no chance he'll see the inside of a prison?"

"I thought you wanted to talk about yourself," Jeff said.

"Why?"

"Well, you don't seem happy."

"I don't like to be bullied," I said.

"You going back to the office?"

Instead I drove home. Showered and changed, frothed some milk and made a half-assed London Fog. Put on Kellylee Evans's album of Nina Simone covers and sat listening with the sliding glass door open to accept as much of a breeze as the July afternoon could muster.

After a while I got out my MacBook and went to work.

If going after Rhodes was too dangerous, there were other angles to work. The list I'd given Shay contained several of them. Add the identity of Kevin's father and the circumstances of the party Rhodes and Chelsea had attended. I started with the most basic and most metaphysical question: Who was she and where did she come from?

Vital Statistics had sent Gail Kirby a copy of Chelsea Loam's birth certificate. I also had her adoption papers. Born to Anne Loam and an unnamed father, Chelsea Anne Loam was brought into the world at Vancouver General Hospital, delivered healthy if a little underweight. Our mothers had shared the same maternity ward. Chelsea's adoption history was well documented—stints in Oakvale Girls' House, a year out with a Mr. and Mrs. Forrester, back to Oakvale and then to a smaller facility called the River Run Academy, and then at age thirteen adopted by Lew and Gail Kirby.

I thought back to when I'd asked Gail why she'd adopted an adolescent. She'd said, "It sounds like masochism, doesn't it? Willingly taking in a thirteen-year-old?"

"Most adopters want younger kids," I'd said.

"I did it for Caitlin's sake," Gail had explained. "I couldn't have more of my own. She was having a rough time of things. I thought it would help for her to have a sister. So we talked it out as a family at the dinner table. I convinced Lew. Caitlin loved the idea."

I wondered how quickly that had changed. A sister in the abstract is different than one you have to compete against.

The internet is vast but not all-knowing. I couldn't find much on Anne Loam. Like her daughter, whatever she'd done with her life hadn't been well documented. After a while I went to the private detective's best friend, the Yellow Pages. There weren't many Loams, six in total. I dialed all of them.

Four nos in quick succession, a could-you-get-back-to-me, and a disconnected number. I waited half an hour and dialed the fifth number again. A Wayne Loam answered on the second ring.

"Y'ullo?" he said.

"My name's Dave Wakeland, I'm a private investigator. Are you by any chance related to an Anne Loam, or a Chelsea Anne Loam?"

"Sorry, you're a what?"

"Private investigator, sir."

"This about inheritance, some dead relative?"

"Sort of," I said. "Do you know Anne Loam?"

"I know she was my sister. How much are we talking?"

"Mind if we do this in person?"

"No complaints on my end."

"Should I drive to you?"

"You'll have to, my van's got starter troubles. But I'll make it easy on you. Know the Tomahawk? That's five minutes from me on foot. What say I meet you there at two."

"Suits me," I said. "If you have any documentation about Anne Loam . . ."

"I'm not a documentation type guy," Wayne Loam said. "But I'll see what I got."

"Photos, anything."

"See you at two."

I gassed up the Cadillac at a Husky on Broadway. As I waited for the automatic payment machine to spew out my three feet of receipt, a text came through. It read: THIS IS KEN. SORRY TO DO YOU LIKE THAT.

I climbed behind the wheel, texted: SORRY NOT GOOD ENOUGH.

WHATD BE GOOD ENOUGH was his reply.

I still needed two hands to text. I pulled into the air pump space and wrote YOU KNOW WHAT I WANT.

NOT GOING TO HAPPEN. ·

I pulled over at the corner of Clark and Terminal. I punched in I NEED TO KNOW ABOUT THE PARTY.

Everett's answer took a while. I watched some teens dribble a basketball across an industrial park. I looked up at Ken Lum's white neon cross that presided over my part of the city. It was unlit at this time of day and turned west so I could barely see the writing. But I knew what it said. An old biker tattoo design, now reclaimed as neighbourhood art:

```
        E
    V   A   N
        S
        T
```

My phone jumped in my hand. Everett had texted me back: NOT FROM ME.

THEN FROM SOMEONE ELSE. I was quick.

PUTS ME IN A BAD PLACE.

It took me a while to write but I was happy with my response: HAND IN GARBURATOR BAD OR JUST AWKWARD?

Broadcast silence for seven whole minutes.

ILL LOOK INTO IT came the response.

13

DRIVING TO THE NORTH SHORE entailed retracing the day's steps and passing through Coal Harbour, then onto the Stanley Park Causeway that cut through the park and led to the Lions Gate Bridge. The other side of Burrard Inlet was a different city. Compared with Vancouver proper, North Van seemed wealthy and green and removed from the grit and hustle—"pleasant" was an apt descriptor—but it had its own atmosphere, its own legends. Its own ghosts.

I outdid the speed limit by twenty klicks, making up for the time I'd spent texting Everett. I had music going through the Caddy's stereo, Ingrid Jensen's *Vernal Fields*, her muted trumpet on "Ev'ry Time We Say Goodbye" a mellow burn.

Coming off the bridge it took me a minute to find the road that would take me to the Tomahawk grill. I remembered my father taking me there, remembered splotching crayon colours on the placemats.

The Tomahawk served up lumberjack food, barbecue, burgers and eggs, and did it as well as could be done. As for the decor— log cabin exterior, totem poles—it was hard to pin down. An almost century-old restaurant that serves organic beef burgers named after famous coastal chiefs ought to be hard to pin down.

It was six past two. Aside from an elderly couple and the wait staff I was alone in the place. I sat and ordered a Chief August Jack burger with a Boylan's cola.

A quarter of an hour passed. The next customer that came in was tall and broad-shouldered and wore a red trucker hat and a Gore-Tex jacket despite the heat. He nodded at me and sat down.

"I googled you," Wayne Loam said. We shook hands. "I was here a few minutes early and you weren't around so I went and got my mail. Ordered without me, huh?"

The waiter set my burger down, took Wayne Loam's order. "Help yourself," I said, indicating the fries.

"Don't mind if I do." The waiter brought him a cup of black coffee. "Thanks kindly."

"You probably guessed there isn't a fortune waiting for you," I said.

Wayne Loam nodded. "These type visits are always extra hassle."

"Other people have asked about Chelsea?"

"Sure," he said. "I always tell them what they can do with themselves, so many words."

"But not me?"

"You asked about Anne. You asked about my sister."

"Anne Loam went missing too?"

"No," he said. "But yes. She was taken."

"By who?"

"Government. Who else?" He slurped his coffee. "Yeah, she was taken to one of those residential schools. One day two guys show up in a government van, out of the blue, and take her. I was off hunting with my cousins when they came, else I'd'a been nabbed, too."

"Fuck."

"That's the word for it. When Anne came back she wasn't near the same. Took her a long while to get comfortable being around people, get back to dancing—Anne couldn't dance to save her soul, but try and tell her that. Then, just when things looked up, along comes Chelsea. Not that we all didn't love her."

"Who was Chelsea's father?" I asked. I'd lost my appetite. "Did you know him?"

"Anne was real good keeping that secret," Loam said. "But I found out. He was slipping her money."

"Who was he?"

"Thomas Mulcahy. Father Tom. Real nice guy. He used to talk to me after the service. Took an interest in me, which was probably just him taking an interest in Anne."

His food arrived, a Yukon breakfast, bacon and scrambled eggs. He chewed slowly. "Yeah, we used to talk about me going into the seminary. Wasn't too keen on the celibacy part. Guess neither was he. He said he'd write me a letter of recommendation for the college in Canterbury. The story of how I found out he was the daddy's pretty good."

It was. Father Mulcahy had trusted Wayne with the church bookkeeping. Wayne had excelled in mathematics—"not calculus, but stick a dollar sign in front of it and I can do most anything with numbers." He'd worked out a rough formula for church donations. "I forget it exactly but it was something like, number of attendees times a buck minimum donation, minus the number of kids, minus the number of really stingy people like the Clays, minus the people who couldn't afford to spare anything."

During the summer attendance dropped, until late August. "People who'd done an entire season's worth of sinning were now suddenly taking their kids, getting ready for the school routine."

Attendance doubled but donations plunged. Wayne couldn't figure it. His system had been accurate to within five dollars for the last eight months. And then suddenly it wasn't just off, it was exponentially less.

When the next week's yield was even shorter, he grew suspicious. And he noticed his sister Anne with new baby gear.

"Not stuff people had kicking around their homes and might've donated, but high-end Hudson's Bay type stuff. And not only baby stuff but dresses. Anne had this blue dress. Sheer. Like right out of a *Chatelaine*."

Wayne confronted Anne on her thefts. Anne denied it. Said the money was a gift from an admirer. Wayne connected the dots.

"I talked to Father Tom. I was pretty naive. I asked him why he didn't marry Anne and get some other job. He cried. First white man I ever saw cry."

"What happened to him, Mulcahy?"

"The darndest thing," Wayne Loam said. "Soon as I let him know I knew, he got an urgent call back to Canterbury. I go to his office to chat, Father Tom's stuff has been cleaned out and Father Radomsky's moving in. No goodbye. At the time that hurt more than what he'd done to Anne."

"How did Anne come to put Chelsea up for adoption?"

"That would be, what, eighty-something? Eighty-three?" The waitress refilled Wayne Loam's coffee cup, asked if I wanted anything. I told her just the cheque.

"Anne met a fellow named Billy Micheaux and wanted to go off with him. Billy was Anishinaabe, a bit younger, real good-looking. No shortage of women, white black red, you name it. I think she thought without a kid they'd be free to go off together."

"And did they?"

"Yes and no. For a time. But then she came back. By then she was in her forties, been kicked around a bit, so to speak, and she started getting real forgetful."

"Alzheimer's? Dementia?"

"Forgetful," Loam repeated. "Plus she regretted giving up Chelsea Anne. Talked about getting a lawyer and trying to get custody back, but with her forgetfulness and other bad habits she never got around to it. Couple years in Riverview and then back here once they shut that place down. She passed about eight years back. Buried next to my mother and other sister."

"She and Chelsea ever connect?" I asked.

"Well," Wayne Loam said, "here's what happened. Maybe fourteen years ago I got a call same as you, asking the same questions you did. She said her name was Chelsea Loam and did I know anything about her mom or her mom's family. I told her pretty much what I told you with a few family things that you wouldn't find interesting, and I wouldn't tell a stranger, no offence."

"You told her who her father was."

"Sure. By then he'd passed too—plane crash. I asked her did she want to come by the property, meet her mom. She said only if her mom wanted her to. I asked Anne and she said, 'She wouldn't want to meet me, after what I done to her.' Both of them kinda hurt, but shy. Plus Anne's bad habits. So they never got together even though they lived on opposite sides of a bridge. That's the Loams for you."

"Anyone else ever ask about her? Chelsea, I mean?"

"Policemen," he said.

"And?"

"I have a rule," Wayne Loam said. "I don't talk to police. You're First Nations and you talk to police, sooner or later you wind up in police custody. Then your odds of surviving drop a significant amount. So I don't talk to cops, or splash 'em with urine if they're on fire."

"Fair discretion," I said. "I used to be a cop."

"Your father, too. A fellow can learn anything off that Google."

"What else did it say?" I asked.

"That you're pretty fair with your clients, but as a cop you were kinda quick with the old riot baton."

Without prompt the waiter had brought Wayne Loam a slice of apple pie with whipped cream in a dish on the side. He offered me his fork but I shook my head. I'd pushed my plate away, elbows on the table.

"I'm twenty-nine," I said. "I've been seven years in this other line of work. I don't know I'd do things differently."

Wayne Loam patted his chest. He flipped open his wallet but I'd already given my credit card to the waiter.

"I'm twice your age," he said. "My kids're older than you. And their kids are half your age. Them and my scoundrel of an ex-wife is what I got for family. Anne was my sister and Chelsea would've been my niece. There was a lot I could've done for them—a lot more. But I decided early on that family wasn't the same thing as blood. I got cousins and such, but I don't consider them family 'cause they don't come around anymore. Family are the ones who want to be there. And Anne when she got back couldn't stand being with us for very long. Plus her bad habits, and me trying to raise two kids. She didn't seem to need me. Of course now I think she really needed me and maybe couldn't bring herself to say. I wasn't there for Anne, is the bottom line."

"Family's tough," I said emptily.

"And what gets my goat is, I've been burned by the church, and the government—well. But I still go every Sunday and I still pay my income tax. And if you hadn't've phoned I wouldn't've thought of my sister."

We walked out and had cigarettes standing in the gravel parking lot. It was still hot, the sky still cloudless, but late afternoon had become early evening almost imperceptibly.

"I guess I'm hoping that you helping Chelsea is like me helping my sister," Wayne said. He coughed the first drag of smoke out of his lungs. "That sounds sappy, huh?"

"It does sound a bit Hollywood Zen."

"All the same, I hope you find her. I hope she just got tired of everything and lit out. Living wild somewhere, no priests and no cops. No one trying to do things for her."

I said, "If I find her like that, I won't disturb her."

We finished our smokes. I drove him to his place, a sprawling half-acre with an old colonial. The wooden skeleton of a half-finished porch had been grafted to the side of the house. A woman stood on the porch tending a barbecue. Two teenage boys sat lounging on plastic chairs. I could hear Ry Cooder off a tinny boom box.

I dropped Wayne Loam off and watched him rejoin his family.

14

HOME. I MADE A STIFF BOURBON and Schweppes and fired up my stereo. I looked around the bare-walled apartment with its overstuffed bookshelf, couch and end tables culled from thrift stores and auctions. The TV with its collection of films I never watched. The Xbox that had sat unplugged since my half-sister's last visit to the city. Leaning against the couch was a framed Alex Colville print of no small value, which I hadn't bothered hanging up. Marie had given me a birthday present of a Sidney Paget poster, Holmes and Moriarty teetering over Reichenbach Falls. It sat in its tube mailer atop the fridge, never unfurled.

The apartment revolved around the Rega turntable, the Meridian power amp and Klipsch speakers. I chose Esperanza Spalding's first record, gave it a quick clean with a microfibre brush. People retreat into their record collections because sound is the least voluntary sense, the one most often overwhelmed. To control sound is to control mood.

I had Blue Note reissues, European imports, 180-gram audio-phile editions. Stacked in a pair of wooden Forcite crates I'd purchased from an army surplus and lined with moleskin. Not a massive collection, but a well-curated tour through soul jazz and outlaw country, with a foray into nineties Seattle that was longer than healthy. Frog Eyes, Mad Season, Sleater-Kinney, Jackie McLean.

I set the needle down into the grooves. Spalding's cover of "Ponta de Areia" with its syncopated bass line came over the Klipsches, heavy and warm. I sank into the couch and watched the ice cubes in the drink melt.

The pattern of living out your parents' lives without learning anything, without avoiding the pitfalls that had brought them down. Wasn't that an almost universal fear? And yet who ever avoided that completely? Anne Loam separated from her family, Chelsea from hers, Kevin from his. In a way Chelsea had been the most fortunate. She'd ended up with people who loved her. But was that enough? Maybe her fate had been written into her blood and tissue, in a place that a foster family's love couldn't reach.

My father had been a street policeman, Constable for Life. Someone who'd found in violence a comfortable, casual friend. He'd died unglamorously in a freak turn of events. I'd tried to resurrect him by becoming like him. It was a bad fit. When it came to violence I didn't have his tact or discretion.

Side A ended. With my patio door open I could hear from up the block the sound of a tenor saxophone. Someone at Commercial Station, playing for change. I listened to that while I chose a follow-up, something darker, angrier. I pulled out Soundgarden's *Screaming Life* EP. Not their best, but I'd lent Jeff my *Badmotorfinger* and hadn't seen it since. I dropped the needle on "Nothing to Say," Kim Thayil's lumbering guitar tone perfect for steering oncoming depression into profitable rage.

Blood—violence and family. It was too much to fathom. But I'd made one decision.

I texted Ken Everett. AT THE INN?

NOT NOW came the reply.

NOW. RIGHT NOW.

No answer.

LEAVING RIGHT NOW, I texted.

DONT BE STUPID. NOT THE TIME. NOT THE PLACE.

CANT BE HELPED.

I waited for an answer. When it didn't come I turned off the stereo, locked up and threw on a coat. I left the drink untouched on the floor. I was in the hall when the phone rang.

Everett said, "You know how much shit you got me in?"

"One straight answer's worth."

"Your head bolted on right, Dave?"

"Asks the Exiles hangaround."

"I am a cunt's hair away from my patch," he said. "Throw my old sparring partner a bone. Didn't consider this. This is a world of trouble. You don't even know."

"So tell me."

"Believe me, I fucking asked about what's-her-face. I didn't even ask, I broached the fucking subject. All a sudden Rhodes got quiet. Next day his bodyguard visits me, asking all about you."

"You'd told me a tenth as much about Chelsea Loam as you said to the bodyguard, this'd be over."

"Dave, I don't *know* anything. You don't talk about his business. Only way you'd find out is by asking Rhodes yourself."

"I plan on it," I said.

"Dave—"

"Don't bother trying to talk me out of it," I said. "I know it's stupid. You just play dumb like you don't know anything about it."

"He told me, Rhodes did, I hear from you, I should tell him. He knows I'm outside taking a call. You show up—"

"So tell him," I said. "Tell him I can't let it drop. Tell him the media and police don't need to be involved. Tell him I'm not threatening him and I'm not looking for revenge. Answers only."

"Dave—"

"Tell him that."

I hung up.

I drove out to Burnaby once more. Past the PNE Fairgrounds and the Hastings Park racetrack. Past Anton's, a line of impatient customers waiting for a table even at this hour. Past Brown's Books and a bar called Oscar's. Past a strange block of one-floor

storefronts, all of them selling bridal wear or industrial appli-
ances. If I'd continued up Hastings I'd end up on Burnaby
Mountain, below the castle-like Simon Fraser University. Streets
pulse and thrum like the strings of an acoustic bass, and bizarre
arrangements of buildings could be a type of architectural poetry.

Deep thoughts for someone heading to get his face kicked in.

As I passed another Safeway, Everett phoned. I put him on
the speaker.

"Okay," he said, some of the agitation gone from his voice.
"I told him."

"And?"

"There's a pub near the Inn called the Mountain Glen. It's at
the foot of Burnaby Mountain, at the end of a cul-de-sac, kind
of out of the way."

"I know it," I said.

"There's an upstairs and a downstairs. I'll meet you upstairs."

"And Rhodes'll be there?"

"That's all he told me to tell you."

"See you then."

"Be polite, Dave."

I followed the SFU bus line off Hastings and onto Pandora.
I left the main road and weaved through an unlit housing
tract. It was as if an unwritten curfew had been passed on that
neighborhood. No noise, no one in the street.

The Mountain Glen was done up like a cross between a
Bavarian tavern and a longhouse. Inside it was all sports
bar. Screens everywhere, functional seating. Cheap Pitcher
Tuesdays, Wing Wednesdays, other promotions for other days.
It was packed with an equal mix of students and older sports
fans. The TVs played highlights.

The toilets were upstairs. Going up I ran into a traffic jam
of frat-boy-types on the narrow landing. They manoeuvred
around me, lost in their griping about the Canucks.

The top floor had more tables than booths. Dead centre was
a table for four. Ken Everett sat facing the staircase.

His left eye bulged. The lid was closed, the skin purpled and rubbed with a liniment I could smell over the sweat and beer. He swivelled his head furtively. He recognized me. Otherwise he didn't react to my presence. Everyone else seemed fascinated by me. The volume dropped as I took a seat.

I gestured to the shiner. "Go a few rounds?"

He was drinking his usual Black Tooth Grin. His hand didn't close around the glass, but was holding it daintily, pinky extended. I caught sight of the metal cast over two fingers.

"You're real hilarious," he said.

"Rhodes do that to you?"

My back was to the washroom. Everett's good eye travelled past my right shoulder. I looked over in time to see the man from the house seat himself to my right.

He smiled at me. The kind of smile that means farewell. His hands unfurled the napkin-wrapped cutlery setting in front of him.

"How are things?" I asked him. "First-time homeowner?"

"We've had our words," he said, unfolding the napkin, setting aside the fork and spoon.

I looked over at Everett. Everett wasn't making eye contact with the man. I asked Everett, "Is Rhodes coming or isn't he?"

"He's taking his dogs for a piss."

"So he'll be coming back here soon."

"He's here already," said Everett.

The washroom door opened and out strode a bullet-headed mastiff followed by another. They were slobbering and their nails clawed into the wood floor as they fought against the pull of the choke chains that held them back. Behind them, taking his time, with the other ends of the long chains wrapped around his forearm, was Terry Rhodes.

He was short and wore denim, wore his silver mane of hair long and unruly but his beard kept cropped and dyed ink black. Bad teeth in a wide grin and small grey roaming eyes.

Most of the patrons had slipped away, either out of revulsion from the dogs or a keen apprehension for bad shit about to go down. A few stayed in their booths, and I noticed at least one cellphone camera held at the ready. Rhodes didn't care.

The only open seat was next to Everett, across from his unnamed enforcer. Rhodes grabbed the back of the chair and dragged it carelessly in a semicircle around Everett's back. Everett watched the dogs. Rhodes dropped the chair next to me, straddled it backward so he could rest his elbows on the back. Our knees were touching.

One of the dogs, the slightly bigger one, was nuzzling Everett's knee. Its slobber-coated mouth ran up against Everett's thigh. With his good hand Everett gingerly and discreetly pushed the head away. Immediately the dog's oversized head retraced its path toward Everett's crotch. Everett began pushing it away again but Rhodes shook his head.

"Let Fuck have at it," he said.

Everett put his hands on the table. The dog sniffed and reared up to set its paw against the inside of Everett's knee, splaying his legs out wider. Its head banged against the underside of the table. I watched the dog's back. It was all one muscle, covered over with scars and patches where the fur didn't grow. The other dog lay with its head folded on its forelegs and generated drool.

The first dog's head poked out between the table and Everett's abdomen, pushing Everett back. The paw trailed up to Everett's throat and down over his breast and Everett, in a fit of terror and revulsion, flung the dog off him. His shirt had been torn and the flesh beneath scraped white.

"Sorry," he said to Rhodes, and then without being bidden he repeated it to the dog. "I'm sorry."

"Kenny," Rhodes said, "if you don't want Fuck up in your face, give him something else."

Everett complied, extending his good leg. The dog mounted him, pistoning its haunches into Everett's shin. The remaining patrons turned away and vacated. Even the iPhone paparazzi were overcome by a sudden flight of decency and withdrew.

Rhodes's enforcer stared down at his table setting, his hands folded at a perfect ninety degree angle. Rhodes watched the dog with glee.

"'At's it," he purred. "Give it to her. Give it to the bitch. 'At's it."

He looked over at me.

"Love dogs," he said. "Love everything about them. Love how they eat, love how they fight, how they fuck. Don'tcha love the way a dog just—fucks. It don't care where or when. It gets the urge to fuck something, it fucking fucks it, fucks it hard. No talk, just slams it in. That's fucking nature, that's how things are meant to be. Waitress."

The two servers in their black dresses had removed themselves to the edge of the stairs and were whispering. Deciding who it would be. Both were blonde. The one with a pink streak in her hair shook her head, frantic. The other, taller girl took pity on her and came up to our table.

"That meat you got downstairs," Rhodes said. "Sitting on the bar."

"It's for our meat draw," the waitress said. "Tickets are two dollars, three for—"

"Bring us up the T-bone."

The waitress didn't hesitate.

"I'd like a Vodka Collins with celery," Rhodes's enforcer said to her back as she fled.

Fuck wound down and let go of Everett's leg. Everett stood up. He looked at his soaked and soiled pant leg. He headed for the washroom.

"Kenny," Rhodes called out.

Everett stopped.

"Leave it."

Everett paused. Looked at the wood floor. Returned to his seat.

Once he'd sat, Rhodes said, "I'm just joshin' you, Kenny. Go get cleaned up."

Everett stood and once more crossed the floor of the bar.

"Kenny."

Once more Everett stopped. His hands were balled into fists. Even the dislocated fingers were wrapped in on themselves, the metal cast bent.

"Kenny," Rhodes said. "Kenny Boy. Just wondering. Was it good for you too?"

Rhodes laughed and waved his hand. Everett about-faced and walked into the washroom door. Rhodes laughed harder. Everett turned the handle and went inside.

"That was Fuck being gentle with him," Rhodes said to me. He slid a hand down the taut cord of muscle attached to the dog's back. "Wasn't that you being gentle, baby? Wasn't that? Yeeeessss."

The dog growled at him and shrugged off his hand. Rhodes dropped out of his chair instantly, his weight landing on the dog. He cinched his arm around the dog's throat. He bit the dog's ear.

"Gotta be the pack leader," Rhodes said to me. "Never let 'em forget."

He pulled himself into his seat. He pointed at the other dog.

"Holy don't challenge me. Holy just lives to watch. All pious watching his brother give it to some bitch. You got dogs?"

"I did," I said.

"What was its name?"

"I didn't name her."

The waitress brought over the steak, still in its packaging. Rhodes lifted it off her tray and flung it to the dogs. They tore through the plastic and Styrofoam, Fuck taking the lead, the blood pack still attached to the slab.

"What'd you call her?" Rhodes said.

"I told you, she didn't have a name."

"I mean when you called her, what did you call her? Call her 'dog'?"

"Yeah—'dog,' 'pup,' 'you.'"

"Coyotes get her?"

"Lymphoma."

"Bad ending," Rhodes said. "Speaking of bad endings—Kenny told me you're Matt Wakeland's son. That right?"

I nodded.

"He was a surly old mick."

"Scottish Presbyterian actually."

"Point being he was an old bastard even when I was a kid nickin' titty mags from the chink grocer, my first week on the coast. One time he beat the balls off me, you wouldn't believe."

He stroked Holy's coat as the dog gnawed at the table leg. Fuck had carried off the bone.

"You as tough as he was?"

"I'm a better dresser," I said.

"You boxed amateur. He train you?"

"I used to lose a lot. He wasn't exactly Cus D'Amato. And I don't like fighting."

"Different kinds of fights," Rhodes said. "You know your old man wouldn't take a dime?"

"I know."

"Not even a beer on the house. And him a beat cop dealin' all day with hypes and whores."

He looked around, saw an abandoned beer on a nearby table, stretched over and downed it.

"One time," he said, "he ran me in for drunk and disorderly. And I'm rocking my vest, patches out. No doubt anyone's mind I'm an Exile. I get bounced from stir the next day. I go have a few, then look for Constable Matt to set him straight on who he can and can't arrest in my city. That stubborn motherfucker, know what he did?" Rhodes shook his head, grinning nostalgically. "Saps me and runs me in again. We do the same dance about four times in a row before I leave to take care of something else. Now what do you call that?"

Everett rejoined us, taking the seat across from Rhodes's enforcer, removed from the dogs.

"I'm serious," Rhodes said. "What do you call that? Is it toughness? Is it stupidity? What's that called?"

"Doing the right thing," I said.

"Explain to me how that's right," Rhodes said. "That fourth time I threatened to fuck his wife in front of him—guess that'd be your mom. And I'd'a done it too if this Quebec City thing hadn't've come up. And still he busts me like I've said nothing, like he doesn't think I'm the type that follows through."

"There was no figuring him out," I said. "I mean, he used to watch *Hee Haw*."

"My old lady got me this dog trainer video," Rhodes said. "Fucking thing is my bible."

One of the dogs squatted and squeezed out a coil of feces. It nosed a scrap of Styrofoam restlessly.

"I know a dipshit ran his whole crew off *The Art of War* or one of those dink manuals. Me, everything I do comes out of nature. In nature you got an alpha and a pack. You stay alpha by being the toughest and best, and when you're not toughest and best, then you're not the alpha and you don't deserve to be. Can't be two alphas. Everybody's got to stay in line."

Rhodes's enforcer drank his Vodka Collins, staring languidly around the room like a bored date. The empty booths, the sports paraphernalia, the waitresses all but cowering. He took all this in, disinterested.

"I'm guessing this is an analogy," I said.

Rhodes belted me. It was open hand and it stung. I felt something press into my side. His enforcer had a blade at my rib cage. He was still looking around the room.

Rhodes stood and leaned on the table. Jabbed a finger in my chest.

"I don't do analogies," he said. "I *am* the fucking alpha, and everyone does what I fucking say. And if I wanted Charley to gut you like a marlin in front of those two spooked cunts then that's what's going to happen."

His chair had toppled to the ground. He righted it, sank back down.

"Now what do you want from me?" he said.

"I want to know what happened to Chelsea Loam."

"Don't know her, never saw her."

"She used to sometimes go by Charity."

His fist struck the side of my head, knocking me toward the knife held by his enforcer. My shoulder struck his. I felt the knife's slight puncture.

"What in fuck's wrong with you?" Rhodes said. He took out his wallet, peeled off fifties. "Is it money you want?"

"I get by," I said.

He struck me with a left. I turned my head but I didn't block it. It took me out of the chair, onto the floor. The dogs were barking. Rhodes kicked them away. He clouted me across the top of the head as I tried to stand and soccer-kicked me in the solar plexus. My lungs emptied. I flopped onto my back, trying to pull in oxygen. Rhodes placed the heel of his boot across my jaw and applied pressure.

"Do you not understand how easily I could get rid of you? Of everyone that ever knew you? There's not that many. Dear old mom, couple ex-girlfriends, ex-boyfriends, some low-rent cops, your gook partner and his wife. You not existing would be simple. Do you not get that?"

The pressure on my throat relaxed slightly.

"I get it," I said.

"You didn't know that before today? Wanted to see if I was what I said I was?"

"Didn't have any doubt," I said.

"Then what?"

"Thought I'd appeal to your sense of decency."

Rhodes crouched over me, looking at his enforcer.

"See, Gains, this is what I'm talking about. What do you do, you get a guy like this?"

"Pretty straightforward," the enforcer said. Charles Gains. I recognized the name.

Rhodes took the knife from Gains and held it to my throat.

"Tell me you're leaving this alone," he said to me. "Tell me or I'll make you chew on your own eye."

"I'll stop," I said.

"Say it like you mean it."

"I'll stop."

"Like you mean it. Like—akh."

Puzzled and disgusted, he stood up and let the knife fall. It bounced off my stomach and slid to the floor. Rhodes sat down and swept a hand through his tangled mane.

"Unbelievable," Rhodes said. "You really wouldn't've stopped."

He looked over at Gains, who had retrieved the blade.

"See that's what I've been saying, Charley. That same stupid stubbornness. There's gotta be a way to put that to work for us."

"Or not," Gains said.

Rhodes moved his wrist horizontally, signalling why bother?

"It's not like he's a threat. Sit up."

I did.

Rhodes bent down to look me in the face, his hands rubbing over his knees and thighs. Everett still in his seat, watching us, watching the dogs. Gains unconcerned.

"Charity," Rhodes said.

I coughed. "That's her."

"And you think I killed her, that's why you're here."

"Did you?"

Rhodes seated himself in my chair. Up close his shock of hair was a smattering of ivory, yellow, silver, slate. I passed a hand over the puncture in my side to make sure it wasn't significant. Rhodes grinned at me like a clay idol.

"Fact is I didn't," he said. "Fact is, night of the party, we did our thing and she left upright and breathing. Never saw her again."

"No clue where she went?" I asked.

"Clues," he said to Gains in a scoffing tone. To me he said, "I don't deal much in clues. You spend time with her family?"

"Some," I said.

"Think she's special?" Rhodes spat on the floor. "The amount of slit out there just like her, you could buy it by the pound.

"And I *liked* her," he continued, his voice dropping in volume, softening. "She gave good head, she didn't steal too much, and she had her habit under control. But all that don't make her unique. They all got sob stories."

"No one else at the party she connected with?"

"How do I know? You got dope and a cock, sooner or later a junkie whore's gonna get 'round to you."

"But she was with you. Wouldn't that keep her from inter-acting with too many people?"

"I get any woman I want when I want," Rhodes said. "What they do when they're not sucking my dick doesn't matter to me. Anything else you'd like to ask?"

"She have any STDs?"

"Ask her doctor."

"Anything more you could tell me?"

I grabbed the table to pull myself up. Rhodes kicked out at my arm. I fell back, sprawled on the ground. I felt boots landing on my ribs and shoulders. He bent down and seized a handful of my hair, raised my head up and drove it back into the floor. My vision turned into a swim of colours.

While he put the boots to me he kept saying, "Is it worth it? You fucking challenge me, for some whore? It worth it now?"

The dogs howled.

I turned over onto my stomach, tried to push off the floor. I felt the weight of Rhodes's boot between the shoulder blades, grinding me into the floorboards. I coughed. Something warm and wet streamed over my neck.

"Just 'cause I didn't kill her doesn't mean I wouldn't've. Or that if she shows up alive I wouldn't still. You got your answer, bitch. Far as my involvement, and my crew, that fucking ends it. Turn over."

The foot left my back. I rolled over. The back of my head rested in a puddle of what I knew to be another man's piss. My vision cohered. Rhodes stood over me, his enforcer behind him holding the leashes.

"This is the last time we ever see each other," Rhodes said. "You ask for me again I'm sending Charley here to kill you. And that's not a threat—I know you're not smart enough to understand threats. It's a plain-ass fact. I can't have you fucking things up."

Then they were out of my vision. I moved to sit up and a last, final kick struck me in the groin. I doubled over and screamed through clenched teeth.

"And another thing," Rhodes said, leaning over me, sounding cheerful. "It's Kenny Boy's new job to keep you out of Exile business. You cross me, he comes after you. And Charley goes after him. Just thought of that now—not bad, uh?"

He left. I heard the sound of the dogs receding into the noise on the first floor.

I used a chair to pull myself up. I took off my wet jacket. I noticed Ken Everett still sitting in his chair, a half-finished Vodka Collins in front of him.

"You realize how fucking lucky you are?" he said.

If it had been raining, I could have washed by standing outside, stripping down, and to hell with what people thought. But even with the sun long gone it was hot and dry.

I did the best with what I had in my car, which turned out to be some serviettes and a cold cup of tea. I drove home to shower.

Rhodes hadn't killed Chelsea Loam. Claimed he hadn't, anyway. He seemed to be telling the truth, but then maybe I was deceiving myself. Maybe I didn't want to think that I'd suffered a beating and humiliation just to have my ear pissed in—hardy fucking har—by a biker.

Everything hurt but everything seemed functional. I thought about revenge but the concept didn't apply to people like Rhodes. Some people, some families, pay and pay. Others pay nothing. Rhodes would never have to get accustomed to life in a prison cell. Even if someone killed him, Rhodes's death would only be a recycling. A different sack of meat and water and bad chemicals would take over. Everett had been right—I'd gotten off cheap.

At my apartment I soaked and soaked under the shower,

using every cleansing agent I had. I dried off and stood naked in my apartment as the steam-fog rolled out of the shower and dissipated in the long empty room.

The case had started with a killer's interview and had ended with one. Rhodes had been my last good lead. The case wouldn't solve. It would end up on a shelf next to the Ghosh file. I'd take it down once in a while, make some calls, tell whoever cared that I was doing what I could. It hurt. It hurt like hell. But some cases never close.

Cases. I was doing what the authorities did—treating her as a thing. A collection of scraps of paper, captured images and faint recollections. Chelsea Anne Loam had lived. She'd been one of the billions. Maybe that didn't entitle her to anything. There's so many of us, it's hard to maintain the belief that any one of us matters. Maybe impossible. We value our own life, our friends, those near us, those that look like us. But maybe that speaks only to our vanity, our need to see reflections of ourselves everywhere.

That was smug nihilism and it was very convincing. My biological parents were cultists and as a result I don't take anything at face value. And I know the idea of a person having a soul is laughable, obscene even, given this world of mass destruction, of epidemics, of fast food genocide. It is unprovable and it is silly and I hold on to it, clinging, with all my terrified strength.

PART TWO

DANS UN CAFÉ

15

ORSON WELLES ROUSTED ME FROM MY SLEEP. During a week-long burst of tedium, I'd misused company property to make ringtones out of old Mercury Theater radio plays. It had provided a sore distraction from a lack of distractions. What I heard was Welles as Macbeth hollering about Birnam Wood be come to Dunsinane. I sat up, feeling the bruises on my stomach scrape each other, and groped for my cell.

"This is me," I said.

"David Wakeland?"

"Yes ma'am."

"This is the wait staff at Veritas, we have an unpaid bill?"

"It couldn't wait till morning?"

"Sir, this client ran up a four hundred dollar tab. We have her here in the restaurant."

"So what do you need a PI for?"

And it slid into place.

"Is this woman's name Shay?"

"She refuses to give a name, sir. She told us to phone, said you'd settle her bill for her. Otherwise we'll be forced to notify the authorities."

"I'll come down," I said. "You still across from the courthouse?"

"Yes sir, in the hotel lobby."

I dressed and drove downtown. Vancouver dies after one. Nothing is open, no noise is allowed. Speeding through streets which are usually congested to hell, you get the feeling of driving through a scaled-to-life model of Vancouver, plastic and unpopulated.

Lawyers need a place to congratulate themselves. In Vancouver that place was Veritas. Opposite the Supreme Court building, the swank cocktail lounge sometimes featured good piano jazz. The restaurant was closed, the great fireplace dark. Chairs had been placed on tables. I rapped on the glass door. A tired-looking woman in a peacoat and scarf unlatched it. She passed me one of my cards, the one I'd given to Shay, with my cell number pencilled on the back.

Shay was sitting by the dead fireplace. She stood up as I stepped inside, a look of triumph and relief on her face, a look that told the two employees, *See? I told you he was real.*

"Dave," she said, hugging me. I was engulfed by lilacs and cigarettes and cheap vanilla. She was wearing a feathery purple jacket zipped all the way up, white jeans, heels.

The waitress who'd been standing guard over Shay while the other opened the door passed me a bill on a tray. It came out to four hundred and twelve dollars in VSOP, single-malt Scotch and champagne. I handed over five hundred dollars in twenties, withdrawn from an ATM machine. The two tired waitresses rang it up, cashed out and split the tip.

As one set the alarm, the waitress who'd answered the door asked me, "So it's true what she said about her working for you on a big case?"

I looked at Shay as we stepped outside. Shay smiled. I looked back at the waitress and told her it was.

"She's one of our better operatives," I said. "Without her, we wouldn't have recovered the Montrose Diamond."

The waitresses glanced at each other, impressed.

In the car I said, "I've only been a PI seven years, so I'm not authoring any textbooks yet. But a good rule of thumb I've found

is, if you're working a big case, you don't go around telling people you're working a big case. Tends to be counterproductive."

Shay shrugged. "I'd run out of lies. It's not like they'll tell
anybody. They just wanted their money."

"So this was work?"

"Sure."

"My kind of work?"

"You want me to say it wasn't a hustle, it wasn't a hustle. Feel
better now?"

"The truth makes me feel better."

She let out a one-syllable bark of a laugh.

I said, "Who were you drinking with?"

"Just a guy."

"He skip out on you?"

She was fixing her makeup in the side mirror. Her purse was
open on the dash. It looked like a square white leather envelope, GUCCI branded on it with sequins. Bad stitching and a
twice-repaired strap.

"Here's the thing," she said. "I really appreciate you coming
through for me, and I'll get the money back to you soon. You
can drop me at my door. Would you like a blowjob before I go?"

I looked her. Her expression was glossed over, emotionless.
"No," I said.

"Gay?"

"Where'd this come from?"

"Look," she said, with the frankness of an inveterate liar.
"You know you're not getting your money back. And I do appreciate you helping me avoid adding to my sheet. So if you want
to pull over, I got a dam in my purse somewhere. Or not. Or
you could come upstairs."

Upstairs I sat on her Ikea couch and ran a hand over my hair.
She was in the washroom, pissing then showering. I looked
around the flat.

It was dirty and hadn't been painted in a long while.
Photographs taped onto the yellow walls. Shay and a woman,

Shay and a man, Shay with two children. Better times. On the opposite wall was a Marie Laurencin print, pale women running with wolves. An old CRT television, its bulk propped on a plastic three-legged stool. Mattress thrown down by the kitchenette.

Shay came out of the washroom wrapped in towels, brushing her teeth.

Her apartment didn't have a balcony, just an old double-paned window with a layer of film and grease between the panes. The window was propped open by an old beige air conditioner. Beyond that I could see the darkened outlines of other windows in other buildings. A few lit up, curtains drawn.

"Did you find out anything about my missing woman?" I asked.

"Well, I tried asking about her."

She sat down on her couch and lit a cigarette. It was a Dunhill, different than the vanilla Bullseyes she'd been smoking at La Grange. She offered me the pack.

"A date left 'em here. Might as well smoke 'em."

So we did. The smoke hung in the room, curling around the light fixtures in the stucco ceiling.

"No leads at all, then?"

"Do you really want to talk about this?" she said. "Because I thought you came up for the other." She removed her cigarette long enough to chew on her thumbnail. It was a parody of seduction, erotic all the same.

"I don't know why I came up," I said.

She blew out a cloud of smoke and set her face in a practised look of innocence. Ran a hand down into my collar and caught sight of the welts. "Someone hurt you?" she asked.

Before I could answer she'd stood up and grabbed my wrist. Her bed was close. Her bedsheets yellow, fetid and warm. I took a step with her, eased down onto the mattress.

The towel around her shoulders had fallen, exposing tan lines, freckles and scars. Damp, her hair clung to her neck in a single mass.

Everything hurt but it didn't stop either of us.

—

My cigarette had flared out. I placed it in a clay pot in the centre of the table, the pot holding a tobacco museum's worth of crushed filters. I would rather have laid there on her mattress, but Shay seemed to want me gone.

As I struggled back into my clothes I asked her who she'd talked to.

"Mostly older people, people who'd been around at that time. There's a lady named Geena who sort of remembered her but couldn't tell me much. A few others."

"No word on Kamikaze, her pimp?"

"He wasn't with her. Doesn't remember her."

That caused a double take. "You spoke to him?"

She was looking back over her shoulder toward the window.

"Yeah, but like I said, he doesn't know anything."

"Where is he?"

She hesitated, then said, "He has a place on Alexander. By the water. But I'm totally sure—"

"I need to ask him myself," I said.

"For what?"

"'Cause he might be lying."

"He wouldn't lie to me."

I realized she wasn't looking toward the window, but to the knockoff Gucci sitting on the coffee table.

"You have a history with him."

"Not really." She tilted her head to her shoulder. "Sort of."

"Can you introduce me to him?"

"Not now."

"Tomorrow?"

She didn't answer, entranced by what was in her purse.

"Tomorrow?" I said again.

"I'd really rather not," she said.

"You could give me his address," I suggested. "Where he hangs out. His name even."

"No, I'd have to explain things, or else he might think I narked on him."

"He wouldn't hit you?"

"No. No. Totally not."

"So tomorrow?"

"Fine. Can I—" She turned back to look at me. "I'll need some more money," she said.

"Wouldn't this fall under services rendered?"

She'd been fingering one of her small silver earrings. Now she let her arm drop insolently so that it slapped against her thigh.

"Can I get the money or not?"

"A little more," I said. "How about twenty?"

"Come on."

"Well, what do you think's fair?"

"How 'bout two."

"Hundred? *You* come on."

"At least fifty, then."

"Fifty. After the meeting. From this point on, it's cash and carry."

She sucked in air. "Okay. Then let's set it up real early, like first thing. Why'on't you meet me out front at eleven and we'll go see him."

"Kamikaze."

"Right."

"I'll be here at eleven," I said.

She drummed her fingers on the door handle. I stepped into the hall and she began to shut the door. I held up my hand.

"I'm sorry," I said.

"Whatever."

The door clicked snug in the lock.

16

IN THE MORNING I phoned Jeff and told him I wasn't coming in, that I had to see about something. I went back to sleep until nine. During the night my body had exploded in bruises, reminders of the thrashing Terry Rhodes had given me. Walking was painful.

I shuffled down Commercial Drive to Tangent and had eggs and hash browns and a pot of tea. I lingered over my toast and an emaciated wheel of orange. I paid up and drove to Shay's apartment.

During the day the area was bustling. I parked by the old Woodward's building, now appropriated as part of Simon Fraser University's arts campus. Classrooms and hip cafés and grocery stores and a London Drugs. A block east, among the hotels and bars, a street bazaar of people selling outdated electronics, clothing, trinkets and books. I walked on.

Shay met me outside her apartment. "It's not far," she said.

I followed her across Water Street and down to Alexander. We passed the dockyards that abutted the train tracks, the enormous cranes unutilized, no cargo ships in sight. Past the sugar refinery, the detox, a handful of new restaurants with wait staff in formal wear who gazed at us optimistically through clean glass doors.

Past the turnoff for CRAB Park, we stopped outside a white-painted complex of staggered terraced apartments that gave the building the look of a giant ivory staircase.

"It's super-pricey," Shay said. "But wouldn't it be great to be in there?" She pointed at an adjacent structure of weathered, blue-painted wood. "That's an artist's colony. They even have a kiln in there, right next door. Isn't that badass?"

We rode the elevator up to the fourth floor. Our destination was the suite at the end of the hall. Shay walked ahead of me and knocked three times. She held me at arm's length, out of sight of the peephole.

"Yo," came a groggy voice from inside.

"It's me, Kazz. Shay."

The door opened. A gangly man in boxers and a T-shirt leaned out. The shirt was rumpled and had holes, but I could make out the slogan. It said THIS IS WHAT SEXY LOOKS LIKE. The man looked at Shay and looked at me and scowled further.

"Going shopping?" he asked.

"Not today," Shay said. "It's for my friend. This is Dave. Kazz."

Kazz nodded at me. "'Sup."

"Can we come in?" Shay asked.

Kazz threw his hands up as if he'd lost a major argument. He retreated into the apartment. Shay and I followed.

The suite had a high ceiling and a view of the water. He had nice things, nice art on the walls, but everything was coated in soot and dust. A glass end table had been rolled between the leather sofa and a wall-mounted plasma screen. On it sat a hash pipe, a propane torch, an empty cereal bowl and an Xbox controller. I got the feeling that was an accurate cross-section of Kazz's interests.

He was past forty, his bald spot offset by a thick stubble that ran down his neck to his chest. A faded FTW tattoo circled his left forearm. Flames covered the right.

"Bud and mushrooms," he said. "Those I got. Anything heavier I'd have to make a trip. How 'bout a Dell laptop, new in the box?"

"I just want information on a woman," I said.

Kazz scowled in Shay's direction.

"I told him you didn't know anything," Shay said. "He just wants to hear it from you."

"I know my rights," he said. "This is entrapment. It's been entrapment ever since you stepped in here."

"I'm not a cop," I said.

"This is about Chelsea." He sat on the padded arm of the sofa. "I don't know anything."

"But you knew her. You were her pimp."

"I was her boyfriend. We were heavy in love. We were thinking about marriage at one point."

"I heard you were abusive to her."

"Fuck that."

"I'm not sitting in judgment," I said. "I need information on where she might've gone."

"She's just gone, man."

"So you don't know anything."

"Sweet F.A.," he said.

"She leave any papers, things, anything at all?"

His eyes darted instinctively to the short hallway that connected the living room to the bedroom and closet. He covered this up by rotating his head and yawning as if working a kink out of his neck. But I'd caught the look and he knew I'd caught it.

"Nothing," he said. "There's nothing here and I don't know nothing. So buh-bye." He waved sarcastically at me.

"Could you tell me a bit of background? Where you met her, at least? What she was like?"

"Those are painful memories," he said. "And I don't like this Gestapo interrogation you're pulling. I'm legally within my rights. I asked you to go."

I drew out a business card. "I'm working for Chelsea's foster mother. If you'd feel more comfortable talking to her—"

He swatted the card out of my hand. "Son, I asked you to go. I'm not asking anymore. Now get. The fuck. Out. Of my domicile. Before I press charges."

He backed me toward the door. Looking over at Shay he added, "Don't ever bring anyone around again or else don't *you* come back."

"I knew that wouldn't go well," Shay said as we retreated to the staircase. "I knew he didn't know anything."

"Yeah," I said.

We walked west up Alexander toward my car.

"He's really not a bad guy," Shay said. "He just doesn't like talking about Chelsea. Guess her leaving really hit him hard."

"I can tell."

"But he's not usually like that. He writes these songs sometimes that are really, really imaginative."

At the Cadillac I handed Shay five twenties. "Sorry to ruin things with him," I said.

"He'll be fine after a few days. He's a Leo. Leos are all hotheads."

"You buy from him?"

"No. Not usually. Once in a while."

"Where you off to now?" I asked.

She smiled and shrugged. "Woman About Town. Places to go. You?"

"It's tea time. Might get a bagel, look at the water."

"Enjoy that." She started backward up the street. Waved to me. "No hard feelings."

"None."

I waited till she rounded the corner. I opened the glove box and brought out the steno pad and pen I used to chart my mileage. Then I popped the trunk. Inside was a tool box, and in the tool box were tools. I took out an old-school Mag-Lite, the kind that used three D-cells and weighed as much as a length of lead pipe. It was my father's, and it brought a sentimental smile to my face.

I put the flashlight in a grubby Canadian Tire bag and made my second trip down Alexander. Kid Diogenes, prowling the city with his lantern on a quest to find one honest man.

I caught the door to Kazz's apartment building, trailing behind a grocery-laden couple dressed in refugee chic. When I knocked on Kazz's door I grasped the bag in both hands and tried to look sheepish.

Kazz opened the door. "Fuck is it?"

"Forgot her keys."

"Fucking typical." He let me move past him into the room, toward the sofa. He hadn't paused his game. I watched his avatar stare dumbly at a pixelated wall.

Kazz stood with his arms folded. I waited until the door shut. I grasped the flashlight and shook away the bag, which wafted lazily to the parquet floor.

He looked at me and blinked and I tapped him on the temple with the grip end of the Mag. He dropped to the floor and stared up at me, insolence replaced by panic.

"What the hell," he said, scrambling away from me and knocking his head into the butcher-block island. "Wait. Help. *Help.*"

"You don't want to go that route," I said. "Go have a seat on the sofa and let's talk."

"Help—"

I held up the flashlight. "On the couch."

He crawled over and pushed himself into a sitting position in the middle of the sofa. He threaded his fingers together and sat with both hands in his lap.

"Let's start over," I said. "My name is David. What's yours?"

"I have rights," he began.

"Yes, but we're not talking about you. The subject at hand is Chelsea Loam. You're what we might call a secondary character. Now what's your full name and date of birth?"

"Why?"

"So I can check you out, dummy."

His hand went to his pocket. I held up the flashlight. He drew his wallet out ever so slowly. Placed it in my left hand.

Brandon Kenneth Trevino didn't have a driver's licence. I put his SIN card, Care Card and Amex on the counter and snapped photos with my cellphone.

"Let's start with the first time you met Chelsea," I said. "Where was that?"

"Meeting."

"What kind?"

"I'm not s'posed to talk about it or anyone who goes."

"But a twelve-step meeting, roughly." He shrugged in affirmation. "How long had you been going, and how long had Chelsea been going?"

"She'd been there longer than me. But she, you know, lapsed a few times."

"And you?"

"I was fierce into it for a while. But the meetings made sense. I mean, nowadays I just smoke weed and a little coke, *rarely*, like at a party. I was kicking smack then, and doing okay till Chels and I hooked up."

"And she lured you off the straight and narrow."

"No BS. Chels would go through these shame cycles—that's one of the terms I learned, it's where your shame drives you to kick, but kicking's hard, and pretty soon you fuck up, and then the shame kicks back in and you want to cop. She'd do that all the time. 'I got to get clean I got to get clean' Monday morning, 'I got to get high I got to get high' Tuesday night. Ask anyone who knew her."

"So who knew her?" I asked.

"Everyone. But close friends she only had a couple."

"Names, full last and nick."

"It's been more than ten years."

"That's right. You've had plenty of time."

He chewed his lips. "Dolores Gunn. They were friends."

"And who's Dolores Gunn?"

"She's a bartender on Main. I want to say the Waverley but I'm not sure. I'm sober now, I avoid those places. By now she might've quit."

"Anyone else?"

"There were a lot of girls around," Kazz said. "I wasn't, like, formally introduced to all of 'em."

"Names."

"Lila, Vee, Casey, Kimmy—Kimmy might've been after Chels. Ask Dolores."

I jotted the names on the back page of my mileage log.

"Anyone else? Any men that hung with her?"

"Vee, before the op, but besides him—her—can't think of any."

"So just you in terms of men."

His eyes narrowed. "That an insult?"

"It's a prompt."

"Of course there were men, but that was business. She had regulars but I didn't know them. I kept the skeeves from bothering her."

I wrote it all down, then worked the pen through the coils at the top of the pad. I put the pad aside. I said, "We're going to have a talk now about being a pimp."

"I said before that I wasn't a pimp."

"Yes, you did."

Kazz turned his head around the room. His gaze rested on the many fine things in his bright, high-ceilinged apartment. He sighed. I was patient.

"Okay." He slapped his knees. "Let me say first, it was a time of aggravation and turmoil in my life. I was angry, I was fixing."

I nodded.

"Did I always have a job back then? No. And Chelsea lived with me, yeah, and yeah she paid some bills, but I wasn't a capital-P pimp. I didn't have a stable. But I looked out for her, sometimes, sure. There's creeps out there."

"In terms of clientele. She was a good-looking young woman."

"Yeah," Kazz said. His mouth quivered and he clenched his jaw. "Gorgeous at one point. Still a hard seven when she disappeared. I got her this costume, 'Native Princess.' Sort of a Disney Pocahontas thing. Little warpaint. Older white dudes paid through the ass for that. German tourists? Currency exchange downtown never saw so many Deutschmarks."

"The day she disappeared," I said. "What do you remember?"

"Waiting," he said. "Waiting and waiting. It'd been a good morning, some money had come through from my dad. I'd bought three papers of H and two of coke, plus I'd fixed earlier. I was gonna share with her when she woke up, which would've been noonish. Figured we'd fix and lie in bed all day. Only she wasn't there when I got back. I waited till I started coming down, then I did one of the papers. That was how the next few days went—me waiting, trying to hold onto some for her.

She never came back. Never heard from her again. Love of my life," he added.

"Anyone ask about her?"

"The cops, for a while. I got calls from her mom, once or twice from her sister. But I was kicking, and I didn't need that kind of negativity in my life. After that I tried to move on."

"Besides the cops—anyone ask about her, last few years? How about Terry Rhodes?"

His eyes widened. "The Exiles? Fucking hope not."

"What about Anne Loam, her mother?"

"I remember Chels mentioning they were trying for a meet. I told her it was a bad idea. Someone gives you away, then gets in touch years later, it's to shake you down for money or make themselves feel better about what they did. Chels didn't need that noise."

"What about her son?"

"Kevin?" He shook his head adamantly. "That's never been conclusively proven, him and me." Through the windows I could see to the harbour. A cruise ship lurched away from the dock. The sound of canned samba music carried as far as the shore. High times in the Caribbean for someone other than Brandon Kenneth Trevino or myself.

Kazz hazarded to stand up. "That's the story," he said. "I kicked smack. Now I deal a little herb, help people make connections, manage a couple of bands. I'd kind of moved on, when you brought all this back up."

"Sorry 'bout that," I said. "We're almost done."

"Almost?"

"There's one more thing, and I think you know what it is."

"I honestly have zero clue what you're talking about."

I said, "When I was here before, with Chelsea—I mean, with Shay—I asked did you have anything of Chelsea's. You said no but you looked over there."

I pointed with the flashlight in the direction of the closet and bedroom.

Kazz bolted for the door. I got a hand on his throat and tossed him toward the sofa.

I got hold of the Xbox console and ripped it free from its wires, sent it hurtling across the room. A bronze statue of Ganesh sat on a black-painted Greek column. It was being used as a keyring holder. When the console hit, the statue crashed hands-first into the floor. The column rolled back and forth in a semicircle. The Xbox bounced off the wall unspectacularly.

"Let's get this over," I told Kazz. I brandished the Mag-Lite.

"It's all that's left of her," he said softly.

"There's nothing left of her. Which is why I'm taking it."

He stood up and walked to the closet. Opened it. Crouched down and moved some clothing off a shoebox. He brought the box back to me. I set it on the counter between us and flipped up the lid. Inside were two folded sheets of paper, some silver jewellery, and a thick quarto-sized book.

I put down the flashlight and unfolded the papers. They were sketches, a cityscape and a face. The first was done as if standing kitty-corner from the Carnegie Library, the perspective distorted so that the tall financial buildings of the city centre seemed to wrap around the more detailed, low-slung buildings of the Hastings-Main corridor. A mouth, square-cut steel fangs devouring up a neighborhood.

I knew the face in the second sketch. It was Chelsea Loam, the Chelsea Loam of the police mugshots, gaunt and diamond-hard. The clean linework and subtle hatching enriched her physical characteristics, made their hardness seem in service of some deep-hidden warmth. The sketch somehow had more soul than the photos did.

I leaned into the counter and imagined her on a wet street corner in May, shivering in a fringed buckskin coat, waiting for a strange car to cruise by, slow down, unlock the passenger door. A line of strange cars, each taking something, leaving her tokens redeemable for poison.

Both pictures were signed AK-47.

"Know the artist?" I asked Kazz. He was also leaning on the counter, twisting on the ball of one foot, then shifting to twist on the other.

"Some trick," he said.

"They're good."

"Well, why don't you just take 'em, then?"

I held up the jewellery, two simple crosses on thin chains, which I saw were pewter and not silver.

"Chelsea make those?" I asked.

"We did together. Well, I fired it for her."

"Do they have sentimental value?"

"It all does, man. It's all mine."

"I'll need to borrow it."

He snorted. "Borrow."

His eyes fell on the book.

It was a ragged-cut journal with a cover of padded vinyl. A nylon band to keep the pages together. Once I slid it off, papers began falling out, slips and scraps that had been shoved between pages. Ticket stubs, directions, printouts. I turned to a random page.

> *. . . just that kind of day, like walking through a sprinkler. Makes me want to clean. Clean the apartment. Clean my shoes, the blue Fluevogs that I noticed have gum on the sole. Clean myself. Clean up my act. Maybe I'll soak in the tub. Spend the whole day in there until my skin turns raisiny and I have to get K to carry me out.*

> *Meeting w/ G.O. tonite. Last of my regulars. He'll go on about his wife again I know it. How she doesn't understand him. Maybe if you didn't perv on girls younger than your grandkids, maybe she'd understand then. G.O. sweet and pays good but not too bright. Not much wattage in the headlamp as Gail says. Should phone her. Should phone Kevin. Maybe after. Bath now. Wash my sins away ha ha ha.*

I put the book down, ran a hand over the creased vinyl. The book felt as if it had a charge. As if it were a very real piece of her.

Kazz had picked up the Mag-Lite.

I looked over at him. "Really?"

"Get out and leave everything. This is personal property and I know my rights."

"Put it down, dummy."

He held it for the most studied and epic of defiant poses. Then his arm sagged and he set the flashlight on the counter.

"Good. Now who else has seen this?"

"Seen it?"

"Did you show it to the police?"

"I don't cooperate with fascists."

"Why hide it? Why keep it at all?"

"I loved her."

"Was the plan to blackmail someone?"

"I loved her. Really. Why's that so hard to believe?"

"Your One True Love disappears. You don't go to the cops. You got her journal—her bad trick book—in a shoebox in her closet." I tapped the book. "I could buy true love if you were trying to crack this. Visit these johns on your own and try to find out who took her. You know who G.O. is?"

"No," he said. "I get too emotional when I read Chels's stuff."

"Putting aside the Most Lamentable Tragedy of Star-Crossed Chelsea and Brandon, and going from my gut, there's two viable reasons a guy like you holds onto a book like this. Both come down to power. Either you're afraid of someone named in the book, or this is blackmail material."

"You seem to know everything," Kazz said.

"I read a lot."

He turned to look out the window. The cruise ship had chugged out of sight. He watched the Seabus ferry the midday travellers to the North Shore.

I backhanded him. He stared at me dumbly. I slapped him again. I raised my hand to slap him a third time and he cowered and held up his hands.

"What'd I do?" he said. A child's question, spoken in a child's voice. His whole life laid bare in three words. Kazz Trevino had taken an unfair beating early enough in life that the unfairness of it had stuck with him.

"Blackmail or insurance," I said. "Which."

"I thought maybe there'd be some money in it. When Chels was younger and better looking she had all these regulars, like call girl style. That was before her habit really crept up on her. She didn't give me names—she'd say, 'I got a date with Mr. George,' that sort of thing. She had rich clients, some famous ones. She was so stupid about it, she didn't get their names all the time. Sometimes she didn't even know who they were. Then we'd be sitting in the Ovaltine and she'd see, like, a finance minister on the front page of the *Sun*, and she'd go, 'I used to see him.' So stupid."

"Who'd you blackmail?" I asked.

"Nobody. I can't make heads or tails. Some of those initials stand for nicknames. More I looked, more they seemed to lead nowhere."

"What about AK-47?"

"Dunno," Kazz said.

"Guy or girl?"

"Guy, I think. Think he's some sort of artist."

"You get that from him signing his name on two pieces of art?"

"Man," Kazz said, "I didn't exactly care whose prick she was sucking. I just handled the money."

I packed the book and drawings back into the shoebox. I put the Mag-Lite under my arm. I left him the two pewter necklaces.

"We covered a lot of ground," I said. "I'll bring all this back when I'm done."

"Nah," he said. "Fucking trouble's all it brought me. *You* keep it."

17

MY PLAN WAS TO HOLE UP in the office with a pot of tea and itemize what I had. The world of Chelsea Loam had been as bleak and sparsely populated as a Beckett play. Now there was a deluge of names. The bartender Dolores Gunn; Lila, Casey and Kimmy—possible coworkers; Vee—coworker, friend, possible post-op transgender person; AK-47—artist, possibly male; G.O.—elderly trick with money. There would be others. And all of them would know a different Chelsea Loam.

But most significant was Chelsea herself. Her voice and her thoughts. Her obsessions. Her regrets. The journal was a document of her mind in those months before the disappearance. How intimate printed words could be.

At the office Shuzhen herded me into the small conference room, where Jeff sat facing a trio of smart-dressed corporate types. He looked up, glad to see me, until he noticed I was wearing street clothes. Jeff was wearing his power suit and a tartan tie.

He stood up and introduced me. "This is the man himself. Dave, this is Pat Carnahan, Don Utrillo and Tommy Ross. They're from Solis."

Utrillo was the oldest, early fifties, and seemed determined to keep up the same level of enthusiasm as Carnahan and Ross. The baby-faced Ross had a bronze complexion, a plastic smile. Carnahan had the hair of a Lego figurine.

"Dave was out on surveillance detail," Jeff said. "Which is why he's dressed like a homeless person."

I was wearing a T-shirt and jeans and a flannel overshirt. What I normally wore. I grabbed a powdered donut from the centre of the table and sat behind Jeff. "You got to blend in," I said.

"Carny was asking about the Salt case," Jeff said. On the legal pad in front of him he'd written PATRICK CARNAHAN— SENIOR VP and put two asterisks next to the name. He tapped the sheet.

So I told them the story of the Salt case. I'm a good enough raconteur when I want to be. I impressed upon them the horrors of finding the decomposed corpse of a teenager. That's what they wanted, the gory parts. I elaborated. I embellished. My audience oohed and aahed and ughed when I told them about the second corpse, the abductor Chester Breuning, bowels voided, neck crushed flat by the heavy rope.

"Know what?" Carnahan said. "That would make a great, great movie."

"A guy finding two bodies?" I said.

"Well you'd have to add some story to it. Like maybe it's your kid and you swear revenge."

"Ooh ooh ooh, you know who'd be great in that—playing you?"

"Seventies Redford," I said.

"Liam Neeson."

"I'd watch Neeson in anything."

"And you know who could play Jeff here—"

"How 'bout Jackie Chan?"

"How 'bout Jet Li?"

"How 'bout Bruce Lee?"

"How about Bruce Li?"

Laughing as it got ever more ridiculous. Jeff laughed loudest of all.

When they were gone I said, "Don't ever make me do that again."

"You think it's fun for me?" Jeff said. "If shit were sushi everyone would eat it."

The shoebox was by my feet. I stooped and picked it up.

"He didn't mention it," Jeff said, "but Ross set the Winnipeg dates. You fly out next Wednesday."

"There are other things going on."

"Yes," Jeff said, "which take up time, I'm very aware. But this is serious money and they asked for you personally."

"Who? Carny? Your good pal the Carn-meister?"

Jeff folded his hands. "There's this invention called money," he said. "And it doesn't grow on trees, but it seems to grow in the pockets of assholes. And to get hold of it, sometimes you need to—"

"Become an asshole yourself?" I said.

"—put up with things. Like insults. Like distractions. I put up with you running your cases."

"Case."

"That's my albatross. And fine. It's important to you, I respect that. But there's got to be some"—he circled his wrist, searching for the word—"reciprocity. You have to be reciprocal."

"I can't spare four days from this."

"Yes, you can."

"I know I've been a bit remiss," I said. "I know you've had to pick up the slack. I appreciate that. But let me solve this. I can solve this."

"Maybe," he said. "She's been missing for thirteen years."

"Eleven."

"Does it matter if it's next week or the week after? And if you do find her—say it all works out happily, and the girl is alive and well in some hippie artist's colony on Sechelt—can you tell me honestly you won't find another case that *has* to be solved right now?"

He stood up and stacked the dirty coffee cups on the table inside each other. Light brown coffee sloshed out over the rims. I watched the rivulets run over the countertop, toward the edge, until Jeff caught the liquid in his napkin and swept it back to where it could be sopped up.

"Can you not see, Dave, that you keep doing the same thing,

again and again, and each time expecting a different outcome?"

"There's no other way," I said.

"You lack perspective," Jeff said. "You care too much. I was like that. This Winnipeg trip'll be good for you. Get you out of the city for a while. You'll get to see the Coke can. Will you do it?"

"I'll think about it."

"All right."

"Jeff?"

"Dave."

"If I go, I'm not going to see the Coke can."

Jeff said, "I think they have a zoo."

Around four Marie stopped by to take Jeff to an early dinner. Evidently they'd reconciled. I called the Waverley and learned that Dolores Gunn had the night off and would be back tomorrow. I didn't leave a message.

I phoned Martz next, asked him to introduce me to his friend in Sex Crimes.

"You insist," he said. "But she's an eight and a half and you're, well, counting your personality I guess I could give you a high four."

"Ha ha."

"And without your personality, a low six."

"Don't you have an old woman to tase, Ryan?"

We'd meet Jane Henriquez tonight at the Alibi Room on Alexander and Main. I gave Martz the names I was interested in. After more zingers from the Policeman's Big Book of Humourless Jokes, I put the phone down.

Dolores Gunn. Chelsea's coworkers and friends. That left the diary. Before I opened it I set it down on the empty desk and drank a glass of water. And I thought about what Jeff had said. He'd spoken the truth. But then I wasn't convinced that being true and being right were exactly the same thing.

I'd come this far. I opened the book.

But I didn't read it. I turned the pages and looked at the scraps of paper and paraphernalia tucked away. There was no discernible order to the pieces. Yet each piece was a memento of a life—a ticket stub from a Canucks game, a bar bill from the Commodore, scrawled directions from Kazz's apartment to a West End restaurant long since demolished. Several pictures of Kevin, school photos mainly, one of him with Pavel Bure. And a folded sheet of writing paper torn from a coil-bound notebook.

The paper listed cars and vague descriptions of men. BLUE PRELUDE ASIAN 30S BIG GOLD WATCH. BLUE CELICA WHITE BALD BLUE EYES. PLATE LDG XXX. One simply said BLUE VAN MULLET.

A bad date list, either Chelsea's or one passed on to her. The women would keep track, swap stories of abusive or violent or stingy johns. Problem clients, predators. In an environment neglected by the outside world, those women had developed their own mechanisms to protect themselves and share information.

It was something to take to Henriquez.

I wasn't ready to dip into Chelsea's thoughts. I looked up Dolores Gunn's home number instead. On the fifth ring someone picked up.

"I don't know this number."

"My name is David Wakeland. I'm—"

"Don't know you."

"—a private investigator working—"

"Don't. Know you."

"—for the family of Chelsea Loam. Can we—"

"I don't talk to strange men on the phone. Sort of a rule."

"It's important."

"You want to talk, come see me at the Waverley. I'll be back tomorrow."

"You sure we can't speak now? I could come to you, your place, your terms."

"Walk in my place, limp out. I told you no strange men. Those are my terms."

"See you tomorrow, then."

The Alibi Room had squeezed into a building that had once held the Archimedes, which had been frequented by cab drivers and the occasional off-duty cop. The patrons of the Alibi Room were younger, had more money and better taste in beer.

I expected Jane Henriquez to be Latina. In point of fact she was an Amazonian blonde, almost milky pale, and her family was from Salamanca and Copenhagen. Martz was smitten. In a well-cut pantsuit and glasses, her hair trimmed short, Henriquez dressed to offset men's attention and failed. Like all sex crimes cops, she had the hollowed-out stare of someone who'd gazed too often at things that can't be unseen.

"Ryan mentioned that you'd been in contact with Sharlene Nelson. How is Shay?"

"She's been a help," I said.

Henriquez seemed surprised. "Out of the goodness of her heart?"

"I've been paying her."

"Her habit's deep. Any money you give her is going straight for narcotics. Be aware of that."

"I don't control how she spends her money," I said.

"No, only how you spend yours. I'm just stating a fact. Did you two want to eat? Because I really don't like the vegan choices here."

"How 'bout nachos?" Martz said.

I handed Henriquez the sheet of notebook paper I'd discovered stuffed into Chelsea's diary. She unfolded it, studied it.

"A bad trick sheet," she said. "An old one. Where'd you find this?"

"Among Chelsea's things," I said.

"Chelsea Loam, Charity." Henriquez stared at the sheet. "She's been on the missing list over a decade. This just surfaced now? I'd like to know where you found it."

"Tucked into her diary."

"You have her diary?"

I nodded.

"I think you should turn it over to me. Or Missing Persons."

"Yeah, I could take that," Martz said. He'd been studying the menu.

"I'm not prepared to do that right now," I said.

When the waitress came by I ordered nothing. Henriquez ordered nothing. Martz ordered nachos and a pitcher of Fat Tug. When asked how many glasses, Martz said three.

"This diary," Henriquez said. "Does it mention who might've killed her?"

"Not by name. The book's in shorthand. And anyways, we don't know she's dead."

Henriquez looked skeptical but didn't argue the point.

"I think VPD'd have a better chance decoding it," she said. "Which is not a slight against you. We simply have more specialized personnel."

"None taken, but the diary stays with me for the time being."

"Do you really want to impede a police investigation?"

"Show me there is an investigation first."

Martz said, "That's not fair."

"To hell with fair." I caught my voice rising above the noise of the bar. I said, more quietly, "Everywhere I go I hear from people who don't want to talk to you. Think that's coincidence? You've alienated the people you should be protecting."

Neither said anything.

Exhaling, I said, "I need some sort of overture from the VPD right now."

"Like info on those women you mentioned," Henriquez said.

"As a start."

The waitress brought Ryan's pitcher and set glasses in front of us. Henriquez put her hand over hers, blocking Martz's pour. I let him buy me the pint.

"Different professional standards," Henriquez said. She sipped her water. "Lillith Jeffries, Lila, died twelve fourteen oh eight, cardiac arrest linked to cocaine and amphetamine use. Kirsty Clarkson, Casey, died nine seventeen oh nine from a GSW, linked to an unregistered firearm in the possession of Lonnie Clarkson, her husband. Charge of second-degree manslaughter laid. Kimberly Sung, died eight six of two thousand eleven, body recovered from Vancouver harbour. Note left on her bike, a Kawasaki Ninja, found parked in the middle of the Burrard Bridge. Witness saw her jump."

She'd stared straight at me while reeling off the list. No papers in front of her. No emotion in her pale blue stare.

"No links between the deaths?" I said.

"Overdose, domestic violence, suicide. Unconnected."

"All dead."

"The odds of survival don't favour sex trade workers," Henriquez said. "I did locate Marjorie Vee, birth name Milos Vrenna. She works at Spirit Bear Coffee up at SFU and she told me she'd be willing to talk to you."

"Appreciated," I said. "Can you run those descriptions on Chelsea's bad date sheet, tell me who these men are?"

"The records on dead women are easier to pull compared to those of living men. Does this at least earn me a look at Chelsea's diary?"

"This book is my only edge," I said. "If I learn anything I'll share it. But I'm not comfortable putting it in police custody at this time."

"Then this has been a waste for me," Henriquez said.

"Not a total waste, hopefully," Martz said.

"Why not share? Why not have as many people looking as possible? Isn't it a bit egotistical for you to insert yourself as a custodian between this evidence and the proper authorities?"

I said, "If you're asking do I have an interest in this, abso-fucking-lutely. Maybe it's only ego, but there are things at play I can't talk about."

"Self-serving if not self-aggrandizing," Henriquez said. "Can you at least *try* the proper channels?"

I tapped the table, on which rested the date sheet and my notes on the four friends of Chelsea Loam.

"Think what you just said," I told her. "Five women. One is still upright. What does that say about the proper channels?"

"You're not suggesting a conspiracy," Henriquez said.

"I *wish* this was a conspiracy. I wish you'd told me all these women were killed in the same way, by the same person. The idea this is all the work of a lone, frothing supervillain would make me ecstatic. I *envy* conspiracy nuts. The idea there's a master plan would be a comfort—because there is no plan, no one at the helm. How are you s'posed to get in the ring against entropy?"

"It's a very nice speech," Henriquez said.

"My point, I hand the book over to you, things take a certain course. I lose my only foothold and I assume certain risks. Maybe it's got to be like that, but I'm not certain it does. Not yet."

"Risks?" Henriquez asked.

"Risks. There's a couple guys out there. If they knew about the diary they'd probably want to take a gander themselves."

"So this is about self-preservation."

"It's about finding a way through," I said.

"You don't have the right—"

"No, just the means."

I'd exhausted my goodwill. I got up to leave. Henriquez followed me out. Martz, naturally, followed Henriquez. On the pavement Henriquez said, "You're not the only one who cares about this situation. I'm in the trenches every day."

"What trenches?"

"You wouldn't understand."

"I understand there's a couple guys I got to worry about."

"Because they're stronger than you? Because you can't be sure what motivates them or how they're going to treat you?"

"That's right."

"Now imagine that's forty-nine percent of the population," Henriquez said, "and you can perhaps begin to understand how these women felt."

18

THE NEXT MORNING I left my flat in East Van with a Thermos of tea and the diary. I bought fresh rolls and raspberry compote at the Farmer's Market at Trout Lake. It was a Saturday. The absence of clouds and the sweltering heat gave the city a listless feeling, already palpable in the late morning sun.

I walked down Commercial Drive toward the waterfront. I enjoy the Drive, with its conglomeration of misfits, its restaurants, ethnic hair stylists, funky cafés and Legion halls. I like Black Dog Video and I like Cafe Deux Soleils, where on a warm night you can walk by and hear amplified snippets from the open mic poetry slam (*stare at yo' dick, stare at yo' dick*) and in the morning you can see children playing on that same stage as their mothers breakfast. I like the barbershops and ristorantes that hint at the Drive's history as Vancouver's Italian enclave. There are good sushi joints and the best espresso.

But Commercial blends into the industrial waterfront, and a left brings you onto Hastings or Cordova. Past the needle exchange and the bad hotels backgrounded by the towers of finance that loomed so ominously in AK-47's drawing. I passed West Coast Reduction and nameless storehouses and watched a Chinese woman gather cans and bottles strewn across Oppenheimer Park from last night's debaucheries.

My destination was Victory Square, with its coliseum seating arranged around the cenotaph. I chose an unoccupied stretch of concrete, parked myself and poured some tea. I people-watched. I sent a homeless man on his way with two of the rolls. I contemplated cigarettes, since I hadn't brought my own.

Only when I couldn't think of further distractions did I open the diary.

It's difficult, for me at least, to feel sympathy for anyone who constantly gets laid. That probably says more about my own peculiar blend of shame and lust and self-pity than about the other person. There is a feeling, being a man who's never had all the sex and love he's wanted, reading the perspective of a woman who felt smothered by an overabundance of those things, of wanting to say, at least you have that. At least you are connected to others, even if it's not in the way you'd prefer. At least at least at least.

And yet she was in torment—even I could see that. Caged by her habit and her sex in a cycle of trading one for the other. Caged by her love for a damaged son and a damaging boyfriend. Caged by an endless line of men all wanting their own needs quelled, willing to pay, quite willing to see her disappear once their cocks had deflated.

And her own blindness to it all—her inability to see that Kevin was lost to her, that Kazz was doing the opposite of looking out for her. That her descriptions of tricks, with their eccentricities and hang-ups and grotesque or irregular bodies, only fronted a stultifying *sameness*. As if each required something different. But then maybe they did.

> *Back from a date with C.P. Met him at one of A.K.'s*
> *parties. He came up to me and asked about butt sex,*
> *the etiquette of it. He said when he was a boy he'd done*
> *it to another boy and wanted to see if it was different*
> *with a girl and would pay. Now writing this on the*
> *toilet trying to get the rest of his gunk out of me. Can*
> *still feel his tongue rough like a cat's on my bum.*
> *Laughed about it with Kazz. He says I should put a*
> *camcorder in my purse so we can watch and laugh*

*about it later. He says there might even be $ in it. I told
him if he wanted me to be a film star I could always go
back to JJ's. He dropped the subject.*

*R.W. unlike anyone I've met. Makes my cry every
time. After the date he pays me extra to lie there and
answer questions. Do I have a family, what do they
think of what I do, if I was a mom would I want my
daughter etc. etc. Same questions every time and I still
tear up. Wonder if I told him we don't have to fuck,
we can go straight to questions, would he appreciate
it? I'm convinced that's what he pays for. The fuck is
meh to him. But maybe he needs it to feel normal. Not
saying I don't love Kazz but when I think of A.K.
I can imagine a sort of different life. He and I and
Kevin in a place above his studio on Cambie. I could
model for him, or muse for him as he calls it, without
the other distractions. What would I do for $? Maybe
get a student loan and get some sort of childhood
educator certificate—wish we had internet so I could
check the Langara website and find what that degree
is called. Something where I could work with Kevin
and maybe 3 or 4 other special kids and really help
them. Then come home to A.K. and muse. Not that
he's a husband type or I'm a wife type but it's my
dream and I can be as unrealistic as I darn please.
Kazz called. C.G. on his way. Scared of C.G. Scared of
T.R. Ice and fire, those two. Don't like their clubhouse.
Don't like their parties. Want to do my date or two
dates and go home and cop. Casey said T.R. just
watches. Told her on the bed on her knees and then she
felt paws on her back. Don't want don't want don't
want he's here.*

Rhodes's initials came up again.

Not what I thought. Exiles parties all right. All T.R.
wanted was head. Paid well and gave me two free
sheets. Asked if I wanted to come back. I said yes.
Asked if I wanted to make serious $. I said all $
serious. T.R. laughed and said I was too smart to be
taking dates, I should be his accountant. Actually not
a bad guy.

And:

Slow ass night UNTIL. Sat around with T.R. and crew
watching that movie with whatshisname. Cousin Vinnie.
Seen it before. There's a part where this guy's hitting his
kid and the movie stops and the kid as an adult says over
the screen, something like, "It's okay he hit me because
we all take a beating time to time." And T.R. says that's
not a beating. Called the father a faggot and stalked out
of the room. Comes back he's taken off his coat. Not
saying a word. Picked up a half-full bottle of Crown
Royal and smashed it on the head of one of his own men.
His name's Skeet I think. The bottle doesn't break like it
does in the movies and everyone laughs. T.R. hits him
again and keeps hitting him and on the fifth or sixth time
it breaks. I couldn't look away. Skeet's close to this other
biker named Delmar who's actually a nice guy. Delmar
gets up to pull T.R. off Skeet and C.G. kind of shakes his
head and Delmar just stands there while T.R. beats his
own guy for no reason. Just about kills him for all
intensive purposes. I got a cab and got out of there.
Called Delmar today. Thankfully Skeet's going to be fine.
Have to call T.R. soon, explain why I wasn't around to
give him his beej.

It was noon when I packed away the book. Impossibly, given
the heat of the day, my tea had cooled. I walked to Malone's and

ordered a double Bulleit and a pitcher of ice water. I stood at the bar waiting, thinking how nothing my problems really were.

"How goes the struggle?" the bartender said as she put together the order, complete with a generous handful of unrequested citrus wedges in my ice water pitcher.

"Could do with some rain," I said.

"Vancouverites." She stressed the *ouver* in a noticeable hoo's-it-gooin'-eh? "Canadian" accent. "You complain about the rain until you don't get it."

"I never complain about the rain," I said.

"'Tire city don't know nothing about weather. Don't even have weather, not like Manitoba, not like Ontario."

"They're welcome to it," I said. "Give me women in gumboots and cigarettes under awnings."

"Talk about weather once you've seen a Manitoba snowstorm, then you can talk."

A woman slouched on a stool behind a fortress of cider glasses looked up. "Without weather," she said, "what'd shitheads like you two have to say to each other?"

I killed two hours in the university library at Harbour Centre looking up leads from Chelsea's diary. I started with the artist because A.K. had come up often in the book, both professionally and unprofessionally. Chelsea had "mused" for him. She'd "made love" with him. She'd also "dated" him and "dated" several friends and acquaintances of his. He had a studio or exhibition space somewhere on Cambie Street. He had signed his sketches AK-47.

The website of Alex Knowlson had this to say about Alex Knowlson:

"An acclaimed artist and cultural historian whose work embraces a heady new omniscience. There are no places, no faces, no races; instead one is left with an aestheticized liminal space that puts at its forefront the spectre of post-colonial alternate histories in order to challenge, refute and resist the Neo-Liberal complacency of postmodern consumer culture."

On the third time through I actually understood what that meant.

My knowledge of painting consists of two trips to the VAG, one semester of Art History (precipitated, naturally, by a girl who'd also signed up for the course) and my mother's print of Daumier's Quixote and Sancho which hung in her sewing room. I know little of the last forty years of art, other than there must be some.

That said, I liked Knowlson's work. His earlier sketches—his "AK-47 period"—were undoubtedly of Vancouver, a Vancouver filtered through a chiaroscuro wonderland of exaggeration and menace and swagger. I liked those the best because I felt I'd eaten in those lonely diners with their rain-sopped neon signs. I'd worked those streets.

His later work—the omniscience stuff—was more conceptual. Grids and polygons. Two-dimensional renderings of three or four dimensions. The collision between the soft rounded human forms and the precise angles and vanishing points of the environment. It was jarring and bewildering and I liked it, too. And I believed those images still to be of Vancouver, a Vancouver of the mind as opposed to his younger self's vision of a Vancouver from the guts and loins. Like early William Gibson novels, Gibson's Japanese sprawls a more accurate Vancouver than anyone else's.

The site gave no address or contact information, only a photo of the studio, close to the Cambie Street Bridge. That seemed like a studied bit of I'm-not-in-it-for-the-money preening. I thought of phoning Shuzhen to dig up the number for me, then remembered what business I was in.

In a moment I had Alex Knowlson's cell number and the hard line for the gallery. His cell phone went straight to message.

"Hi, you haven't quite reached Alex. In all likelihood I could come to the phone right now but I choose not to. Perhaps I don't know your number. Perhaps I don't feel like it. If you're offended by that, hang up now. Or leave a message." Beep.

His gallery-workspace receptionist picked up on the first ring.

"All Knowledge Gallery," came the chipper salutation.

"My name is David Wakeland, I'm a private investigator and I need a moment of Alex Knowlson's time."

Maybe she hadn't heard me, and maybe she'd prepared her answer before I'd spoken. "If you're looking for tickets you'll have to contact the university."

"Tickets to what?" I asked.

"Mr. Knowlson's talk tomorrow night. Art and the Demand for Public Space. It's sold out, or close to it."

"He do a lot of those talks?"

"He does the right amount," she said. "It's important to him to give back and to participate in the dialogue. What was it you wanted to talk to him about?"

"An acquaintance of his named Chelsea Loam. This is my cell, he can phone me back on this number."

I caught the Skytrain to Main Street–Science World and walked the short distance down Main to the Waverley. It was four o'clock and the bar was mostly empty. An overweight man with a shaved head and tattoos manned the bar, which seemed the centre of light and heat in the quiet universe of the Waverley. I paid for a gin and tonic and picked out a red Naugahyde booth where the barkeep could deliver it.

Instead of sitting I wandered around the horseshoe-shaped seating area, taking in the musty smell, the soiled green felt of the billiards tables. Old men nursed pints of yellow beer and stared at silent television screens. The back door was propped open. I could see outside to the parking lot, where a trio of hirsute men pulled off the world's least covert drug deal.

My drink arrived at the table before I did. I sat and pulled out the lemon wedge and the straw. The gin had an industrial tang to it. I sat and waited for Dolores Gunn.

Time passed. The barkeep brought me another gin and tonic and asked if I wanted a discount taco platter. Someone had ordered and changed their mind. I snapped at a few cheese-soaked tortilla chips, sipped my drink and watched on the TV as a city that wasn't Vancouver geared up for the summer Olympics.

When the barkeep made his next round he asked me one of those barkeep non-questions that encourages safe chatter.

"How 'bout those Games?"

"Better there than here," I said.

"Not a fan, huh?"

I shrugged. "I might watch the boxing. That kid Hunter's supposed to be the next Frazier."

"But they're hyping him as the next Ali."

"Hype is hype."

"True that."

I thought of bringing out the diary and studying it, but I didn't want Dolores Gunn to know of its existence. Maybe if her memory was good and she was willing, I'd ask her to help me give full names to the sets of initials: G.O., C.P. T.R. was Rhodes, A.K. was Knowlson. C.G. would be Charles Gains, Rhodes's enforcer. "Ice and fire, those two."

The sports show had gone to its expert panel. I was watching idly when a shadow slid into the bench next to me, wedging me into the wall. Another shadow sat down across from me, a look of pained determination on its bruised, familiar face.

"Hello, Ken." I looked to my left, noticed the pattern of scars on the man's scalp where hair no longer grew. "Hello, Skeet."

"Wakeland," Ken said. "I don't know why you couldn't leave things the way they were."

"I don't either."

"You thought Terry was pissed before. He gets a call from this dealer who says you took something from him that Terry's going to want. Any idea what that could be?"

I didn't look at the nylon lunch bag Skeet had knocked to the floor by my feet. "Nope."

"This guy's shitting his pants 'cause, first place, he's got to tell Terry this diary exists, then he's got to explain how he lost it. And the only reason he tells him is if Terry finds out from someone else he'll clip him."

"How exactly is Terry Rhodes mixed up in this if he didn't kill her? Was he lying to me?"

Everett ignored the question and put one hand out on the table. "Let's have that diary, Dave."

"Think, Ken. Why would I bring it with me?"

Everett set his elbows on the table and rubbed his temples. "Nothing's simple with you."

Skeet said, "We take him to his office, he brings us the diary. Simple enough."

"It's not at the office," I said.

Ken hit the table. My gin jumped and sloshed. "You really going to make me ask, Wakeland? Fuck is it?"

"I mailed it to myself," I said.

"That's not believable."

"Sure it is. I have a P.O. Box."

"Where?"

"Belarus."

"Do you think I want to do this?" Everett said. "'Cause I don't. But you're leaving me no choice."

"Why should you have a choice? No one told you to join a biker gang."

"All right." Everett took a pair of slow breaths that seemed to strengthen his resolve. "On your feet. We'll search your car first."

"I walked here," I said.

"On your feet."

I held up my index finger, one moment. I used the same hand to pick up my drink and pour it into my mouth, ice cube slivers and all. I used the same hand to bring the glass across my body and into the face of Skeet. And when I did that the glass shattered.

I clambered over him for the back door, weaving through tables of stunned patrons. Everett's right hand caught at my shoulder. I spun back to hit him, turning right into his fist. We clinched, staggered, collided into the Golden Tee Golf machine. I broke away from him, brought my fists up.

I had height on Everett, had the longer reach. And I knew his patterns. Brush off the jab and then wait and slip the heavy

overhand left. I slipped it and caught Everett above the eye—
I felt seventeen again.

In that half-second of self-congratulation I didn't register
a bloody-faced Skeet behind me, his arms wrapping around
my torso, enfolding me in his mass. He propelled us forward,
toward the wall. My feet stumbled and dragged until the impact
of brick and biker ripped the air from my lungs.

My forearm scraped against Skeet's face as I tried to unpin
myself. I would've had better luck boring through the brick. I
got a breath in. Everett approached from the left side, a trick-
ling cut over his eyebrow. A fight-stopping cut, I thought. If
this were a fight with rules.

"Fuck it," Everett said to Skeet. "Bring him back to Terry."

"Got the zap straps?" Skeet wheezed.

"In the car. He tries anything, here and there, snap his fucking arms."

I was jostled and steered toward the exit. A low drawl of a
voice said, "Leave him here."

It wasn't a woman's voice but it was a woman speaking. She
was squat and solidly built, with long dark hair. She wore a
bartender's apron over a red plaid shirt and dark jeans. Cradled
in her arms was what looked like an antique stagecoach gun,
double-barrelled, with two triggers. Her finger rested across
both of them.

"Don't get involved," Everett said casually. But he didn't move.

"My place of business. I'm involved."

"Know who we are?" Skeet said.

"Cunts," the woman said. "Cunts I'm nicely giving a choice
to. Leave or stay for the cops, who Barry's calling now."

Skeet's grip on me loosened and I shrugged him off. I stepped
away from them, out of the line of fire.

"It won't get left like this," Everett said.

"It better, you expect to walk out of here."

The clamour of an ambulance siren filtered into the bar and
registered with everyone in it. I looked over and made sure the
lunch sack was still by the base of the table.

Everett and Skeet withdrew.

I sat down, hands on my knees, and breathed.

The woman came over, holding the shotgun with the barrel pointed up.

"You should get going too," she said. "Don't go up against those type of men 'less you got a big fucking blunderbuss. 'S'all they understand."

"You're Dolores Gunn," I said. "I'm—"

"I know," she said. "I get the paper. You can kind of take care of yourself, for a kid."

"They might come back," I said.

"No. They know not to pull shit in here. They'll probably try for you again, though. Must have something they want."

She sat down with a wheeze of pain and set the scattergun on the table. Barry the bartender swept by with two glasses and took the gun away with him.

"He really call the police?" I asked.

"What do you think?"

She tipped her glass back and consumed it in one gulp. I tried mine. It was tap water.

19

"YOU KNEW CHELSEA LOAM," I said.

"I did know her."

"Her foster mother hired me to find her."

"'Leven years too late, but a nice gesture."

"Can you tell me anything about her?" I asked. "How did you know her?"

"You're all business," she said. "Let's go to my office. Prying ears and all that."

Her office was a cubbyhole of beige-painted brick, one wall stacked with empty liquor bottles, newspapers and recyclables against the other. In between, a small desk and two chairs. We squeezed in.

Dolores spoke thoughtfully, her eyes roaming the office.

"Chelsea was the nicest girl I knew. Too nice for where she ended up. You need to be hard to last, and she wasn't all that hard. But she made friends. Everybody liked her."

"How'd you meet her?" I asked.

"You meet people working a bar. Lila might've introduced us. Or now I think of it, she'd been ripped off by some dealer and she asked me to arbitrate. Get her money back."

"I know what arbitrate means," I said. "You do that sometimes?"

"For a fee. Girls, 'specially girly-girls, need muscle once in a while. They usually get a guy, but that complicates things.

He wants to be her pimp, or he falls in love and wants to 'rescue' her. With me they cut out the bullcrap. I charge a flat rate. Fifteen percent, no strings. Just like a business manager."

"Who was this dealer?"

"Name was Kamikaze. He and Chelsea later hooked up, but back then he just wanted money."

"And later on he didn't?"

She smiled grimly. "Then it was money and pussy. Not 'zactly a pimp but not like he was looking out for her."

"Can you tell me about the people she moved with?"

"Not the girls," Dolores Gunn said. "Their business is their business and you prob'ly wouldn't understand anyway. Ask me about the men."

I asked her. "Alex Knowlson," I said.

"Want my opinion or Chelsea's?"

"Both."

"I think he's like every other artist. He has an idea about the 'Downtown East Side' based off TV and what he reads. And he comes down to 'create art' and 'speak the truth.' But it's all about him. He makes a few bucks, people in Ontario go, 'Gee, poorest postal code in Canada blah blah blah,' and none of it changes anything. Alex was nice enough, and God is he handsome. But he's a colonizer. He don't live here."

"And what did Chelsea think of him?"

"That he was Christ risen."

Dolores Gunn laughed. She reached into her desk for a tin of chewing tobacco. She administered some to the corner of her mouth, offered me the tin. I waved it off.

"So," she said between chews. "You're gonna find who killed her?"

"If I can. If she's dead."

"What else would she be?" she said. "Some fuckin' man."

I didn't know if that comment applied to me or to whoever had killed her. Both, maybe.

"Can you tell me anything about Terry Rhodes?" I asked.

"I can tell you that you pissed him off."

"How does Chelsea fit into that? Was he just a trick?"

"The chapters like to throw parties. They need girls. Chelsea sometimes went. You got paid, plus there was usually free coke. But the ones who went all the time, they ended up fucked out. Takes a toll, being around those violent bastards. I'd never do it myself, it was me. You're outnumbered, you're out of the city in one of their party palaces and you got no control. That's what does a girl in, being out of control, and your habit getting bad enough that you don't care."

"That what happened to Chelsea?"

"She wasn't that far gone, but not that far from being far gone, either."

"Did Rhodes single her out?"

She stopped chewing. A bubble of brown spittle formed at the corner of her mouth. "You think it was Rhodes? Or that big goon he's always got with him, Charley Gains?"

"I think," I said slowly, "that he didn't kill her but knows who did. Knows something, anyway."

"How'd you figure that?"

"I asked him."

"And you're still here," Dolores said, impressed.

"Thanks to you."

"Don't worry," she said. "I won't tell anyone your ass was saved by a girl." And she laughed.

"You seem like you have some leverage over them."

She put her thumb and index finger together a half-inch apart. "Some."

I nodded. I stood up. My body felt like it had been pulverized with hammers and glued back together with faulty adhesive. As if a sudden move would dislodge an ankle.

"Do you know someone Chelsea would know with the initials G.O.? Or C.P.?"

"Tricks?"

"I think so."

"Think one of them killed her?"

"Possible."

"Don't know them," she said. "But I got a question for you."

"Shoot."

Her voice dropped. She inched closer. "When you find him—"

"If. It's never a sure thing, these type of cases."

"—are you going to kill him?"

I was bothered she'd said it out loud, as if as long as it stayed in my mind I could pretend I hadn't thought it. But the thought had seeped in.

I said, "I honestly don't know."

"Why's that? Chelsea doesn't count the same as some little white kid?"

I didn't answer.

"You don't feel you got the—guts," she said, pausing so I'd know she'd thought of saying *balls*, "leave a message at the Waverley."

If Everett was going to come for me, I'd need cardio and I'd need a weapon, neither of which I had any interest in acquiring. Nevertheless, I woke up at six and jogged the outskirts of Clark Park, which bordered on Commercial and had enough of an incline. I went home, stomached some bran flakes and drove out to Langley to buy a gun.

I walked the aisles of a big-box retail sports retailer, through camping gear, crossbows, bookshelves lined with guides to crimping your own cartridges or brewing your own deer attractant. Firearms were at the back of the store, trigger-guarded, under glass.

The beefy kid behind the counter pulled guns from the display case with the studied don't-give-a-shit movements that are the armour of minimum wage employees. I examined a .38 revolver similar to what my father had carried, and a row of carbon-fibre Glocks and Sigs that reminded me of my own service weapon. Still, I preferred revolvers, with their die-cast parts and simple firing mechanisms. The movement from six-shot wheelguns to the plastic-and-springs automatics with their high-capacity clips said everything about the last two hundred years of North American history.

I looked farther along the counter, at the novelty section. Dirty Harry–sized .44 Magnums with eight-inch barrels, pink-painted "women's" pocket guns. Silver-plated six-shooters covered with elaborate scrollwork, complete with hand-tooled pig leather cartridge belts and casings. A carnival of freak show guns in all sizes and proportions.

The kid smirked. "I think you want something more practical."

"What I want," I said, "is a gun I'll never have to fire."

"Intimidation factor," the kid said, nodding. As if he knew the first thing about firearms, and wasn't simply repeating what he'd heard from whoever had previously held his job. "I got a nice .357. More than enough stopping power. Plus it can take a .38 special load, which saves a bit of coin."

"How 'bout that one?" I pointed beyond the .44.

"You don't want that, that'll break your arm."

But he took it out of the case and set it on the counter. It was a hand cannon, comically oversized, with a simple rubber grip.

"I don't recommend it," the kid said. "First, it only holds five shots, plus it'll cost you ten bucks *per cartridge*—'less you reload your own. The recoil is, well, there are videos online that show the kick. It's pretty hilarious. Plus there's the price."

I tapped the business end of the gun. "This was pointed in your direction, would you get the message?"

The kid said, "Bro, that was pointed at me, I'd lose your email."

I stowed the gun in its case at the office, then had Shuzhen mail the diary. Years ago I'd acquired an American postal box in Blaine, mostly to avoid cross-border shipping costs. I posted the diary to myself at that address.

Jeff and Marie arrived, and we rehashed the argument over my table. Marie told me there were some incredible rolltops that could be had for a steal at the rosewood furniture shop on Broadway.

"Or if not a rolltop, Dave, how about a trestle desk? Saw-horses instead of feet. Ralph Lauren makes a great trestle for about thirteen hundred—"

They'd brought back lunch for the office. The four of us sat and went through cartons of lo mein, pork cheek and peppers in black bean sauce, wonton and rice and a half-order of duck.

"Are you going to need a ride on Wednesday?" Jeff asked.

"What for?" I said through a mouthful of cheek.

"Winnipeg. Ride to the airport."

"I'll bus it," I said. "It's just the ninety-nine and then the Skytrain."

"Do you have a suit?"

"You've seen me wear it."

"Well, you can't wear the same suit," Marie said. "He's already seen you in it once."

"Who has?"

"Tommy Ross."

"So what if he has? I have to amuse him by dressing different?"

"You have to be presentable," Marie said.

"Professional," Jeff added.

"Right. You're not only representing yourself."

"You're repping the business."

"Think of him as money."

"Right. Impress the money."

"And behave yourself."

I put up my hands, surrendering. "Hell with it. I'll buy another suit."

"Go with him," Jeff said to Shuzhen. "Make sure he doesn't pick out something stupid."

Shuzhen replied in Chinese and the two of them laughed. I didn't catch it but I knew who was the butt.

Before I left I told Jeff about the gun. Bringing one into the office was a decision the two of us should've made together. He said as much. I gave him one of the keys to the trigger guard.

I picked a smoke-grey blazer off the rack. The tailor made notes on what to take in or let out. Mostly let out. He found a pair of matching dress pants for me and we repeated the process. Shuzhen sat and played games on her phone. When the tailor had signed off I presented myself to her, wearing the suit coat over my T-shirt like Don Johnson.

"Well?" I said, striking a pouty-faced pose.

"You need shirt and tie," she said.

"I got three at home."

"Jun Fei said for you to get new ones."

One black shirt and one red tie later we were on our way back to the office, my street clothes folded in a bag at my side.

"How many pairs of underwear did Jeff tell you to make me buy?"

She laughed but answered seriously. "No underwear. Buy that yourself."

We neared Harbour Centre, a vast brown obelisk housing a mall and offices and a satellite campus of SFU. I pointed at the saucer mounted atop the building. "Ever been up there?" I asked.

I bought two overpriced tickets and we rode up, up to the observation deck where we had a three-sixty view of the city and harbour. It was the opposite of what Alex Knowlson had drawn. We were up above, like a floating, benevolent deity, looking down at the insignificance below. No streets look dirty when viewed from on high. Nothing looks out of place. Like a glimpse of an order the brain can't fathom, as if a lab assistant had held a white rat high above the maze it was destined to run through.

"Beautiful," Shuzhen said.

She took pictures. I phoned Jeff and reassured him I wouldn't be a sartorial disappointment to the good people of Winnipeg. Jeff said he'd never doubted it.

Watching his cousin collect photographs, I wondered how Jeff felt about our partnership, now a year in. "Does he like his work?" I asked Shuzhen.

"Jun Fei?"

"Yeah. Is he happy with the business?"

"Worried for you," she said.

"He shouldn't be." I added, "I don't want to disappoint him."

"Not so much disappointed. He thinks you're good at one thing. He's a little bit good at a lot of things. His way works for him, but sometimes he thinks you focus too much. Because *he* can't focus."

"I can imagine." Jeff had been a satellite kid, sent by his parents to another continent to learn English and get an honours degree in economics. Given a BMW and an apartment in Richmond and told to earn it by thriving at what they'd chosen for him. Families like his had found the culture shock of Western academics more easily assailable than the Gaokao and government bribery.

Only Jeff had been sidetracked—or corrupted, depending on which parent you spoke to. More adept at picking up language and customs than parsing Keynes and Friedman, he was practical, personable, hands-on. His success had somewhat defrosted his mother, though the introduction of Marie had promptly plunged her back into Arctic winter.

Chen Jun Fei was his own man. He was my partner. I was happy with that.

I bought Shuzhen a pop and took the elevator down alone. At the university's help desk I bought a ticket for Alex Knowlson's lecture. They'd had a cancellation. I was lucky. The receptionist informed me of this twice.

"Alex does one of these talks every year and they're always very well attended. He puts on a good show. You know he's an alumnus?"

She tried to sign me up for an arts diploma but I begged off and retreated to the street where I smoked a dry cigarette that tasted no different than the air and waited for Shuzhen to come down.

20

UNIVERSITIES, LIKE UNIVERSES, tend to expand. There was SFU Harbour Centre, SFU Woodward's, SFU Surrey. Simon Fraser University proper was an ominous grey fortress that loomed over the city from Burnaby Mountain. It was designed in part by Arthur Erickson, whose fondness for concrete and despair helped earn SFU the unflattering distinction of having the highest suicide rate among Canadian universities. In my time there I'd nicknamed it Castle Grayskull.

With its vaulting quadrangle and many ramparts and battlements, the Burnaby campus brought in a supplemental income serving as backdrop for low-budget science-fiction films. Many a student activity had been disrupted by the hammering of set designers, turning the quad into Alien Marketplace or Future Lab. Today it was the corporate headquarters of an evil bio-genetics firm. A giant INGEN-U-TECH crest hung above the elevator doors, and the doors themselves were buffed and shined into flawless mirrors that reflected nothing.

Spirit Bear Coffee was across from the library, in the same complex that housed the Highland Pub, the gift shop, and administration. Working the till was a tall woman who spoke so softly I had to lean over the counter to hear her.

I paid for tea and told her my name. She asked me to give her fifteen minutes, since the other barista was on her break. I strolled the grounds, watched the film crew work.

The temperature was lower on the mountain and there was a hint of a breeze. I crossed the koi pond in the courtyard of the quad, rounded the Terry Fox statue and turned back. As I did I saw Marjorie Vee hike up the stairs, heading toward me.

We shook hands. Away from the till, it was easier to find traces of her birth sex. But she was beautiful, her mannerisms as old-school feminine as my mother's. Her timid smile made me attempt to be gallant, gentlemanly.

We chose a bench with a view of the pond. "I wish we weren't meeting under these circumstances," she said. "Detective Henriquez said you're looking for Chelsea."

"I understand you were friends."

"Yes, she was my good friend. I didn't have many. It was a very tough time for both of us."

A family of four crossed the concrete steps that bridged the pond. The two children paused to crouch and examine the fish. Their mother urged them away from the water with a command to hurry up, a command that couldn't disguise the small note of worry in the last syllable. The water was half a foot deep, the bridge an inch or so above its surface. The woman walked back, gave each child her hand and led them off as if evacuating them from a burning church spire. As they went on, the father's hand fell to the nape of the younger child's neck.

"Crisis averted," I said.

Marjorie smiled. "It's nice to see families."

"What are you studying?"

"Humanities," she said. "Greek and Latin. Kind of frivolous, I guess, but I like it."

"How did you meet Chelsea?"

"At a women's shelter. She was one of the only ones who didn't mind showering with me. The others used to wait till I finished."

"And you connected."

"Oh, yes. She was sweet. She also knew things about how to function in that world."

"Kind of things?"

"Where to get clean needles, free prophylactics, where to go for medical attention, which cops would actually listen to you. My family was upper middle class and I was very sheltered, which I only realized once I'd run away. Chelsea was like a big sister to me."

Marjorie Vee clasped her hands together and rotated the palms against each other, back and forth. Her face lit up with a memory, and for a split second she seemed transported back into the fray of the past.

"One night I was in an awful way. I phoned Chelsea and she met me downtown and comforted me. She took me to a crisis centre. The person running the place wouldn't accept me. Chelsea urged them, first very politely, but then she got cross. She was screaming. She told them if they didn't let me in and treat me like any other woman, she'd tell the entire community. Finally they let me in."

If I'd had a handkerchief I would have offered it to her. She covered her nose, sniffed and wiped at her eyes.

"Chelsea was beautiful like that. She'd help someone without even thinking about it. I try to be like her, but when I do something good and right it's because I've thought it through, weighed my options. Good, for me, is a decision, Mr. Wakeland. With Chelsea it was instinctual. I so miss her."

"Anything you can tell me about her regular clients? The circles she travelled in?"

"When I met her she was very careful. She had a few regulars. She never partied. She would work and then go home and—fix." The very comfort Marjorie Vee had with the slang was distasteful to her. "After she moved in with her boyfriend she became a bit less together. I don't know if it was his influence, or her habit had gotten worse, or problems with her family, or what. The old Chelsea would never have gone to bikers' parties. Maybe it was the money."

"Did you ever hear her talk about Alex Knowlson?"

"Yes," she said. "I met him."

"Decent guy?"

"Chelsea believed so. He and I—I thought his art was very nice. Chelsea told me he thought I was 'asymmetrical.'" She pronounced the word as if it were the ultimate insult.

"I have Chelsea's diary," I said.

"Oh, you mustn't read it."

"I don't have a choice, I need information. You've been one of the more helpful people."

She'd begun to cry. I fetched her a pair of brown paper napkins from the coffee shop.

"I know it's invasive," I said. "I know I have no right. I promise you I'm not using it for titillation or cheap thrills. And if it makes you feel better," I added, "she had nothing but nice things to say about you."

"She was my friend," she said through sobs.

"I know that to be an indisputable fact."

"She didn't deserve whatever happened to her."

"No."

"How can there be a god that lets those things happen?"

She leaned forward, face in hands. I put a hand out to her, gingerly, and when she didn't shy away I rubbed her back, trying to be soothing. A tiny silver crucifix and a St. Christopher dangled from a silver band around her neck.

Her sobs eased. She used the tissue to blow her nose and dab at her eyes. Shame and gratitude and anger and hurt all played across the soft features of her face.

"I'm sorry you had to see that," she said.

"It was warranted. I don't know what can be done for Chelsea at this point. What I can do. But maybe you could help me with a couple sets of initials."

I handed her two photocopied pages with G.O. and C.P. highlighted in buttercup yellow. She read through them and this started fresh tears.

"Do you recognize those initials?" I asked. "Can you tell me who they are?"

"Sorry, I need a minute." She smeared her tears into her

cheeks, closed her eyes and counted down from twenty, inhaling and exhaling a long breath for each number.

At one she opened her eyes and smiled, the kind of smile that shows the world the smiler is braced for anything, or at least attempting to be.

"Ready," she said. "Sorry. C.P. the C.P. George O. Yes, I recognize them. Chelsea gave out nicknames and then shortened them to initials. George was a man she'd meet in Oppenheimer Park. An older man, fifties, I guess. I saw him once. Chelsea told me he was rich, a businessman or something."

"George his real name?"

"You'd have to ask Chelsea." Her lips quivered.

Before she could lose focus I charged ahead. "What about C.P.?"

"I don't know the initials, but those *were* his initials. She called him 'C.P. the C.P.' because he was a Crown prosecutor. She was always joking about how if she got into a really bad scrape, she'd get C.P. to help her."

"Ever see him?"

"No, but Chelsea told me what he looked like. She said he was handsome but he had a—curve to his equipment."

"Huh."

"It wasn't that Chelsea hid things from me," she said, hastily. "We didn't talk shop much. There were other things to talk about. We laughed a lot."

"Can you think of someone who wanted to hurt her, someone she might have angered?"

"No, no one. Her sister was mean to her, but that was mostly for Kevin's sake. She didn't feel Chelsea was a good influence at that point. Once the drugs had—changed her."

She bit her bottom lip.

"This sounds kind of pat, but the only person who seemed to want to hurt Chelsea was Chelsea. Not that she was suicidal— I would have known—but the decisions she made and didn't make. She was very gung-ho to reunite with her birth mother, but she was scared. After a while she stopped talking about it. She said, 'If my mother loved me she'd've gotten in touch already.' She acted sometimes like, I don't know, like things were already over for her."

"If you think of anything else." I gave her my card. "Or if you need anything."

"Thank you. I hope you find her." She squeezed my hand, her own as dainty as Irish linen. "I think you will."

"Hope so." I stood up, buttoned my jacket.

"Do you have a good track record of finding people?"

"Pretty good."

"Have you ever seen *The Big Sleep*? I adore that film. Lauren Bacall." She said the name reverently.

"Dorothy Malone," I said.

She smiled and nodded, waved and walked down the steps, across the courtyard, back to her post in the coffee shop, her posture perfect, honest, unbent.

21

HOTELS USED TO EMPLOY their own in-house detectives, at least the more reputable hotels did. Most still have security teams, but for problem clients and strange occurrences, they outsource.

Good news for business, bad news for nostalgia. I liked the idea of being an old man in a rumpled suit, dozing in the lobby with my hat pulled low. Instead I was treated to a phone call at three in the morning, my second to last night before Operation: Tedium in Winnipeg kicked off.

The call was from the night manager at the Chateau Vancouver, asking could I come down right away. I asked him if his definition of right away included a shower and a caffeinated beverage. He told me he'd brew a fresh pot and have it waiting.

I'd been up late looking up rich businessmen in the Lower Mainland with the first name George. Even narrowed down with a possible last name starting with O, there'd been too many. I'd done better with C.P. In the last twenty years there'd been two Vancouver-based Crown counsellors with similar initials—G. Calvin Palfreyman and Eladio "Chucho" Perez.

Perez had his own practice now. He'd been part of a landmark case on tainted evidence admissibility, and he gave the odd lecture at UBC. He was in his early sixties now.

Palfreyman was forty-nine, still working as a prosecutor but poised to strike out for himself. He had worked on the case against Terry Rhodes and the Exiles' Vancouver Chapter, the same case that had yielded the surveillance photos of Rhodes and Chelsea Loam courtesy of defence counsellor Tim Kwan. That raised questions in and of itself. I wondered cynically if they weren't all involved—Rhodes, Kwan, Palfreyman. Perez, too. Everyone and everything. It didn't seem logical, but then, how had the rot sunk in this deep?

Earlier that evening I'd shown up at Woodward's for Alex Knowlson's talk, only to find it pushed back a day due to "circumstances beyond his or our control." The administrator had given me her best these-things-happen face, and said "It's Alex Knowlson" as if he were a force whose will was beyond the comprehension of mortals.

I phoned Knowlson's gallery and told his receptionist I wanted an audience with him tomorrow after the talk. If not, I'd make it known to the proper parties—I was thinking the police, she was probably thinking the media—that Alex Knowlson had refused to cooperate with the investigation of a missing sex trade worker in the neighbourhood he claimed to represent. She told me he'd need at least an hour for glad-handing. Could he meet me back at his gallery later tomorrow night, after eleven?

I was scheduled to fly out early the next morning. But I said fine.

Twenty minutes after the phone chirped and Orson started his spiel about Dunsinane, I was in the Chateau's foyer, wearing my T-shirt inside out and the same pants as yesterday. Dress professional, Jeff always said. But after 10 p.m., Jeff's cell went straight to message.

What the night man told me was this: an hour before, there had been a loud crash from the seventh floor. Twenty minutes later the guest in seven fifteen fled, carrying the suitcase he'd checked in with but not bothering to check out. Which was not a problem in this age of credit cards and internet check-ins. What was a problem was the noise coming from his room, a thumping and thrashing that had frightened the night maid. The hotel staff demanded police intervention. The manager was hoping that wasn't necessary.

And why was he hoping that? I wondered as I took the elevator up, a steaming cup of hazelnut roast in my hand.

Because Mr. Seven Fifteen is a good client.

Because this has happened before.

I'd brought my tool box with me, which included box cutters, bolt cutters, tape, cleaning agents, first aid supplies, a litre of distilled water and my father's Mag-Lite. I felt foggy and distracted, as people do at three thirty on a Tuesday morning. I was anticipating blood.

I made my way through the opulent maze of hallway to seven fifteen. I knocked and heard the thrashing of restrained limbs, not trying to free themselves but trying to make noise. I swiped the key card the night man had given me and opened the door.

It opened about four inches. With the door partway open, muffled voices could be heard. I reached around to move whatever was obstructing the door. My hand brushed cold metal.

It was a tripod, its back leg jammed under the door. By swinging the door toward me with my arm still stuck through, I could move the tripod forward into the room, allowing me to do the same.

Inside, Shay was lashed to the bed facedown. Arms secured behind her back, one leg tied to each bottom bedpost. Mr. Seven Fifteen had used zap straps. One of them circled her throat and another connected the neck strap to a light fixture on the wall behind the headboard. The plastic had dug into her ankles, leaving thin bracelets of blood. The smell of sex hung in the air.

On the floor, hog-tied and flopped on his back, was a blond youth with the longest, thinnest penis I'd ever seen. Both of them were gagged.

I closed the door and took a slow swig of coffee.

The tripod had no camera mounted on it. As I opened the tool box I looked around for other traces of Mr. Seven Fifteen. The chair and wastebasket had been moved away from the desk, out of the camera's line of sight. I looked in the wastebasket and found several wads of toilet paper and a mangled condom.

Once I freed Shay's wrists she struggled and tried to remove the neck strap. I took off the gag. Our eyes met and she relaxed, breathed. I slit the neck strap and told her to hold still as I cut the leg restraints.

When she was free her limbs spasmed, restoring circulation and exulting in their freedom. She bounced off the bed and ran stiff-legged to the washroom. I heard the tap running.

I gestured for the kid to roll over so I could cut him loose. He stared at me uncomprehending. I grabbed his shoulder and turned him three quarters face down. His cock made a plop as it flopped on the floor. I cut him free and eased off the gag.

"Dude, thanks," he said. He smelled like marijuana and baby oil.

"You okay waiting for the shower? I can phone the night man, see if there's a free room."

"I can wait," he said.

So we waited. I drank my coffee. He made no move to cover himself up. Steam began to leak into the room.

"So is this a regular thing?" I asked, breaking the silence.

"It was just s'posed to be a video shoot, man. Joe just lost it."

"Joe is Mr. Seven Fifteen?"

"What? Yeah." He grinned. He had the ruined teeth of a heavy freebaser.

"Any last name?"

"Just Joe."

"And what's your name?"

"Marius."

I introduced myself. I said, "So this guy Joe, he picks you up, offers you some cash to perform while he watches and directs."

"Yeah. I've worked with Joe lots. This was our first time with Shay."

I realized there were no clothes in the room, men's or women's. I searched through the drawers, under the bed. While I did this I asked Marius what had gone wrong this time.

"Shay went wrong. That chick would not stop talking price. 'I didn't realize you were gonna film it—that's extra.' 'Tied up—extra.'" His Shay impersonation was pretty accurate. "Joe reached a point, he's like, 'For what I'm paying you I could get two Koreans.' But Shay kept at it and Joe finally gave in. Then I was like, 'Why should I get less than her?' I mean, I'm sort of the star. So Joe gives in, promises us each two grand. Once we finish we're like, 'Okay, time to cut us loose now.' Instead Joe ties us up even more. Then he took our shit and bailed."

I tilted my head toward the washroom door.

"While you were restrained, did he try to—"

"No, he didn't even like her that much. Said she had small tits and looked too old."

He avoided meeting my gaze. "Did he try something on you?"

Marius nodded. "A handjob. But with the restraints and everything, plus that dude was crazy old. He put it in his mouth and—can we not talk about this?"

"Sure. Do you want to press charges?"

"Like with the police? Why?"

Eventually Shay came out of the shower, in towels. Marius bolted in to replace her. She sat on the bed and pulled her knees up to her chest. I called the night man, told him what I needed. He asked if I was serious. I told him bring two of everything, just like Noah, down to the belts and hats.

"And how was your night?" I said.

Shay didn't laugh. I reminded myself that not everyone brushed over their pain with humour.

"Why'd it have to be you?" she said.

"I'm just glad you're okay."

She'd staunched her bloody ankle with toilet paper. I lifted my first aid kit out of my tool box and bent down to put on proper bandages. She snatched the kit out of my hand, spilled the contents on the bed and smeared a heavy dollop of ointment over the raw skin. So much ointment that the first bandage wouldn't adhere. She threw up her hands and dropped it. I used a towelette to wipe away the excess ointment, peeled a larger bandage and applied it. Before I let go of her foot I patted the arch.

"Good as new," I said.

She snorted. She'd seemed near tears and then almost willed herself into anger, hands bunching and unbunching the bed-sheets. I pulled out a garbage bag and did a last sweep of the room.

"Nice tool box," Shay said. "You got a spare change of clothes in there?"

"Not needed," I said.

"So we're gonna waltz out naked? Or did you call the fuck-ing police?"

"Nope," I said.

It was the night man himself who knocked on the door, bringing the uniforms and more coffee. He bowed formally to Shay, and did a double take when Marius came out of the wash-room, using a hand towel to dry off his pits.

"Let me state unequivocally," the manager said, "the two of you are barred from these premises."

I took off my coat and wrapped it around my wrists, the way the police do when they want to spare someone the indignity of appearing in handcuffs. The night man doled out the uni-form items parsimoniously to Shay and Marius.

"So I'm Joe Seven Fifteen," I explained. "I'm drunk and I smashed up my hotel room. Your security people are escorting me out. It's only because I'm a good customer you don't call the cops." I latched up the tool box and pushed it toward Marius. "You take this when we leave. Does anyone want coffee before we go?"

Both of them looked too young, too thin and too short to be security guards. In Shay's case the long arms of the shirt had to be safety pinned into sleeves, and the hat fell cutely down over her brow. But at first glance we'd fit with our story: a drunk escorted out by two rookie rent-a-cops.

"Those uniforms cost," the night man reminded me.

"Believe me, I'll be collecting from Joe after I drop these two off."

He put a card into my pants pocket, just one more in the night's sequence of uncomfortable, intimate moments. "Here's his particulars. Joseph Partridge. He lives with his wife in the West End."

"Of course he does," I said.

The four of us rode the elevator down to the lobby. The staff was preparing the continental breakfast. A few early birds lounged over coffee or scoped brochures. EXPERIENCE CAPILANO SUSPENSION BRIDGE and the like.

Shay and Marius each took an arm and I did my best impersonation of an irate lush. I sobered up as I reached the Cadillac, and we piled in. I drove them east, home.

Marius directed me to a cheap hotel in Strathcona. I dropped him, told him if I recovered his belongings I'd leave them at the front desk.

He shook his head. "Don't bother, the desk man'd just steal it anyway."

Shay was sitting in the back seat staring at the floor mat. As I pulled away I said, "All right, Miss Daisy, your turn."

"You're going to that asshole's house?"

"Soon's I drop you off."

"I'm coming with you," she said.

"That would make a bad situation worse. The easiest way—"

"That fucker restrained me," she said. "I hate that. I fucking hate it." She sobbed and then was quiet for a minute. Then she lashed out. Her fists beat impotently on the leather headrest, on the window, the seatback. She tugged on the door handle. I coasted to a stop. But she didn't want to get out. The handle yielded and broke off in her hand and she flung it at me. It scraped my elbow, leaving a small faint seam that pearled blood.

We were kitty corner to her building.

"Go sleep," I said. "Get some breakfast. Another shower maybe."

"Joe's," she said.

I shrugged.

"Joe's."

Joseph Partridge lived near Kits Beach. His house was nothing special. Two storeys, vinyl siding, some sort of polycarbonate roofing tiles. At this address it would sell in the mid seven figures.

Two cars in the driveway, a Grand Cherokee and a BMW coupe. Lights were on behind the curtained bay window.

I parked one house down, pulled a roll of toilet paper from the tool box, wound some around my hand.

"I have a way I like to handle these situations," I said.

"Long as he pays."

"All right." I handed her the toilet paper. "How much phlegm can you muster?"

I put two wads of TP coated with lung butter inside a freezer bag. I told Shay to wait in the car. I went up the driveway, trying to recall the names of flowers in the Partridges' garden. Azaleas, chrysanthemums, pink roses. I rang the doorbell.

A woman in a blue terrycloth robe came to the door. She looked pleasant and tired. She asked in a whisper how she could help me.

"Ma'am, my name is David Wakeland. I'm an independent arbitrator hired by the North American Association of Hoteliers. Could I please speak to a Mr. Joseph Partridge?"

"He just got home a few hours ago," she whispered. "I can't disturb him."

"I think you should, ma'am. Sorry to bother you so early but I'm operating on Ontario time. If we don't get this resolved it becomes a full-fledged dispute and then it gets needlessly ugly. I don't think he meant to defraud the Great Northern hotel chain. Ask me off the record, seems like a case of crossed wires. That's where I'd prefer to leave it. But I can only do that if I speak to him in the next"—I checked my phone—"forty-eight minutes or so."

She of coursed and closed the door. I waited, looked at the garden. Were those nasturtiums? The door opened again and Joe Partridge stood there, belting on his pants.

He was about six feet, muscular under a plain white T-shirt. A soup strainer of a mustache and a pair of oddly angled ears were his only distinguishing features. Other than the moose slippers on his feet.

"Something about a hotel?" he said.

"Yes sir." I repeated my spiel and reiterated that it was all a misunderstanding. Mrs. Partridge carried an empty coffee tray into the kitchen. I told Joe Partridge I'd left my clipboard in my car and would he follow me out? He said sure. His wife reminded him to shut the door or else Balthasar would get out.

"Come to my goddamned house," he muttered as he followed me. "Some kind of threat?"

"You have a nice wife," I said.

"She knows all about the films. We watch them together."

"Does she know you direct them?"

He spat in the flower bed. "So she thinks I buy them on trips. Not like there isn't worse floating around."

"There's just something about Betacam," I said.

"Nothing I do is illegal. I pay well and the actors are all over the age of consent. I make sure they use condoms and I never let them hit each other if they don't agree to it. I really don't see what the problem is."

He noticed Shay sitting in the back seat of my car. Shay noticed him. Flipped him the bird.

"I guess the problem is you tying up two people and leaving them to rot."

"That's pure melodrama. They were never in danger."

"You had restraints around her neck."

"Look," Partridge said. "She practically begged me to use her in the film. Then she became combative and held up filming with insane demands."

"So did Liz Taylor."

He folded his arms. "What is it you want to make this go away?"

"Seventeen thousand dollars."

"Too steep."

"Plus all your zap straps plus your camera."

"You should have a balaclava on, asking for all that. Highway robbery."

"It's a compensatory gesture," I said. "Ten to the hotel for damages and loss of revenue from associating it with lewd actions. Two to each participant, which is what you promised them."

"And the other three?"

I smiled. "Five hundred for every hour of sleep this bullshit cost me."

Partridge shook his head. "I'm not paying," he said. "This is a shakedown. I'll phone my lawyer."

I held up the Ziploc bag.

"DNA swabs from the room," I said. "Your fingerprints on the zap straps I recovered. We go the lawyer route, I'll be presenting these in both a civil action by the hotel and any criminal proceedings brought on by your sexual abuse of a young man, and abuse via coerced proxy of the young woman in the car now. Allegedly," I added.

He stood with his arms crossed looking up his driveway, which seemed more like a face-saving gesture than real deliberation. He knew my price was cheap. Cheaper than justice. He said, "I'll get my chequebook."

He went inside and came back with a leather binder and a gold fountain pen. Before signing he opened the trunk of the Beemer and pulled out his kit—zap straps, camera, lights. It was neatly compartmentalized and looked like ordinary luggage. He set it down, closed the trunk, and leaned against the roof of the car to make out the cheque. "Their clothes?" I asked. He shook his head, gone.

I'm not good with technology. I was down on one knee turning the camera over in my hands, looking for a memory card slot. I didn't hear the door of the Caddy open. I looked up when I heard agitated footsteps.

Shay had my Mag-Lite. I watched her sly-rap Partridge on the back of the skull hard enough that his jaw bounced off the roof.

I keep handcuffs in my tool box. Shay had them out. She cuffed Partridge's left wrist to the side mirror and kicked him, and grabbed the Mag-Lite from the ground and hit him again. Partridge was left-handed and he brought his right up feebly to ward off blows to the face.

"How do you fucking like it?" Shay said. "Like being tied up? Feel good?" She worked down his pants and his tighty whities.

She held the flashlight over him. "How 'bout I shove this up *your* ass? Like that?"

I pulled her off of him. I could have done that sooner. Maybe it was shock. Or maybe, when you see someone commit a serious crime in the name of revenge, inchoate, reasonless revenge, and you feel no urge to stop them—maybe that's how you know it's true love.

22

I HAD THE SITUATION DEFUSED in nine steps. These were:

   a) Flinging Shay away from Partridge.
   b) Fetching the handcuff key.
   c) Telling Shay to stay back as I
   d) unlocked Partridge's wrist, then
   e) retrieved the chequebook,
   f) made sure Partridge signed,
   g) placated an incredulous Mrs. Partridge
      with a wave, then
   h) took possession of the cheque and
   i) beat a retreat with Shay, my tool box and
      Partridge's camera bag.

"I can run the cash over to you when the banks open," I told her as we followed Georgia back downtown. She sat in the front seat, playing with the lock peg on the door.

"I can wait," she said. "How 'bout breakfast?"

I pulled into a White Spot. I ordered an omelette with the closest thing they had to Twinings Earl Grey. Shay deliberated and settled on a Belgian waffle with fruit and whipped cream. We were boothed between old ladies, truckers, families. Shay put her hat next to her in the booth, shook out her hair. She'd ordered a juice but she didn't touch it.

"'Member that time you walked me to school?" she said.

I searched for the memory and couldn't find it. "Not really."

"It was maybe grade four. I was living with my dad. This was about a month before we moved out to Aldergrove. I saw you walking up Laurel Street and I rushed after you. 'Member I made you put your arm around me?"

"Right," I said. "You grabbed my arm and hugged it with both your hands. I thought you were rubbing snot on it."

She laughed. "You were a stupid kid."

"That's a hurtful thing to say and probably true."

"Anyway," she said, smile fading, "I did that 'cause my dad used to follow me to school in his car. Like, drive real slow, but hang back. As if I wouldn't notice my own dad, tailing me in the family station wagon."

I sipped my tea, wondering where this was leading.

"You were tall for your age. I thought, if he thought I had a boyfriend that would get bigger than him soon, then he might stop."

"Stop what?"

"Following me. What have we been talking about?"

I didn't know. I didn't say anything.

"You know what this has all been about, David, me coming with you, not going home?"

"Money."

"No," she said. "It's 'cause if I go home I'm gonna get high. I know I'm going home sooner or later and I know what I'll do when I get there. And I can't help thinking, what am I doing to myself? My lungs hurt. I got bad teeth. Plus what could've happened last night, you hadn't showed up."

Our breakfast arrived, along with smiles and solicitations from the waiter.

"So what do you want to do?" I asked.

"I want a real job. I want to help people. Maybe like a counsellor?"

"What's keeping you from that?"

"Me."

She nudged the dollop of cream into the doughy grid of the waffle and spread it thin.

"When things were really bad, I'd always tell myself I was a hustler, not a hooker. I don't know if you can appreciate the difference."

"A hustler has agency," I said. "A hustler's in control."

"Right. It's you getting what you want out of the rest of the world, instead of taking what the world feels like giving you. I'd see girls turn tricks for bus fare or fight over pipe resin, and I'd laugh at them and think that'd never be me. I was gonna do what I wanted all the time, for the first time in my life. No one was gonna own me. Can you understand what it's like to have someone treat you like you're their property? The stuff I've done. Can you imagine actually letting someone piss on you for money?"

"Not for money," I said.

"No. Course not. You're always in control. Nothing rattles you."

"I don't feel that way," I said. "I used to run my own business. Now I'm partners with this guy who's got much more business sense, but treats me like a junior partner. Or like a mascot." I looked at her, over our trays of food. "Not that it's the same as what you're talking about."

"That's a choice you made," she said. "And okay, maybe I made choices too, but there were other factors."

"So what can you do now, today, to keep yourself from going home and getting high?"

"Nothing," she said.

"What about a program?"

"Six weeks, a lot of Jesus talk, a lot of so-called strategies for the real world that some guy's reading out of a book. Then it's back on the street and best of luck. They care more about an empty bed than about helping you."

"So what's the solution?" I said.

"Take me back to your place and lock me in a room and don't let me out until I'm clean, no matter how sick I get. Please."

"Wish I could," I said. "But I have to fly out to Winnipeg tomorrow morning."

"No one ever has to fly to Winnipeg," she said.

"That's my feeling, but according to Jefferson Chen, the fate of our business hangs in the balance."

"Couldn't you get someone to stay with me? Someone who'd be as ruthless as you would?"

"That's a short list," I said.

At my place Shay asked if she could take another shower. I changed the bedding and took extra pillows and a blanket over to the couch. I opened the sliding door so the hint of an August breeze could trade places with the shower steam. With *Sunday at the Village Vanguard* playing on the turntable, I sat down with my laptop to work on the G.O.-C.P. problem.

The offices of both Perez and Palfreyman had sent me emails to the effect that, while they really, really appreciated my taking the time to write them, they were dreadfully, dreadfully sorry that lengthy correspondence couldn't be achieved with every interested party. They were only men, after all. I sent them identical responses, saying in essence, That's quite all right, I'll try you at home, and if that fails, I'll post my questions on YouTube.

There were G.O.'s a-plenty in Vancouver, thousands if I took in the entire Lower Mainland. I thought of phoning the office and having Shuzhen make up a list for me. I thought back to how G.O. was described in the diary: older, married, well dressed, kind. Chelsea had written about him with a measure of respect and familiarity, as if he was well known, his name common knowledge. Not a celebrity, perhaps, but a known figure. And that was the rub—a known figure eleven plus years ago. It was difficult to remember who'd been prime minister or president then, let alone the names of wealthy businessmen.

I fell asleep turning the name over in my head. I dreamt of nothing.

When I awoke a pillow had been shoved behind my head and the laptop was closed on the floor. Shay was standing by the bookshelf, tapping each volume at the right angle between pages and spine.

"I keep my money in the cash box beneath the sink," I said.

"Shh . . ." She went on tapping. She had on one of my T-shirts, sticking with the baggy, too-long security guard pants.

She finished her tapping and turned to me. "You have a hundred and thirty-eight books."

"Not counting the box of paperbacks in the closet, or the ones at my mother's."

"How many have you read?"

"Not many. I keep them to make people think I'm smart."

She picked one up at random. *The Muhammad Ali Reader.* "Ever read this one?"

"Some of it."

She seemed to be doing a thorough inspection of the room, moving across the bookshelves and into the study. Then she inventoried the stereo set.

"This is maybe inappropriate," I said, "but if you ever get in the position where you need to take something to borrow or, y'know, pawn, could you please leave the records? I had a bitch of a time finding a clean copy of *The Boatman's Call.*"

She didn't nod and she didn't put on a how-dare-you expression. "What were you listening to earlier?" she said.

"Bill Evans. He's a piano player. Maybe the greatest white jazz musician of all time."

"Making him what, four hundredth overall?"

I laughed. She sat down at the table and turned the chair to face the couch.

"I peeked at what you were working on," she said.

"And?"

"She's lucky to have you looking for her."

"Nice of you to say."

"I mean she's lucky to have someone care enough to find out what happened to her. Not everyone has that."

Shay looked out through the patio at the city, corralled by distant mountains. "Sometimes I hate this place," she said. "Even though I can't imagine living anywhere else."

I sat up and twisted my neck to read the time off the stove. "Four already. How do you feel?"

"Like I should get high," she said. "I need some clothes and vitamins and things. Will you grab them for me? If I go up to my apartment I'm going straight for my stash."

"Give me your keys. I'll drop you off first, then get to the bank so I can cash that cheque and disperse the money to the proper parties. Then get your stuff and bring it to you. Should have just enough time to make Alex Knowlson's talk."

"The art guy? He's part of this case?"

"Everything's part of this case," I said.

Drop off, bank, hotel, front desk of Marius's hotel, Shay's apartment (flush flush flush goes the dope, stamp stamp stamp goes the pipe), London Drugs, then finally over the river and through the woods, back to my mother's house on Laurel Street.

There were strikes against it as a place to kick a drug habit, especially for Shay. Chief among them was that it was in the neighbourhood she—we—had grown up in. Anyone who's tried to go back to a childhood home knows that at best it's disconcerting and at worst, it sets you adrift from your own sense of self-history. That was a danger.

But it was peaceful and there were quiet places to walk, and ultimately one room is as good as another. And it had my mother, whose disciplinarian's kindness would prove an asset. If Shay could survive that house on Laurel Street, the wide world would present nary a problem.

My mother was on her porch tapping pipe ash into her planter box. The first thing she said as I came up the steps laden with groceries and garment bags: "This is you punishing me, isn't it?"

I kissed her cheek. "She needs help," I said. "She asked me if

I knew someone ruthless and mean. You'd feel bad if I called anyone else. And you can probably use the company."

"Your half-sister was out last week."

I unlatched the screen, held it open with my knee as I opened the door. "How's she doing?"

"She's having a hard time with school."

"Grade twelve, that's natural. She got any idea what she wants to be?"

"A private investigator," my mother said, closing the door behind us.

The house was warm and dark. The smell of chicken stock and celery hung in the air. The TV segued from *Law and Order* to a maxi-pad commercial, glowing smiling women pouring out blue liquid. I took my shoes off without undoing the laces and earned the first of a long evening's worth of remonstrative glances.

"I put your friend in the guest bedroom," my mother said. "You can take her stuff up to her."

"You could have given her my old room," I said. "More space, at least."

"Women don't like basements, David."

Her voice grew distant and echoed as she carried on our dialogue from the kitchen.

"Now, I didn't know you were coming, so I didn't make anything special. But I defrosted some homemade soup. We've got rye crisp and we've got bread. You can like it or you can lump it."

"Did that sign arrive?" I asked.

"What sign?"

"The one for over your front door. One that says '*Arbeit Macht Frei.*'"

She stopped her kitchen bustling to stare at me. No trace of recognition that it had been said in jest.

"Don't make jokes about that," she said. "Your great uncle died fighting those people."

"He died in a POW camp. Probably did in by his own men for serving them soup in August."

"David." Turning the word from a proper name into an admonishment.

I took Shay her clothes and meds and moisturizers and everything else I'd swept off her counter and into a Safeway bag. She was sitting on the corner of the paisley-patterned guest bed, leafing through photo albums of dead people and children.

"She has a whole scrapbook of newspaper clippings about your exploits," she said.

"My exploits."

"And check this one out."

My mother had filled two plastic pocket pages of the album with photos of a smiling handsome couple changing the diaper of a bawling infant in an Optimus Prime sweatshirt.

Shay tapped the third photo. "That's your dick," she said.

Indeed it was, protruding from the smooth body like a gnarled and misplaced thumb.

"In her spare time," I said, "my mother is a child pornographer."

"I think it's nice. You have this whole record of who you are. And your real parents, you have to be glad to have pics of them before—" she paused. "Before whatever happened to them."

"They're still alive," I said.

"Really? I thought—"

"They were part of a church, ardent followers of the Reverend Something-or-Other. It's a long story."

She looked at me expectantly. I sat down on the bed.

"He was a counsellor," I told Shay. "I was their second kid. The oldest, Kyra, joined the church's youth brigade. She was—the church called it an accident, some fault of hers in following their purification program. When my parents found out, they split. Disconnected from their friends, from everyone they knew. That pretty much killed their marriage."

The photo in my lap showed the dark-haired woman in a knit sweater and skirt, the tall redheaded man who I'd heard all my life I was a dead ringer for.

"When they divorced she remarried, had another kid, moved back to the prairies. He lives in a shack on Gambier Island."

"When'd you last talk to them?" Shay asked.

"Probably when they were wiping my ass in that picture."

"You don't miss them?"

"No."

She expected more of an answer. I added, "What I miss is not having a big sister. That would've been cool. Someone to drag me to concerts, borrow cigarettes from, help me cheat my way through school. I would've liked that. I hate that I don't have that."

"But your parents," Shay said. "You never tried to get in touch?"

I took the book from her and closed it and set it down.

"The other day I talked to this guy, Wayne Loam," I said. "Chelsea's biological uncle. He said family is who's there for you. I'd never articulated it that well. My birth mother's older sister and her husband are my parents. The other two made their choice."

"Maybe I'll phone them up," she said impishly. "How would that make you feel?"

"It wouldn't make me feel anything," I said. I looked at the Sears clock over the dresser. "At night that thing ticks like John Bonham. You might want to pop out the battery. I've got to go."

"When will you be back?"

"Saturday, hopefully. Anything I can bring you from lovely Winnipeg?"

She did her best to think of something.

23

I WAS LATE FOR THE LECTURE, but lectures never start on time. Grad students were selling wine at a tableclothed desk in the hall. Copies of Alex Knowlson's art books were for sale and perusal at the next table.

The theatre was packed with academics, art patrons, students and other members of the city's cultural vanguard. Once the rounds of cool applause for the event sponsors and coordinators were out of the way, the place roared—roared—as Alex Knowlson took the podium.

Even at a distance I recognized that he possessed the gravitational pull of celebrity. The unease in his movements broadcast as unease with fame. But it was a practised discomfort. Success sat easier with him than he perhaps realized. Like a punk rock front man turned actuary. At some point the thing you pretend to be becomes the thing you are.

Knowlson's lecture lasted fifty minutes and began with a solemn acknowledgement that we were conducting this meeting on unceded territory belonging to the Coast Salish peoples. He took his time excoriating, in turn, the feds in Ottawa for slashing arts finding, the city council for giving themselves raises at the expense of social programs, the art community for resting on its haunches during a time of undeclared class warfare, and the international community for putting economic interests ahead of humanitarian ones.

The gist of his speech was that, as money poured into the city, corporate interests would continue to overtake communities. The result would be the speedy demise of the city's arts scene. "You can't outsource poetry," Knowlson said at one point. The crackdown on graffiti—"the last vestige of true democracy"—coupled with real estate prices forcing out local studios, meant that important voices were being silenced. Something had to be done, and it fell to us, right now, right this minute.

Question time. A devout-looking student approached the audience mic and asked if Knowlson had any advice for an aspiring artist like herself, and those like her in the crowd.

"Care," he said. "Just care. I don't care what about."

Raucous, rousing, wall-to-wall applause.

"Art is misunderstood," he said. "A painting isn't art because it's a painting, or because it fetches two hundred million at Christie's. And it's not worthless because the quote-unquote art community deems it so. Some of my favourite paintings are forgeries."

Laughter and profound murmurs.

"What art's function is—apologies to Oscar Wilde—is to smack us upside the head. Sometimes delicately, sometimes severely. If you do that well, and follow that principle regardless of where it leads you—well, you'll probably make a few dollars somewhere down the road, and someone important will probably call you subversive pinko scum. But there are worse things to be. Just so long as you care."

Afterwards Knowlson hung around to press the flesh, sign a few programs, accept a plaque from the dean of arts. A few students and rich people wanted their moment with him, and he did his best to indulge them. He was an hour and a half late in leaving, but finally he did, heading up over the Granville Street Bridge to his darkened gallery.

I gave him five minutes to settle in before I knocked on the glass door.

"You were at the talk," he said, inviting me in. "How did you find it?"

"I'm not ready to march on the Bastille," I said, "but I liked it."

"Out of curiosity, what would it take for you to march on the Bastille, to use your phrase?"

I didn't have an answer.

"How corrupt does a system have to get before anarchy is preferable for a working-class professional like yourself?"

"I don't believe in anarchy," I said.

"Which tenet do you find hardest to swallow?"

"That it exists," I said. "Sooner or later someone always takes control."

"So better them than the people?"

I put my hand over my heart and leaned back as if shot. "You got me. I don't know anything about politics. I came to ask you about Chelsea Loam."

"That's a subject that deserves a drink," he said.

I followed him through the unlit gallery to an aluminum spiral staircase that led up to a loft, half office, half salon. The workspace was neat and spartan, with framed pieces on the wall, one that looked like the Declaration of Independence copied out in brown Crayola. The salon side of the room was a jumble of papers, ashtrays, books with Post-its peeking out from between pages, envelopes and camera paraphernalia and empty glasses. Knowlson took two tumblers from the sideboard and poured a dram into each one.

"Friend of mine in Scottish parliament brought this over," he said. "Only MPs and their staff can purchase it. I don't have distilled water, then you could really appreciate the subtlety."

We clinked glasses. Alex Knowlson saluted the pictures on his wall. I appreciated the subtlety just fine.

He sat and crossed his legs and swept a few locks back from his eyes. "Where to begin with Chelsea Loam," he said. "She helped make me and in return I did . . .far too little. At the time, of course, it seemed the other way around. If I'd known then what I do now about the political implications of appropriating the stories of those in the sex trade."

"Mind translating that for those of us without master's degrees?"

He grinned. "You're more intelligent than you let on," he said. "A lot of my earlier work attempted to capture what it was like to live in Vancouver's poorer areas. I was practically living out of the Carnegie Centre, taking my meals with addicts and prostitutes. The year before I'd been absolutely destroyed by a painting of Degas's that hangs in the Musée d'Orsay. *L'Absinthe*, or *Girl in a Café*. Do you know it?"

"Sort of," I said.

His hands flew to a volume by his feet and he found a photo of it. A woman neither beautiful nor homely, sitting at a small table, staring at a goblet of green liquid as if it were the only thing sustaining her.

"There's beauty but no sentimentality," Knowlson said. "People initially thought it was a warning against the over-indulgence of spirits. I'd pass people on Cordova, different means of escape but that same finality of expression, that acceptance of despair. And I sought to capture that."

He paused and drank, then seemed to realize he'd paused to give his story effect, and laughed to himself at his own theatricality.

"What I figured out in later years," he said, "was that while my intentions were good, I was reinforcing certain stereotypes about the people that live here, especially the women. Society sees them as valueless, drug addicts and prostitutes and the mentally ill and all the other reductive stereotypes. When you factor in that many of these women are aboriginal, or Métis, or mixed race, you have a perfect storm of racism, sexism and colonialism. And my intentions aside, people were misreading my work. 'Oh, another junkie prostitute, another drunk native.' They were missing the humanity with which I was trying to imbue my subjects—but then perhaps so was I. Perhaps I was so eager to become the Great White Protector, Champion of the Downtrodden, that I had done the exact opposite of what I'd intended."

"So that's why: 'No faces, no races, no spaces,'" I said.

"Right," he said. "Departicularize. It's the only way to avoid all possible chance of misrepresentation."

"I like your early stuff better," I said.

He laughed hard and leaned back in his chair. "So do I," he said.

"How 'bout this?" I handed him the sketch of Chelsea's face. He took it and laid it on the sideboard and smoothed it, then returned to his seat, holding the picture and scrutinizing it for a long time.

He let out a moan. It didn't seem theatrical. It seemed as if someone who'd once been important to him had reappeared, bringing with her a rush of memories that had overwhelmed his heart.

Alex Knowlson stared at the picture sadly. I was in no hurry.

And then of a sudden he was jolted to awareness of where he was and who was with him. He apologized. "I was remembering when she and I did this."

He held up the picture.

"I started it from memory one day while waiting for her outside Performance Works. It was between Christmas and New Year's. She showed up late, not really dressed for the snow. Addicts don't always dress weather-appropriate. Once she'd arrived I made her sit there while I sketched in the fine details. It took two hours. She was just about blue by the end of it. But she didn't move once. She insisted on getting the picture right."

"If she'd run away on her own," I said, "would she have taken it with her? Because I found this with a diary, and I don't see her leaving both behind."

"Her diary," he said. "Does it mention me?"

"Very favourably."

He stood up and paced to the desk. "What right did you have to read that?" he asked. He seemed upset, but not at me.

"Would you rather she called you a shit?"

He stopped pacing. "Perhaps," he said. "You have to understand, things changed all of a sudden for me. I met my second wife. I'd just started reading Hegel. I was invited to go back to Europe as part of a rolling exhibition of post-colonial talent. And when I came back I had a young son and things were different.

Chelsea was different, too. More desperate. She wouldn't stop with the phone calls. She'd write me notes and drop them through the doggy door. I was so fucking sick of her, sick of the way she desperately wanted to be around me. I'd tell her to do something as a joke and she'd take it literally and do it. Like, 'Go offer a blowjob to that fat old man sitting over there with his wife.' And she would. As if she enjoyed having me degrade her."

Knowlson gestured to me. "Come over here."

He turned on the bank of lights over the desk. He pointed up at the strange scrawled parchment framed on his wall.

"She did that," he said.

I looked closer, caught the brush strokes and the uneven smears of paint. It read:

I know you've been busy but I've
been reading that book you gave me
and it's really wonderful and I kind
of understand what he's saying but if you'd
help me with this one part I just can't

The frame cut the last line off.

"'Get it,'" Knowlson said. "'I just can't get it.' I never gave her my copy of *Camera Lucida*. She stole it from out of my wife's car."

"Was there something wrong with her hands?" I asked.

"No," he said. "The original letter is framed in behind that. I told her if she wanted an answer she had to get a big piece of parchment, mix together some of her menstrual blood, stick a brush in her ass and rewrite it."

"Why?" I said.

"Because I didn't think she would do it. And she did."

"But why in hell would you frame something like that?"

"It's a perfect mixture of obscenity and passion," he said. "It's the most powerful piece in this entire gallery."

He refilled his glass, offered me some. I didn't respond. I stared from him to the note and back.

"You think I'm a son of a bitch," he said.

"Yep. I think you betrayed her as much as it's possible to betray another person."

"She gave it to me willingly," he said. "Wanted me to hang it up. The line between pornography and art is entirely a social construction."

"You know who Kevin's father was?"

"Kazz, I assumed. She'd given Kevin up before she met me."

"Hear her talk about someone with the initials G.O.?"

"No," he said. "She did mention someone named George, I think, but I don't know much about him. One of her clients, maybe."

"How about C.P.?"

He started to disavow, then caught himself.

"Cal Palfreyman," he said. "His wife used to be a benefactor for our studio. I think Cal and Chelsea might have met at one of the showings. Cal's a prosecutor. Was he one of her clients?"

"Just a set of initials," I said. "She ever talk about bikers?"

"Not to me."

It was past midnight. I was tired again. I owed Shay a phone call but decided to put that off until morning.

"I might have more questions," I said. "I'll leave them with your secretary."

"I hope Chelsea turns up," he said.

"With friends like you looking out for her, how could she not?"

I spun my way down the staircase and crossed the dark gallery and let myself out.

Jeff Chen drove me to YVR early. The sun wasn't up. We took his convertible, the top down. The cold air swooped and shrieked over our heads as the car picked up speed, sounding like so much white noise.

"Any case-related business I should be aware of?" Jeff asked.

"I'll do what I can from Manitoba," I said. "Don't let anyone touch that diary for any reason."

"How could I? It's in Blaine."

"And don't tell anyone that, either."

"Anything else?"

"Check in on my mother. Make sure Shay has what she needs. Don't give her money unless I okay it."

At the terminal I called her. "So early," Shay drawled.

"Everything's okay?"

"I guess."

"See you Saturday."

"Safe flight, or whatever."

I checked my messages. Gail Kirby's daughter had texted me. MOM NOT WELL WANTS TO KNOW ANY NEWS?

NONE, I wrote. BACK SAT.

The final boarding call went over the PA. I bought a couple of newsstand paperbacks and a Dr. Pepper. Then I jogged for the gate, then ran, and made it in time. And everything worked out perfectly.

TOMMY ROSS knew how to have fun, and knew how to make all the girls wet and begging for it. He told me this several times over the course of our trip.

I wasn't sure if I was in town as Ross's guest, his bodyguard, or his pet. What he wanted from me was, first, to enjoy myself, and tell him if I needed him to buy anything for me, anything at all; and second, to help him out, get the drinks, open the limousine door. But that was only with the ladies, so they'd know who was funding this venture.

Ross had rented an Escalade limousine, a sleek white monster that would dwarf and humble anyone who dared question who was The Shit. That was not up for debate: The Shit was Tommy Ross and the world would accept it and start taking dictation.

The Roving Party Headquarters—The Shit Central—picked me up at nine from the parking lot of the Comfort Inn. Ross was already in the bag. He emerged through the sunroof like a strange new deity, pointing at me as if bestowing some terrible, life-threatening honour: Come with me, Mr. Wakeland. Together we will drink up the night and fuck the entire city, and when we're done you can take your place at the foot of my sarcophagus as the other peons seal tight the pyramid doors.

"Buddy," he said to me as I climbed in. He was sitting next to a thin Asian woman in a silver lamé wrap. Ross had half of a tuxedo still on. They were drinking Goldschlager. Ross would point and gesticulate using the bottle.

"This is Tammy. Tam, Dave. How you feeling, buddy? Ready to tear this town a new one?" He pressed an intercom button. "Terence, man, take us to the best club in town."

Restaurants and gas stations flew by on the other side of the tinted window. Winnipeg was sweltering, even with the sun melting into streaks of gold.

"So what kind of things you want to do?" Ross said. "You like strippers? Want to get some food? 'Cause it's whatever you want, buddy."

"How about a coffee shop? I started a pretty good Sue Grafton on the plane." G is for Get Me the Fuck out of Winnipeg.

Ross snorted. "Maybe later. Right now we need some hot bitches and some more tunes and a hell of a lot more Goldschlager."

He splashed some into a water glass, handed it to me. No ice. I watched the flecks of gold dance in it. Like drinking a snow globe.

On one armrest was a stack of CDs that slid across the seats as Terence negotiated the stretch through the maze of downtown Winnipeg. The music ranged in variety from Nickelback to Night Ranger. "Pick your poison," Ross said, sweeping an arm at the selection.

One drug-themed compilation had an Iggy Pop track. I put it on. Ross air-drummed along to "The Passenger."

The neon letters of the club came in view, with a line of well-dressed people in silhouette below. Ross struggled into his jacket. Tammy helped him fix his tie. He finished his drink and told Terence to stop right in front and be back in an hour.

Terence, who drove with the one-handed grip of someone with more practice than patience, told Ross there was a lot down the street and he'd wait for him there.

"Fine," Ross said. "But when we come out I want that limo right on the curb, bam, like it is now."

I asked Terence for the limo's phone number and told him I'd text before we left the club.

"Good thinking, buddy," Ross said. "Mind getting the door for me?"

I did, standing stoically as Ross and his escort made their red carpet entrance. Tammy had forgotten her purse. As I leaned in to grab it I heard Terence muttering to his steering wheel.

The club music was a series of sonic booms, accompanied by the guttural rumble of a blown subwoofer. People danced. I sat at a VIP booth holding Tammy's purse, watching Ross ply his trade.

To his credit Ross had a smoothness with people. He could follow three conversations at once. He could make jokes that, while not funny, goosed the conversation along. He was something of a maestro in making the vague promises that would move women to follow him.

Soon he'd cut three women out from the pack, one with a boyfriend in tow. So now there were seven of us. The boyfriend was in jeans, a collared T-shirt and a chain wallet. He grew surlier the happier his date got. Ross bought champagne and Courvoisier and told the booth what he did for a living. It was a boring two minutes but it allowed him to drop in his net worth and car collection. He made frequent toasts and poured the liquor himself. The girls got drunker and the boyfriend got surlier. Ross and one of the girls danced. Tammy danced with the other girl. The couple argued. An ultimatum was made. A bluff was called. The man stormed off while the woman slumped in the booth.

"I don't know why some people don't want to have fun," she said.

Ross and Tammy came back from the dance floor and I couldn't swear they hadn't switched partners. Laughter, ass-slapping, another round of drinks. The quartet was happy and they lured the girlfriend or ex-girlfriend out of the booth and we headed to the limo.

I rode up front with Terence. He had the CBC on. Genocide, uprisings, terrorism. The prime minister was calling for an end to something. The back of the limo filled with weed smoke.

"Guess you boys are from BC," Terence said.

"Dope give that away?"

"That, and you act like you above this place."

"I got business back home," I said.

"That not your business in the back seat? Kind of bodyguard are you?"

"A reluctant one," I said.

We hit another club, although in layout and patrons, Terence might as well have rolled once around the block. I opted to wait by the car and smoke. Terence stretched and leaned against the front panel. He'd played for the Roughriders before tearing a quadricep, and had done some bodyguarding before his chauffeur licence came through.

"Hated bodyguarding. Quit the second week. Old teammate hooked me up. Fullback, two point three mill contract over four years. Talking *stacked*. Like your boy in there." He pointed to the club.

He opened his lunch pail, took out a sandwich and an orange. I offered him a cigarette. "Two years four months," he said.

"What was it made you quit the bodyguard racket?" I asked. "Being around your rich friend?"

"What it is," he said through a mouthful of orange, "is too many people wanting to be gangster without wanting to do the work to be hard."

He chewed thoughtfully and added, "My girl says she misses the money, but damned if being a chauffeur doesn't bring in almost the same, once you factor in the tips."

"This whole corporate world irks me," I said.

"I feel that. But miss enough meals and it starts to look pretty damn attractive."

"Shit." I caught sight of the boyfriend, or ex-boyfriend, stalking over toward the stretch.

He paused and looked at me as if he was going to ask a very silly question. Then he turned and walked into the club, held back by the bouncer long enough to flash his ID.

I rushed in after him, plunging into black light and lasers, the sweat-fog of attractive people. I scanned the dance floor, didn't see Ross. I caught sight of a square head that might have been the boyfriend. I followed it in, pushing past couples, breaking embraces.

And then a strobe light kicked in and I lost the boyfriend, although it could have been someone else. There was a bar with a waterfall and the private booths stretched behind it. I caught a flash of silver lamé on a hip disappearing around the falls and I jogged over.

Ross sat in a roped-off booth with the women all across from him like a row of golden-haired dolls. Two of them looked tired. An empty pitcher sat on the table. Tammy slid in next to Ross, carrying more drinks.

From the other side of the waterfall came the boyfriend.

I stepped over the rope. As soon as I did a big bald bastard put his hands on me. He was doing the bouncer shuffle—"We can talk about this, sure, but as I listen you're going to back-peddle toward the door."

While the bouncer was distracted with me, the boyfriend slipped over the rope and approached Ross's table. He put his hand out and seized his ex-girlfriend's—definitely now his *ex*-girlfriend's—thin pale wrist.

I slipped the bouncer's grasp and beelined for the booth. Hooked an arm around the ex's shoulder and pulled him away. His breath had a gasoline reek and his cheeks were red and puffy.

"—of your damn business," he was saying to me.

He took something from his pocket, something with a handle. His other hand grabbed for my lapel.

I jabbed him in the face and when his arms went up I hooked him in the side above the hepatic nerve. The Micky Ward special. The ex dropped the way Sanchez did to Ward, straight down, folding in on himself.

A butterfly knife fell from his hand and tapped the toe of the bouncer's shoe. Ross stared at the man, at the knife. He cheered and climbed out of the booth. The bouncer had picked up the knife and I was explaining things to him, stationary this time.

I thought Ross was going to congratulate me, a lot of back-slapping and toasts. Instead he walked to the crumpled ex-boyfriend and kicked him in the face.

Tammy had an iPhone. It absorbed her attention as we waited in the parking lot of the Executive Plaza, a monolith of brass trim and light fixtures that looked like melting crystal. I read my Grafton and Terence listened to the CBC.

After two hours Ross came down alone. His hair was mussed and he was down to an undershirt and dress pants. As he climbed in I caught a whiff of mingled perfumes and sex.

"I want to teach you something," he said solemnly. "Take a look at this." He held up a credit card, embossed with the words EXECUTIVE and EXPENSE and stamped with a hologram of a soaring eagle.

"This is not a card," he said. "This is a key. A key that opens any door. Any bottle. Any pair of legs."

And he laughed and returned to his jovial self, and told us how he'd fucked two of them while the third lay passed out on the adjacent bed. Evidently one of the participants was the ex-girlfriend of the man I'd decked.

"If he hadn't've been such a douche I wouldn't've gone after her," he said. "How about that punch? Wham right in the side. I gotta learn how to do that. Where to?"

"It's your party," I said.

"Know where I really want to go? Let's go out to the reservation. They probably throw sick parties out there." Ross rapped on the divider. "Terence, man, take us out to the res."

"Bad idea," Terence said.

"Terence." Ross pressed his platinum card into the glass. "Take us out to the res, man. Time to kick this party into fourth gear."

"Which res?" Terence said.

"Sorry?"

"Which res."

"One with the Indians on it. There another kind?"

"There's different reservations for different peoples," Terence said patiently. "Assiniboine, Cree, Métis, which ain't strictly speaking—"

"I don't fucking care," Ross said. "Take us to the party." He snapped his fingers in epiphany. "Where do the Indians go to party when they come into Winnipeg? Yeah, take us to an Indian bar. The *best* Indian bar."

I don't know if Terence tried to comply or decided to teach Tommy Ross a lesson. He headed toward the North End.

Ross cuddled an arm around Tammy, who was wrapped up in texting. He said to me, "We having fun?"

"Could use that coffee shop," I said.

"Ah, fuck coffee shops. Bunch of turtleneck douchebags working on their screenplays."

A broken clock, I thought.

"I liked the way you handled that," he said. "No-nonsense, just deck the bitch with body blows. What martial arts do you know?"

"I took junior karate for a year at the Douglas Park Community Centre, but I was awful. I learned a few things boxing."

"Boxing's cool," he said. "Yo Adrian. But I want to learn MMA, jujitsu and stuff. I really want to devastate people if they try and fuck with me. You ever watch MMA?"

"I liked the Gracies," I said.

"One time I was at this party," he said. "Guy had Exiles doing the security. Now those dudes are hardcore. This guy starts mouthing off and one of the bikers walks over to him and folds him in half. Like closing a briefcase. Awesomest thing I've ever seen. And you know who it was?"

I said I didn't.

"Charles 'Ill-Gotten' Gains himself. Two-time light-heavy champion."

"What party was this?" I said. "Who hosted it?"

"Who cares? Charles Gains, man. He's a badass."

"He's very scary," I agreed. "Who hosted the party? Was it a corporate event, or—"

He snapped his fingers a few times. "You know who it was for? George Overman, the Discus Solutions guy."

I felt the plate tectonics of the Loam case grind and shift, if not exactly erupt in revelation.

"The name is familiar," I said.

"He owns a few franchises, an auto mall. I'm sure if you—"

The vehicle stopped. Terence announced that we were here.

The place was called Holloway's Hideaway. It was situated in a concrete desert of parking lots, industrial sites. Decades-old neon advertised Michelob and Coors Regular. It was a country bar, with all the country charm of a double-barrelled shotgun.

"Perfect," Ross said. "Time for some real fun."

As he and Tammy climbed out, Terence lowered the divider. "So's you know, I'm on the clock another thirty-five minutes. There's a cab stand four blocks down that way. I got the card somewhere."

"How rowdy is this place?" I asked.

"They're good folks, most part. And you're strapped, so you shouldn't have problems."

"Strapped as in a gun?" I asked.

"Kind of bodyguard doesn't have a gun?" he said. "I know, I know, a reluctant one. Take care of him, man."

The inside of the Hideaway was simple enough. Red carpeted floors, solid pine benches and booths. A bar in the centre of the room, a historical display of beer bottles in a greasy case above the bar. TVs turned to pre-Olympic hype, baseball and darts. Row of pinball and shooter games on the far wall. Cigarette dispenser by the john.

It was halfway busy, the clientele about an even mix of aboriginals and whites. A few veteran types, some in wheelchairs.

The women were older, harder, and when one cornered me and said she'd suck my dick for a twenty and I said no thank you, she laughed and asked if I was a fag.

"Totally," I said.

She laughed again and crowed to a couple of denim-jacketed buddies that it was a rare night that the joint would be graced by the presence of *two* gays. "Not counting you two," she said, sparking off a round of merriment.

Ross was at a booth, elbows on the table, looking like a college freshman about to taste his first alcohol. He peeled a twenty off his roll and tossed it in front of me. "I'll have an Old Fashioned, she'll take a Screwdriver, and whatever you're having."

I crossed the empty dance floor. The bartender, a punk chick with alabaster skin, filled out the order capably without once glancing at me. When I returned to the booth, two women had joined Ross. One was native, one white, both closer to my mother's age than to Tammy's or mine.

I put down the drinks and Ross handed me money to bring Patti and Margot what they wanted. Which turned out to be cream sherry and a Boilermaker, respectively.

I fetched the drinks again. When I came back Ross was ready for a refill. He slid out of the booth, told me to sit, and handed me a bundle wrapped in a sticky garbage bag.

"Present," he said.

Inside was a carton of untaxed cigarettes.

I sat down and told the two women, "Run your scam but don't hurt him."

"Relax," Patti said. "We like him. Don't we?"

"We like you, too."

"Tommy Boy was telling us about you."

"You killed a man tonight."

"Folded him in half."

"Hands like lethal weapons."

"Like that movie."

"Right, with what's his name. What *is* his name?"

"Mel Brooks."

Ross came back and we switched places. I hovered around the table, bringing drinks and watching the door. When the ladies of the manor left to powder their noses, I sat and asked Ross what his endgame was.

"Ever fuck two women at once?"

"No."

"Well, I'm'n'a be the first guy to ever fuck twice two women and on the same day. My cock will be a Guinness record."

"Make sure it's at your place, at least."

"This is my place. My favourite place."

"Take them to your hotel room. Get a cab. Don't go home with them."

"I know what I'm doing," he said.

He peeled off eighty dollars. "Will you take the Tamster home? She says she lives a few blocks from here." He tossed the money in front of her. "A tip, on top of your cut from the agency. Always good to keep a spare."

She pocketed the money, not thanking him. I offered her my jacket and as we left the Hideaway we passed Patti and Margot, smiling sweetly as they supplanted us.

We took quick steps along the sidewalk as traffic roared past. Trucks mostly, intervals of bright light, rumbles, then silence. It was balmy but the temperature was dropping. Tammy clasped the jacket around her as we walked.

"Been escorting a long time?" I asked.

"Not really."

"Pays good?"

"Some nights."

"We don't have to talk."

"Okay."

Tammy lived in a second-storey flat above cheap and battered storefronts. A bailbondsman, a thrift store. There was a covered bus stop on the opposite corner. Not much else.

She slid the coat off her shoulders, handed it to me, and wordless, left.

I speed-walked back to the Hideaway.

On the curb, folded, where the limo had been, was Ross's sport coat. I checked the pockets. Cellphone, Cialis, car keys, cocaine.

Ross was no longer in Holloway's. The bartender told me he'd called a cab. She didn't know where to. I called one for myself, guessing, hoping he'd taken them to the Plaza. I wondered if the blonde girls would still be there, and if so, would there be a scene. But Ross hadn't come back to the Plaza. He hadn't left word. The golden trio had left hours ago, two of them carrying their nearly comatose friend, a parade of mussed hair and mini-skirts that the desk clerk remembered well.

"Whoever your boss is, he's my hero," he told me.

I tipped him twenty to call me if Ross appeared, gave him twenty more to pass the message on to whoever relieved him. The same taxi driver was dozing, his cab parked in the roundabout. I knocked on the glass and told him to take me back to the Comfort Inn.

An LCD display built into the passenger's side headrest played nothing but commercials. Soft drinks and online poker. The driver told me about the rash of stabbings a few years ago that had led to the installation of panic lights in all the cabs in the city. He told me he was ready for someone to just try starting something with him, just once.

At the motel, I took the stairs up to my room on the fourth floor. There, on the bed, Ross was being ridden by one of the women in reverse cowgirl. A fungal smell hung in the air. The other woman stood over them, holding up a pen, tracing their movements like a demented conductor.

I didn't even try to decode the scene. I let the door glide shut on its pneumatic hinges. I walked to the lobby and found a comfortable chair, put the coats over my lap and tried to think about George Overman and Terry Rhodes and Shay and Chelsea Loam.

Before I passed out I realized that Patti or Margot, whoever had been standing over the other two, had been aiming a Wakeland & Chen novelty pen cam, capturing the writhing of Tommy Ross and the woman for posterity.

—

Second verse, same as the first, a little bit louder and a little bit worse. So proceeded my second night in Winnipeg.

As the third night wound down I watched Tommy Ross and two Greek prostitutes take turns potshotting rats with a .22 target pistol as they stood on the back bench of the car. I was driving a vintage drop-top Eldorado that Ross had rented, with the idea that if I was going to stay sober anyway, I might as well drive. Ross had bought a suit of purest white and a nautical hat, and had insisted on being addressed for the entire night as Admiral. The girls, with their slippery Mediterranean accents, were calling him Animal. We were parked at the Winnipeg landfill. They were very drunk.

"Take a drink, Seaman." He thrust a bottle at me. Ross had bought a two-litre Coke, dumped out three-quarters and topped the bottle up with Goldschlager. He had almost finished it. I considered the dregs and handed the bottle back to him.

"Driving, remember."

"How dare you refuse a direct order." He stood and leaned over the seat to where the women stood in the back, plugging away at the scurrying shadows. He kneaded the shin of the girl with the gun. "First Mate Nia," he said. "Ensign Wakeland has disobeyed a direct order."

"Have him walk the plank, Animal."

"This ship cannot condone mutiny. You have my permission to shoot the lad."

All three of them laughed. Nia was holding the gun in a proper two-handed stance. She swung the barrel around and down until it was pointed at me. "Pew pew," she said.

Then she shot me.

It's that easy to kill someone. Back of the head, middle of the chest. With a small-calibre round, there might not even be an exit wound.

There was shock and pain. Then mayhem. Nia dropped the gun and shouted that she hadn't meant to pull the trigger, that she'd been joking. The other girl screamed. The Admiral stood dumbfounded.

I touched the outside of my right thigh. A growing dark spot on the suit fabric. A graze, but enough blood to make me worried.

We tore out of the dump, Ross cautioning me to yield up the steering wheel, Nia begging forgiveness. The vintage Caddy had a modern GPS. I punched in HOSPITAL and followed the soothing female voice: "In one hundred metres, left turn, go straight, right on sixteenth."

I missed a turn. "Recalculating," the voice said. Ross urged me to pull over so he could drive.

"Seriously, you don't have to prove you're tough."

"It's not toughness," I countered, "when everyone else is shitfaced."

We passed the emergency entrance, its red neon illuminating a nearby strip mall. I glided the Eldorado up to the door, took too long putting it in park. The GPS told me I was a fool. Nia ran in and before I could work myself out of the car, two paramedics had me by the shoulders, lifting me up and helping me into the waiting room.

There are rules and procedures for dealing with victims of gunshot wounds. I filled out some forms, and was briefly questioned by a uniformed pair of Winnipeg's finest. When I sheepishly told them that my rifle misfired while I was shooting at tin cans, they accepted the lie without question.

The wound itself was little more than a graze, quickly swabbed and dressed. The doctor told me I was lucky.

Nia and I split a cab. The Tylenol Threes kept the pain to a manageable throb. As the taxi turned into the Comfort Inn parking lot, Nia's cell rang. Her ringtone was a Cyndi Lauper tune I'd have in my head for the rest of the night. She answered, nodded, passed the phone to me.

"Buddy." Ross sounded boisterous, though his tone was undercut by a delicacy he hadn't exhibited before.

I told him not to worry, what my story had been. He sounded relieved.

"Guess you need some rest, huh?" he said.

"I could use it."

"I got you a room here at the Plaza. Tell the cabbie to head over here. You can rest up, and we'll bring the party to you."

"Nice thought, Tommy," I started to say. But it didn't matter where I stayed. And why not let him pay for a suite, when he'd fucked my room up, literally?

Ross was waiting by the valet's station, along with the other woman whose name I still didn't know. The women wore party hats and held streamers in their hands. Ross had donned a Jughead crown, gold, the kind you'd find in a kid's meal at Burger King.

As I eased myself out of the cab, Ross grabbed an arm to steady me. He doffed his paper crown and moved to put it on my head. I shrugged him off.

"Not really up to partying," I said. "Just a clean bed for a few hours."

"Sure, sure, no problem. I think, though, we should have a drink, take a minute, the four of us, and appreciate how much worse things could have turned out. One drink. Okay?"

Ross had booked the room that adjoined his own. Rather than unlocking the door to mine, we followed him into his room and he unlocked the sliding partition. He had two bottles of champagne on the sideboard, bucketed, on ice.

"Hope you like Cristal," he said. "It's what the homeboys drink. Nothing but the best."

I took a flute and clinked glasses with the others, took a sip and set it down. I had an ashy taste in my mouth so bad I would have drunk spittoon polish. One of the women hooked her phone into the suite's sound system and began scrolling through her playlist. Ross leaned toward me as if to collude.

"First off, I'm sorry," he said. "I only wanted to vent a little steam. The job is stressful as hell, and when I cut loose sometimes I don't exercise the soundest discretion. So—"

"I'm not going to tell on you," I said.

"No, no, of course not. Didn't think you would."

"I'm going to go to sleep and tomorrow I'm going home."

"That's cool, I understand." He nodded, relieved. "So. Party then, huh?"

"Go ahead."

As he stood up I asked him about George Overman. He almost didn't place the name. Puzzled, he sat on the armrest of the chair.

"Is this connected to some case?"

"Probably just me keeping my mind off the pain," I said. "You said you met him?"

"Once at his party and then once years later at a fundraiser. His son Nick runs the company now. Nick didn't seem like a bad guy. The old man—well, to be honest I don't see what the fuss is about."

"What do you mean?"

"Well, at that dinner, they wheeled the old man out, everyone gave him a standing O, and some people even lined up to take pictures with him. I mean, I get it, I totally appreciate that he built that company out of nothing. But he doesn't run it anymore. His son doesn't, either. They just 'see to their interests,' that kind of thing. The guy I met was just another old man."

"When was this?"

"Six years ago, maybe."

"How old would he be now?"

"Seventy-something, at least. Old is old."

"Thanks," I said.

Ross nodded and tackled one of the girls, laughing, onto the bed.

—

I woke on my bed but not in it. The wound was swollen and raw. I reached over the sleeping form next to me and pawed at the bedside table for the tablets. My hand struck the thin tube of anti-inflammatories but couldn't find the stouter bottle with the pain meds.

Light seeped in around the edges of the blinds. It was noon. Nia breathed peacefully on the other side of the bed, wrapped in her coat. My wallet sat on the writing table next to the television stand. Everything else of mine was at the other hotel.

I limped to the washroom and washed my face. I was still in my dress pants, a small but noticeable puncture partway down the right pantleg.

The door between rooms was open. Next door Ross and the other woman were entwined beneath the sheets. Both snoring. Spilled out across the top of the credenza were my Tylenols. Some of them.

I limped into the room to gather them up but thought Ross might have something stronger. Some Percocet, maybe, or a morphine drip. I looked around and didn't see anything. I tried his washroom.

He had two identical shaving kits. I opened one and found nose trimmers and Selsun Blue. The other was a veritable pharmacopoeia. Vicodin, Percs, ecstasy, codeine—the grass is always greener—and a pouch of Rohypnol.

Two white tablets remained in the pouch. The older kind, that dissolve colourlessly. I tipped them into my hand. I remembered finding some on the person of a rapist who'd worked the parking lots around Jericho Beach.

I pocketed the pills and found the pen cam in Ross's pants on the floor. I left the hotel and shuffled out into daylight, trying to see Winnipeg for what it was and not just an absence of Vancouver. Hot and dry, but like Vancouver, struggling to figure out what it owed to itself and what face it would show to the world.

It was time to go home.

I got back to the suites in time to intercept the breakfast trolley. Ross was propped in bed. The women had both left.

"Morning," Ross said.

"Afternoon."

He shrugged and smiled. "I figure, whenever I wake up, it's morning. Is that breakfast?"

I put the cart next to him. He sipped at the orange juice. I looked from the spilled codeine tablets to him.

"You drink, you end up doing a lot of things," he said in lieu of an apology. He put the tablet on his tongue and took a sip of his cappuccino. "Might as well start early."

I pulled a chair over to his bedside. I put the empty pouch of Rohypnol on the bedstand. I watched him realize what it was, saw him realize its significance.

Mute, he stared at his feet. A child caught by his mother hucking rocks at sparrows' nests, that was how his face read.

"I don't know how long this has been going on," I said. "I don't know how many women."

"It's not like that, Dave."

"Does Utrillo know about this? Or the other one, Carnahan?"

"No."

"You're sure?"

"There's nothing to know about," Ross said. "It's depression medicine. I get depressed."

"Triggered by the word 'no'?"

Ross rotated his glass of orange juice on the tray with the concentration of a safecracker. I waited him out. When he looked up at me he'd found an expression that was halfway contrite.

"A friend gave them to me. Said they help uptight people relax. You were with me. Did any of those girls resist? Say no? Any of them complain about me footing the bill?"

"Hard to complain when you're doped to the gills."

"I never—"

"You're telling me if I call those blonde girls, get them tested, not one of them's got any of this in her system?"

Ross's juice had regained his attention.

"If they do it's something they probably took themselves." He looked in my direction without making eye contact. "Tell me how we make this right."

"You're the one with the key that opens everything."

"Money?"

"Phone up the girl, make her an offer."

"I meant you," Ross said. He smiled eagerly. "You and your partner need the business. And Solis doesn't need any unnecessary aggravation. Let me do what I can to make it happen."

I thought it over.

"Ten thousand," I said.

Ross grinned. I held up my hand.

"On the condition," I added, "that you turn the rest of your travelling pharmacy over to me."

"I can do that."

"All those pills."

"Sure."

"And tell me honestly if the other people at Solis knew about this."

"None of them, not a thing. I take full responsibility. And thanks, bro."

"I am not your fucking bro."

He came back from the washroom with the shaving kit. Tossed it on the bed. Sat down on the edge in his tighty whities, drank down his orange juice.

"I'll let you take a shower," I said, gathering up the kit. "Last day of vacation, long flight ahead."

Once I heard water running I hobbled down to the lobby. The concierge looked up from his computer as I placed the kit on the desk.

"A present," I said.

"For me?"

"For the police. Turn it over to them when they ask. Only them." I brought out the pen cam, cracked its plastic case and removed its flash drive.

"I'm sorry, are you a guest here?" The concierge's hands were poised over the keyboard.

"A guest of a guest," I said. "Ross, the Solis account."

Clack clack. "Of course."

"Can I charge long distance calls to the room?"

"You sure can, sir." He hit one and handed me the receiver.

I phoned my mother and got no answer. She did a twice-weekly brunch at the casino with a few of her friends. She'd probably be gone the whole day.

Don Utrillo's office manager put me right through.

"Mr. Wakeland," Utrillo said. "How's Winnipeg?"

"Growing on me," I said. "There's a situation here with Tommy Ross."

"Tommy. What's up with him?"

"He's been doping women and taking sexual advantage of them," I said. "Found some roofies on him, among other things."

"What's any of that got to do with us?"

"Nothing, except he's been doing it on the company expense account, in the company suite. I figured you could be the one to phone the Winnipeg PD, tell them your security staff alerted you to this rogue employee's behaviour. Ensure cooperation and so on, keep the corporate image clean."

"You're very considerate," Utrillo said.

"Wakeland & Chen strives to consider the angles the others don't," I said. "When you call, tell the officers Ross's dope kit is at the front desk, along with a video file. Tell them to fast-forward through the gymnastics to the part where he confesses and absolves the company."

"I'll do that."

"Tell them to test the girls he was with. Tell them if they look at the very bottom of the shaving kit they'll find two of the pills. Ross should be preoccupied until they show up."

"You handled this absolutely right," Utrillo said.

"Yep."

"If you need something you can call me."

"Do you know how I could get an audience with George Overman?" I asked.

"Discus Solutions?"

"That's the one."

"I could make a call," Utrillo said. "Guess having him as a client would add to your prestige. Remember, Solis business comes first. We don't plan on sucking hind tit."

"Absolutely," I said.

"Great. Excellent. See you back here in civilization."

In front of the Comfort Inn, waiting for the airport shuttle, my cell rang. Jeff Chen, eager to learn what feats I'd surmounted to get Utrillo to sign off on our contract.

"Had Ross arrested," I said.

I explained things to him. Jeff found it funnier than I did. It cost me a minute of long distance cell time before he could reign in his laughter.

"And now I get to finish the Loam case," I said. "No distractions."

"That was the deal. Although—"

"No 'although.'"

"Has Caitlin Kirby talked to you?"

I tossed the plastic husk of the pen cam into a discarded Slurpee that sat on the rim of a nearby trash bin. "What about?"

"Her mother's in the hospital," Jeff said. "Gail Kirby had some sort of respiratory failure. She's been comatose since last night."

NO MORE PAINKILLERS. My guts lurched on touchdown. Early evening and not a cloud in the sky.

I took the Skytrain through Richmond, over the Fraser River and into the city centre. I got off at Broadway–City Hall and lugged my carry-on into the foyer of Vancouver General Hospital.

I'd called my mother and learned that Shay had left Laurel Street the previous day. To go score? I wondered, but asked instead if Shay seemed better.

"If by better you mean happier, then I guess so. She had a rough go of it. I gave her space, and after two days she seemed to be doing better. She asked a lot of questions about you as a boy. She's nice, David."

"Shay say why she left?"

"Just that she had business to take care of. Plants to water."

I thought of the dead ficus on Shay's windowsill, the clay pots with their dusty grey soil and mounds of cigarette butts.

"All right," I said. "I was worried you might have chased her off by making that onion and cheese loaf."

"You said you liked my onion and cheese loaf."

"I miss having that dog around to clean my plates."

"Where's the nice David?" my mother said.

"Try Winnipeg."

At the front desk of VGH I asked which room Gail Kirby was in. I bought tea and a bagel at the hospital canteen and rode up to the observation ward. Caitlin was keeping vigil. She had a knitting project with her and fed her needles as she spoke.

"Here to check on your two hundred thousand dollars?" she asked. "Believe me, you should be worried. If something happens to my mother you won't see dime one. I'll contest your contract. I'll contest it even if it costs me two hundred and one thousand in legal fees."

I eased into the seat on the other side of the bed. Caitlin stared at her lap.

"All you had to do was tell her a good story," she said. "Some pleasant fiction about how Chelsea died in her sleep and was buried up in Haida Gwaii or some other faraway place. A car wreck. Even an overdose. Now it's too late."

"She asked me to find the truth," I said.

"The truth is what every truly dishonest person hides behind. The truth is Chelsea is dead, somehow, some way, and this woman here isn't. And she was poorly the last few days and all she could ask about was Chelsea. I tried to lie to her but she knows me too well. She would've believed it coming from you."

"If I start lying to clients," I began.

"Oh, fuck your policy. One client. One sick woman who could have gone to her grave with a nice thought about a daughter that didn't care for her, didn't care for herself enough to take care of herself. I lived a lie as Kevin's mom for years and it was the most honest thing I've done. Don't tell me you're above a lie."

There was no retort or rejoinder that could make her feel worse. Caitlin saw her own emancipation lying on that bed. What she was saying to me might have been true. But to make a happy lie out of Chelsea's life would be its own special sin.

"George Overman," I said. "Eladio Perez. Calvin Palfreyman. Do you know any of those names?"

"What does it matter? Haven't you heard anything I've—"

"Yes," I said. "I can't say you're wrong. But it's not what I do. Until a judge throws out my contract, I'm employed by your mother."

She hesitated. No doubt she thought I was wrong, but part of her must have been curious. "I've heard of George Overman," she said. "His company donates to some of the same foundations Gail does. The other two I've never heard of."

"Terry Rhodes?"

"Him I've heard of. Nothing good."

Caitlin turned her attention to the cotton swabs and water which would keep Gail's mouth from drying out. Caitlin would be there to do that. She would take the time.

"I hope she doesn't suffer," I said.

I cabbed home, feeling sore, lethargic from the heat, worn down by arguing with Caitlin and with myself. I set down my carry-on and drank tepid water from the tap. I turned the lights on around the apartment, checked the barred windows and the patio. Everything was how I'd left it.

My mailbox held the usual assortment of supermarket flyers, condo brochures, catalogues from the Adult Education Annex. And an envelope, slipped in with no postage, no address. The typed note inside read IT'S GOOD TO HAVE FRIENDS. Ken Everett, telling me there would be a return engagement.

I wondered what Everett's punishment would be for failing to wrest away Chelsea's diary. Maybe he'd never make it above hangaround, a stooge for life. Well, his choices had led him there. He'd vested his faith in the wrong hierarchy.

I sat on my couch, listened to the hums and clicks that made up the zero level of silence in the apartment.

Since I left the city, what I'd wanted was to be back in my bed. Now here it was, feet away, with its comforting Hudson's Bay sheets. And it held as much interest for me as the toys a child already possesses interest him on his birthday.

What I'd really been looking forward to was coming home

to a woman who'd become healthy and whole again and who owed that in some part to me. And in return owed me what? Love? Maybe I was just that arrogant and foolish. There are no damsels. No knights errant either.

What I wanted was to save somebody.

My eyes closed and I fell back on the couch. I didn't dream. I didn't let the phone rouse me, even on the third set of chimes.

In the morning I took a long hot shower, then walked a block up Commercial to see how my leg felt. I bought breakfast at the Portuguese grocery. It was late afternoon when I checked my messages.

One was from Jeff, the gist of which was, Why aren't you at work today? One from Shay's number with no accompanying message. One from Caitlin that was hard to make out. I phoned her first.

The dialing noise that signified ringing sounded eleven times. No message. I hung up and hit redial.

When Caitlin did pick up she said through sobs, "Gail passed. I guess you don't need to worry anymore."

I called Shay next. She answered promptly. "So you lived to tell the tale," she said.

"What happened with you?"

"Me? I'm doing better than I have—"

"You're still using?"

Pause. "Can we have this conversation in person?"

"I'll come to you," I said.

Jeff had left a cryptic message, so I drove to the office first. Shuzhen had left for the day. Marie and Jeff sat on her desk eating cherries. They seemed very glad to see me.

"It's a surprise," Marie said, taking my hand and leading me to my office. Jeff walked behind, telling me again, way to go on the Solis case, nice job turning in Ross and making it work for us.

They'd removed my table. In its place was a stately L-shaped desk with an oiled hardwood veneer, a hutch on one side with row upon row of drawers and cubbyholes, and a lowered draw-bridge to hold a keyboard.

Marie walked me through the many features and options. "...and if you need more surface area, the hutch comes off like—unh—like this. And feel the felt on the bottom of the hutch! That's to keep it from scratching the wood."

"Where's the table?" I asked.

"The table? David, look. Jeff and I—"

"Put it back the way it was," I said. "Please."

"She shopped everywhere to find you the best," Jeff said.

To its credit, the desk was of solid construction. When I plunged the hutch down into the centre of the writing surface, it was the hutch that disintegrated, bursting into a mess of wood splinters and tiny handles. I kicked at the desk and broke off the handy little drawbridge, and finally toppled the thing, and stomped it until one of the stout mace-shaped legs snapped off.

I picked up Chelsea Loam's file, which had been neatly squared and placed on the distant corner of the floor.

"How fucking dare you," Marie said.

"The thought is appreciated," I said.

I took the stairs down, and kept going down, down Hastings, down Water, wishing the weather would do something, wishing the heat would break. The city seemed engulfed in sweat and excess. People ate outside on restaurant patios, swilled their sweet cocktails and pale blond beers, set fire to cigarettes, the smoke from which hung fat and lazy above their heads.

I walked to Shay's apartment. The elevator was out. I took the stairs two at a time.

She answered the door. She let me in. Music on her stereo. Neil Young doing "Albuquerque."

"All right," she said unprompted, "but let me go first. Yes I left and yes I used. But that's not the same thing as using. See, I can't go cold turkey, I've tried and I don't do well. But I've cut back. I was using every day before. Now, I used yesterday morning and haven't felt like it since then. It feels like it's down to once a week. I don't know if you can appreciate that, how big a difference it is, how much better I feel. You can see I look better, right? What you and your mom did really helped me. But here I go running my mouth and monopolizing the conversation. Did you want to say something?"

A pale collarbone jutted out through the oversized V-neck of the shirt she wore. Her hair was an unruly tangle that obscured one ear and a part of her jaw. Frail and unbreakable, the two adjectives that always came to mind when I thought of her. Never more apt than now. She did look better.

I nodded to her. I did have something to say.

"I don't want to judge you. I'm not fit to judge anyone. The ugliness I've seen, the hundred million ways people can be shitty to each other—it paralyzes me because I know I'm no better. I want to fuck without consequences same as every-one else. Maybe it's sex and maybe I'm in love, because Christ knows I've thought of nothing besides you and this other woman who's most likely dead. And to put all our ugliness on the table, I have what you need for your habit and I can be what you need to do away with it. My weaknesses nicely align with yours. I have money, not billions but a steady income. I'm healthy. I'm good at what I do. I made the 'notable mentions' list of *Vancouver* magazine's Top Thirty Under Thirty. I'm loyal and I have a sense of humour and I have love to give. I know what it is to be lonely and I won't take you for granted. If that's too much then give me what you can and I'll learn to live with the rest of it. And I'll try not to fuck things up."

I didn't say any of that. I didn't say a word.

I reached for her, that underwater feeling of every movement lugubrious and tense, anticipating rejection, sliding through disbelief as my hand found her cheek amidst the tangle of hair, found her willing and accepting the touch. I brought our mouths together. The warm exhalation of breath on my cheek, in my mouth. A hand moving up to set its thumb above the collarbone, an arm moving diagonally across her spine, down to graze on the slope of buttocks. Kissing and breaking that kiss. Feeling her hand rub at the back of my neck, the other arm reaching up to link with it. Her body harder than it should be, mine softer.

We toppled over together onto her unmade bed, kicking up a perfume of a dozen smells that were all of her, fragrant and acrid, bitter, sour.

I ripped at her shirt, delighted to find it the only garment she was wearing. Her hands held me back from undressing myself. She unlooped the belt mechanically, professionally. She caught herself and smiled. Her hand rubbed into me through the fabric, searching me out, taking her time. With a rough tug she freed me from jeans and underwear both. Stroking it, sitting on it, fitting the condom over it, and it into herself, controlling every motion, slapping my hand down playfully as I groped up through her armpit to touch the smooth plane between her shoulderblades. And I held back until there was no doubt this was more than payment or gratitude, and I drove into her, violently seeking salvation.

Later I woke in the swamp of the bed, feeling for her. I heard the rush of water and saw the light cast on the far wall in uneven streaks from around the misaligned door. I walked to the window naked. Looked out through the grillwork. Late, all sorts of sordid activity on the streets below me. I lit one of her awful cigarettes and dropped it down to bounce off a newspaper box. No lights on anywhere but street level.

I knocked on the washroom door and she invited me in, into the small square of mildewed tile. I put my arms on her, feeling the water alternate cold and hot. I was hard again. I braced her at the meeting point between wall and tile. She told me what I'd forgot but I was kissing her and she didn't let me go, and I thought, I don't care, give me whatever sickness you have.

PART THREE

FAREWELL MUSIC

25

THE CITY MOVED languorously through August. Clouds formed and teased the possibility of rain. Even that empty threat was enough to send the tourists scurrying for cover. Summer in Vancouver: a collection of hot grey days, a haven for bad ideas and wildness of no particular use.

My apartment on Broadway became our staging ground. Shay had her flat. I had the office. Sometimes we met downtown for dinner, strolling down Robson like any other couple.

Shay was warm and wickedly funny. She worried about her teeth, about aging. She could pick out four or five Beatles tunes on piano. She'd hated taking lessons but hated more the way her mother had agreed to let her quit, as if confirming a lack of talent and dismissing a whole array of possible futures. Her father was dead. Her mother had severed ties.

I told her my secrets, too. We became repositories of each other's best stories, dreams and humiliations. She wanted to teach or counsel people, but not children. Young adults and people who could benefit from her experience.

I told her I wanted to own a house.

"In Vancouver?" she asked, as if the thought of someone under forty being a homeowner and not born to wealth was as far-fetched as time travel.

"Same area as I live now. It can have a few years on it, and I don't care about the yard. But it has to have a porch. Something about sitting on your porch in the rain, having a smoke. That's what I want."

"That is a perfectly appropriate dream," she said, "for a seventy-year-old man."

Her habit remained hidden. She had money from the hotel settlement and never asked for more. When we spoke about drugs our conversation cooled.

But there were subjects enough to fill hours of talk. She'd say things for effect, insert non-sequiturs into her anecdotes, or suspend them and change tack completely, trusting me to follow the unspoken leaps taken by her mind.

So I spent the first part of August in pursuit of two women. Then the diary came calling.

To his credit, Jeff Chen made the first move for reconciliation. He phoned a day after the table incident and asked for a sit-down with the three of us, he and Marie and myself. It was a short conversation. I apologized. They accepted. We talked things out.

I spent my first morning back fixing my new desk, or more accurately, cobbling together a makeshift table out of the wreck-age. Anti-vanity, Marie called it—the idea that you can get by with the tools at hand, yet feeling fraudulent and inauthentic if the tools at hand happen to be expensive or gaudy. She was right. I couldn't convince myself I was still doing work that mattered if I was posed behind the Executive Deluxe.

So much of everything is bullshit.

I was circling around three men, trying to get interviews without divulging what I had. G. Calvin Palfreyman's assistant professed that her boss was positively deluged. Eladio "Chucho" Perez had a full voicemail loop and a summer home on Bowen Island. George Overman didn't own a phone and didn't make appointments, and all inquiries went through his son.

The sentence "I want to talk about your connection to a miss-ing sex trade worker" might open some doors. I was hesitant to take that approach. If I threatened to make that connection public, men like that would have investigators of their own looking into me. A guilty, terrified millionaire would raze a city to keep his secrets. I had Shay and Jeff and my mother to think of. For those first weeks in August, I'd wait them out, work through back channels. For once I'd do things with a minimum of collateral damage.

I didn't hear from Everett or Rhodes. I hadn't gone to the police or tried to use the diary against them. Maybe I didn't matter.

Utrillo had arranged a security consultation with George Overman's son Nick. Jeff had decided to come with me, probably in the hopes of doing actual, profitable business. The Overmans had bought up three housing tracts in a cul-de-sac around West Forty-Ninth, making them neighbours of an ex–Governor General, the mayor, two retired Canucks and a hip-hop artist. A perimeter of laurel bush enclosed the Overman compound. The houses were of different styles and dimensions, but had been sided with the same gold-tinted aggregate, giving them a warm if outmoded look.

As we started up the driveway I tapped Jeff's elbow and directed his attention to the sidewalk near the bushes. Dozens of amber caterpillars clung to perforated leaves. Many of the branches swayed with the weight of the creatures.

"Try one," Jeff said. "Chinese delicacy."

"Seriously? Raw?"

"You're too gullible," he said.

The bushes enclosed a massive yard, built up with symmetrical planter boxes for flowers and vegetables. A Vietnamese woman in a broad hat knelt between tomatoes and kale, attacking weeds by plunging her hands into the rich black soil and removing the offender, roots and all. She smiled and nodded to me in recognition. It was Mrs. Tranh, Gail Kirby's housecleaner.

"Your daughter in school today?" I asked.

"Studying. Always busy." She held up some of the earth. "Me too."

"Looks lovely." It smelled of warm manure and basil and soil. A sprinkler chittered away deeper into the property.

Nick Overman let us in. He was forty-two, slender with a well-groomed beard, dressed in a camel-coloured shirt and white slacks. He shook my hand and bowed to Jeff. The two of them traded sentences in Mandarin. I caught *ni hao* and *zao an* and something that sounded complimentary.

He led us through a house stocked with dark antiques, silver and glass. Every bookcase in the library had a glass door. The desktops were glass. A sliding door partitioned off the living room. He had the turntable setup I dreamt of, a McIntosh tube amp and a Linn Sondek, big JBL cabinets raised off the ground. Carelessly stacked vinyl, Jimmy Buffett, Steely Dan.

Nick Overman poured us each some water from a crystal decanter, then sat in a plush sueded chair that seemed to sculpt itself around his body.

"Security is an interesting business," Jeff said, "because it's a business built on peace of mind. Not having to worry is what we aim to give our clients. Sometimes it's an alarm system, sometimes it's a bit more elaborate than that. But our guarantee is, by the end of our consultation you will know exactly what you need to get yourself to a place of feeling totally tranquil, totally secure."

Jeff then launched into phase two of his spiel, which involved a brochure that listed statistics on breaking and entering, burglary, home invasion and arson. He recast Vancouver as a Gomorrah of crack dealers, rapists, victimizers and scum, all hard-wired with an unquenchable lust for the blood and fortune of the Overmans. By the end, even I wanted to rethink my home security options.

Before Jeff could launch into phase three, wherein the Overmans avail themselves of Vancouver's leading security experts, Nick Overman held up a hand and said, "Whoa there, before you continue, let me explain something."

"Of course," Jeff said.

"My security needs are maybe different from your other clients'."

"Part of what makes Mr. Wakeland and myself experts is our ability to adapt to our clients' needs," Jeff said. "Which we recognize are fluid."

"What I mean is, I'm in no danger." Nick Overman walked to the sideboard, loaded with the kinds of whiskeys and liqueurs that liquor stores keep in display cases. He opened one of the drawers and fiddled with his keys. When he turned around he was pointing a gun toward us.

It was a large-calibre automatic, a .45 maybe, black. Nick Overman pointed it at the floor.

He said, "This is how Pop handled security. This one time a burglar strolled into our house while we were having dinner. Back when you could leave a door unlocked in this city. He comes down the hall, sees us, we see him. Just another dope fiend. He starts giving Pop this shuck-and-jive story about how his friend's house looks just like this. My dad, he stands up and shows him the gun he used to carry around, this silver wheel gun, and begins checking the loads, calm as could be."

Nick laughed in anticipation of the punchline.

"The fiend backs up, starts saying, Oh, I'm sorry, don't hurt me, I'm only doing this to get some medicine for my sister. You got to believe me. And my dad says—cocks the hammer back real easy—says, I will believe anything you say, provided it ends with you hightailing it out of here and never coming back."

"Your father seems like an interesting guy," I said.

Nick Overman put the gun back in its drawer. "I think so," he said. "Pop did all right for himself. He's earned some peace. Which is one of the reasons we're not a normal household for you boys' line of work, and why I wanted to tell you that before you get worked up. Go on, please."

"If I can hazard," Jeff said, "your father lives with you."

"In one of the houses out back," Nick said. "My ex lives in the other, on paper. Alimony reasons. Mostly the kids stay there, now that they're old enough."

"How's your father's condition?"

"He has a woman living with him, a nurse. When he sticks to his meds he's almost all there."

"But there have been incidents," Jeff said. "Now, you have a loved one who might be acting strangely, wandering the property. So motion sensors, alarms, things of that nature aren't effective solutions for you. Have I read that right?"

"Succinctly, Mr. Chen." Nick added something in Chinese.

"Not a problem for us," Jeff said, "though it would be for our competitors. They get their products from a wholesaler. But Wakeland & Chen establishes relationships with the manufacturers themselves, which means customizability. Total control of features and specs. Now, a lot's been said about face recognition technology, but here's the thing."

I interrupted at a good moment to ask if I could look over the grounds. "To give us a better idea of the customizability," I said. I patted my leg. "Also, I suffered a gunshot wound the other day. Doctor's orders to stretch it every ninety minutes."

"Of course," Nick Overman said. "I hope you took care of whoever shot you."

"You wouldn't want to trade places," I said.

26

THE SUN AND THE WATERING BYLAWS had baked some of the green out of the Overman yard. It was still trimmed diligently, nourished and kept free of dandelions and clover, but the interstitial space between the houses had the look of a slightly yellowed golf course.

The smaller, rancher-style house was George Overman's. A pair of crooked plum trees had deposited their fruit on the back patio, spattering the concrete with red-purple stains. Empty ice cream buckets sat near the trunks.

Imagine a captain of industry who finds that all his wealth and renown only hedge him in. He seeks his joy in the company of a young prostitute. He becomes a regular, and more than that, a protector. As her life spirals away from her he seizes control. Devotes his money and resources to all manner of cure, from rehab to acupuncture to Freudian talk therapy. She recovers. They realize, perhaps, what they have is a form of love. The captain's wife passes on and his son takes the helm. The old man retreats to his family compound, to be comforted and fed plums by this young, no-longer-troubled woman, who for propriety's sake he takes to calling his live-in nurse. The two of them define happiness for themselves, gently disconnected from the world.

It was beautiful enough that it should have been true.

Looking through the patio door I saw a silver-haired woman bustle through the making of a crustless egg salad sandwich.

She poured a glass of water, filled an egg-poaching cup with an assortment of medication, put all of this on a tray and carried it into the living room.

When she came back I knocked on the door, startling her. She wore a yellow peasant dress and a jade orca pendant around her neck. She was twenty years too old to be Chelsea Loam.

"You startled me," she said. "Are you one of Nicky's friends?"

"My partner is talking to him. We're consultants. Could I have a moment with Mr. Overman Senior?"

"I don't know about that." She looked me over. I smiled, unshaved and in my unpressed suit.

"Two seconds, just to pay my respects."

She consented, listing rules on duration, tone and appropriate topics. She explained to me his dementia, which for the most part was benign. There was a calloused look to her, though, that made me wonder how often she'd borne the brunt of his abuse. Everything I'd researched about Overman had mentioned his ruthlessness. How he'd fire the bottom third of his sales force every year. How he'd made his son start in the shipping yard and work his way up like anyone else. But nothing mentioned the man himself, or what was left of him now that he was no longer fit to compete. I wondered how Nick Overman had convinced his father to yield control.

"Georgie, visitor," the nurse's singsong voice announced. The living room had two televisions blaring, sports highlights and soap operas. Overman sat in a Barcalounger, feet up, controls and half a sandwich on a mobile tray rigged to rest over his lap. He snapped the soap opera TV off as I followed the nurse into the room.

"Who the hell are you?" he said.

Coils of hair grew like ivy from his head. He was liver-spotted, mottled pink and orange on his face and the backs of his arms. His coughs were frequent and unpleasant, and each one set the nurse on edge.

"My name is David Wakeland," I said. "I'm a private investigator. My partner is talking to your son."

"You want something from me?"

"I want to talk to you."

He coughed, shooing away the nurse. "That's ... something," he said. "Nick's the one to talk to if you're looking for a contract. Private dick, huh? You work for who, 'zactly?"

"Myself."

"That's a good place to be at your age. You're what, thirty-two?"

"Thereabouts."

"Successful?"

"That depends on what you tell me."

His cough dislodged something brown that he spat on his plate. It had been brought on by laughter.

"Everyone wants the wisdom," he said. "Problem is, no one listens to it. I was the keynote speaker at UBC, few years back. Room full of a thousand business students and their teachers. I say, show of hands. How many of you ever started a business? Couple dozen hands go up. And how many of you turned a profit on that business? Say, half the hands go down. Now, how—water please, Marian."

His nurse brought in a pitcher and silently refilled his glass.

"How many of those businesses lasted a year? Two years? Not a hand was still up. These were kids your age, with master's degrees, and their teachers. I tell 'em, it's too late. You got to start young and you got to make mistakes while you're young enough to recover. You got to have the discipline to keep things afloat when not a single customer wants what you're peddling. You can do that when you're eighteen, twenty. Not so much when you're twenty-eight. I ask them what school Ray Kroc got his master's from. They go duh-duh-duh Ray Kroc, who's that? Maybe some of them knew the name. I tell them, you learn anything of value in this world, you learn it by doing and watching. I was their age, I knew what colour tie Ray Kroc preferred. I'd wear the same type shoes. I tell them, you spent fifty grand on a degree, say you were me, would you hire yourselves?"

He laughed and coughed and spat again.

"No one's as dense as an educated man," he finished.

"What I came here for," I said, "is to ask you about a woman you used to know. Chelsea Anne Loam. She went by Charity. She's been missing eleven years."

"My memory's not ten out of ten," he said. He'd wiped his mouth with his fist, but left his fist up, obstructing my view of his expression. His eyes were sharp.

"She was a sex trade worker," I said. I described her.

"And you think I used to see her," he said.

"Eleven-plus years ago, yes. She wrote about you in her correspondence. Favourably," I added.

Overman used his next occasion to cough to wipe at his eyes.

"Charity ain't free," he said. "She used to say that when I paid her. Has someone hurt her?"

"I don't know," I said.

"Was it that useless tit of a boyfriend?"

"Don't know."

"So what do you know, let's start there."

"You first," I said. "Tell me what she was like."

He chewed the corner of his mouth, nostalgia slowly replacing his hostility.

"What she was like. Beautiful. Sweet. Looked a bit like Cher from Sonny and Cher. Same long neck. My Indian Maiden is what I used to call her. She had this coat—"

"I know about the coat," I said. "I'm more interested in what your routine was like."

"We'd meet in Oppenheimer Park. I'd pick her up. I kept an apartment in town, but when Nick started college he moved in. I took her to the Four Seasons. She liked watching these snooty bastards bow and scrape."

"No arrests, run-ins with other clients?"

"When I do something I do it carefully and I do it real well."

"So what happened?"

His hands dug into the soft arms of the chair. "It wasn't about the money," he said absently. "When I noticed what was happening to her I gave her more, told her to look after herself.

Goddamn it." He beat his fists on the chair. Marian pulled his tray away, deftly, and left the room.

Overman pointed at the nurse's retreating back. "She'd like to believe I was always like this," he said. "A weepy old man who watches soap operas all goddamn day. Like I never wanted my dick sucked."

"Chelsea Loam," I redirected.

"Such a beautiful kid. We had so much fun. And then she started aging, in that way druggies do. She used to have a great ass, big old hips. Then she was down to nothing, so thin and brittle I felt I'd break her. Her hair started turning grey. Lines on her face. She joked that she was catching up to me."

"So you cut her loose," I said.

"No," he said. "She was still my little Indian Maiden. She knew how to take care of me better than anyone. But it was damn sad watching her go the way she did. Goddamn drugs."

He cleared his throat, and looking for somewhere to dispose what was in his hands, rubbed it on his shirt front.

"Do you smoke cigarettes?" he asked.

"Sometimes."

"What brand?"

"Gauloises blues when I can get them. Or Parliaments."

"Machine gunner cigarettes," he said of the latter. "Give them to me. Lighter, too."

I handed him my pack and matchbook.

"The sooner you quit, the less of this you'll have to look forward to," he said. He made a show of crushing the pack in his fist, but carefully tucked the mangled pack into his pocket.

"You didn't stop seeing her," I said, "so what happened?"

"When something depreciates it loses its value or utility. The market adjusts, 'less it's mitigated by the goddamn government."

"You realize you're talking about a person," I said, my voice rising.

"I'm talking about a transaction," Overman said. "And anyway it was Charity's choice. She could've had me exclusive, I would have paid. Gladly. She ran herself down. As a consumer, I adjusted."

"Which means what?" I asked. "No more Four Seasons? You put her up at a Travelodge?"

"Yes," he said. "We picked a nice motel out in Surrey and things went on as they did."

"And afterwards, you get her a nice Ray Kroc burger, send her on her way with some bus tokens?"

"I was as mad as you are," he said. "What we had used to be an experience. She used to enjoy it—hell, maybe not, but she'd pretend. By the end it was spread her legs and stare past me at the goddamned ceiling. You tell me, is that worth a premium price?"

I wanted to overturn his lounger, step on his throat, and watch black sludge trickle out of his mouth. "Tell me how you learned she disappeared."

"One day I showed up and she didn't. I called and left a message with her tit boyfriend and she never returned it. I figured she'd overdosed. And I'll tell you to your sancti-fucking-monious face, I was goddamn glad. She'd become a burden on me and my marriage and wasn't worth the hassle. I never shed one tear for her."

"Your son ever meet her?"

"Nick knew I had a side piece. You think Chelsea was the only one? She was the one I paid for, but there were others. Lots."

"Tell me about Terry Rhodes. Didn't you hire him to do security?"

Overman snorted. "The company did, once or twice, for parties. We'd hire great bands—Clapton one year—and get the Exiles to work the door. Those were some wild parties."

"Nick know Rhodes?"

"He met him once or twice. Bikers scared him. Nick didn't grow up scrapping like I did. He did away with those parties. He's a better man than I am. Runs the company with a steady hand. He's very prudent, very sharp. The best of me and my wife."

"Did you know about Chelsea and Terry Rhodes?"

Overman paused, nodded. "I warned her not to go to those parties. When they're sober and working, those men are unpredictable. In their own clubhouse, they can be . . ." His neck stiffened, his eyes considered mine. "You think it was Terry?"

"He told me it wasn't him."

"And you believe him?"

"Not especially," I said. "Considering our relative positions at the time, if he'd done it I think he would've told me."

"Then who do you suspect?"

"I hoped she'd be here with you," I said. "The way she wrote about you, I thought you'd've looked after her."

"You can't look after people who won't look after themselves," he said.

"Maybe," I said. "Or maybe they need looking after the most. Enjoy those cigarettes."

I found Jeff and Nick Overman on the front lawn, where the two of them stood chatting in Chinese. Nick shot me a look of wry indulgence; Jeff, one of embarrassment.

"Sorry," I said. "The chance to meet him was too great to pass up. He's a Vancouver legend."

"In business circles he is," Nick said. "How's my father doing today?"

"Enjoying an egg salad sandwich and watching his TVs."

"Good. He can be unruly."

"Must be tough to be the son of someone so well respected," I said.

"It's not without challenges, but I've had it good, compared to a lot of people." His mouth pursed in a stoic smile. "It's a myth I worked my way to the top without his help. What really happened, I worked my way to the middle, enough to demonstrate to him that I was capable. I spent most of my twenties apprenticing in Zhuhai at our factory, learning Mandarin. Those were my favourite years. Since then I've had it relatively easy, though I'll tell you"—he chuckled—"getting my kids to care about business and work instead of Nintendo, that's a job for Sisyphus."

"How old are your kids?" Jeff asked.

"Liam is fourteen, Georgina is twelve this month, and my second wife is expecting. So yeah, full house. Houses, I should say. You?"

"My fiancée and I are working on our first," Jeff said. "Dave here is single."

"A swinging bachelor," Nick said, giving me a square's idea of a lascivious grin. "Good looking guy like you, women must be falling in line."

"They must be," I said.

By the time Jeff had started the ignition he was swearing.

"Why does every white person who learns five words of Chinese think we have some sort of mystic connection?"

"He sounded fluent to me," I said.

"Because you're an expert. Decade in Zhuhai and he can't count to twenty."

"How'd business go?" I asked.

"He said he'd think about it."

"Give him a pen cam?"

"No," Jeff said. "I was too angry."

"Why did he set you off when Ross and the others didn't?"

"Because," Jeff said. "That was business and this was me helping you."

"I don't get it."

"My dad told me, if you get the money, it doesn't matter what they call you. It sounds better in Chinese. The point is, the money is a symbol of respect. Jawing with Nick Overman, knowing there's no money in it, I feel like—"

"Like?"

"Like a Wang Jingwei," he finished.

"Oh," I said, when he'd been silent for a long while. "A Wang Jingwei, of course. Don't bother explaining further."

"Wang Jingwei was *hanjian*, a traitor," Jeff said. "He sold out the Kuomintang to the Japanese. It's an insult, something you call a person who works against their own people."

"Like Quisling," I said.

"Sure. When I worked for Aries, he'd put me on any case that involved Asians. I'd interview people in Chinatown and they'd call me Wang Jingwei. And sometimes when I'm listening to someone like Nick Overman, and I'm smiling and nodding and pretending to care, I feel like maybe they're right."

"Sorry for putting you through that," I said. "When I'm working only for money, that's when I feel like a traitor."

"You feel like a traitor when you're successful," he said. "I've seen you torture yourself on the Jasmine Ghosh case, and now this one, not to mention the Salt kid and what happened with that."

"What's your point?"

"If you're such an amazing detective, Dave, why do you spend all your time on cases that don't solve?"

I didn't know how to answer that.

"You could tell, Dave, by reading the Ghosh case, that she wasn't ever going to appear. Couldn't you?"

"Yes," I said.

"And now you work a case where the client is dead and the client's daughter is refusing payment of our last invoice, and the missing woman hung out with the fucking Exiles, and there's a chance you could get hurt."

"Christ, Jeff, what else can I do? There's no one else."

"How many years do you plan on doing this? Twenty? Thirty?"

"Until I have a house with a porch," I said.

"Thirty, say, which is generous considering your tendencies. Say you turn down every case that feels like it won't solve. Say you take that time and apply it to cases that will solve, and that won't endanger you. How many people will you reunite with their families, how many answers can you bring to loved ones? All those people you could actually help, and not to mention will pay you, you're turning all of them down because you're too obstinate to say when you're beat."

"You don't think I can solve this?" I said.

"Whether you can solve it is Not. The. Fucking. *Point.*" He hit the dashboard hard enough to leave a dent in the vinyl. I'd never seen him lose control to that extent.

He took a few breaths.

"If you put your effort into unworthy things, you bring about unworthy results. That's another of my dad's sayings that doesn't really translate."

He looked at me sympathetically, hoping for comprehension. A frustrated teacher making one last attempt on a heedless student.

"You're like a man standing in a freezing river trying to catch a fish with his bare hands. If you can do it, that means you have more skill than those of us on the shore with our rods and nets. But you'll wear yourself out. In a few years I'll be running the company, telling clients stories about how great you were. But we'll both know that you made a choice, Dave. You're on borrowed time, and I'd be a bad friend if I didn't point that out."

27

THE CRACKS BEGAN to show while Shay and I were wandering the showroom maze in Ikea, that great primary-coloured Disneyland for the menopausal.

I'd borrowed the company van to help my mother refurnish her guest room in time for my half-sister's arrival. River was starting at Langara in the fall and would need a computer desk and a bed. "A fresh start," my mother called it. There'd been some unidentified trouble with River in the small-town prairie hellhole her family had moved to. She'd always liked Vancouver, and everyone involved thought it would be good for her.

My marching orders were to pick up the furniture, paint the bedroom, regrout the upstairs bathtub, and tell her that becoming a private investigator was not the right career path for a girl with her brains.

My mother had fallen behind in the kitchen showroom, the temptation to pick up a few odds and sods for herself simply too great. Shay stuck with me as I pushed the buggy. I'd already reached my tolerance threshold for particle board shelving with goofy names.

In the rug and drapery section Shay made a joke about carpets matching drapes. We watched people pick curtain rods as if the wrong choice would lead to shunning and ruin. Her eyes alighted on a bin of sheepskin rugs. She picked up one and nestled her face amidst the white fur.

"Feel it, it's so soft." I ran my hand over it and stroked her cheek. "We have to get one."

"At least one."

"One each," she said.

"His and hers."

"And look," she said, letting out a delightful squeak. "Cowskin. Now feel that. Seriously, you need one of these for your floor in the worst way."

When she opened her arms to unfurl the rug to its full shape, her joy ceased almost immediately. It wasn't oval or rectangular, but rather the cloud shape of a hide that has been removed from a once-living animal. She let it fall into the bin, full of other skins, and we made our way out.

Once we'd returned to my mother's house and my mother had turned in for a nap, I sat on the floor of the freshly painted room and slit the tape on the flat-packed desk and vanity. I handed Shay the instruction manual. Together we began performing the some assembly that was required.

"Something on your mind?" Shay asked.

"No. You?"

"Not really. Are you around tomorrow?"

"I have to return the van tomorrow morning. Figured I'd put a few hours in. It's getting close to my monthly meeting with Jasmine Ghosh's father. I should make sure everything's updated. I'll be out of there by noon, and I'm yours for the rest of the day."

"Good," she said.

"I do have to go away the day after," I said.

"Where? Why?"

"Bowen Island. I need to talk to a man about a woman."

"How long will you be gone?"

"Just the day."

"Can I come?"

"Sure."

"Do you want me to come?"

"I insist," I said.

"Don't make fun of me."

"If you want to come, you can. I'd like it if you would."

"It's a nice place, Bowen. My dad took me there when I was young."

"I've never been," I said. "Never had a reason. Weird how that works. Something wrong?"

She was clutching the instructions in two hands, clenching her face to hold back tears.

"This can't last," she said.

"What can't?"

"Any of it. It's too good."

"How can anything be too good?" I asked, putting my arms on her waist from my sitting position. But I knew what she meant. Furniture shopping, day trips, the little moments other people took for granted. They felt wrong, like a simulation. Worse than that. It felt like the moments were real but we were the frauds, and sooner or later someone would revoke our passes. And I knew she was right. It wouldn't last.

"Let's take a real vacation," I said.

"To where?"

"Where would you go if nothing was holding you back?"

"If I had my druthers?" she said. "Easy. Gay Paree."

"How soon can you pack?"

"We can't go to Paris, Dave."

"Sure we can, it's one ten-hour flight away. That's five Sandra Bullock movies and we're there."

"I don't have a passport."

"They're not hard to get."

"But with my record."

"You're not a murderer. I know a woman that runs a Remove Your Record business. She owes me. We can get you to Paris, that's where you want to go."

"All right."

"Okay?"

"All right."

She sat down, folding herself around me. We forgot about the instructions for a while.

It's a short ferry ride from Horseshoe Bay to Snug Harbour on Bowen Island. You pay on the Mainland for a return trip, about ten bucks. The boat docks among the yachts in the marina. You walk over the ramp and see winding trails hewed out of the forest, produce stands, restaurants with umbrellaed patios offering cold beer and seafood. Heaven, you think. Then you remember that there isn't a property to be had for less than two million, and far from being kind-hearted rustics, the islanders are real estate swindlers, corporate sleaze, tycoons, stock manipulators. And lawyers. Lots of lawyers. Bowen Island is a refuge for the undeserving.

Shay accompanied me. So did my mother and half-sister. I toted a cooler behind them up the trail. River and Shay walked ahead, River lecturing her on bird species, Shay feigning interest.

Past the salmon run with its spawning ladder, the trail took us to a lakeside, with a few picnic benches and an outhouse a healthy distance from the water's edge. The water was still and dappled with leaves. River wasted no time kicking off her flip-flops and wading in. My mother wasted no time admonishing her.

I'd brought lunch, and fixed up a sandwich for the road before leaving the three of them at the lakeside. I backtracked down the trail to the paved winding streets. The residences varied from cabins and trailers to art deco mansions. From the hill I could see across the water to the finger-like peninsulas of Gambier Island.

The property owned by Eladio Perez had an A-frame and an old Airstream trailer, the latter balanced on a pyramid of cinder blocks. The house had been treated, years ago, and now the wood was a faded sickly grey. A clothesline hung between the trailer and house. A BMW and a Mazda pickup were parked on a driveway of equal parts gravel and pine needles.

In lounge chairs arranged around a firepit sat a fat shirtless man, two women in exercise gear, and a short thin man in tennis shorts and a polo tee. This was Eladio Perez.

The shirtless man was talking and the others were poised for laughter. They heard the crunch of my steps and looked over at me, all but the shirtless man, who barrelled through his anecdote before turning to see what had cost him his audience.

"Are you lost, sir?" Perez asked, electing himself spokesman for the group. "Can I get you something?"

"A moment of your time, please." I handed him my card.

"You've been leaving the messages." He turned and gave a nod to the others. "You tracked me here?"

"Not exactly the ends of the earth," I said. "And it is important."

He relented. "Let's go inside."

A considerable percentage of the A-frame's square footage was given over to a main floor office. Perez had an ample desk, file cabinets, a law library, a separate desk for computer, printer and fax. If he spun his chair around, Perez could see out the kitchen portal to the driveway and road.

"So." Perez drummed out a ratamacue on the desk. "You're a PI, you're looking for a girl, you think I know her. I don't. You said she was a sex trade worker. I handled sex cases for several years, but that was back in the mid-eighties. Probably before you were born, or just after. Wild time to do that work, but I'd quit by the time your girl started. Chelsea Loam's her name, huh?"

I nodded.

"Nice name, as names go. But I don't know her."

"She went by Charity," I said.

"I'm sure she did. But if I'd known her through the office I'd've known her full name."

"No chance of a non-professional association?"

"You mean my profession or hers?"

"I mean you maybe see her at a party sometime?"

Perez leaned over his desk. "I told you I don't know her," he said. "Never saw her. Don't know how you've connected us."

"Your initials," I said. "She knew a prosecutor with the initials C.P."

He smiled. "My old man called me Chucho," he said. "That's 'cause he was Eladio Senior. He said there was something weird about calling your own name to come in to dinner or to go to bed."

"So there's no way you could have met Chelsea?"

"I have a pretty good memory," he said. "You came out here because of initials that aren't even initials?"

"I'm not trying to take this into court," I said.

"Obviously."

"Just trying to find out what happened to her."

"North America happened to her," Perez said. "Everyone wants a share of the good things in life. No one wants to pay full price. That balance has to come from somewhere, and it's from the people who can least afford it. Like Ms. Loam. Sad but it's how it is."

"So it's not worth looking into?" I asked.

"My point was only that if you're looking for someone to blame, Physician, heal thyself."

"I brought photos," I said, not knowing how else to continue.

"I've already said I don't know her. Do you think I'm lying? If I am, do you think a photo will change things?"

I put the photos charting Chelsea's transformation on the desk. The two sets of eyes stared at him.

Perez picked up the photo of High School Chelsea, blonde and smiling. "Mestiza," he said. "At least half native. Something else in there, too. The blonde hair—in the black community they call that passing, dressing so you blend into the dominant culture. Her age I bet she was already conscious of what she was doing, how she wasn't like the others. Something you maybe didn't think of: she'd feel like she didn't fit in among white folks."

"I guessed as much."

"But she'd feel equally fraudulent with people of colour,

especially natives. 'Not Indian enough,' issues with status cards, tribal membership—blood quantum. All that would be equally daunting."

He put down the yearbook picture, gave a perfunctory glance to the mugshot, and passed both back to me.

"That's how I'd read her," he said. "Caught between two cultures. I felt like that, my old man coming from Cuba." He tapped the pictures and smiled. "I like this girl. I wish you luck."

He led me back outside. The others had killed the fire and were thrusting foil-wrapped potatoes among the coals. The smell of fried meat was coming from the trailer. I felt something land on my neck and draw blood.

Back at the lake, my mother was sitting with the cooler and cutlery while River and Shay traversed the far end. We could see them, the two women checking River's birdwatching guide-book against what they spied in the trees.

"How'd your business go?" my mother asked, handing me a plate of salad unbidden.

"Ah . . ."

"It's good for you."

I shovelled a bit up with a Tupperware fork. "Another dead end," I said.

"Don't speak with your mouth full."

"You can't hand me food and ask a question at the same time."

"I'm just saying, David. If you eat like that in front of your friend."

"You should see the way she eats."

"Never mind," she said. "You're happy. Everything is okay. And you'll talk to River?"

"I will."

"Because that's not a life for someone as smart as her."

"But it is for me?"

"Never mind," she said. "Why don't you set up the cribbage board and I'll take some money from you?"

I did, and she did.

—

On the ferry ride back, my mother snoozed, lying across two seats. River and Shay made plans to hang out, for Shay to show her around the city. I looked out at the southernmost finger of Gambier to our left. I could've mentioned to River that her mother's first husband lived there. Had a cabin and electricity, hunted and gathered berries and laid prawn traps and had the rest of his supplies shipped in every month. My father, by some definitions. I didn't say anything. I turned and watched Vancouver approach.

28

"YOU HAVE SIX MINUTES," G. Calvin Palfreyman said.

I'd accosted him outside of court, in the long white atrium with the sloping glass wall. The B.C. Supreme Court building was another of Arthur Erickson's creations. It looked like a combination greenhouse and military base.

Palfreyman was finished for the day. His suit coat was slung over his arm and his tie had been loosened. I'd watched him hand his court gown to an assistant. With his armour off, he looked like a retired general, or an abdicated dictator. His hair was a square slab of gunmetal, his mustache two neat triangles of iron filings.

I introduced myself and told him what I wanted to learn from him. At the mention of Chelsea Loam, his eyes narrowed.

"I have nothing to say. I don't know the woman."

He started past me. I kept pace, held up the photos for him to check out. He kept his gaze fixed on the parking lot.

"I'm not trying to leverage you or embarrass you," I said as we crossed the street. "I know you know Terry Rhodes. She was with Rhodes. I think you know what I'm talking about."

"Is that who you work for?"

"No."

"Son," he said, drawing himself up as the door handle of his Lexus came in reach. "The wrath of the British Columbia Crown Prosecutor's Office is about to descend on you. I've refused officially, and now you've got my answer anyway. I don't know the woman. Proceed further and we enter my territory."

I stepped between him and the car door, keeping my hands behind my back.

"Sue me," I said. "Bring it all out into the light. This point, I'd pay to see you put your lawyering against the things I know."

We stood there awkwardly. Palfreyman was the first to break eye contact. His hand found the lever on the door. His eyebrows raised, asking, May I? I stepped away from the door and allowed him to open it.

"Maybe it doesn't have to go to court," he said quietly.

I watched him drive off, my anger lingering like so much exhaust.

Gail Kirby had few relatives other than Caitlin, but her employees, friends, and the beneficiaries of her charitable work seemed to number in the hundreds. Her ashes were interred on a marble wall in Peace Arch Cemetery, a few klicks from the American border.

The funeral was non-denominational, or maybe pan-denominational. The speakers included a rabbi who administered the Kirby Scholarship, a representative from the Ukrainian Orthodox Church who had gone to school with Gail, and a minister who worked downtown, who I knew to say hi to.

I learned from Rabbi Sarah Lefkovicz that Gail had wanted to name the scholarship after Chelsea, but that had seemed strange since Chelsea hadn't shown much interest in higher education. They'd been working on setting up another award, for mature women returning to college. That award would be named for Chelsea instead.

I met family friends who remembered Chelsea and Caitlin as happy teens. I heard good things about Chelsea, how smart she was, her artistic aspirations. No one kept in touch with her after she left her foster mother. I heard repeatedly what saints Gail and her husband were for taking her in.

It was Caitlin I'd come to observe. She wore a traditional black mourning dress, accompanied by her partner Nettie, who wore a black pantsuit and tie. They stuck close. Several times during the eulogies I saw Caitlin clench her hand for support.

As the funeral ended I saw a tall bald man approach and shake Caitlin's hand. He offered his hand to Caitlin's partner. She glowered at him. The bald man drove behind them back to Gail Kirby's house, where the wake had already begun.

I watched the man. Evidently he was supposed to be here—meaning whatever falling out he'd experienced with Caitlin, propriety dictated he pay his respects, and pay them through the wake as well as the funeral. He shook hands and traded condolences, swigging imported beer and keeping out of Caitlin's orbit.

Ladies from the church had brought perogies and borscht. The gathering grew maudlin and sentimental. Rich food and booze, memories of the dead—I felt a vicarious melancholy. I hadn't known Gail Kirby long. I'd utterly failed her in the task she'd assigned. I was still at it, though. Maybe she would have appreciated that.

As the wake dragged out, Caitlin saw me but didn't seem surprised or angry. I wondered if the end had purged her of bitterness.

Nettie was a think tank economist based out of Ottawa. Caitlin would be moving there soon. Nettie seemed nominally moved by the funeral, and agitated by the bald man. When their two conversational circles were linked by a boisterous aunt, they both politely retreated to neutral corners, like fighters obeying a referee.

Caitlin and Nettie withdrew from the living room. To a sober crowd, that would have been a sign the wake was over. People were cooking and popping open wine bottles in the kitchen. On the back deck, children were sipping pop in their formal wear and making each other laugh.

The bald man had been throwing back beer steadily. When Caitlin withdrew he seemed on the verge of following her, but someone passed him a mug of wine—Gail's good crystal had already been claimed—and he was forced into a symposium on how the internet was ruining reading skills. Finally he was permitted to disengage.

I shook my conversation partner and made my way up the staircase, well behind the bald man.

I put my ear to the door. They were arguing. Caitlin's sobs punctuated Nettie's abrasive whisper and the drunken challenging tone of the bald man.

"Not talking about that," I heard him say. "Not the issue. I'm talking about certain promises."

"That money is Caitlin's. It stays Caitlin's."

"Why'on't you stay out of this, for once in our lives? Eight years you've been hovering, afraid I'm gonna take Cate away from you."

"That's not true. Caitlin, tell him that is not true."

"Why'on't you let Cate answer for herself, then? Cate, tell her. We had certain promises."

"That was forever ago, Frank."

"So now she's dead and you're free to break your promise to me."

"You son of a bitch."

"Stay out of this. Caitlin?"

"No, Frank."

"See? She said no."

"Fine. That's how it's going to be. Guess I'll call a press conference then."

"Don't be an ass, Frank."

"How many times do I gotta say it, shut your damn mouth."

"I will not shut my—you need to leave, Frank, and never call us again."

"Make me."

"You shit."

"Caitlin can make me. All it takes is cutting one cheque. I'll leave and keep my mouth shut."

I opened the door. I found the three of them arrayed as I'd expected—Caitlin in a chair, with Nettie's arms on her shoulders. Frank blundering about the room, but keeping his distance.

"Hell are you doing here?" Frank said.

I said to Caitlin, "You're out of toothpicks. Would you like me and Frank to go grab some?"

She nodded slightly. Nettie nodded vigorously.

"The three of us are having a business meeting," Frank said.

"Let's you and I talk first," I said, beckoning. "Outside"

I followed him downstairs, watched him make polite good-byes. I could see his fists flexing the way mine did when I wanted to hit something.

In the carport he said, "It's only fair to warn you, I know Krav Maga."

"How's he doing these days?"

He cracked a very thin smile. "Backyard's probably a better place for this," he said.

We walked single file around the back. He slid his blazer off and hung it over the gate. He pocketed his cufflinks. He undid his collar and played out his tie until it was one long strand of pleated silk. "Head or gut?"

I grabbed the lonely fringe of hair at the back of his skull, head-butted him and broke his nose.

He fell on his ass, bleeding and sputtering. I waited until the flash of head pain had faded, then wiped my forehead with a serviette. I handed another to Frank and instructed him to elevate his face. I helped him into a lawn chair facing away from the house and sat near him. I told him I'd put a few questions to him and then take him to the hospital.

"Shoulda known you were a cop," he said. It came out, "Shoulda knowed you wah a cob."

"I'm a private investigator."

"Even worse. I hate private eyes. I hate private eye movies. Dashiell Hammond can kiss my ass."

"Easy now. How do you know Caitlin?"

"We were engaged."

"When and how did that end?"

"What does it matter? She's not into men anymore."

"With your charm, how is that possible?"

"This hurts," he said. "It could be broken."

"It is. What were you blackmailing her for?"

"Family secrets."

"The best kind. Tell me."

"It's about her kid, Kevin. You know he wasn't Caitlin's?"

"Keep talking."

"It was her dope fiend sister's. But do you know who the father was?"

"You?"

"I have standards."

"Tell me, then."

"Who do you think?"

I thought that over. "What's your proof?" I said.

"My proof? My proof is it's true."

"How'd you find out?"

"You think being a private eye makes you smart? I can do what you do. Any time I watch a detective movie, I can spot the killer within ten minutes."

"So you have no evidence," I said.

"I could get some. DNA and all that."

"How much were you asking for?"

"Forty. Which I know sounds like a lot, but I've kept mum for more'n fifteen years. Caitlin didn't want Gail to know."

"You're never going to bring this up again," I said.

He smiled cynically. "Are we bargaining now?"

"This is not a bargain," I said. "Nothing you do involves the Kirbys or Loams from here on out. You mention this to anyone and I'll ruin you."

"Ruin me," he said. It's hard to maintain bravado through a broken nose, and he didn't quite pull it off.

"Every secret you have," I said. "Cheat on your wife or your taxes, look up animal porn, steal office supplies, it will come out.

There will be naked pictures of you mailed to everyone in your address book. You'll be afraid to jerk off lest it's recorded for posterity. Every secret. You can shut up or you can make another half-assed play for Caitlin's money and lose everything."

He took a moment to nod, then told me he wanted to go to the hospital now.

On the way I asked him how he could tell who the killer was within ten minutes of any film.

"Easy," Frank said. "It's always the woman."

I asked him to elaborate.

"If it's directed by a guy, he's probably got woman issues. Who doesn't, right? If it's a chick directing, she probably wants to prove how tough and independent women are, so making a woman the killer is actually like a badge of honour."

"Better a killer than a victim," I said.

Back at the house I told Caitlin what had gone down. I'd dropped Frank at St. Paul's and parked his car. I'd cabbed back. She reimbursed me the fare.

"You know none of it's true," she said. "When Kevin needed blood there were tests done. None of the Kirbys were a possible match."

"You seemed like you were going to give in," I said.

"Because I didn't want it brought up, not while things were going well for Gail. She shouldn't've had to deal with Frank Ainsley. And once those accusations came out, they're all people would remember."

"So you don't know the father," I said.

"No. I don't think Chelsea knew."

"So there's no chance? None?"

She sighed and rubbed one of her arms. "Maybe a very slight chance," she said. "I'm realizing more and more that Chelsea's experience and mine were so very different. I could have been a better sister to her if I'd realized that."

"You did fine," Nettie said, brushing her hair from her temple back behind her ear.

"It's never enough, is it," Caitlin said.

I left them and walked out, putting away my wallet. I passed boxes of heirlooms, family photos, newspaper-wrapped trinkets. The house would be empty by the summer's end. I got behind the wheel of the Cadillac, thinking, if it's true, god help the dead son of a bitch.

29

WHEN I GOT BACK to my apartment, I found a note on the fridge saying Shay would be back later. She'd left her handbag, taken her purse. The cloth Crown Royal bag that held my laundry money was empty.

I called Jeff and cancelled our double date. I mixed a bourbon and water. Put Isobel Campbell and Mark Lanegan's *Hawk* on the turntable, stretched myself across the couch, and used my laptop to find out more about Frank Ainsley.

The *Sun* newspaper archives had a photo of Caitlin and Ainsley, looking on as Gail Kirby and the mayor of Surrey shook hands and grinned at each other. Ainsley had his hand across Caitlin's back, cupping her shoulder. Caitlin's attention was fixed on her mother, her smile wide, disregarding Ainsley.

And that was Ainsley in a nutshell, on the periphery of players but not one of them. I tried to connect him to Perez, to Palfreyman. He hadn't been convicted of anything large. I had slightly better luck tying him to Overman. The accounting firm he'd apprenticed at featured a testimonial from a Discus Solutions executive on its website. Still nothing direct.

Ainsley's scam had been ugly and meagre and simple. Making Caitlin's adopted sister disappear wouldn't seem to fit into his plan—would actually complicate it. I couldn't see him kidnapping Chelsea or harming her. But I also couldn't see him leaving off Caitlin, despite my warnings.

Ainsley and Caitlin had broken off their engagement after Chelsea's disappearance, while Caitlin was raising Kevin. I thought of phoning Caitlin to ask why they'd split, but figured she deserved time to mourn. It was enough to know that he was an asshole and needed watching.

I heard keys jingle and someone stab the door lock a couple times before sliding it home. Shay came in breathless, smelling of cigarettes and dance sweat, perfume and something else.

"Hey there," she said. "Working? How's that going? Got some leads? Get some clues?"

"It's all right," I said. "How was your night?"

"Good. I mean, I know we had that thing, but my girlfriend is in town, and we just—you know how it is."

"Sure."

"What? What, Dave?"

"Everything's fine," I said. "Want to go for a walk?"

"I just got in. Thought I'd take a shower. Is that still all right?"

"Course. Why wouldn't it be?"

She moved to the couch and threw a leg over my lap, sat down, cinched up her dress. "Are you pissed at me?"

I tossed the computer aside, put my hands on her hips to steady her. "I don't get pissed at you."

"No matter what?"

"Sure."

"Not even if I smashed all your precious Nick Cave records?"

I kissed her throat. I felt her fingernails dig lightly into the back of my neck.

"None of it matters," I said.

"That's nice."

"Just as long as you stay pure till our wedding night."

I felt her body convulse with laughter. She swatted the back of my head, stood up. She smoothed her skirt, teasing with a caricature of a prim coy smile.

"How 'bout I take my shower and you take your walk and I'll meet you in bed?"

It was the third Wednesday of the month and it was summer. Welfare Wednesday, some people called it. The police called it Mardi Gras. For people who scraped by the other twenty-nine or thirty or twenty-seven days of the month, it was cause for celebration. On the Drive, people would be carousing or drunk. On the side streets, where I walked, people sat on their balconies, or the porches or stoops of their rented subdivided houses. I passed a trio of men leaning on the tailgate of a Dodge Fargo, passing around a joint and laughing. I saw a married couple pushing a stroller, their other child walking behind them with a Slurpee held with both hands. I watched women crush out cigarettes in cereal bowls, on porch steps, on the iron banisters of their third-floor apartments. I heard a clicking sound and saw the light from the street lamp hit the reflective surfaces on a bicyclist as he passed us, the road his. As I turned up the alley toward my building I heard a man singing, plaintive and dirge-like, carrying out from the upper windows of a mosque.

The next morning I met with Ritesh Ghosh, Jasmine Ghosh's father. I had no good news for him. The case would not solve, no matter how much time was added to the hours already logged, by the police, by me, by everyone I pestered.

Mr. Ghosh took it all with a good nature that would have astounded the Stoics. Every time we met he had some plan to extend the search, to broaden the criteria. As long as it didn't involve psychics, I was happy.

This month it was sex changes.

"I know she was only nine when she disappeared," Mr. Ghosh said. "But I've been reading testimonials from people as young as five who knew they were unhappy in the gender they were born with. What if she found someone who would pay for the surgery? Maybe she thought we wouldn't understand."

I drank my tea and set the cup down on one of his elegant crocheted coasters. Jasmine Ghosh would be sixteen now.

I had digitally aged pictures of her at eighteen, some even older to account for drug use and hard living. When Charlie Parker died at thirty-four, the medical examiner guesstimated his age at sixty.

What Mr. Ghosh wanted were new designs, forwarded to all the relevant agencies, showing Jasmine as a man.

I told him it wasn't a problem. I knew digital artists who'd done forensic reconstruction. It wouldn't be cheap, to do it right, but then what was?

"You know price isn't the issue," he said. "Just make sure it's two different artists. You know how subjective art can be. The same range of ages and hair styles, too. Please."

"It'll get done."

"And please bill me. I'd feel better if you'd accept something."

"I'd accept another cup of tea," I said.

It took him a significant effort to climb out of his chair to fetch the teapot. He was aging, his movements becoming arthritic, delicate and measured. I followed him to the kitchen, worried he might fall.

From the other entrance I saw a shadow slink by, heard hard steps on carpeted stairs. Mrs. Ghosh.

"You're not married yet?" Mr. Ghosh asked me.

"No."

"But you're seeing someone?"

"I am," I said.

"That's lovely. What does she do?"

"She's an adventurer."

"Really! She and you must get along perfectly, then."

Jasmine Ghosh and Chelsea Loam. Both had left behind damaged families, empty chairs at the dinner table. Maybe Jasmine had come from a happier family, had been too young to realize how the world would let her down. Jasmine would never know that people like Terry Rhodes could walk through this world, untouched by the systems we erect to shield good people from the likes of them. Chelsea knew. And for that her disappearance was just as hard.

It seemed wrong that it could be a bright day, with a warm breeze fluttering through the communal garden on the corner near the Ghosh's house. The world should stop and acknowledge all those who weren't here to enjoy it. There should be a reckoning. Instead there was the sway of carnation blossoms and a beautiful woman in dungarees crouched to check the yarn and stakes that kept her tomato plants vertical. When the world ends, the fact that the world doesn't end is an obscenity.

I'd left my phone in the car to recharge. Jeff had texted me, relaying a message. Dolores Gunn wanted to see me.

30

"I FOUND SOMEONE YOU SHOULD TALK TO," Dolores said, meeting me at the front entrance of her tenement building, nodding as we passed a neighbour. The elevator didn't work. We huffed up to the fifth floor.

"Ten years and this never gets easier," she said between gasps. "All that time and you're the third man who's seen the inside of my place."

"I feel special," I said.

"Chelsea was special. Only reason I'm doing this."

She had three locks on her door, and I was grateful for the time it took her to get them all open. By the time she let me in I had my breath back.

It was a small apartment, messy and filled with the cloying smell of overripe fruit. Plants covered the balcony, encircled the television. Next to her bed, a stack of magazines and chapbooks leaned against the wall.

Sitting anxiously on her couch was a man who looked about sixty. He seemed ready to throw himself over the railing if Dolores closed the distance between them.

Dolores brought a bottle of near-beer from her fridge and uncapped it without offering one to me or the man. She tossed the cap into a margarine tub on her counter filled with them.

"I'll be late for my daughter," the man said. He was fastening and unfastening the clasp of his digital watch.

"So tell him already."

The man looked at me like I was a new kind of terror. He wore chinos and a Mr. Rogers sweater.

"Who's this?" I asked Dolores.

She took a swig of O'Douls. "Ask him," she said. "Ask him anything."

I asked him.

"She bring me here because of the girl," he said. "Because of what happened. But I don't know anything."

"His name's Dyson Law," Dolores said, "and he speaks better English than he's letting on. He bought Flynn's Tavern in Poco fifteen years ago, turned it into the Law Courts. What's it called now, Dice? After he sold it the new owners demoed the building, put up a strip mall with a fancy little alehouse with plastic seats. But it was the Law Courts when Terry Rhodes and his boys hung there, wasn't it, Dice?"

"They came in sometimes," he said. "They drink and party. I can't get them to leave."

"Not till you tore the place down. Tell Dave here about Chelsea."

"She was there sometimes," Law said.

"Dyson. Come on."

"There with Rhodes," he said. "She partied a lot with him."

"Who else?" I said.

"His bodyguard, the quiet man."

"Gains."

"Yes," he said, shuddering.

"Anyone else? Any lawyers? Police? Any businessmen?"

"All types."

"But with Rhodes and Chelsea specifically? Any connection there?"

"I don't remember."

"He's not being honest," Dolores told me. She loomed over the couch and Law squirmed, expecting to be hit. "Terry Rhodes wasn't just some customer. He was part owner. Had the run of the place. That not true, Dice?"

Law nodded, miserable.

"See, Dice loves dice," she said. "He lost big at pai gow. He lost big at big two. He owed money to some people with Hong Kong connections. Rather than go into hiding, he went to Rhodes to broker a deal. They get paid back, Dice and his family get to keep their heads and feet, and Terry Rhodes owns a controlling interest in the Law Courts. That about right, Dice?"

Dyson Law nodded again.

"So you can imagine what he knows," Dolores continued. "Crown prosecutor would love to get Dice to talk, but he's afraid. Of Rhodes, of the Hong Kong boys, of the police. But he's not as afraid of me as he should be."

She bent over Law. Law flinched. She picked a piece of white fluff out of his hair.

"Tell him about Chelsea," she said.

His face quivered but Law said nothing. Dolores slapped the side of his head. It wasn't a womanly slap. It was the kind that could dislodge teeth.

"Give it up to him or I'll peel you like an Anjou pear."

It occurred to me, perhaps too late, that I'd wandered into the midst of a kidnapping.

Dolores held her palm out to me without breaking eye contact with Law, the way a surgeon would to a nurse. "Toss me a knife from the second drawer down," she said. "There's a big Stanley that keeps a good edge. On second thought, maybe the serrated. Yeah, definitely the serrated."

Law talked. He'd given Rhodes the offices and back rooms of the Law Courts, setting up his own office in a storage closet. Law heard some of the deals Rhodes was running—other protection schemes, busting out restaurants, defrauding insurance companies. Rhodes let his dogs have the run of the kitchen area, and soon all the Law Courts offered were nachos and hot nuts. It was Law's turn to bust out, and he did. The Law Courts were disassembled, the stoves and fixtures auctioned off. Law now worked for his father-in-law.

Rhodes spoke only in general terms, delegating to others. But one business he handled personally. He'd installed extra phone lines and office equipment for that purpose. That business was women.

Or it involved women. Law wasn't sure. One night Rhodes told him to go out to the dance floor and fetch Charity. Law tried to but she refused to come along with him. He relayed that to Rhodes and Rhodes stormed out and dragged her back to the office. Law was sure it was Chelsea Loam because years later he'd see her face on posters and remember that night, and remember that was the last time he saw her in his club.

Rhodes dragged her back to the office and slapped her. She was pouting like a disobedient child. Law didn't think she looked scared. Just miserable.

Law was an amateur photographer. Rhodes told him to bring his Polaroid. He told him to snap pictures of Chelsea, a front and side shot. "And make sure she looks fuckable," he'd instructed.

He told Chelsea to lose her top and she'd sassed him but ultimately complied. Her body looked unhealthy, famished. Law had her strike a supermodel pose, suck in her cheeks, look over her shoulder with a side view of one breast.

Rhodes handed her a twenty and sent her away. He took the three best pictures, arranged them in a triangle, and photocopied them onto one sheet of paper. He dialed a number and said, "I'm gonna send you something you'll like," hung up, and faxed the sheet.

"You have to tell me where he took her," I said.

"I only know that much."

"Then fucking guess the rest." I was shouting.

Law had retreated into the couch. Even Dolores was staring at me. I made an effort to compose myself.

I rubbed my forehead, thinking out loud. "Okay. Rhodes is too high up to be a pimp, unless the clients themselves were high up. He was sending women to them. Auditioning them. Told me he didn't kill her. Probably knows who did."

They were watching me as I paced.

"Overman's the obvious culprit. Liked his sex, knew Rhodes

from the parties. Can't see him killing Chelsea or having it done, but that's off meeting him as an old man. Can't rule out his son. Maybe killed the old man's mistress to keep his family together? That leaves Perez and Palfreyman. Sex I could see them going to Rhodes for, but would they kill to protect their careers? Not like they're judges. Maybe they thought they had a chance to be. Maybe maybe maybe. Who am I not thinking of? Goddamn it."

I sat down. Dyson Law inched away from me on the couch.

"The problem," I said, "is that if you have money and position and a friend like Rhodes, you can do anything you can think of with no consequences. How could you trace that back if it's only Rhodes that knows? He wouldn't share that kind of juice even with his cronies."

"So let's go ask Rhodes," Dolores said.

"I guess I have to if I want to know."

She snapped her fingers in front of my face. "I was just joshing," she said. "I'd sooner take a shot at killing him than getting him to talk. Least if you killed him you'd only have to worry about Gains and all the others. 'Less you killed them, too."

"I don't want to kill anyone," I said.

"What about whoever did for Chelsea? You wouldn't take a gun to him?"

"I just want to understand," I said.

I stood up. Dolores grabbed my arm, spun me so I was square with her. As she spoke her hand dug into my shoulder.

"You're telling me after you find out who did for her, proved you're a big-shot private eye, you're gonna say 'That's it,' let that man get away with it?"

"He already got away with it," I said. "Nothing's bringing her back."

"He's got to pay and he's got to pay hard and he's got to know 'zactly what he's paying for."

"You're talking murder."

"Which goes on every day and doesn't seem to bother folks when it's poor coloured girls. But some rich white man—and you and I both know that's who it's gonna be—he gets a free pass? Where's your sense of justice?"

The hall door was open. Dyson Law was gone.

31

RHODES, TERRY. The fucker was in the phone book.

I thought about what to do with that information. I thought about it as I lay next to Shay in bed, listening to her quick, regular breaths. I thought about it the next day as I drove out to Richmond for a word with Tim Kwan.

He and his cohort were attending the opening night of a legal professionals conference, held in the ballroom of one of the swank hotels out by the airport.

I had my lawyer wrangle me an invite. Shauna Kensington, mother of twins, had as much interest in a conference titled "Negotiating the Fields of Justice" as watching ants cart away a dead mole. We walked in with the kids between us, she identified me as her plus one, and the three of them ran back to the world of cartoons and juice boxes.

I had one question to ask Kwan. Seeing his company at the event, I didn't even need to ask that. I nodded to him and turned my attention to G. Calvin Palfreyman and his resplendently dressed wife.

"Word with you, C.P.," I said.

He introduced me to Mrs. Palfreyman, told her he'd be back in two secs. He asked Kwan to make sure she didn't associate with the wrong people.

"This is going too far," Palfreyman said. We left the ballroom and walked out into the courtyard, away from the awnings where clusters of people traded cigars and lawyer jokes.

"I know what you did," I said. "Tell me about the case against Rhodes."

"It fell apart," he said. "Hearsay and a lack of substantial physical evidence. Not to mention the procedural errors of those overeager cops. My boss wanted to charge him anyway, considering how much money the government pumped into surveillance and such. But it's a loser case, not even worth the political points he'd make laying charges."

"You know Rhodes was selling women?"

"Selling them? You mean pimping them?"

"He had photos of Chelsea Loam faxed to an unknown number. She disappeared soon after."

"I knew they should've been up on the fucking fax machine," he said.

"So you've read the case file?"

"Of course," he said. "Everyone in the office wanted a piece of the Rhodes case. There are guys who'd come out of retirement to get that accolade. But it's a loser case, as I told you."

"How often did you see Chelsea?"

"Never. I told you that, too."

"But what's the real answer?"

He turned his head to make sure no one else was in earshot.

"Look," he whispered, "I met her at some stupid art show. I saw her a few times. I was lonely and I was on the outs with my wife."

"Poor you."

"I used to drive down Hastings as part of my commute. Sometimes I'd see her on my way back late at night. One day I stopped to talk to her, she offered and I was weak and said yes. A few months later I broke it off. I told my wife, I cut a cheque to a marriage counsellor, and I've been working on making amends. I did not harm her or do anything wrong except pay her for sex. I don't know what happened to her."

"When you saw her photo with Rhodes in his case file—"

"I was worried she'd be called as a witness," Palfreyman said. "Of course I was. I imagined some scene where I'd be called in to handle her testimony. She'd pretend not to know me, and then say it in the middle of the courtroom and ruin me. So I was relieved, yes, when I found out she was missing."

"You had Kwan show me the photo. You wrote the note telling Gail Kirby to talk to Ed Leary Nichulls."

"Yes and yes."

"You felt guilty."

"I'm Catholic," he said. "The day I don't feel guilty for something, my mother will disown me. When I heard Gail Kirby was looking for Chelsea, I wanted her to get some closure. I've talked to Nichulls. I know a true psychopath when I see one. I thought the Kirbys would ask, and he'd deny it, and his very denial would be the proof she'd need."

"She would infer her daughter was dead," I said.

"Yes, with no need for further proof. When I learned she'd hired a private investigator, I knew you wouldn't quit. Anyone who gets paid by the day stretches things out."

"So you had Kwan run the same ruse, with the picture of Chelsea and Rhodes."

"A piece of real evidence. A picture that tells you everything about a woman and the danger she'd put herself in. I thought you'd see that picture and your fear of Rhodes would curtail your investigation."

"Kwan owes you."

"He's a bright young mind. When I start my own practice next year he'll be invaluable."

"I believe some of that," I said. "This had nothing to do with easing Gail's mind and everything to do with keeping your own ass out of the fire."

"They're not mutually exclusive. One action could have brought about both results. You, of course, were more diligent than planned. Or suicidal."

"I like flattery," I said. "What I'd like more is a copy of the Rhodes case file."

"Too fantastic to consider, even facetiously."

"I need something."

"Make it something else."

"The night that photo was taken. I want a list of all calls made, from all the Law Courts' numbers. Transcripts of those calls if you have them."

"The wiretap evidence was inadmissible. It's not part of the official case."

"That poses a very interesting dilemma that I don't give four-fifths of fuck-all about."

He shook his head. "Can't do the wiretaps. Maybe I could do the phone numbers."

"Of all the lines, especially the backroom ones."

"It'll take some time," he said.

"Then you'd better get on it."

We rejoined the soiree. I watched Palfreyman head to Kwan and Mrs. Palfreyman, kiss her cheek, laugh as someone hit the punchline of an anecdote he hadn't listened to. I left through the back.

There was business to be done, a conference call with Utrillo to take, two forensic artists to hire for Mr. Ghosh. The next day at the office I dispatched all that and was having lunch when Shuzhen ushered in Shay.

"She's a bit snooty," Shay said as I closed the door.

"She's just jealous."

"That's right," she said, kissing me. She pointed down at my take-away. "Curry? Can I have some?"

"Just in the neighbourhood?" I asked as we sat down.

"Pretty much," she said between mouthfuls of rogan josh. "Actually I wanted to ask you something. You remember Marius?"

"Yeah."

"Well, he's leaving town soon, going to Halifax, and he's having this sort of going away party at the Backpacker's Lodge, and my girlfriend and I are going, and he asked me could I drop that money off for him, seeing as how he's leaving."

"What money?"

"The money you got from Joe."

"He asked you for that?"

"He did, yeah, since he's leaving." She laughed as if sensing what I was thinking. "You don't have to worry. That was only because Joe paid us for the movie. His dick is gross. I mean it's big, really big, but he doesn't get fully hard. It's like having a mushy cucumber inside you."

"I trust you," I said.

"You should, sweetie."

"It's just that I gave him his money already."

Her brow knit. "That's strange. Are you sure he got it?"

I called my email up on the computer screen and turned the monitor so she could see.

"Dear Sir," she read. He'd managed to misspell both words. "Thank you for all you done for me. I never will forget it. I will use the money smart. Thank you."

I said, "He goes on to offer me a discount if I want to watch him jerk off."

Shay read through it again.

"Hunh," she said. "That's so weird. Maybe he forgot."

"Maybe."

"Do you think that's what it was?"

"Do I think he forgot two thousand dollars?"

"So what do you think?" she asked.

"Are you trying to get me to say I think you're lying?"

"Is that what you think?"

"What do you want me to say?"

"Who wants you to say anything?"

"You know that if you need money you can ask for it, right?"

"For two thousand dollars?"

"Is that how much you need?"

"Either I can ask or I can't, so which is it?"

"Why don't you tell me what it's for?"

"Why are you doing this to me? Do you want to hear me beg?"

I leaned back in my chair, thought it over, brought my cheque-book out of the drawer. "Fine," I said. "How 'bout four hundred?"

"How 'bout two thousand?"

"Six hundred."

"Nine."

I wrote it out and tossed the book and pen across the desk to her. "Why don't you fill in the memo part and explain what it's for?"

She lobbed the book at me. "You fucking asshole."

"Right. I'm a fucking asshole because I don't want to see you kill yourself."

"You knew who I was when you fucked me."

"Think about where you're at. You're thirty."

"Twenty-nine, same as you. Don't talk to me like you're my dad."

"I'm sorry you had a shitty childhood but they're all like that. It's not permission to drop off the side of the world."

"You don't know anything," she said. "Big fucking deal who thinks he knows what's best for people."

"Maybe you should consider I do know what's best for you. All the decisions you've made in your grown-up life, how have those worked out so far? You feel good about yourself?"

"I feel like shit and you're making me feel that way."

"But a lid of coke will solve everything."

"It makes me feel good," she said.

"Who the fuck told you you should feel good? You shouldn't feel good. Life is about eighty percent shit. You should accept that and quit charging your good times to the people who love you."

"Do you think I love you?" she said.

I sat back and spread my arms. "Who knows? Maybe it changes day to day."

"You gave me money and were nice to me. And I fucked you for that."

"You're saying you see me as a john? I don't think you sleep over or make breakfast for too many johns."

"Not a john," she said. "In our business we call people like you marks. We get a place to stay and money, and in return we fuck you. It's better than being on the street, safer, but same deal. It lasts until the money runs out. Or the mark falls in love."

She was laughing, hysterical, triumphant. "You're a mark. That's all you are to me."

"Get the fuck out of here," I said quietly.

"Mark. I fucking played you."

"Out."

She slammed the door hard enough that it rebounded instead of closing. I heard her laughter out to the hall and down the stairs.

The chequebook lay on the carpet like a lapsed curse or a slain desire.

I spent the night drinking in Veritas, the lawyer's bar. I didn't want to be around anybody. When that closed I cabbed to the Narrow, an underground bar on Main that took cash for bottles of Kronenbourg. I listened to the playlists the bartenders came up with, their MacBook hooked into the speakers, heavy on Mudhoney and LCD Soundsystem.

After I closed out the Narrow I walked home along Broadway, singing to myself about neon lights and glitter and magic.

32

THE DRINK WORE OFF AROUND NINE. I got up and pissed and popped three of Shay's acetaminophen and crawled back to bed. I woke up with slices of August sun baking my chest through the barred window of my bedroom. I got dressed because there was nothing else to do.

A mess of scrambled eggs and plastic cheese, a quart of pulpy orange juice. I was choking down my second pot of tea when my phone went off, vibrating across the top of the fridge like some mutated science experiment. I answered it with a whispered "Yeah?"

"I'm speaking to Mr. David Wakeland?" The voice was booming, tinged with a foreign lilt. Filipino if I could trust my ears.

"Yes, you are," I said quietly, hoping the voice would modulate its volume accordingly.

"You're related to a Beatrice Wakeland?"

"She's my mother, yes."

"I'm so sorry, Mr. Wakeland," the voice said, sounding not at all sorry. "Your mother has suffered a stroke. You are her emergency contact, yes?"

"Where is she? VGH? I'll be right over."

"Yes, do come," the voice said. "She seems to have avoided the most debilitating effects, although there are more tests to run. She will be here for a while, I'm afraid."

"A week? Months?"

"At least a week for the full battery," the voice said. "We encourage family members to bring things from their home. Photos, pillows. Things the patient would easily recognize. It helps their memory and brain function and their overall comfort. Would you like me to read you a list of approved items?"

"I get the gist," I said. "Is my half-sister there?"

"Who?"

"She's staying with my mother. Her name's River."

"Right. If we see her we'll tell her you're on your way."

I grabbed keys, wallet, threw a flannel over my grubby shirt.

I called River's cell and left a message. I saw I'd received a text from Shay. It was dated the previous night.

WE SHOULD TALK. I SAID SOME THINGS. LETS TALK. PLS CALL.

Peace talks and détente. Yalta and Potsdam. I tried to think of what I wanted to say to her, what would be healthy.

Everything would have to wait.

I'd driven halfway to VGH when I remembered my mother's stuff. I made an abrupt left. I had an idea of what she'd like to wake up to—some flowers from her garden, arranged in the crystal vase my father had given her for their anniversary. Maybe a Hummel, the one with the brother and sister fishing. Would she want jewellery? Photographs?

Chagrin washed over me. I knew her better than I knew anyone, and I couldn't figure out the four or five items she'd want by her bedside.

And where was River, who was still technically underage? Would she go back to Alberta without an adult to stay with? Would she stay on as my mother's caretaker? What kind of life was that for a kid dealing with her own problems?

Hell.

The house looked the same. I parked in the first spot I could and detoured across her neighbour's lawn, stepping carefully over an accumulation of dog shit. I almost rang the bell.

Inside and up the stairs to the bedroom and—

Dogs.

Mine had spent her last months in this house and I was used to the smell. Wet, earthy. But the house hadn't smelled like that for a year, not since I'd ripped out the carpeting. I breathed in the smell of the creatures, not my dog, and heard tittering laughter. I sank onto the step.

"Come on down here, Davey Boy," Terry Rhodes's voice called from the kitchen.

Rhodes, Charles Gains, two other large white men and a stout, grinning Filipino man filled the kitchen. Rhodes's right hand was wrapped in the leashes of his dogs, which lay like sphinxes on the marble. They all looked happy to see me.

"We were getting bored," Rhodes said.

The stout man tittered. It was his voice I'd heard on the phone.

I stood frozen. Not out of fear, though there was plenty of that. Out of indecision. Running, retreating, would only delay what was coming.

I looked for guns. I didn't see any. A knife on one of the flunkeys' belts. And the dogs. My handgun was unloaded and locked up back at the office. It might as well have been in Burundi.

"The old bitch is at the casino," Rhodes said. "This half-sister of yours gonna come looking for you?"

I shrugged. "I'm very popular and well regarded."

Another titter from the stout man. Rhodes uncoiled the leashes. He lit a Turkish cigarette.

"There's no reason everybody in this room can't stay above ground," he said.

"Don't bullshit me."

"Fair enough. I'm going to kill you. But first we're gonna talk."

"Good," I said. "I have lots of questions."

Rhodes laughed. The others joined in, the stout man hardest of all. "I got a few for you," Rhodes said. "Starting with this diary I been hearing about."

He put his hand over the skull of one of the dogs. "Sicced Fuck here on poor old Kazz to get a straight answer as to what's in there. Funny thing was, he wouldn't talk to my guys. He was too afraid of what you'd do to him. You, the badass private dick."

Rhodes crouched and rubbed the dog's jowls affectionately. "Course he talked eventually, once Fuck here persuaded him. Cost poor old Kazz a ball."

"Guess that ends his chances of being a high-wire balancing act."

More laughter from them. Keep them laughing.

"Funny guy," Rhodes said. "I never saw your pops crack so much as a smile."

"What the hell do you want?" I said.

"That girl's diary for starters."

"You're not afraid of that," I said. "A book with a bunch of initials in it? You beat a million-dollar surveillance case."

"I want it," he said. "That's reason enough you give it to me."

I heard the front door behind me. I turned. Ken Everett and Skeet filled the door frame. Everett held a shotgun, pointed at the ground in front of him. Skeet held a fistful of zap straps.

Rhodes echoed my own thoughts.

"And guess who's in the middle," he said.

Everett stared at me and nodded. He looked past me at his boss and his boss's bodyguard and three of his own. His eyes settled on the dogs at Rhodes's feet.

"Put one of those around his wrists," Rhodes said to Skeet. "Another on the feet and you connect 'em with a third."

Skeet didn't move. His eyes flitted to Everett.

"Kenny Boy," Rhodes said. At the back of his voice, maybe for the first time, was fear.

Everett tilted up the gun and pointed it toward Rhodes.

"Fuck the whole lot of you," he said.

He pulled the trigger and shot a fist-sized hole through one of the dogs.

In the narrow enclosure of the hallway, the blast hit my ears with a painful slap that killed my hearing. Everything that came after played out in silence.

I saw Rhodes throw the leashes and move back behind his men. Holy leapt over his dead brother and bounded toward Everett. The three lackeys flattened themselves against the kitchen wall. And Charles Gains smiled and stood his ground.

I heard the gun go off again but I didn't look. I was out of the hall, scrambling into the living room, crouching. The living room windows were covered over by screens. Both staircases were on the other side of the house.

I saw a dark shape back into the room and crouch. Rhodes. He looked up in time to see my fist land right on his eye socket, total follow-through. He fell backward onto the floor and I landed on top of him, taking the breath out of both of us. He had an iron grip but my right hand was free and I hit him in the face, thinking Pacquiao, thinking young Foreman, how he could jolt the heavy bag clean off the hook unless his trainer steadied it. I couldn't hear anything. I broke my fist on Rhodes's face.

Something like a concrete vise seized me around the neck and ripped me off of Rhodes. It was the arm of Charles Gains, cinched into my throat.

No air. Wavy patterns overlaid my vision. I hit him in the ribs with my elbow but it didn't earn me any give. I tried it again. Falling back, he wrapped his legs across my stomach from behind. I couldn't move.

Goodbye movement. Goodbye air. The wavy patterns grew into waves, loud ones that buffeted the breakwaters of my skull, smashed over it in loud hissing sprays. Then it was too dark to sense movement. A watery blackness and nothing more. And then goodbye to even that.

33

Chelsea.
I gave it a try, darling.
Maybe there was more I could've done.
It sure didn't feel like it.

I failed you
Just like the city failed you
And failed however many more like you.

They'll never find the book,
I'd never give it to them.
It's all that's left of you.

Overman, Palfreyman, Knowlson, Kazz
A dance of johns
A line of pricks and predators
And you the one breaking the law.

Chelsea
I'm sorry
I failed you
I tried.

Wanted so badly to find you
Alive
Older and at peace
Perhaps on the Island
Some douchebag artist's colony
Making sand dollars into mobiles
Or frying bread and pemmican for German tourists.

If I'd found you
(And it's easy to say now it's over)
I would have told you who I am,
What I was here for,
Who loved you enough to want you found.

I would have listened
And if you'd said no,
Leave,
I would have listened.

But
  Maybe
      I
          Just
             Want
                To
                    Believe
                I'm
             Not
          Like
        All
      The
Rest—

34

HOODED LIKE A FALCON. It took me a long while to comprehend that. I was trussed up and on my side, with some sort of fabric shielding my face. My knees were against something inert that could have been someone else. One knee felt warm and wet, which meant I'd probably pissed myself. We were travelling.

I rolled forward, taking pressure off my hand. I flailed out with my legs and head, trying to map the dimensions of the trunk, if it was a trunk. I was jostled. We seemed to be moving at an incline.

I could hear April Wine and then Bachman-Turner Overdrive. The Stampeders, "Sweet City Woman."

Maybe this was Purgatory.

The incline remained steady. The tires spun on gravel instead of pavement. I was jostled. The person behind me shifted. I called out but no one answered.

I got used to breathing again, to having time move forward. The pain in my hand and the darkness became facts rather than universal laws. I even slept a little.

The vehicle slowed and bounced along. It stopped. Two doors opened and slammed shut. A key scraped the metal below the lock before the trunk opened. Cold air flooded my nostrils.

I was lifted out and set down on gravel. The other person was heaped next to me.

"Dig now?" a voice said. The stout, laughing Filipino man.

"We dump them in the cellar," an unfamiliar voice said. "Wait for Terry, see if they find that book. Save the digging for later. Right now it's beer o'clock."

"For us."

"Yeah."

"Not so much for them."

He cut the trusses, leaving my wrists and ankles bound separately. I was hoisted to my feet. They steered me inside. We went down a staircase. I waddled, leaning on the rail.

"Have a seat anywhere," one of them said. I felt a boot to my back and I spilled out onto dirty cement. I heard laughter.

The door closed and locked. I found a wall to lean against.

When the door opened I listened for footsteps on the staircase. There weren't any. I heard the voice say, "On three," and count to three. There was a grunt of exertion, a second of anticipation, and then something landed near me with a meaty thud.

The door locked once again. I shrugged off the bag. I stared at Ken Everett. He was dead all right. We were both soaked in his blood.

The cellar, as they called it, had a high ceiling and cement walls. The ceiling was unfinished, with slabs of pink insulation stapled to the wood. The staircase was raw lumber with no guard rail. It had flooded before, leaving a smell of must and rot. Dead leaves had been swept into the corners.

One of the pillars had a sharp-looking edge. I backed into it, rubbing the plastic of the zap strap vertically until the friction frayed it. My wrist was sore but didn't look infected. I'd need it set soon.

I wondered how badly I'd hurt Rhodes. Probably not at all.

I unbound my ankles. There was a light fixture, but the switch was on the other side of the door. No tools around. I went through Everett's pockets. He had cigarettes but no source of fire. His wallet was there. Fifteen dollars, a driver's licence, a photo booth snapshot of himself with his daughter balanced on his knee.

It hit me who I was looking at. What he'd tried to do for me.

No teeth or claw marks on him. His neck had been snapped. But maybe that had happened when they'd dumped him.

I took the stairs and tried the door. There wasn't a handle on this side.

The cellar had no windows, but I could tell it was late afternoon. A million tiny slivers of light shone through the wood. Those slivers dimmed and it was late evening and then night.

Maybe they wanted me to cry out and beg.

I was thirsty. I kept thinking of a nice double bourbon and ice water. A few hours after the sun went down the temperature plummeted. I stripped off Everett's jacket and draped it over myself. An hour later I took his shirt, too. I pushed the leaves into a small bed and sat down in them, leaning against the wall.

So. What. Next?

In the late morning two men came down the stairs, the stout man and one of the tall white thugs. They looked amused, seeing me swaddled in the dead man's clothes. Both had guns and the thug had a shovel balanced on his shoulder.

"Get up." The thug toed Everett's corpse. "Pick him up and take him up the stairs." To the stout man he said, "Stay behind him, Freddie. You see him drop the body it means he's trying something."

"Or he's tired," I said. I stooped over. The body was dead weight, the joints rigored. I put Everett's arm across my shoulders and dead-lifted. It was a good way to lift the weight without putting pressure on my hand. Everett's feet dragged on the lip of each stair as I carted him up. Each step required finding a new fulcrum, lest we topple over the side.

At the top the thug held the door and I hauled Everett over

the threshold. Freddie stepped through, drawing the door shut without aiming the gun away from me.

"Out to the back," the thug said.

The cellar was beneath a one-storey cabin, all vinyl and plastic but finished with a wood veneer. As I dragged Everett out through the sliding door I saw other cabins. I counted four plus an aluminum shed. They were arranged in a semicircle, around a gravel turnaround that led out to an access road.

Behind the cabins was a thick undergrowth of blackberries and ferns that sloped down and seeped beneath a dark green canopy of Douglas fir. Beyond that an escarpment. Below us a long green valley. We were on the other side of one of the Coast Mountains.

It was warmer in the sun. Freddie instructed me to drag Everett's corpse. We moved through the brush to a clearing bordered by a rotten section of fallen tree. Freddie hacked at a few tendrils of encroaching blackberry.

The thug mimed dropping the body. I did. He pitched the shovel at my feet.

"Six down and three across," he said.

I picked up the shovel, gripping it left-handed and using my right to steady it. I broke ground.

"Fling the dirt over there." He pointed to the other side of the log.

I began work. The sun kept rising. By the time it was at its apex I was lathered with sweat and more than two feet into the ground. My shovel clanged off something harder than soil.

Freddie left and returned with a deck chair, a bottle of fruit juice for himself, and a Coors Light for the thug. They took turns sitting and standing. Freddie left again and didn't return.

I tried widening the hole but I couldn't work the spade further. "Rock," I called up.

"So pick it up and move it," the thug said.

"It's too big and I got a busted hand."

"Christ," he said, making it sound like an exasperated sigh. "How big are we talking?"

"I don't know."

He swore. "Climb out of there. Leave the shovel."

I did. He stood over the hole, looking down at the exposed clump of rock. He kept the automatic trained on me, but used the other hand to bring out his cellphone. He dialed with his thumb.

"Freddie. Who do you think? It's Cody. Yeah, we got a problem with a rock here. What I need is you to watch him while I take care of this. Right, the rock problem. I don't know, shoot it? You're the digging expert. Well, how long? Can't you pinch it off and come deal with this? Christ. No, I'll do it myself."

He tossed the phone onto his chair. I asked for permission, walked a few paces and pissed on some ivy.

When I turned back he motioned for me to stand near the hole. He aimed the gun down at the rock.

"That's a bit dangerous," I said.

"Thanks, Safety Minister. What's your idea?"

"If we can dig under and leverage it, the two of us could lift it out."

"That's stupid," he said. "Cover your ears."

I turned away and ducked. He shot off three rounds. When the smoke and dirt had floated off, the rock was much the same as it was.

"Fine," he said. "Leverage it or whatever."

By widening the hole I could get the shovel under it and loosen it. Cody climbed down and tried to pick it up. He didn't bend his knees. I told him to rock it back and forth and I'd feed the shovel underneath.

It would be easy to brain him with the shovel, I thought. I looked up and saw Freddie perched on the edge of the hole, thinking the same thing.

I wedged the shovel underneath, and together we pried the rock out and heaved it up onto the lip of the hole, where Freddie helped roll it out of the way.

Cody climbed out and drained his beer. He kicked the rock, as if to rub our victory in its face.

"Any chance of some water?" I asked him.

"Sure," he said. "When you're done."

Some hours later, with the sun still in the sky, I stood over an oddly shaped but feasible grave.

"Now what?" I asked.

Cody stood drinking out of an Evian bottle, still holding the gun on me. He drank it down to the dregs and backwashed a little and tossed it to me, watching with amusement as I gulped it down.

Freddie came out with a bag of cold convenience-store burritos. He tossed one to me the way you'd toss a mackerel to a seal. I peeled it in a frenzy. Nothing from the Gotham Steakhouse ever tasted so good.

They dropped the wrappers into the hole. I did the same. They instructed me to roll Everett's corpse into the hole. I did, stooping down to fold his hands over his chest and straighten out his legs. I made sure his eyes were closed. Not that any of that mattered. I remembered he was Catholic, or had been. I crossed myself with my closed fist the way I'd seen him do before every fight.

I started covering him over with dirt. Cody kicked the water bottle in to join him.

When it was done I felt worn out and clammy from the dried and redried sweat. I had blisters on my hand and could taste only dirt. I sank down onto the log to rest.

"Now the second one," Cody said.

35

"WHY YOURS, EBENEZER!" cried the Ghost of Christmas Future. Black Pete in the Disney version. I remembered renting that tape when I'd babysat River one year while my mother went Christmas shopping. I remembered how River squawked as the spirit flung Scrooge into the grave, and how my mother had chosen just that moment to return home.

I dug the second hole more carefully, yet faster. I ached. My broken hand was filthy. I wondered who else was buried out there among the evergreens.

I'd thought the diary was keeping me alive. Rhodes would guess that I'd probably stashed it somewhere only I would be able to retrieve it. I'd thought that was why I hadn't been mutilated.

But no, he didn't care about the diary. This was his method of slow execution.

This grave was easier going. Fewer rocks. I managed to keep the sides somewhat square.

It grew dark. Cody and Freddie set a mosquito lamp near the edge of the hole.

My shovel chuffed. I thought I'd struck another rock. I bent over to wipe away the dirt.

It was a shard of bone that had been splintered or shaped into a spear end. Shorter than the breadth of my hand, and as I felt it, deliberately tooled.

I pocketed it as Cody walked to the edge of the hole to investigate the break in shovelling rhythm.

"Climb on out," he said.

"I'm not finished."

"Yes, you are."

"It's not as deep as the other one."

"It'll do," he said.

I climbed out. He was standing away from the light, holding a different, short-barrelled gun at hip level.

"Go tell 'em it's done, Freddie," Cody said. Freddie folded the lawn chair and took it with him.

"Strip," Cody said to me.

"All the way?"

"That's what 'strip' means."

I took off the flannel, the T-shirt, unbuckled my pants. I stepped out of my shoes, rolled down my boxer briefs.

He gestured with his leg to kick the clothes into the hole. I bent down and threw them in, palming the spear tip, taking the smallest of satisfactions from the planed and chipped surface of the bone.

"Socks, too?" I said.

"It doesn't matter."

He pointed the gun. I felt a cold stream of water hit my face. The shock of it made me drop the spear tip. The shock wore off and it felt good, and I managed to get some of it down my throat.

Once I'd scrubbed myself, Cody let the gun fall to the ground, which turned out to be the nozzle of a garden hose. He led me back toward the cabin.

I heard footsteps and whimpering. From the cabin to my left emerged two figures, walking the way we'd come. The four of us passed. I recognized one of the figures as Charles Gains. He had a knife in his hand, tapping the blade against his leg as he walked. In front of him, with his hands bound, was Skeet, Everett's partner. He was blubbering.

As we passed he looked over at me. "Please," he said.

Gains didn't look at us at all.

I was shoved onto the basement stairs and the door locked behind me. I sat on the bottom stair and rubbed my shoulders for warmth.

Four long shrill screams rang out amidst the soft noise of the forest. A little while later I heard a coyote echo them.

I collapsed on my bed of leaves and felt the temperature fall.

Nothing happened the next day. When I needed to shit I banged on the door. No one answered. I dumped in a corner behind the stairs and covered it over with handfuls of dry grey dirt.

The temperature rose, though not by much, and then fell along with the light. My feet were numb. I huddled and kept watch on the door, wanting and not wanting it to open. It didn't.

The next morning I banged on the door again to no avail. I paced around the room to keep my circulation up. I examined the floor and walls for secret passageways and structural faults and found none.

It was past noon when Gains came down. He was wearing black sweatpants and a prune-coloured sweatshirt. He tossed something at me that skittered across the concrete. The pieces of the spear tip, which he'd broken and dulled. They looked like alien teeth.

He held the door and gestured for me to walk through it. I did. He stopped me and locked the basement door and then shoved me out of the cabin.

"I'm not going to beg," I told him.

Gains's expression remained neutral, as if he hadn't heard me.

Outside an Econoline van had pulled into the space between cabins. Freddie and Cody stood nearby. I caught sight of myself in the van's mirrored windows, caked with leaves and cement dust, hair wild, like Edgar in a production of *Lear*.

"In you go," Cody said. He unlatched the back door and beckoned me to climb inside. No seatbelts, no seats, just two steel benches facing each other.

Terry Rhodes sat on one bench, looking like his face had been pieced together by a surgeon's assistant's son. He regarded me with an expression dulled by painkillers.

I climbed in and sat opposite Rhodes. On the floor between us was a carry-on bag that looked very similar to the one I'd taken to Winnipeg.

Gains climbed in, shut the doors and sat next to me. Rhodes rapped on the cage that separated the driver from his cargo. The van started moving.

"Last time we spoke," Rhodes said, "you were about to give me the diary."

"Was that where we left off?"

"This guy," Rhodes said to his bodyguard, "is the genuine article. He's not giving up anything. You were right, Charley, we should've nabbed the mother. My fault for being old school."

"Yeah, it's your ethics that are the problem," I said.

He sighed and smiled in that combination that can mean only true exasperation. I seem to bring everyone there, given time.

Rhodes said, "If I were as bad as you think I am, you'd be in pieces now."

"I assume that comes after you get what you want."

He shook his head. "This is what I want."

He grabbed my hand and crunched it. It hurt like hell. Gains clamped down on my other arm to prevent reprisal. The pain brought tears to my eyes and I bit through my own lip.

"What I want," Rhodes said, tightening his grip for empha-sis, "takes a back seat to what makes me money. You're going to make me money or I get to watch my friend Charley pop your eyeball out and feed it to you."

He let go of my hand. Gains didn't let go of my arm.

"Now," Rhodes said brightly, "there's a time to prove to the world you're not a sissy, and there's a time to value your body parts and the pleasure they bring you. You got"—he looked out the cage and the windshield at the flat township we were mov-ing through—"four blocks to make that call."

"Tell me who's paying you to retrieve the diary," I said.

"No. No more questions from you. Yes or no?"

"Yes," I said.

"Yes what?"

"I'll get it for you."

"It?"

"The diary. I'll get Chelsea Loam's diary for you."

"Yes, you will," Rhodes said.

The driver made a right into a small crescent-shaped strip mall, the buildings done up with log cabin facades. There was a coffee shop and a Home Hardware, a Mac's and an animal hospital. We went around back. The driver had a time manœuvring the van so its back end was close to flush with the back doors of the clinic.

"You should ask him about the apartment," Gains said to his boss.

"What about the apartment?" I asked.

"We sent some guys to your place," Rhodes said, "thinking maybe the diary was there."

"It isn't."

"I fucking know that," he snapped. "The boys told me the place looked like someone had already gone through it. A lot of stuff's gone—TV, computer. I gather you probably had some sort of stereo system."

"Records?" I asked.

"They said everything that wasn't gone had been smashed."

The driver opened the back doors. I didn't recognize him. Another beefy tattooed cracker who thought aviator shades and a goatee made him as cool as Robert De Niro in *Heat*. He looked more like a professional wrestler with a policeman gimmick.

Shay wouldn't even have had to break in, I thought. She had the key. And you can always find someone willing to help you cart away someone else's stuff.

"This means one of two things," Rhodes said. "Either this is a robbery with no connection to our business, or this is some other crew after what's mine, and they took your shit to make it look like a robbery. If that's the case, and they got the book, you tell us. We'll tool up and find them. Maybe even get some of your shit back."

It's not related, I almost said, thinking that if someone said that to me I'd suspect the opposite was true. They'd tear Shay's world apart looking for something she didn't have, and they'd find her eventually.

I pulled on a pair of pants from the carry-on bag, slid into fresh socks. I said, "It doesn't matter either way. You'll have the diary in three to five days and it won't matter."

"Three to five days?" Rhodes said. "You're grabbing it for me after we're done here."

"Can't today," I said. "I can make the arrangements if you have a phone for me, but it'll take as long as it takes."

"Where is it?"

"Washington State."

We went through the back part of the clinic, past cages of yipping, baying animals, into an examination room with a high bench wrapped in tissue paper.

"We'll go across the border," Rhodes said. "You me and Charley. Half the time they don't even check."

"Two career criminals and a guy who's been missing for days? That won't draw suspicion?"

"There are other people I can send."

"Or you can be patient. Get everything you want with no one the wiser. What's five days?"

"You're trying to stay alive, you're better off giving me what I want now."

"No I'm not," I said.

Rhodes had a reluctant grin. "You should be working for me," he said. He looked over at Gains. "Kind of crook you think Davey Boy would make, Charley?"

Gains said nothing.

"Charley's reserving judgment on you," Rhodes said. "Okay, run it down for me."

I told him I'd need to phone to have the book mailed. It would take standard delivery time, coming across the border.

Customs would inspect and deem it unimportant, as every authority figure had deemed every part of Chelsea Loam's life unimportant. I would retrieve it, hand it to Rhodes, and we'd go our separate ways.

"You don't have it delivered to your apartment?" Rhodes said.

"Not with my neighbours."

"That book's either in my hand or destroyed on that fifth day."

"Or sooner," I said.

He nodded. "Let him use your cell, Charley."

I had to dial the operator to get a number for the mail service in Blaine. When I was patched through, I asked the clerk if my package had arrived.

"Sure has," she said. "Most people have stuff mailed here from the rest of the States, then schlep it back to Canada. You're doing things bass ackwards."

"Don't I know it. Could you mail that package back to the return address?"

"I guess," she said. "What class?"

"Standard."

"First," Rhodes said to me.

"That'll draw attention and it won't be any faster."

"First."

"First," I said into the phone.

"Right. Insurance?"

"None."

"Your gamble. I'll need a credit card."

Rhodes instructed Gains to give me his American Express.

"It'll take three to five," the clerk said when I'd finished giving her the number. Gains snatched his card back.

"I can wait," I said.

Once I hung up, Rhodes told me I'd be staying at the cabin until it arrived. I told him I'd live with that. He said I'd have to.

The veterinarian came in, a short native woman in scrubs and an immaculate smock. She gave Rhodes a detailed explanation of the damage done to his dog. She called it Holly. She said

Holly was sedated, and the Euthasol injection was at hand.

"Let's do this," Rhodes said. His expression was maudlin. That and the bruises made him look almost pitiable.

"I'm the first thing they see when they come out of their mother's cunt," he told me, "and I'm the last thing they see when the light fades."

"That would make you—"

"A god to them." He smiled. "It's a special kind of fear and awe and love. Can't beat that into them. Wish to God I could do the same with women."

I contemplated that. Rhodes left and another vet came in. She looked like the mother of the last one, and none too pleased to have us roaming her clinic. She took me through the stations of disinfecting, X-raying and finally setting my hand. The cast was crude, the plaster coarse.

"Sorry I don't have any painkillers for humans," she said, handing me a small vial of pills. Gains confiscated them. She stalked off, shaking her head.

Gains tipped the pills onto the paper-covered seat.

"You will," he said to me.

"Pardon?"

"Beg," he said. "You'll beg. I can tell the ones who'll beg and you'll beg."

"Because of the pills?"

He held up his left forearm, displaying a long pale scar. "I broke my arm. The bone stuck right out of the skin. I was fourteen. I didn't make a sound."

I picked up the pills and dry-swallowed one. "And it's been a steady ascent from that point on, huh?"

He hit me in the stomach and I fell backward, retching. The pills rolled across the floor. Gains crushed one with the toe of his steel-toed boot.

"I want you to try and escape," he said.

36

THEY DROVE ME BACK TO THE CABINS, Rhodes sitting in the front seat with his shades on, saying nothing. He and the Big Boss Man drove off in the van, leaving me with Cody and Freddie and Gains.

I didn't see Gains for three days. Cody and Freddie alternated watching me. When I knocked on the basement door it was usually Cody who answered.

I saw more of the property in those days. For lunch they'd let me up to the kitchen and sit me down at a Formica table. I had gas station burritos and egg salad sandwiches and all the dirty tap water I could stomach.

Twice a day they'd lead me out and shackle my arms and ankles with zap straps and let me wander around the property. The straps impeded swift movement, and the enterprise allowed me all the dignity of a cat tethered to a clothesline. But I got a look at the trails that led around the property, that wound up toward the summit or neared the escarpment.

Leaning close to the edge in the second before Cody ordered me to waddle back toward them, I saw down to where the gravel met the main road, kilometres below us. Below that, the edge of a town.

They brought down a plastic wash basin and a bottle of hand sanitizer. I was allowed to keep the clothes and the carry-on bag.

They even found a square of thick foam and a ratty blanket for a bedroll.

For toilet matters I'd knock on the door. Freddie would tie my ankles and lead me out to an aluminum storage shed. Between the empty rows of shelves was a genuine flushing toilet, the floor around it covered in rubber car mats. Freddie would slit my wrist straps, I'd do my business. When I was finished I'd present my arms to him to be rebound. They made sure there was nothing in the outhouse of use, nothing sharp.

When I asked for reading material they gave me the owner's manual from a Dodge Dakota.

I listened to Freddie and Cody during my exercise break. The rules of incarceration were familiar to them. They got a kick from being on the other side. Freddie had been a paramedic at some point, and had worked on a farm. He laughed when he was nervous or confused. Cody griped about his pay, his status in Rhodes's organization. He griped that Gains had been left to oversee them, and he griped that Gains didn't talk to him.

"He's just spooky," Cody said. "I think he's sittin' in that nice house, cross-legged, waitin' for Terry to call. Why's he need the nice house to do that? Meantime I'm shittin' in a hut."

"Why'on't you ask him to switch with us?" Freddie said.

"Right," Cody said. "You know, I don't think I've ever seen him show interest in a girl?"

"Maybe he's gay," Freddie said, and tittered.

"Terry'd never hire a homo." Cody picked up a pine cone and launched it over the escarpment. "There's just something not right about him, isn't there?"

"He scares you," Freddie said.

"Know what? Least I can admit it."

"I'm not afraid of anyone."

"Sure you're not."

"I seen worse killers," Freddie said.

"Like your friend Nichulls?" Cody snorted. "That's not tough. That's psycho."

"You don't know anything," Freddie said.

When Freddie left and Cody was leading me back to the basement, Cody said, "Thinks being chummy with a serial killer makes him hot shit. Terry only keeps him around as a favour."

"To who?" I asked.

"Nichulls. They were all friends, back in the day. Amount of time they spent out at the Law Courts, or the clubhouse, you'd think they were family. Giving Freddie a job is Terry's way of looking after his friend."

"Or paying him back," I said.

"Paying him back for what?"

"Keeping quiet. Taking the blame."

Cody shook his head. "Terry's no serial killer. He does what he has to. He doesn't get anything out of it."

"Maybe he's a facilitator," I said.

"A what?"

"A middle man. Someone does murder, someone else owns a junkyard, he puts them in touch."

"You're lucky he didn't hear you," Cody said. "He's not a middle anything. Terry's at the top."

"Everyone answers to someone," I said.

My guards had different habits and ways of doing their job. Cody was lax, talkative. He forgot procedure and ordered me along. He was bored easily and the novelty of guard duty quickly wore off. Often, if he took me to the outhouse, he wouldn't bother to bind me. Freddie stayed mute and stuck to the rules. If I took too long he'd knock on the walls of the shed. He kept his knife out.

Cody was ignorant of what Freddie and I knew: once Rhodes had the diary, once I wasn't of use to him, he wouldn't hesitate to kill me. Which meant sooner or later I'd have to escape.

The evening of the third day, long after the sun ducked down, I knocked on the basement door. Cody always answered those calls during the night. He'd be groggy and cut every corner he could to get back to bed. He was also roughly my size, and wore comfortable-looking shoes.

I had my shirt on inside out, to look like I'd just woken up. I had two pairs of socks on. My flannel was draped around me. I'd pocketed the pills and Everett's cigarettes, though neither seemed of immediate use.

I knocked incessantly, loudly. Cody didn't come to the door. I thought no one would. When I finally heard the bolt slide back, it was Freddie, squinting and cross.

"Washroom," I said.

"Wait for the morning."

"I need to go now."

"Wait."

"It won't wait," I said. "You can't serve grease and plastic every meal and expect me to hold it."

Freddie sighed and shut the door in my face. A moment later he reopened it with his shoes on, the zap straps in hand. His knife stuck out from his belt. I'd drawn the wrong guard. Already my plan was showing its seams.

He led me outside across the cold earth and slit the straps on my wrists. I waited for him to slit the ankle straps. He didn't move.

"I need leverage on this one," I said.

"Leverage?"

I mimed squatting, trying to spread my feet apart and being stifled by the ankle straps. He smirked and cut them. I entered the outhouse and heard him affix the padlock.

I was five minutes. As I flushed I lifted the porcelain lid off the water tank, delicately, so the grinding sound of removing it was lost beneath the evacuation of water. I worked the lid up under the back of my shirt, so it was partly tucked into my jeans. The lid felt cold and slimy. I put the flannel over it.

Freddie rapped on the side of the shed. I slid open the door, killing the light. I stepped out.

I held my hands out obnoxiously, as if telling him which limbs to bind first. Instead, he crouched and began threading a strap between the two fastened around my ankles.

I put my hands on my head and looked resigned. When his eyes dropped to focus on his task, I scrunched up the flannel so I could get my fingers on the edge of the lid.

Shifting my weight slightly caused Freddie to drop the strap. He looked up briefly to shake his head and then back down. It was dark and he was feeling his way.

I swung the lid over my shoulders and connected on the back of his head, laying him out. The sound of porcelain hitting bone was loud and strange in the still night.

Freddie moaned softly. I took his knife and slit the straps, dragged him into the outhouse. I was sweating now and my hand throbbed beneath its cast.

His shoes were too small to be of use. He had nothing in his pockets except a key ring, and I couldn't see any vehicles. I padlocked the shed. I took the straps and ran across the ivy-covered ground toward the edge of the escarpment.

A steep trail cut down to the bottom, heading into the trees. I picked my way carefully. As I reached the bottom I saw the grey curve of an access road, down another steep drop to the left. Beyond it, the small glowing circuit board of the town.

I crossed over a ditch with a trickle of creek water running through it. The foliage became denser, harder to negotiate. The dry leaves and branches made moving silently difficult.

Before me was a steady decline that would lead to the road. The trees thinned out and I'd be visible during much of the way down. If I chose to go right, I'd stay reasonably camouflaged by the trees, but the craggy ground would make it a more arduous descent. Worse, the treeline skirted the town, so if I wanted to head there I'd be running across two kilometres of open field. There was no third option.

I started down, stumbling from tree to tree. The ground seemed boggy and footing was unsure. I fell, planting myself on my back as I slid down unglamorously, catching hold of an exposed twist of root to stop the slide. The next few steps I made were tentative.

I was thinking how stupid all this was. If I'd just given them the diary. It had been foolish to think there was something like justice for someone like Chelsea Loam.

Chelsea.

Maybe it was better never to know. Maybe it was fitting. In a way, the truth lets you close off all the possible answers, the criticism, the questions. Maybe her absence needed to linger over the city of Vancouver, haunting it, rebuking it at every corner for not caring about her, for caring too late.

I saw high beams distant on the road below. I paused on the slope. A Jeep came in view. The engine was unmuffled and as the Jeep idled the driver left it running.

A flashlight played up and down the road and into the bushes nearby, and then up the slope, near me, past me.

I squinted and made out Cody, standing in the roofless Jeep, swinging his flashlight wildly. He held a pistol in his other hand.

He swung the beam to the bushes and stayed focused on that spot. I could almost hear the dialog in his head, arguing whether or not to check it out on foot.

Another set of lights, another Jeep. This one pulled up alongside the first. Cody turned and aimed the light into the other truck before turning it off. Gains was at the wheel.

The two drivers discussed something. I saw Cody point at the bush and Gains say something. Cody sagged. He walked to the bush and poked at it with the barrel of his gun. Gains stood with his arms folded.

Far from where Cody was prodding, I spotted movement. I saw a black bear leave the cover of the bushes and start up the slope. As it cut closer to me I backed up, slipping, sending a shower of dirt and leaves down the slope. Cody stopped and strained his light across the clearing, but missed the bear. He returned to the Jeep.

I pulled myself up and behind the nearest tree. The bear ignored me and lumbered uphill into the brush. Cody drove the first Jeep away. I watched the lights dwindle.

Gains sat in the Jeep with the lights off for a long time. I couldn't see where he was looking. I heard him start the engine.

Gains banked the Jeep hard right, the front wheels almost driving into the narrow ditch that separated the slope from the pavement. He backed up the Jeep until the rear fender nudged the guard rail on the opposite side. I heard him race the engine.

The Jeep lurched and peeled rubber and sprang across the road. It cleared the ditch and moved up the slope. Gains steered it between two old bowed trees and only then did he hit the high beams.

Brilliant light bathed the stretch of slope where I hid. The light was blinding and I looked away. When I hazarded a look back the Jeep was empty.

Directly below me I saw Charles Gains haloed by headlights, his vacant eyes trained on me as his body propelled him toward me, at me, up the mountainside.

37

THERE'S A MOMENT before a fight when you learn whether or not it's going to be your night. You stand in the ring, shuffling your feet to keep up your heart rate. All your training, all the variables you've tried to spin in your favour, it's all behind you. You stare clear through your opponent into the rest of your career. You know.

When you see a glimpse of doubt, a sag of a shoulder, or someone so eager to hurt you they forget their training, the rest of the night plays out like a dance, ending inevitably with the cut over the eyebrow, the flurry that guarantees you a lead on points, or rarely, the other man knocked flat on his ass.

And when you look over and see only your own best-intentioned failure reflected back at you—there's no loneliness like that. Like you've been cut from the herd and staked out as a sacrifice to a god that no longer exists. The rest of the night is a pointless bloodletting, an attempt to reconcile your safety with your pride.

Watching Gains sprint toward me, I realized what so unnerved Cody and others about him. Gains had never experienced that sense of defeat. He'd never confronted the part of himself that was weak and yielding. He'd never had to.

In that split-second I weighed my options and took stock of my position. I was exhausted and malnourished. My hand hurt. I had a knife.

Gains seemed unarmed. He was in peak shape and ready for this. He could have signalled Cody to join him, and maybe he did, but I had a feeling he'd chosen this confrontation.

I could retreat back up the hill and head across the trail, keeping to the forest and bypassing the town. I might get somewhere. Or I could make a stand, with the altitude and a blade my only advantages over strength and skill and will and experience. Pointless fight or pointless flight. I headed up the slope back toward the forest.

It was like running up sand. In places it was easier to go bent over, using my hands. I told myself not to check over my shoulder until I'd reached the top, but I did. Gains had closed some of the distance between us.

At the top I went through the nearest bush, trampling over and through it, brambles whipping my face. The ground dropped and I saw water pour from a culvert. I looked behind me, saw Gains. Closer now. The bastard didn't even seem winded.

No path now, straight through unending brush. Between sweat and the branches and the darkness I could see nothing. Every branch that scraped my neck was Gains clutching me.

I broke through the bushes. I could see in front of me, at eye level, the steeples of treetops. The bushes and treeline ended within two strides of a cliff that led down to rock and forest.

I broke left, skirting the edge, looking for a way down that didn't involve a plummet.

A kilometre along, the cliff dipped. I saw a line of chain link inscribed over the mossy rock. Here was a man-made buildup of stones, propping up this section of cliff face so erosion and time wouldn't rain it down on the road below.

The road. Not an access road but a multiple lane strip of blacktop. I paused and tried to still my pulse so I could listen for Gains. Instead I heard water.

I kept close to the hip-level fence as I skirted the edge, continuing left. In front of me and below, the drop-off became sharper as the road hewed closer to the cliff face. There was a stream on the other side of the road, moving in the same direction I was.

The break I was looking for came where the cliff receded. It hadn't done so naturally. The stream widened far below, and the road had been squeezed. Part of the cliff had been blasted to add more flat space for widening the blacktop. The rubble had been piled up in a steep but descendable slope of boulders and smaller stones, netted over to prevent a rockslide. I could get down there. Not easily. Not with Gains above. But maybe fast enough to make it down before Gains noticed my direction had changed.

I climbed over the fence and sat on the cliff edge, and finally worked up the courage to push off.

I fell about six feet, my good hand scraping the rock wall. I landed at the beginning of the slope, on hard-packed dirt that rattled my jaw and sent a sting of numbness down my leg. I slid down to the first rock and held myself there, feeling it sway precariously as I shifted my weight. If I fucked up now I'd ride the whole pile down. If I survived that, every creature on the mountain would know my location.

I picked a boulder a short distance below me that looked solidly embedded in the cliff. I delicately transferred my weight, moving diagonally, in case any of the stones I upset decided to show their appreciation by tumbling down after. Silently I picked my way down the scree.

From the boulder, I lowered myself onto a stretch of mid-sized stones. There were no footholds, none that lasted. The entire slope seemed to shift and rearrange itself as I made my way down. Without warning everything around me dropped. The stones bounded happily to pelt the larger rocks below.

I felt my foot hit something solid. I paused, considering how to get the rest of me down onto the zeppelin-sized boulder below, short of triggering a rockslide.

I inched down, feeling along with my heels, using my hands to keep myself spread over as much of the surface as possible. I wished I'd been able to keep awake during physics. Distribution of mass and kinetics were vague concepts. I resolved that when I made it out I'd buy some books, maybe take a night course.

My other foot touched down on the zeppelin and the rocks below me chose that moment to move. I slid and found myself straddling the large boulder. I scrambled over that and dropped down, this time using my arms. I landed on sharp stones that jabbed through the socks. A walk down those and a feeble leap over the ditch and my feet touched the still-warm pavement.

Looking back up, with the moonlight behind me, the entire slope gleamed like a jeweller's idea of heaven.

Follow the river, follow the road. It was the most direct way to the town. It was also over manicured ground that left no cover. It was where I'd look for me, if I was them.

Still, it was tempting. I started that way and only stopped when I saw the twin slash of headlights approaching.

The forest continued on the other side of the river. The river-bank was black stone, moss-covered and shiny. The thought of plunging into cold rushing water and wading across was unappealing. My feet stung and I was already chilled.

From my earlier vantage point above the cliff, I'd noticed a spot maybe two kilometres back where the water flow hadn't been as fierce, and the banks seemed easier to negotiate. I could cross there, elude the high beams, throw off Gains if he was still following me, and use the tree cover to creep near the town by daybreak.

It sounded good. Or it sounded as stupid as anything else I could think of. I started that way, keeping off the road despite my feet's strong preference for smooth ground.

It was a fearful place, the wild, even this artificially straightened, paved and preserved swath of second-growth forest. The night seemed capable of spewing forth anything.

Seeing darkness stretch on in every direction, seeing it take the forms of liquid and air, seeing animals with a kinship to night that you would never have—you could feel the impulse that campfires and trading posts sprang from, villages, nations. Civilization was cowardice made tangible, a graffiti the fearful used to overwrite the truth. The fleeting feeling I'd felt looking across Vancouver Harbour, that this would someday all end— this, the darkness, was what would replace it.

I trudged across the rock toward a place to ford the river, thinking of what meal I'd have when I made it home. A well-done end cut of prime rib from the Keg, marbled and charred on the edges. Baked potato with every artery-clogging topping. Or maybe a curry from Vij's. Bangers and colcannon from the Johnnie Fox with a nice fat-headed pint of Black and Tan. A slice of butter cake from Notte's and a London Fog.

I thought of women I wished I'd slept with, or slept with again, starting with my fifth-grade teacher and working my way back to Shay.

She hadn't been in my thoughts much these last few days. Maybe I didn't know how to think of her.

I know she'd enjoyed those same moments I had—lying together in bed, strolling through the Night Market in Chinatown, all the couple things happy people take for granted. Maybe they'd scared her. There was a comfort in having nothing that could be taken away from you. To suddenly be thrust into a world of fragile moments, enjoyable but out of your control, could drive someone to madness waiting for the drop.

I know Chelsea feared not being loved. I believe Shay feared the opposite.

The rush of water lessened as I moved upstream along the bank. Ahead, two tributaries converged, which accounted for the speed of the river. Above that the ground flattened out and crossing would be easier.

There was a blind corner ahead where the road wound around an outcropping of cliff while the river travelled on. Before I broke away from the road, I looked back to check for headlights. I couldn't see any.

38

AS BEST AS I CAN FIGURE, Gains came out of the brush at the cliff edge, same as I had. There were two directions to go, and it's possible he took the wrong way. It's also possible he stuck to the forest for cover.

Whatever the case, he'd lost me. If he'd been tracking someone in his right mind, Gains might have assumed the cliff continued, sheer, and that I'd backtracked. He'd underestimated my fortitude, or overestimated my common sense.

When he ascertained I wasn't in the forest—and this is just conjecture—he came back to the cliff to look for signs of a fall. If I wasn't in the forest I must have tried to make my way down the cliff face. He'd want a body to present to Rhodes.

I can't put myself in his headspace. I think I bothered him. He'd come after me on foot, with no gun. It had been personal or it had been a game. Likely both. Gains seemed so detached from emotion that finding someone to hate might have made him happy. But that happiness was contingent on bringing me down. As I moved farther away from him, it became exasperation. Charles "Ill-Gotten" Gains couldn't be defeated, least of all by a shoeless nothing with one good hand. I didn't get to win.

So when he saw me below him, making my way up the grass between the riverbank and the road, he was prepared to match and exceed any effort I could make. I wouldn't get away.

I looked up and saw Gains peering at me over the edge.

He was still, perhaps trying to fathom how I'd made it down there. I was limping. I'm sure he noticed that.

My throat was raw, my jaw hurt. My lungs felt like the moisture had been salted and smoked out of them. I didn't say anything. It took all my effort just to give him the finger.

I laughed at my own audacity, and at the blank look of rage that crept over Gains's face. I waved for him to come down.

Gains started down the sheer cliff face.

There was simply no way he could make it. Maybe he thought I'd climbed down here, and somehow controlled my fall. That was what he started to do.

He hung down off the cliff and found a ledge for his feet, swung down till his hands gripped that same ledge, not incautiously but hurried, angry. He made his way a few yards down and I thought, he can do this, the son of a bitch.

Below him the cliff receded inward. There were no more footholds. His legs flailed, searching for purchase. He was supporting his weight with his arms, swinging as if he could drop down and cling to the cliff face itself like some type of creeper.

He tried it but the angle was off, the depression too great. Gains fell with nothing in reach until he hit the bottom.

It was a sickening sound, less a unified thud than the accumulated sounds of a dozen wrapped and fragile things breaking at once. The rocks that greeted him at the bottom were uneven and jagged, and his body was forced to submit to their geometry.

Before impact he'd seemed to hang in the air like a moth with damaged wings. He didn't scream. Even after impact, in the silence, he might stand up and give chase. It wouldn't have surprised me.

After an interval listening for sounds of life, I approached him. I hoped to find a working cellphone, shoes, anything. I had the knife out, which was a pointless precaution. Gains was quite dead.

His legs were a ruin of blood and bone. His back was contorted unnaturally. One arm was broken, but his hands seemed unbothered by the fall. His manicured nails shone off his small hairless hands.

I worked his bloody shoes off. I reached into a pocket and felt nothing but blood. There was a cellphone, lodged in his breast pocket. I had to untwist his torso to get it out.

He'd gone out in a glorious mess, which is what some people seem to want. Maybe he would have regretted not bringing a bunch more people with him. His eyes were open and blood leaked out of his mouth. Underneath the blood the blank expression remained. Gains had met Death head-on and hadn't been impressed.

The town was a stretch of strip malls including the one with the vet clinic, plus a surrounding blot of housing large enough to sustain its workforce. It had the feel of a company outpost. The houses had a lack of creativity, a disdain for yards and all but the most utilitarian community services.

There was a church, though. There are always churches. I knocked on the door but no one answered.

I sat—collapsed—on the steps. Gains's cellphone came to life with a bouncy Virgin Mobile jingle as I hit the power button. Jeff answered his home phone on the twenty-first ring.

"Chen," he said.

"It's Dave. Need you to pick me up. I need some clothes. You might want to bring the gun from the office."

"Can it wait a couple hours?" he asked.

"You have something more important than rescuing your partner who's been missing half a week?"

I heard him and Marie murmur sleepily to each other.

"I'm going to be a father," Jeff said.

I looked around at the tired township, bathed in the first glow of the day, all doors still shut. I heard a car, a newer model, not a Jeep.

"Take your time," I said.

—

I called my mother and told her I'd clean up my mess, and that I'd never go another day without calling her, and that yes I was aware there was a dead dog on her back porch. I called the office, asked Shuzhen for my messages, and asked her to look up something for me. I called Shay but nobody picked up.

Jeff arrived around ten with some Zellers clothes and my ID. He insisted on driving me to the hospital. I told him to forget it. He told me just once he'd like me to not be an idiot about everything.

It turned out my hand had been set badly and needed to be rebroken and reset. What you get, I guess, when you force a frightened veterinarian to perform field surgery.

I was dehydrated, had a bruised windpipe, an infected cut on my left foot and an assortment of slices and scrapes. My first meal back in Vancouver was hospital food.

After that came the dialogues and trialogues with police officers and lawyers. I was questioned about Gains, whose body had been found by a wildlife official.

Ryan Martz tried to talk to me off the record, just between us old friends. He said it looked like someone had beaten Gains to a pulp and tossed him off a cliff. He asked if I'd heard of Gains, if I was aware of his pedigree.

Martz brought up an internet clip on his laptop. It was Gains, younger, executing an ankle lock on a much taller opponent. An amateur bout, filmed with a camcorder. Most shocking was the grin young Gains cracked when his arm was raised. A whole lifetime of victories ahead of him.

"This guy isn't some sick shut-in that abducts teenagers," Martz said as he walked me out of the station. "Gains was known. He has people. They'll be interested in what happened to him."

"I'm sure they'll find strength to cope," I said.

Martz told me about the break-in at my apartment. He told me to make a list of what was missing and he'd help check the pawnshops. He asked if I wanted a brochure full of tips on how to minimize the risk of burglaries.

Don't own anything nice. Or buy everything nice and stay home all the time, cocooned in your luxury. Don't befriend anyone who makes less money than you. Don't associate with unsavoury elements. Move into a bank vault.

I appeased my mother with a visit. I sluffed through coffee and dessert. River drove me home in my car.

"School going all right?" I asked her.

"Meh. It's all prerequisites this semester. Auntie Bea has been nice about it, but it's school, y'know?"

"You want to come work for me?" I asked.

"Seriously?"

"I'm not going to talk you out of it," I said. "You'll have to stay in school, but I'll start you in the office and show you what I know."

"Which'll take all of eight minutes," she said.

I told her she could keep the car for the next day. I got out and approached the patio.

The glass had been broken. The landlord had taped sheet plastic over it.

I slashed it and stepped through, turned on the lights. Rhodes hadn't lied. I could see where his men had tossed the place, upsetting the shelves of the bookcase, overturning cushions. Someone else had taken the things of value.

The TV was gone. The liquor cabinet was vacant. The stereo had been removed and the components taken. The record crates were empty.

But the bed was undisturbed. I changed the sheets and fell into it, and didn't bother getting up for a long while.

39

IT WAS TWO DAYS until I was up to visiting the Overman compound again. I'd spent those days handling business and assuring creditors and other parasites that I was still a viable host.

I'd corresponded with Caitlin, Caitlin's cleaning service, Wayne Loam, Dolores Gunn. And I'd left a message for Terry Rhodes.

It was half past noon and no one was expecting me. I'd been delighted to wake up and see clouds on the horizon, thick, roiling clouds. The weatherman on CBC said there was a chance of rain, but he'd been saying that for months. I think he decided that was a safe bet for Vancouver, recorded all his broadcasts over a weekend in June, and took the summer off.

Nick Overman opened the door. I reintroduced myself and shook his hand. I watched him smile while he struggled to remember me.

"Dan Wakefield," he said. "You're partners with Jed Chen."

"Close enough," I said. "Can I come in?"

He allowed me inside and turned off the TV. He'd been watching sports highlights and having a nip of gin. Did I care for one? I told him some days I had trouble caring for anything else.

"You're here to see Pop," he said, mixing two highballs at the ornate rosewood bar. He had seventy-dollar French gin and no-name-brand tonic. A man after my own heart.

"How's he doing?" I asked.

"He's down for an hour or so. He usually naps before Marian comes back at two."

"Is it all right if I wait?" I asked.

"Sure," Nick said, "if you can sit through some ESPN."

We watched a few minutes of draft picks and golf bloopers, and a roundtable discussion on league expansion. "You're either growing or dead," one personality said. I savoured the gin.

"Nice way to spend a Saturday," Nick said as he got up for refills. "Kids at their practice, wife at her charity thing, Pop getting his rest."

"About your father," I said.

"Is it urgent? I'm sorry. Should I have woken him up?"

"It's fine," I said. "I wanted to ask him about a property he owns. A little group of cabins up one of the North Shore Mountains."

Nick smiled. "Camp Broken Arrow," he said. "That's what I named it as a kid. We used to go there as a family, way, way back. Cheap vacation, nice getaway on weekends."

"I can imagine circumstances where it would be very pleasant to stay there."

"I haven't thought about that place in twenty years," Nick said. "I think Pop sold it."

"He's still listed as the owner."

"Is he?" Nick frowned. "I could check on that."

"I'd appreciate it."

He left the room a minute, came back with a fresh ice tray. He hammered the cubes out and brought the drinks back to the couches.

"I'll be honest," Nick said. "Pop's finances are—well, the word 'labyrinthine' comes close to the mark. He was a good income generator, but his methods were less than meticulous, and occasionally, well." He shrugged. "'Tween you me and the fence post, he associated with some shady characters. Not everything was one hundred percent squeaky clean."

"Like Terry Rhodes and the Exiles," I suggested, "far as shady characters. People like them?"

"Yes," Nick said sharply. "Pop used to get a thrill associating with tough guys. He used them as security for a few corporate events. It was—not a success."

"But he kept ties with them," I said. "Maybe let them use the cabins?"

Nick rubbed his hand over his mouth and chin as if stroking a beard he didn't have. "Now you've got me interested," he said. "Only way to sort this out is to ask him. You've got time?"

"Nothing but," I said. "After this I'm off for the rest of the summer."

"Summer's almost over," he said.

"Good."

He left and I watched him through the living room window, round the corner of the compound toward his father's place. I waited and sipped my drink. It was damn good gin.

He came back shaking his head. "I'm sorry, Marian really has him doped up. He's been having trouble sleeping, more than usual. Started around the time of your last visit. Coincidentally, I'm sure."

"I have that effect on people," I said.

"Refill?"

I didn't stop him.

"Can you answer a question for me?" I asked.

"Shoot."

"I don't know much about finance."

"That's not really a question."

"Your father's got this property and he owns it outright," I said. "No mortgage."

"Sure," he said.

"And with his ailments, plus his messy bookkeeping, his assets, like the cabins, are just sitting there."

Nick nodded. "His doctors warned him. They said he could live twenty years in a garden or two in a boardroom. He made the right choice. In that instance."

"So who pays for upkeep and maintenance on the cabins?"

Nick spread his hands. "As I said, it's a jumble. Maybe the place isn't maintained."

"But your father does no business."

"That's right."

"And you have his power of attorney."

Nick had been sipping from his glass. He paused and lowered it, set it on the floor.

"Which means what?" he said.

"I don't know much about taxes but I know you have to pay them. Property taxes being one example. Otherwise you end up in arrears, penalties mount up, you lose the place."

"It's possible the camp is in arrears," Nick admitted. "I could check it for you."

"I already did," I said.

Nick stood up. He looked down at his drink, at me, smiled. "Bit weak, this one. Top yours up?"

"I'm good," I said. "About the camp."

"This is really bothering you, isn't it?" He slid open the drawer of the bar and brought something out.

"I spent some time there courtesy of Terry Rhodes," I said. "When I looked into the finances of the place, know how many irregularities I found?"

"Considering Pop's penchant for bending the rules, and Terry Rhodes's penchant for obliterating them, I'd say a few."

"None," I said. "Property taxes have been paid regularly. Utilities, too. From accounts controlled by you as administrator of your father's funds."

Nick turned around very slowly. He balanced the tumbler in his hands. As he sat down he stirred his drink with a silver teaspoon. His face became haggard and grief-stricken almost as if on cue.

"My father had a deal with Rhodes," he said. "It's a deal I have to honour. Otherwise Rhodes has threatened a scandal, and the old man wouldn't last through that. Can you understand, if not condone it?"

"All I want is to understand," I said. "I'm no authority. It's your word against mine."

Nick ran his forearm under his nose. "I appreciate that."

"But I do need to understand."

"All right."

"Why did you kill Chelsea Loam?"

Nick blinked. His brow furrowed. He went through a silent film star's repertoire of exaggerated masks of feigned surprise.

"Why would you think I—" he let the unvoiced bit hang in the air.

"Killed her?" I said. "I like the way you phrased that. Not 'why would I do that?' but 'why would you think I'd do that?' And to answer that question, because of how much you wanted the diary. You paid or enticed Rhodes to get it from me. You gave him and his men the run of the cabin for that purpose."

"You're being silly," he said.

"You're the only one Rhodes would answer to. Not because you have more money than him, but because you have clean money, and ways to make money clean. He told me himself he'd've killed me if it was up to him."

"Maybe I did want it back," he said. "Maybe I didn't want some prostitute's lies scandalizing my father."

"It's the twenty-first century. No one's all that scandalized by rich people with wandering dicks. And as much of a busted old minotaur as your father is, he'd probably be proud.

"No, Nick," I continued, "it's not about what the diary contained, it's what it might've contained."

"Meaning?"

"If you thought it mentioned sex, you'd be concerned. But you wouldn't sell yourself to Terry Rhodes. You'd only do that if there was something more at stake—if there was a chance she'd written down something about who killed her."

Nick said nothing.

"Rhodes knew it, too. He knew when he brought Chelsea to you the power you were giving him. And he knew when he learned about the diary that if he told you about it, you'd sell yourself to him all over again. That's assuming you two haven't had a partnership this entire time."

I took a drink, ice slivers amidst the diesel-and-lavender burn of gin.

"And the best part? There was nothing about you in the diary. Not a word. And yet look at all the misery you caused to get it back. At least three others dead, one of them a friend of mine. Just to shut up someone who was already silent."

"It's hardly evidence," Nick said.

"It's not evidence at all. Just the truth—fragile, unprovable, all but useless."

"I didn't kill her," he said.

"Nick."

"I didn't. Swear I didn't."

"I'm a private investigator, not a cop. There's nothing I could accuse you of a big-money lawyer couldn't help you slip. You don't have to convince me."

"Terry—"

"I know his part," I said. "I know Chelsea had a good roster of regulars. As she slipped into addiction she had to work harder and take greater risks to make the same money. Risks like going with Rhodes, seeing who he set her up to see. When he pitched her to you, did he tell you it was sex only, or you could do what you wanted with her?"

Nick didn't answer immediately. He was leaning back in his chair, hands in his pockets. When he spoke his voice had assumed a childish tone, like a son who's totalled his father's car calling from a drunk tank. He'd become small.

"Terry told me it was anything I wanted," he said.

"You meet him at one of your father's parties? He approach you about other girls?"

Nick shook his head. "She was the first and only."

"Terry handle the cleanup?"

"Personally."

"And where's the body?"

"He disposed of it. Told me not to worry about it."

"Could it be up by the cabins?"

"No," Nick said. "Terry said he had a friend who'd make sure nothing was ever found."

I thought of what Ed Leary Nichulls had said. *Real bad people.*

"And in return?" I said.

"I've helped him with some investments."

He wasn't looking at me anymore. I waited for some sort of explanation, a list of mitigating factors. I was young/I was scared/ she was robbing me/she was laughing at me/it was the drugs/ I didn't mean to/things just got out of hand.

I stood up. "Do you know why you did it?"

He looked up at me and said matter-of-factly, "Why do you think?"

"I thought I knew," I said. "She was with your father for a long time. You might have seen them together. You might have only realized who she was after you slept with her, and been driven over the edge by some sort of Oedipal thing. Or maybe you planned it out as revenge, protect the family name. Those would've been my best guesses, but now I don't buy them."

"I didn't know about Pop and her until I caught him crying one day over her Missing poster." Nick rocked his chair and knocked over his drink. We watched the gin soak into the carpet.

"I don't know why I do things," he said.

"Don't equivocate. Tell me why."

Without looking up from the stain on the carpet he told me. His answer seemed to surprise him. His voice was even-toned, lips suppressing a smile.

He said, "I just wanted to fuck something and kill it."

Then Nick shifted his face into a sneer. It was the kind of overdrawn expression that would keep other more genuine emotions from declaring themselves. Masks within masks. How tiresome.

"What's your amount?" he asked.

"What's your offer?"

"Two," he said, very serious. "Paid out over four years. Plus benefits and pension. You'd be head of security. How does that sound?"

"Tedious," I said.

"Think of what you could do with the money. What you could buy. Or how much you could help other people." He held out his palm. "You name a number."

"Twenty-four."

"You can't be serious."

"Chelsea Loam was that age when she disappeared. When you killed her. What's the value of a dead young woman?"

"Prostitute, let's be clear here."

I put my drink down on his glass coffee table. "I don't think we can come to terms," I said. "I'm going to walk out of here and have a cigarette and forget as much of this nastiness as I possibly can."

Nick popped out of his chair. Before I could move he had his pistol pointed at me. "Sit down," he said.

I bent and picked up my half-finished drink. "Think I'll need this after all."

"I wasn't asking," he said. "Sit the fuck down while I make a call."

I didn't move.

He lowered the barrel until it was pointed at my leg, the one Nia had shot, the one I'd favoured when I'd walked into the Overman house for the first time. He pulled the trigger.

Or tried to. It made a feeble metallic clicking sound.

"You did this?" he said.

"With help. You share the same cleaning service as the victim's family. Would you have talked to me straight if you didn't think you had a weapon a foot from your hand?"

He lurched forward and fell on his knees as if struck by divine revelation. His hands spasmed, his neck muscles clenched. He didn't drop the pistol.

Behind him, standing in the kitchen, Dolores Gunn carefully jerked the wires of her stun weapon, removing the spurs from the small of Nick's back. She nodded to me and looked down at the immobilized wretch writhing on the wet carpet.

"You should get out and go find an alibi," she said.

I watched her pull Nick Overman to a sitting position and bind his hands so he was sitting on them. I watched her slide his trousers down, a move which was oddly sexual and oddly motherly. I watched her slip off one of his socks and gag him with it.

I moved to the fireplace and picked up a long-stemmed match. I broke it, struck it, and lit the last cigarette of the summer.

When I left Dolores was sawing through his genitals with a kitchen blade.

40

IT WAS A DAY LATER and Nick Overman still wasn't missing. He would be, though. In time he'd become the city's least invisible dead person. A three-province, two-state search would be conducted. Hundreds of interviews, a tip line. Posters would festoon the city's telephone poles for years.

I was sitting on a bench by the Bloedel Observatory at the top of Little Mountain, the highest elevation within the city proper. I could see into Nat Bailey Stadium below, and all the way to the water and the monolithic cranes by the bay. Mountains, Grouse and the Sisters, loomed beyond that.

I'd hoped Wayne Loam would make it. But it was a work day. Tourists and families congregated outside the observatory. Picnics were being conducted on the sunburnt grass. I watched her approach, puffing up the hill from the bus stop. She was wearing a dark green ball cap and orange-rimmed drugstore shades. A white leather bag was slung over one shoulder. I felt a pang watching her.

Shay smiled as we drew near. She held me tight and kissed my neck and side of my face.

"Glad you're not dead," she said.

"Same."

We drifted down through the picnic area, near the ponds. We found a place away from the children. I set down the battered steel ice bucket I'd been carrying, and the small bottle of butane.

"Do you have it?" I said.

She reached into her bag. "Guess I should give you these first. Probably gave you a heart attack, seeing them gone."

She had my albums, some of them. The important ones.

"I wasn't expecting that," I said.

"I know. I feel shitty about the rest, believe me. The others split my share."

"All of it?"

She smiled. "Some of it," she said.

"And the other thing?"

She handed me the wrapped package. The corner flap had been teased up. Customs had stamped it. The diary was in fine condition.

I knew it had to be done to satisfy Terry Rhodes. His initials were in the book. He'd feel it was a point of pride. I'd given my word.

And still I hated to do it. She'd been honest in her writing, she'd told the truth, and that meant a part of her was that book. It was one of the last traces she'd existed. It was the testament, the will, the Gospel according to Chelsea Ann Loam. To lose it was to contribute to the lack of her in the world. I was a poor custodian if I'd taken it to preserve it, only to destroy it myself.

I pulled out Gains's phone and dialed Terry Rhodes.

"We had a deal," I said. "I'm holding to it."

"Did you really do that to Charley?" Rhodes asked.

"That's a separate matter," I said. "I'm honouring our deal."

"So honour it."

I hung up. I handed the phone to Shay. I started to tell her how to work the camera, but she knew better than I did.

I held the diary up to the lens and flipped the pages, enough to authenticate it. I tore the book down its spine and pressed it into the bucket. I soaked it with butane and set it alight. I watched the pages darken and furl. I prodded it. I made sure there was nothing left but crumbling ash. I held up a handful for the camera.

When it was done I sent the pictures to Rhodes's number and waited for confirmation. I waited seven minutes. He texted back to me with an empty message. I took that as a sign.

Shay and I walked up the hill a few paces and waited for a favourable breeze. When I felt the onset of one I tipped out the bucket. I watched the wind catch the fine ash and lift it up, dispersing it, like a toxic confetti, out over Cambie Street.

I sat down on the grass. I held Shay's hand. We bore witness. We watched it all disappear.

TODAY IS A GOOD DAY. Today the rain falls cold and slick and frightens the tourists away. The parks and benches have all been abandoned. There is an open table in every restaurant. I can stand here by the surf and let the rain batter my fancy new trench coat and paste my hair to my forehead, knowing a hot cup of tea and my office chair are minutes away.

I don't know why this city sees fit to kill its women. I know Yeats once said something suitably fine about the souls that perpetually haunt the streets of London. This place isn't London and I have no idea what haunts us. Will haunt us.

I'll be off this bench and back to the office in minutes. I'll pass by her hotel and glance up at her window, and maybe see Shay, getting her load on, staring down at the scurrying fools below. And I'll pass her library, where desperate people congregate, and her college where my sister will be studying, sitting in a carrel with a view of the street. And her bars. And my office.

At home, in Vancouver, in her lonely places.

AFTERWORD AND ACKNOWLEDGEMENTS

It's been more than three years since the Oppal Commission published its report on Vancouver's murdered and missing women. I don't know what changes are in the wind, if any. The Commission was dogged by controversy stemming from its sidelining of sex trade workers, First Nations groups, the victims' families and loved ones. This marginalization is not new. This, unfortunately, is part of our way of life.

A novel isn't reportage nor should it claim to be. Those wishing for a factual account of Vancouver's troubled history could start with Stevie Cameron's excellent and thorough *On the Farm*.

No one in this book is based on a real person. Any similarities are pure coincidence. All errors in procedure and fact are mine.

In addition to Ms. Cameron's book I'd like to acknowledge Julian Sher and William Marsden's *Road to Hell* and Leslie A. Robertson and Dara Culhane's *In Plain Sight* for helping me see my city differently. I've benefitted from discussions with photographer and filmmaker Mel Yap, Alex Ferguson of Search and Rescue B.C., Barry Vanness at North Fraser Correctional Facility, my brother Josh for his knowledge of Winnipeg, and most importantly, sessions at CRAB Park with my friend, the great Vancouver poet Mercedes Eng. The good parts of this book are indebted to her insight and outrage, the bad parts being mine alone.

A further thanks to Chris Bucci at the McDermid Agency, for having faith in the book; my editor, Craig Pyette, for his painstaking work to get it right; copy editor Tilman Lewis and proofreader Michelle MacAleese; my students at Coquitlam College; my family; and my fellow Vancouver crime writers. I'm indebted to all of you.

S.W.
11/8/15, Vancouver, Coast Salish Territory

SAM WIEBE's stand-alone debut novel, *Last of the Independents*, won an Arthur Ellis Award and the Kobo Emerging Writer Prize, and was nominated for a Shamus award. His stories have appeared in *Thuglit*, *subTerrain* and *Spinetingler*, among others. He lives in Vancouver.